# JENNIFER L. ARMENTROUT

For details about current and upcoming titles from
Jennifer L. Armentrout,
please visit *www.jenniferlarmentrout.com*

# *The* PROPHECY

THE TITAN SERIES

#1 NEW YORK TIMES AND INTERNATIONAL BESTSELLING AUTHOR
## JENNIFER L. ARMENTROUT

HODDER

First published in Great Britain in 2018 by Hodder & Stoughton
An Hachette UK company

1

Copyright © Jennifer L. Armentrout 2018

A CIP catalogue record for this title is available from the British Library

Paperback ISBN 9781473673199
eBook ISBN 9781473673205

Printed and bound in Great Britain by Clays Ltd, St Ives plc

Hodder & Stoughton policy is to use papers that are natural, renewable and
recyclable products and made from wood grown in sustainable forests. The
logging and manufacturing processes are expected to conform to the environ-
mental regulations of the country of origin.

Hodder & Stoughton Ltd
Carmelite House
50 Victoria Embankment
London EC4Y 0DZ

www.hodder.co.uk

# 1

## Josie

*W*ind gusted around me, tossing across my cheeks the short, thin strands of blonde hair that had fallen loose from my bun.

The late-evening air was still cool for early June. At least from what I was used to, having grown up in south Missouri, where it could feel like the devil's butt by this time of year. But I had a feeling it never really got all that hot here in the hills of South Dakota.

Drawing in a deep breath, I focused on a large, gray boulder. Probably been sitting where it was since time began. Lifting my arm, I tapped into all the aether that now poured through my veins, since I no longer had my powers bound by a pair of not so ordinary bracelets.

It felt good to have that power back, especially right now when I wanted to blow stuff up.

I was super irritated at a certain golden-headed *god* at the moment.

Instead of pushing that anger aside like I normally would have,

I *tapped* into it and used it to feed akasha, the deadliest element known to man and immortal. Summoning the air element was something I had always struggled with in the past. Sometimes I'd want to move something and I'd set it on fire instead.

That was why Luke usually stayed far away from me when I was practicing with the elements.

I pictured the boulder lifting into the air and held that image. Power coursed through me. At first, nothing happened, and then the boulder began to tremble as if the ground was shaking. A heartbeat later, the great rock shifted, and then it was like a great hand reached down and pulled on it. The scent of rich soil filled the air as the boulder broke loose from the ground and rose.

I moved the boulder to the left and then to the right. The massive rock slid back and forth like it weighed nothing more than a feather.

I was doing it, but it wasn't perfect. I needed to be able to use the elements immediately, with no hesitation. I lowered the boulder, wincing at the jarring impact it made as it settled crookedly into its hole.

Turning at the waist, I scanned the ancient statues of unnamed gods rising out from tall, wispy weeds, half-expecting one of the many Sentinels or Guards to come rushing onto the low hill, but the field I was practicing on remained empty.

I wiped at the sweat dotting my brow as I turned back to the boulder. Ignoring the weariness cloaking my body, I shook out my shoulders and arms. A huge part of me wanted to take a nap.

I'd been sleeping *a lot* lately.

Supposedly that was normal, even in the early stages of pregnancy. I knew this because I had done some Google sleuthing. Okay. I'd done a lot of reading. Part of me wished I hadn't, because I'd learned about all kinds of things I was just better off not knowing about.

*For you, the reader.*

I'd discovered I'd become a bit of a worrywart.

Because holy crap, there was so much that could go wrong. So much! And that wasn't even taking into consideration the night-mare-inducing birthing stories I'd spent an afternoon reading.

I was traumatized from that.

But there was so much that could happen. What if something happened to this baby? I didn't think it was a crazy question. Normal pregnancies failed all the time, for one reason or another. Hell, some women never even learned why they lost their babies. Sometimes, it just happened and there was no reason.

And like I'd said to Seth, we were not normal.

He was a god, and I was a demigod. His life was crazy dangerous, and mine wasn't any safer. In all reality, my life was a heck of a lot more dangerous than his. He was absolute. Meaning only another absolute being could kill him. That was still scary, but there were only two other beings alive that posed any real risk to Seth.

Cronus.

And Zeus.

But for me?

My heart lurched in my chest. Pretty much any other being that was better trained at physical fighting and was more skilled at controlling the elements posed a risk to me and my child. Granted, as a demigod, I would be harder to kill.

But I still could be killed.

And what if I was seriously injured in a fight with the Titans? What would that mean for the baby? The fact the child had survived the time I was captured by Hyperion proved that this kid was a fighter. No doubt about it, but it was still vulnerable, because I…I was vulnerable.

But I wasn't weak.

Which was why I was out here and not cowering in my bed.

Once again, I summoned the element of air, but this time I

didn't raise my hand.

A moment passed and then the boulder rose.

Good. That was good.

Exhaling through my nose, I *gently* lowered the boulder and then lifted it again.

I kept doing it until my will became an immediate action, until there wasn't a tremble before the rock lifted.

I didn't stop until I did it *right*, and after about a dozen times, the boulder did what I wanted, lifting without hesitation.

A smile tugged at my lips as I stared at the boulder hovering a good three feet off the ground. That thing had to weigh a ton, but I had lifted it off the ground with my mind.

How cool was that?

Even after everything I'd been through and everything I'd seen, there were still times when I couldn't believe any of this was real.

That I was a demigod.

That I was in love with a god.

That I was preg—

A twig snapped, startling me. The boulder fell back to earth, slamming into the ground with enough force to collapse the knee-high iron fence at the back of the field.

"Wow," came the deep, slightly melodic voice. "You dropped that like it was hot."

It was *him*.

He was back.

I spun around, and like always my breath hitched. No matter how mad I was at Seth, seeing him never failed to get my heart pounding. He was...he was simply beautiful, almost painfully so.

He had a face that was so perfectly pieced together, there were days I didn't think Seth was real. Like those broad cheekbones and full lips were molded from clay. And the curved jaw was chiseled into perfection from the finest marble, as was every square inch of his body.

And I would know, since I was well versed in every square inch of his body.

The first time I saw Seth in the stairwell at Radford University, back when my life was normal and gods were just ancient Greek myths, he'd reminded me of a fallen angel. A fallen angel with personal boundary issues, but I'd never seen anyone who looked like him before, but Seth was no angel, fallen or not. He was, literally, a god.

The Appointed One.

The God of Death and Life.

So of course he'd look like a god.

And I didn't care how hot he was at the moment, I was pissed at him.

He seemed oblivious to this, because he smiled at me—that one smile he had that usually caused my chest to feel like it was full of butterflies.

"Have I told you how much it turns me on when you're moving stuff with your mind?" He stepped around several smaller rocks that were piled up on one another. "Because if I haven't, let me inform you now. It really turns me—"

"Don't." I crossed my arms over my chest.

Brows a little darker than his golden hair furrowed. "Don't what?"

"Don't come over here and try to flatter me," I said. "I'm mad at you."

Seth stopped a foot away from me. Confusion settled onto his striking features. "Mad at me for what?"

I stared at him for a moment and then realized he really had no idea that I knew what he'd been doing. "There's something we haven't talked about, Seth."

Lifting a hand, he tucked his hair back behind his ear. "Yeah,

I'm getting a feeling there is."

"I know a lot has happened in the last couple of weeks. Months, even. My entire world has changed. So has yours! I found out that my dad is freaking Apollo and I'm supposed to help entomb some crazy Titans, which by the way, we still don't know how to do. Anyway, everything with my mom and grandparents happened." My voice cracked, and I swallowed the sudden knot in my throat. "And then everything with Atlas and Solos went down, and you became a *god* and freaked out."

The corners of Seth's lips started to turn down.

"Then I got kidnapped by Hyperion, but you found me, which was obviously great and all," I went on in a rush as I kept giving him the highlights of the last several months. "Then we find out I'm pregnant, and then you kill Hyperion, so yeah, a lot of crazy things have been happening, but I haven't *forgotten*."

"Forgotten what?" he asked, those amber-colored eyes of his luminous in the fading sunlight.

Frustration pricked my skin as I took a step toward him. "Where have you been?"

"I told you where I was going." He tilted his head. "I went back to Andros to check in—"

"With Basil," I interrupted. "But that's not all you did, is it?"

Seth opened his mouth, but he didn't say anything. His eyes widened with realization. A moment passed. "Josie—?"

"I didn't forget," I reminded him, unfolding my arms as I drew in a short breath. "And I know checking in with Basil was *not* the only reason why you returned to Andros. I don't know if you forgot that I saw you with her—"

"It's not like that." Seth was suddenly right in front of me. Barely an inch separated us. "When you saw me with Karina, I was—"

"You were recharging. I know." I lifted my chin to meet his

gaze since Seth was a good head taller than me. "I know you weren't being romantic with her or anything else like that. That's not what I'm talking about."

His eyes searched mine. "You know I have to do that. If I didn't have to, I wouldn't. I promise you that."

"I know," I repeated, and I did. When Seth became a god, he finally learned why he'd always struggled with the allure of aether. Aether was what fed the gods' abilities and what made them immortal. It was why the Olympians stayed in Olympus. The place was surrounded in aether. But for Seth? He existed in the mortal realm. The only way he could get aether was by…by feeding just like the Titans did.

"And I wouldn't have had to do it so soon, but after fighting Hyperion and dealing with the damn daimons crawling out of the ground, I needed to."

It had only been two days since Seth had taken out Hyperion, but in those two days, he'd been busy. Hyperion's death hadn't just caused one tear in the mortal realm, allowing daimons to escape Tartarus. Just yesterday, an earthquake had rocked Oklahoma. The mortal world had no idea it wasn't a normal earthquake. We had no idea why there'd been another tear, but we figured it had to do with how powerful Hyperion was. His death was having a continuous ripple effect.

But none of that was the point.

"You didn't tell me the truth," I said. "You could've told me the real reason why you went back there."

Seth said nothing as he looked away. A muscle flexed along his jaw.

"I get that you have to do it, and I'll be honest, I do not like that it has to be one of the priestesses, but I get it. You have to do it." I stepped back, and Seth's head swung in my direction. "But I don't get why you'd lie to me."

"I…I didn't mean to lie to you."

My brows lifted.

"Okay. I just hoped you wouldn't think about what I was doing," he corrected, and that wasn't much better.

"Really?"

"Yes. Really." He sighed, shoving a hand through his hair. "It's not exactly something I'm proud of, Josie."

"Why would you be ashamed? You have to do it. You're a god—"

"But I know you don't like it. I know it bothers you, because how could it not? That bastard fed off you until it almost killed you—killed our child. And you really want to know the exact moment I'm doing the same thing?"

"It's not the same thing." I moved to him, grasping his cheeks and forcing his gaze to mine. "What you're doing is not the same thing Hyperion did, for a multitude of reasons. How can you think it's the same thing?"

Seth's jaw hardened. "So, you're a hundred percent okay with me doing that? Doesn't bother you at all?"

"Honestly? I wish it wasn't Karina, who just has to be utterly gorgeous, that you have to get all up close and personal with, but other than that? No. It doesn't bother me." I dragged my thumb along the line of his jaw as the wind picked up, blowing a lock of his hair across his cheek. "I wish I could be the one who could give you what you need."

"No." Seth slipped free, putting space between us. "I will never use you for that. I will not risk you or our child by using you."

"I'm not suggesting that," I said, ignoring the way his gaze sharpened. "The only part of this that upsets me is that you'd try to hide it from me. That makes it feel like you're doing something wrong. And it makes me feel like you don't fully trust me."

"Trust you? I trust you with my life, Josie. You're the only person I trust."

"But you don't trust me enough to know that I wouldn't judge you? That I wouldn't understand what you have to do?" I reasoned. "You're cutting me out of a huge part of your life that isn't going to magically go away one day. I don't want this to become some kind of dirty secret between us where we're both pretending the other doesn't know about it."

I drew in a shallow breath. "We're going to have a child, Seth. I don't want anything to be between us. Not now. Not ever. I want us to be on the same page. Always."

Seth lowered his hands to his sides. He was silent for a long moment, so long that I had no idea what he was thinking, but then he moved—moved too fast for me to track. In a heartbeat, he was with me, an arm around my waist and a hand at the base of my neck. I sucked in a sharp breath, and Seth caught it with a kiss.

My entire body jolted with surprise. This was no slow kiss. Oh no, this was deep and fierce and it scorched me straight to my core, to my very soul. My hands flattened against his shoulders, but I didn't push him away. I slid my arms around his neck, and the arm at my waist tightened, drawing me flush with his body. The kiss short-circuited every one of my senses by the time he dragged his mouth away from mine.

Seth pressed his forehead against mine. "You're right," he said, his exhale shaky. "I should've told you what I was doing."

"You should've," I agreed, letting my fingers tangle in the soft hair tied back at the nape of his neck.

He ran his thumb along my cheek as he spoke, his voice barely above a whisper. "I don't want anything between us. Starting now."

# 2

## Seth

"You weren't joking when you said you wanted nothing between us starting now," Josie said. "I didn't realize you meant that so literally."

"Was not joking at all." The strand of hair curled around my hand wasn't blonde or brunette. It was a stunning array of colors, from the palest blonde to spun gold. I had no idea how hair could naturally have that many shades in it.

"What are you doing?"

Dragging my gaze from the strangest and most beautiful hair I'd ever seen, I found myself staring down into bright, denim-blue eyes.

Pressure squeezed my chest as my gaze roamed over Josie's face. Her cheeks were flushed pink, which probably had to do with the fact I'd stripped every piece of clothing off her moments before. Seeing all that pretty color to her cheeks almost made me forget about how pale she'd been in the weeks after being held by the Titan Hyperion. She'd been through hell, and there were things I knew she'd kept from me. Things she hadn't shared because she was either not comfortable or because she was worried I'd set fire to half the Western Hemisphere in anger.

The latter was always a possibility.

I had been known to react first and then maybe, depending on my mood, ask questions later.

"You still mad at me?" I asked.

Her head shifted on the pillow. "If I was, I wouldn't be lying here naked. You're talented, but not *that* talented."

I laughed. "I don't know. I like to think I'm that skilled."

"I'm sure you do." Her eyes met mine. "When will you have to do it again? Recharge?"

My gaze flickered to her hair. I liked how she called it that instead of what it truly was. Feeding. Recharging sounded a lot…cleaner. "A couple of weeks. It all depends on if I have to go badass god on anything."

"I want…I want to go with you next time."

I looked at her. "For real?"

"Yeah. Then maybe it won't feel like a secret anymore."

A huge part of me didn't want her there for that, but I'd do it for her. "If that's what you want."

"It is."

"Then it's a plan," I said. "By the way, why were you out in that field today?"

"I was practicing with the elements. Figured that was the safest place for it."

I grinned, but it was quick to fade. "Why were you out there alone, though? Luke could've been with you."

Josie snorted. "Luke doesn't want to be anywhere near me when I'm working with the elements."

"Then you could've gotten Deacon, or even Alex or Aiden. I don't want you out there by yourself."

She arched a brow. "It's not like I went traipsing around outside the University. I was safe."

"Need I remind you that the Covenant walls have been breached more than once?"

"And need I remind you that I can take care of myself?"

"I know you can," I sighed. "It's just not..." Rubbing my thumb over the thick strands of hair, I looked down at her where her hands rested on her lower belly. My damn heart jumped in my chest like it was on a trampoline.

Josie was pregnant with *our child*.

A wealth of raw, contradicting emotions rose up and consumed me. Terror. Happiness. Fear. Anticipation. It was crazy how you could feel so much all at once.

The pressure in my chest intensified. What I was feeling was scary as hell, but it was also the good kind of pressure. The kind that told me I'd do anything to keep her and our child safe. Coat my hands in blood if necessary, and I had. More than once, and I carried very little regret for doing so.

Love outweighed regret.

Something I never thought I'd ever truly feel for another person, and when I first met Josie, it sure as hell wasn't love at first sight. Probably a little lust at first sight. I'd also been disturbed by the fact of who she resembled and who her father was.

Never would've crossed my mind that day in the stairwell that I would end up falling in love with Apollo's daughter. Hell. Kind of wanted to laugh now, but that was what happened.

Getting here, to this very moment, hadn't been easy.

Gods know I'd fought my feelings for her. Timing was shit for a relationship when I first met her. Back then, I had no future. I was being used by the gods to carry out *Remediations*—hunting down and destroying those who'd sided with Ares. And, once the gods figured out how to kill me, I would then get to spend an eternity serving Hades. But that had been when I was the

Apollyon. Now I was a god, and I had a future that didn't involve catering to the whims of other gods.

But it was more than all of that. A lot of it had to do with *me*. Thinking I didn't deserve her. Believing that she'd be safer without me around, better for it. That after everything I'd done and been a part of, I wasn't worthy of love.

Truth was, I still wasn't worthy of *her*, but I was working at it.

"Seth?" Her soft voice snagged my attention. "You okay?"

"Yeah." Lifting my gaze to hers, I grinned. "I'm trying to figure out exactly what your hair color is."

"You're so weird." She untangled her hair from my fingers. "So weird."

Lowering my hand to where hers rested, I swallowed the sudden knot in my throat as the image of her swollen with my child formed. Gods. That killed me in the best possible ways.

"You're beautiful," I said, letting myself look my fill. She was bare to my eyes, all soft curves and flushed skin. "Have I told you that yet today?"

"This morning, and then right after lunch."

"But I haven't in the last hour?"

"No." She rolled onto her side, facing me as she placed her hand on my chest. "We should really get out of this bed."

"Why?" I kissed the tip of her nose. "I just got you naked."

She laughed. "We've spent all morning holed up in this room."

"So?" I dragged my hand over the flare of her hip. "What else do we have to do?"

"What else? We have a lot to do, Seth." Josie snuggled in close, wiggling a long leg between mine, which did absolutely nothing to sway me to get out of this bed.

I swallowed a groan when her breasts pressed against my chest. "Like what?"

"We need to talk with Deacon and Luke and see if they've

finalized their plans to leave for Britain."

Sliding my hand over her hip to her ass, I was rewarded with a quick inhale. "You mean, we need to see if Aiden has allowed Deacon to leave yet."

She laughed softly as she ran her fingers along my chest. "I'm afraid he's going to lock Deacon in a room."

"He might." I squeezed, pulling her hips closer to mine. "Aiden is what you would call overprotective when it comes to his brother."

"Takes one to know one," she quipped.

I pulled back. "What is that?"

The corners of her lips turned up. "All I'm going to say is that I think you and Aiden have way more in common than you want to acknowledge."

Rolling her onto her back, I rose above her. "I think I'm offended."

"It reminds me of these two girls I knew at college." She placed her hands on my shoulders, pressing her nails into my skin. "They absolutely hated one another, and the funniest thing was, their personalities were freaking identical."

I put my weight on one elbow. "Aiden and I do not have identical personalities."

"Doth protest too much?"

Nipping at her lip, I curled a hand around her hip. "Doth talk too much?"

Josie kicked her head back and laughed. "Asshole."

"That's not what you were calling me earlier, just want to point that out." I brushed my lips over hers.

Her chest rose against mine. "Stop trying to distract me."

"Distract you from what?" I asked, my lips coasting over hers as I spoke.

"What we need to do." She gasped when I settled between

her thighs. "Seth—"

I kissed her, silencing whatever good reasons she had for why we needed to get out of this bed, and there were a lot. A shit ton. But I didn't want to think about any of that. Not right now. We had later to deal with reality. It wasn't going anywhere.

As my lips moved over hers, Josie made this breathy sound that told me she wasn't too eager to get out of this bed either. Tilting my head, I flicked my tongue along the seam of her lips, coaxing her lips apart. Not that she needed much persuasion.

Everything about Josie softened under me.

There was a time when I had tried to hold back, but not anymore. I dove right in, the kiss deep and raw as my tongue stroked hers, and Josie was there for it. Sliding one leg up mine, she curled it over my hip, pulling me in closer. The feeling of her against the hardest part of me fried every single one of my nerve endings.

I used to think I was addicted to aether, to that rush of cool power, but I'd been wrong.

I was addicted to Josie.

To the way she tasted. To the sounds she made when I knew she was getting close to release. To the way she called out my name. To the way she argued with me before and after. To the way she just was.

She sucked in a quick breath, and I took it for my own as she looped one arm around my neck. Her hand caught in my hair, tugging my head back. Nipping at her soft lips, I lifted up and stared down at her. Those thick, silky lashes fluttered open. Our gazes locked.

"I forgot what I was going to say," she admitted, her voice breathy.

Chuckling, I kissed the skin under her chin and got back to work on the real imperative stuff. "Must not have been very important than."

"It was." Her hand slipped to my shoulder as I worked my way down her throat. "I'm pretty sure it was really important."

"I know what's important." I blazed a trail to the rosy tip of one breast, tasting every square inch of skin and not missing a single spot. "*This* is very important."

Her breath was quick and shallow. "I'm going to have to agree with you. Just this once."

"Oh, I think it's going to be more than once." Grinning, I lowered my mouth to the taut nipple. Her back arched as her hips pushed up against mine, tempting me to skip all of this and just sink deep into her. I wanted nothing more than that, but I took my time, because today, this lazy afternoon, we had time. I made my way over to her other breast. Wouldn't want it to feel lonely.

I was considerate like that.

Sliding my hand down her stomach, I slipped it between her thighs. Her sharp cry was like a supernova exploding in every direction. I traced the mark between her breasts, the one left behind by Apollo when he unlocked her abilities, and then I started making my way down over her stomach, stopping to nip at the skin just below her navel. Her fingers tangled in the edges of my hair again, and I hoped she pulled.

I *loved* it when she pulled.

Using my shoulder, I nudged her legs apart as I settled there. I looked up, thrilled to see that her eyes were open.

And I *loved* it when she watched.

What I loved more, though? What I saw looking up at her. Such a damn beautiful sight. Her chest was rising and falling in deep, quick breaths, her nipples hard and glistening, and those lovely lips parted, eyes gleaming with desire.

I couldn't help but tease her. "Do you think we should get out of the bed now? You said there were important things to do."

She bit down on her bottom lip.

"That's not an answer, Josie."

Her eyes narrowed. "I think you can find a better use for your mouth instead of talking."

I laughed. "Damn, girl."

She grinned at me as she rose onto her elbows. "Just speaking the truth, *Sethie*."

"That you are."

And so I did.

Josie didn't stay up on her elbows for long. She was on her back, arching and twisting as I took her with my mouth. I drove her to the very edge and then tossed her right over with a curl of my finger on that one spot. Her body was still trembling when I rose, and her hoarse shout was drowned out by mine as I thrust into her, seating myself deep.

I held myself still for as long as I could, barely able to get air in and out of my damn lungs. Muscles in my arms trembled and my stomach clenched. All I could focus on was the way she felt. No matter how many times I was right here, this moment would always be the best, even if I thought that every single time.

Josie folded her arms around me as she stretched up and kissed me softly. "I love you."

"Gods," I growled, kissing her deeply, thoroughly as those three words echoed. I couldn't remain still for a second longer.

I began to move, relishing every second of the way she tightened and pulled at me. What started off slow quickly escalated. I slipped my arms under her shoulders, anchoring her to me as I thrust deep and hard.

She matched me in every way possible, and when I felt it hit her all over again, I couldn't hold back any longer. I followed, dropping my head to her shoulder as a hoarse cry of release shook me to my very core.

"I love you," I said against her heated skin.

She whispered those three words again and they mingled with my pounding heart and roaring pulse.

Neither of us moved for what felt like forever. Hell. A damn Minotaur could've strutted naked into the room and I would've been lying there, but my weight had to be crushing her, so I rolled my ass off, but I didn't go far. I brought her with me, positioning her so she was lying across my chest. I liked her like that. No space between us, hands free to touch her. One found its way to her hair.

*So damn lucky.*

Another three words that kept replaying over and over. The thing about luck, though? It was bound to run out. Always.

I closed my eyes, clearing my throat. "Boy or girl?"

This was a question we'd been shooting back and forth many times over the last week. You'd think we'd get tired of it by now, but we hadn't.

Josie's fingers skimmed along my sides. "Girl."

"Okay." I blew out a long breath. "How about Agatha? It means good-hearted."

"I like it, but I think it's a little old-sounding."

"You're right. Let me see. What about Aileen? It's like Eileen, but special."

She laughed and her breath puffed against my chest. "What does that mean?"

"Torch of light, I believe."

"I like that." She yawned. "What about…Serena? I don't know what it means, but I've always thought it was a pretty name."

"That is a good name." I started to trace glyphs across her back. "We'll put that one on the table."

Josie kissed the space above my heart. "What if…?"

When she didn't finish, I tipped my chin down. "What?"

She didn't answer for a long moment. "What if something happens? Like, to the baby?"

"Nothing will happen to the baby. I swear it on my—" My heart lodged somewhere in my throat, and I moved without thinking. Sitting up so we were at eye level, I clasped her cheeks. "Wait. Do you think something is wrong?"

"No. Not at all. I mean, I think everything is fine. I feel fine, but it's early." She wrapped her fingers around my wrists. "Like way early, and I know that anything can happen in normal pregnancies and we…we don't know if this will be normal. We don't know anything about this pregnancy."

My heart started to slow down. Not by much, though. Christ, I thought I was going to have a heart attack right then, and I was pretty damn sure gods didn't have heart attacks. But what Josie had just said was a hundred percent right. We didn't know much about this pregnancy at all. There had to be a god and a demigod at some point that got pregnant, though. There was no way we were the first.

Crazy how having a kid was something I'd never thought I'd ever want until hearing Josie say those words. *I'm pregnant.* From that very second, this kid—*our* kid—was what I wanted with every fiber of my being. The mere thought of losing this child was like being doused in ice water. I experienced the kind of terror I'd never tasted before.

Scared the shit out of me.

But I didn't want her to stress, though, and if that meant swallowing my own concern, then that was what I would gladly do.

"I'm sure it'll be normal." Wrapping my arms around her, I pulled her to my chest. "It'll be the most boring pregnancy ever."

She laughed as she wiggled her shoulder under my arm, getting as close as possible. "I don't think any pregnancy is boring."

"Ours will be. It'll be so normal, you'll even forget you're pregnant."

Josie shook her head. "Even if the pregnancy is normal, *we're* not normal. I'm not normal."

Knowing where she was going with this, I closed my eyes as I kissed the top of her head.

Her hold on me tightened. "I still have to entomb the remaining Titans. We still have that to deal with and…they aren't going to go quietly into the night. It's going to be a fight, a knock-down, drag-out fight."

I didn't say anything at that moment, because I doubted she'd want to hear what I had to say about her fighting the Titans.

Today had been too good to ruin.

And this afternoon had been so…normal. How I imagined mortal couples spent their time when they had nothing but each other to explore and spend time with.

This moment of normalcy was over, but there were going to be more moments. I'd make damn sure of it, starting with something I wanted to do, something that had been sloshing around in the back of my head ever since I found out she was pregnant.

I wanted to make Josie my wife.

And I was going to.

# 3

## Josie

*F*reshly showered, I toweled my hair dry and then changed into a pair of sleep shorts and one of Seth's shirts, because I didn't expect to be leaving the room and *peopling* any time soon.

Roaming through the small bedroom, I made my way to the window and pulled the curtain back. Night had fallen and stars blanketed the sky. It really was beautiful out here, in the Black Hills of South Dakota, but I actually missed Andros, the island Seth had grown up on.

I wanted to go back there. Soon. Hopefully.

Resting my forehead against the cool glass, I closed my eyes. I…I missed my mom. I missed my grandparents. And I missed Erin, my best friend.

I wished they were here. Not a day went by that I didn't think about them. *They're in a better place.* That's what I kept telling myself. My mom and my grandparents were in a better place, and Erin… Had she recovered from Hyperion's attack yet? I had no way of knowing. My father never hung around long enough for me to ask him. He was in and out, disappearing before I could really say much of anything.

Stepping back from the window, I sat on the edge of the bed. I could really use a talk with my granny right about now. Granted, she wouldn't know much about a demigod pregnancy, but she would be able to, I don't know, tell me everything would be okay.

That I could do this.

That I could give birth and raise a child. That I was responsible and mature enough to handle all of *this*.

And Erin would be right here with me, freaking out alongside me, and she…she would tell me I've got this.

Who knew? Maybe Erin would know something about this pregnancy. After all, she was a furie.

Looking down at myself, I lifted the hem of my borrowed shirt, exposing my stomach. It looked like it had before I was pregnant. Well, not exactly. I did lose some weight while I'd been held captive, but my stomach was still soft and it had never been flat. Ever. But it looked normal.

Which was no surprise. Duh. I couldn't be more than five weeks unless it had been before. Seth and I had always used condoms except for that one time, but condoms didn't always work.

But in a couple of months I would start showing. I poked at my stomach—

The hallway door opened and Seth called out, "Josie?"

Feeling my cheeks heat, I dropped my shirt and hopped to my feet. I skirted around the edge of the bed, hurrying to the sitting room that came complete with a little dinette.

"Hey." Placing a large brown paper bag on the table, Seth grinned when he spotted me in the doorway. "You took a shower?"

I leaned against the doorframe. "Yeah."

"Without me?"

I grinned. "Well, I actually wanted to get the shower

accomplished."

"That wouldn't have happened if I was in there with you." Reaching into the bag, he pulled out a basket of food and then another…and another. "I wasn't sure what you'd want, so I picked up a few things. Chicken tenders. Fries. I got some mozzarella sticks, because I know you like cheese. I thought you could use some red meat, so that's why I ended up grabbing a hamburger too."

My eyes widened as I stared at the buffet of food that was appearing, spread out on the coffee table. Good Lord.

Yet another basket came out, followed by a small white bowl. "And then I know how much you love their bacon, so I got that lady to make a plate. She wasn't at all happy about that, but you know, I can be super convincing—oh, and I figured you needed something green in there, so that's why there's a bowl of steamed broccoli."

Fighting a grin, I lifted my gaze from the many, many baskets of food to startling amber-colored eyes. "Seth…"

"What?" He knocked a strand of hair out of his face. "Is there something else you want?" He took a step back, toward the door. "I can run back to the cafeteria and—"

"No. This is more than enough." Laughing, I pushed away from the door and made my way around the coffee table. "I feel like I'm in an eating competition."

"You'd win if that was the case."

I shot him a narrowed glare, but he was right. I *would* win. Happily so.

Seth chuckled as he picked up the glass bottle of Coke and unscrewed the lid. There was also a glass of water and orange juice. How he'd gotten all this food and drinks here was beyond me.

Must have been another godly talent.

"I don't expect you to eat all of it," he said, glancing up at me through the strand of hair that had slipped free and fallen across his cheek again. "But I do expect you to eat a little of all of it. I don't want you going hungry."

The amount of food he'd brought me could feed a small village and then some. It was a bit excessive, but I understood why he'd brought so much food. Keeping me fed while I was being held captive by Hyperion hadn't been a priority of the Titans.

Seth knew this.

And I knew that was something that had continuously preyed on the back of his mind, as did a hefty amount of guilt. He hadn't known right away that I'd been captured.

Walking to his side, I wrapped my arms around his waist and stretched up, kissing his smooth cheek. "Thank you."

Seth twisted, dipping his chin and kissing me as he caught the end of my ponytail. He tugged on it. "I know you're starving."

Settling back on my feet, I pulled my ponytail free from his grasp. "And how do you know that?"

He cocked his head to the side. "Well, it could be that your stomach was growling like one of Hades's prized hounds while you were napping."

My mouth dropped open. "Was not!"

"Yeah, it was. It scared me, to be quite honest. I'd thought that one of those hounds had made it into our room and was about—"

"Ass." I punched his arm.

Chuckling, he stepped around me and sat down on the small couch. "Seriously, though, this is good, right? If you want anything else, I could go and get it."

Turning back to the selection, I nodded as my stomach rumbled. "This is more than good." I bent, picking up a fry and popping it in my mouth. "I didn't mean to fall back asleep, by the way. Sorry about that."

"It's okay." He caught my hand and pulled me down so I was

sitting in his lap. "When you're tired, you need to sleep."

"I think it was the whole 'working with elements' thing. I was out there for a while."

"You sure that's okay to be doing?"

I lifted a shoulder. "I don't see why not."

Reaching around me, he picked up a chicken tender and handed it to me. "How are you feeling?"

"Okay." And that was the truth. Mostly. "I mean, I'm tired, but I think that's normal with the whole being pregnant thing, even if I wasn't working with the elements earlier."

Seth was quiet as he picked up one of the tenders and bit down on it. "I want you to get checked out. I know you said it's probably too early for a check-up, but how do we really know that?" he asked, squeezing his arm around me. "We don't. So I don't think it'll hurt to talk to the doctor here and see what they suggest."

I nibbled on my tender. "You have a point."

"I know."

"You're just full of yourself today, aren't you?"

He winked as he finished off the tender. "Full of love for you."

Shaking my head, I reached for the soda. "I was thinking the same thing, but I'm not sure they'll be much help. There's no OBGYNs here. We're going to have to go somewhere else and that means we're going to be out there."

Where the Titans could possibly locate me. It was a risk I was willing to take, because I had to. We needed to find someone who could at least guide us on what to expect with this pregnancy.

"I'm sure the doctor will be able to give us basic information, talk about any other situation like ours."

"There has to be another god and demigod who got together and had a baby." Josie pursed her lips. "I mean, from everything I know about the gods, they were pretty horny."

I chuckled. "Understatement of the year."

Josie grinned at me.

"Anyway, I'll go with you, and then we'll take it from there." He smoothed his hand up and down my upper thigh. "We could go in the morning."

"Sounds like a plan." Reaching for the hamburger, I took a bite. A glob of ketchup slid out, but Seth caught it with the tip of his finger. Arching his brow, he licked it off his finger.

"You're like my own personal napkin."

"Yeah." He kissed the side of my neck. "I'm useful like that."

I moved on to the bacon, eating all the crispy slices, because it was the most amazing combination of salty and sweet I'd ever had. I had no idea how they made their bacon here, but eating it was a magical experience.

Seth ate another tender and I even forced a few pieces of broccoli down my throat before I went back to the fries. It was time for these few precious moments of normalcy to end. "So, are we going to talk about it?"

"About?"

I slid him a long look. "About finding the other demigod and figuring out how to entomb these Titans…if that's what we decide to do."

"I thought Deacon and Luke were focusing on the other demigod?"

"They are, but they can't just pop themselves to England to look around for this guy. We really don't want them taking a commercial flight, all things considered."

"Then I can bring them over." His hand stilled on my leg. "And you can stay right here, safe—"

"Seth, I know I'm safe here, but I can't stay here forever." I paused, watching his face. "You know that."

Seth lifted his hand, and a napkin flew out the bag and into his grasp. "I know you can stay here until the Titans have been dealt with," he said, and I stiffened. "Which brings me to your word usage. What do you mean by *if* we entomb them?"

For a moment, I didn't know what he was talking about, and then I realized what I had said. My stomach dropped. There was no "if" involved here. We had to entomb the Titans. Killing them wasn't an option even if Seth had already taken out two of them.

Was that a Freudian slip?

Seth handed me the napkin, and I wiped my fingers off. "Are you aware of another option?"

Tossing the napkin onto the table, I slipped out of his loose grasp and stood. "There is no other option. We have to entomb the Titans. We just need to figure out how."

Seth leaned forward, resting his arms on his knees. "I'm going to be real with you, Josie. I don't want you anywhere near the Titans."

I tossed the ponytail over my shoulder. "Because I'm pregnant?"

"Because you're pregnant with our child and because I don't want you to get hurt," he clarified, watching me. "And I'm not trying to be an overprotective jerk here."

"I know." And I did know that. I started pacing in front of the food-covered coffee table. "Trust me, running out there and fighting the Titans isn't something I'm looking forward to doing, but it's..."

"Your duty," he answered for me, his shoulders tensing. "Fuck this duty shit."

I turned to him, brows lifting.

"No. Seriously. You're a demigod. Great. You were created as some kind of fail-safe, but you control your life." Seth rose fluidly, his arms lax at his sides but his eyes burning with intensity. "This duty thing is utter bullshit."

"Seth—"

"It's the same thing with the halfs. They were born into a world that controlled every step they took, but not any longer. They are free to do with their future as they wish. Why can't that be the same for you? For the other demigods."

"It's different, though." I folded my arms across my chest as I paced in the small space. "Only we have the ability to stop the Titans."

"That's not true." He lifted his chin. "I can stop them."

"Yeah, you stopping them results in massive earthquakes where charred-up daimons climb out of them." I turned, walking to the little kitchen area to expand my pacing path. "That's not an option. You can't continue killing them."

Seth said nothing.

I faced him, my heart suddenly pounding fast, because I was thinking about what I had said moments earlier. Was there a little part of me that wanted Seth to just take them out? Even knowing the potential consequences?

If so, that was incredibly selfish of me.

People would die, innocent people, in the fallout. Wanting to keep my child safe was paramount, but could I live with the knowledge that I had sentenced hundreds, if not thousands, to death?

"There has to be another way," I said, getting my feet moving once again. "One that doesn't require the demigods to go toe to toe with the Titans or doesn't end with you taking them out."

"And how are we going to figure that out exactly?" Seth waved his hand, and the empty baskets ended up in the bag.

I shook my head. "I don't know. Maybe Medusa? She's old and seems to know stuff. I went by the library today to see if I could find her."

"No luck?"

"Nope." I sighed. "But I have a feeling she's only able to be found when she wants to be. Anyway, back to the whole finding the other demigod thing. I think we still need to do that, just in case we don't come up with Plan C."

All the food was cleaned up in moments. "What are the first two plans, just so we're on the same page?"

"Plan A is we entomb the Titans. Plan B is you kill the Titans, and hopefully Plan C will be the perfect plan that doesn't involve either of those things," I explained.

His lips twitched. "I'm hoping we find a Plan C, but let's talk about Plan A for a moment. You don't need to go find this demigod."

Letting my head fall back, I groaned. "And again, I'm just supposed to stay here? Like I said before, you do realize going to an OBGYN will require me to be present there."

"Or it requires me to find said doctor and bring them here."

"Seth."

"What?" He came around the coffee table. "We could get the equipment here and, as you know, I can be very, very convincing."

I unfolded my arms. "Are you suggesting kidnapping a doctor?"

Seth grinned, and it was the bad kind of grin. The one that told me he was up to absolutely no good. "I wouldn't say kidnap. More like convince."

"*Seth.*"

"Josie." His grin spread as he stopped in front of me. "I'm not going to kidnap a doctor. In all honesty, I think we'll be okay with leaving here for short periods of time. Plus, you'll be with me. But going to this town in England? That isn't necessary and it *is* dangerous. The Titans may lie low for a little while, but they are still going to be looking for demigods."

I exhaled roughly. "Especially since they no longer have a food source."

Seth nodded. "You being in the same location as another demigod outside these walls, or Andros Island, isn't smart."

"Is it smart for Alex and Aiden to go, then? Because if Deacon goes, you know they will be with him."

He rubbed his hands up and down my arms. "That's not our problem."

I stared at him.

"I know that makes me sound like an ass, but if Deacon goes, he knows the risk. So do Alex and Aiden." Seth's hands stopped just below my shoulders as his eyes searched mine. "I know you want to be a part of this and you want to be out there, fighting the good fight, but—"

"I really don't," I whispered.

Seth blinked, obviously caught off-guard.

Heat climbed up my throat and splashed against my cheeks. "That's a really terrible thing to admit, isn't it?" I tried to pull free, but Seth wouldn't let me. My shoulders slumped. "In the movies and books, the badass woman is still a hardcore warrior even if she's pregnant. Like Maggie from *The Walking Dead*! She was pregnant, but she still led the Hilltop to battle. With only a revolver. Or maybe it was a different gun. I don't know. But I have super powers, so whatever."

His jaw softened. "Josie, that's a TV show and not real life."

"I know it's a TV show, but if it were a real zombie apocalypse—"

"But a zombie apocalypse isn't real."

"Ugh! I know, but what I'm saying is that the Titans are the zombies and I must lead the—"

"The Hilltop to battle?" His lips twitched.

"I'm seriously going to hit you in like five seconds."

"Sorry," he replied demurely.

I drew in a deep, patient breath. "I mean, a part of me does want to still be that badass. I want to be out there, rounding up demigods, and I want to bitch slap the Titans back into their tombs."

One eyebrow crept up. "Bitch slap them back into their tombs?"

"Yeah," I said with a sigh. "But I also don't want to do anything that jeopardizes this baby. I know we didn't plan this and the whole idea of being pregnant is, frankly, terrifying, but I love it already."

Those eyes of his turned a brilliant amber as he cupped my cheek. "So do I, babe. This wasn't something either of us planned, but I love it with every part of my being."

I drew in a deep, patient breath. "People are going to think I'm weak."

He blinked once and then twice. "Josie, I don't give a fuck what people think."

I opened my mouth.

Seth wasn't done. "And you shouldn't give a fuck what people think. You're not backing down from this fight. You're being smart. You're trying to come up with different options and you're picking your battles. That's not being weak. That's being *wise*."

Pressing my lips together, I closed my eyes as I head-butted his chest. I groaned.

Seth laughed as he slid his hand back to my arm. "What are you doing, Josie?"

"Contemplating life."

"With your head on my chest?"

"Does that bother you?"

"Not really." He folded an arm around my waist. "I kind of like it."

"Good."

He rested his chin on the top of my head. "Can I tell you the truth?"

"Sure," I murmured.

"You're incredibly strong, Josie, and you don't give yourself enough credit."

"Really?" I flopped my arms.

"Yes, *psychi mou*. Everything you thought you knew about the world changed in a matter of seconds and you *adapted*. You've lost your family and you've *dealt* with that." He guided my face off his chest and my eyes to his. "You were captured by Hyperion, not once but twice, and you *survived* that. You found out you were pregnant and you've *accepted* it. And through all of that you never gave up on me. Even when I was an asshole. Even when I left you, you never gave up. You are the furthest thing from weak and I never—*never*, Josie, want you to think for one second that you're weak."

My breath caught. His words… I had no idea how badly I needed to hear them until he spoke them, and what he spoke was the truth. I wasn't weak. Hell, I'd been through some hardcore, serious stuff, and I was still standing here, a fully functional semi-adult. I wasn't cowering in the corner.

"Thank you," I said, stretching up on the tips of my toes. Showing him how much his words meant, I kissed him and then I took his hand. Settling on my feet, I turned him around, pulling him toward the bedroom. "I think it's time we have dessert, don't you?"

Seth's response was immediate, and it wasn't with words. Somehow, he got his arms around me, picking me up and carrying me into the bedroom.

And then *he* had dessert.

# 4

## Seth

The air was thick and stagnant like still, muddy waters as I crouched beside a toppled dumpster. The alley near the gloomy Hotel Cecil had split wide open, leaving a deep, jagged crevice. Embers sparked out of the gaping darkness, and there was a certain musky scent.

Off in the distance, sirens endlessly blared. A constant screeching whirl that had been nonstop since I arrived in Los Angeles to handle the latest "chain reaction" event.

The city was a freaking mess. Fires resulting from the not so normal earthquakes had taken out entire streets and neighborhoods, and what the fires hadn't destroyed, the damn things climbing their way out of these holes were well on their way to finishing off.

Shit.

Couldn't say I regretted killing Hyperion. After what he'd done to Josie, there'd be no entombing the son of a bitch. He had to die, but this... Yeah, *this* was bad.

Unfortunately, killing any Titan was a big no-no. Their deaths triggered catastrophes like the one I was dealing with yet again.

A shadow moved, and my gaze lifted. Across from me, on the other side of the giant tear in the earth, was someone I used to hate with every fiber of my being and, hilariously, the person Josie thought I had a lot in common with.

Aiden "Saint" St. Delphi stepped out from the darkness of a heavily damaged building. In his hands, he held two Covenant-issued titanium daggers.

Once a pure-blood Sentinel, a highly skilled hunter that protected other pure-bloods and hunted monsters the mortal world knew nothing about, he was now something more. A demigod, courtesy of the deal I'd made with the gods Apollo and Hades.

A deal that no longer mattered, but him becoming a demigod, enabling him to spend eternity with…with Alex was one of my rare, finer moments.

*Gods.*

There was a time when I couldn't even think her name, let alone speak it out loud. Not because I had any leftover feelings for Alex. Sure, I cared about her. Always would. But thinking about her had always ended with me flipping through the mental album of what were my *worst* moments.

It was different now.

And I knew what had changed it. Made my past a bit more bearable. There were things I'd never forget and things I'd probably never forgive myself for, but it was, yeah, bearable. And it wasn't just Alex saying she forgave me for working with Ares at one point. It wasn't just that moment when I realized I had people in my corner, people who trusted me.

It was due to Josie.

From day one, she had my back and saw me for more than who I had been, but for who I was…and who I was becoming. Sounded cheesy as hell, but it was true. She was why I was able to start moving on, and she was why I was becoming a better man.

But I was still an asshole on most days.

All anyone had to do was ask Aiden.

I couldn't say I still hated him. Hell, sometimes I wondered if I actually hated him back then. Sure, he annoyed me. He *still* annoyed the piss out of me, but hate? Yeah, not sure. Maybe I just loathed him.

Wait.

Loathing someone was probably worse than hating them.

Either way, we were never friends. He'd been the hero. I'd been the villain. That was how I'd sum the both of us up. Now? I wasn't sure what we were. Enemies? No. Friends? Maybe one day a week.

And we had *very* little in common.

He lifted his chin in my direction. We'd taken care of the charred daimons that had made their way out of the crack, but there was something else down there.

I could sense it.

So could Aiden.

That was why we were hanging around, waiting.

A rock tumbled into the crevice, drawing my attention. The sound of stone grinding against stone came next, and I knew whatever the hell was coming up out of this wasn't some charred, dead-ass daimon. It was larger.

And I was tired of waiting.

Rising slowly, I stalked forward just as a diamond-shaped shadow crested the surface.

"What the...?" Aiden trailed off.

One large paw slammed down on the broken asphalt. Razor-sharp claws sunk in, digging up loose rock as it cut into the alley like a hot knife slipping through warm butter.

As the thing moved into the flickering street lamp, my mouth dropped open. Another diamond-shaped shadow rose, and then another and another until there were five total.

I stood there, stunned into a stupor. "A *hydra*?"

Five heads swerved in my direction, their movements distinctly serpent-like. Their skin was nothing like the charred and patchy skin the daimons were rocking. The silvery sheen glimmered in the pale light, the scales as black as midnight. A second paw came down, and then hind legs. Four heavy paws hit the ground, shaking the buildings.

"You have got to be kidding me," I muttered.

The middle head opened its mouth, hissing and baring fangs—fangs that were about the size of my hand.

"Why don't you tap into some of the special god power and get rid of this thing?" Aiden called out. "You know, before we find out if this thing is hungry or not."

Two of the snake heads swung in his direction. Normally I didn't listen to a single thing Aiden ever suggested, but this was not a creature I wanted to play around with.

"Sounds like a brilliant plan," I commented.

Tapping into akasha was like stepping out into the summer rain after a drought. Every cell in my body lit up with power. Whitish light tinged in yellow curled down my arm, and I let it go.

Akasha streaked across the alley, slamming into the chest of the hydra. Hissing turned into an unsettling roar that rattled my bones. The massive creature spun around, and sure as shit, it had a tail. A long, barbed tail.

The over-seven-foot-long tail smacked into Aiden. I heard his grunt a second before he went flying back into the building he'd just come out of.

Good thing he was a demigod.

I summoned the bolt of energy again, hitting the hydra once more.

The hydra didn't go down like it should've. Two god bolts and it was still alive, about to charge me.

"Shit."

The middle head bared its fang as wisps of smoke flew out of its nostrils. A red glow appeared in the back of the snake's mouth.

Oh hell.

Hydras spit fire? Who knew?

Spinning to the side, I launched myself behind the dumpster as bright red fire scorched where I'd been standing. I rolled across the broken ground and sprung up, reaching for my daggers.

Aaand came up empty-handed.

Shit.

I'd left them on the dresser, because I was a god who could kill every living thing with a god bolt except for, apparently, a freaking hydra.

The dumpster suddenly lifted into the air and flipped over me. A heartbeat later, I was eye to eye with the hydra.

It opened its mouth, and its rancid breath turned my stomach.

"Gods." I staggered back a step. "Your breath smells like a divorced man's ass."

Red light appeared in the back of its throat, glowing. I cocked my arm back and slammed my fist into its jaw, knocking a fang out. The dinosaur-size tooth hit the ground as the hydra yelped.

Swiping down, I grabbed the tooth, and suddenly I was *flying*, ass over teacup, through the air. I hit a pile of trash that had fallen out of the dumpster, sinking through leftover food and, knowing my luck, body parts. Air punched out of my lungs as I hit the trembling ground.

Well, today was not going as planned.

It had been Marcus who'd gotten a phone call from one of the pure-blood communities outside of Los Angeles. The earthquake hadn't damaged their homes, but their Sentinels were engaged with daimons who'd come out of the broken earth. This was kind of—okay, totally—my fault, from the whole "don't kill a Titan" thing, so I figured I'd pop myself to LA and take care of business.

Aiden insisted on joining me, and I suspected it was to stop me in case I came across another Titan and decided to get all kill-kill. Not that Aiden could stop me, but whatever. For some dumb reason, I brought him with me, because why not?

I'd figured it would be in and out, back before Josie woke up, but here I was, clutching a damn hydra fang and with Aiden thrown through a building.

Man, I hoped he wasn't seriously injured. I'd never hear the end of that.

I rolled to the left, out of the pile of trash, as a steady stream of heat crawled along my back. Clutching the fang, I launched to my feet and spun, slamming the tooth deep into the chest of the hydra. Steaming blood spewed into the air.

Rearing back, the hydra swung around. I jumped, narrowly missed getting hit by that damn tail. One of its heads shot out at me, snapping down on the front of my shirt. I jerked back—

Aiden came out of nowhere, proving that he, in fact, wasn't dead or seriously injured, thank the gods. Landing on the back of the hydra, he raised his arm. Light glanced off the sickle blade as it arced high over his head.

I sighed.

Of course, Aiden didn't forget a useful weapon.

He swung the sharp blade down, chopping off the head that had hold of my shirt. The hydra bucked as the mouth loosened on my shirt.

Freed, I jumped back. "Nice of you to join us."

Aiden inched backward as the hydra whipped one of its other heads back, snapping at him. "How in the hell did you not bring any daggers?"

"I'm a god. I shouldn't need them."

"Well, obviously being a god is about as useful as a hole in the head at the moment."

"True dat," I muttered, glancing down at my ruined shirt. "Can you loan me one?"

Tossing me one of the daggers, Aiden twisted at the waist, sliding off the back of the hydra like it was a slide on the playground. He landed nimbly on his feet.

It was time to get down to work.

Together, Aiden and I sliced and chopped until the hydra was reduced to several twitching chunks. Kind of reminded me of sushi when we were all done.

"Well…" Aiden wiped the back of his forearm over his brow. A fine spray of hydra blood dotted his jaw. "That was just disgusting."

I glanced down from the bloodied dagger to the front of my torn shirt. "Yeah, it was."

Aiden stepped around what might've been a part of a leg. "You think any more are going to come climbing out of there?"

"Shit. I hope not."

"For once, we agree on something." Aiden brushed what looked like brick dust off his black tactical pants. "Was not expecting that."

"What? You haven't seen a hydra before? Thought they were like deer. Can't throw a rock without hitting one."

Straightening, Aiden lifted his chin and pinned me with a dark stare. "Smartass."

I smirked.

A can rolled out from the mess that was the alley, bumping into one of the decapitated hydra heads. Aiden and I turned.

An old, wizened man stood there, white hair sticking up in every other direction, beard as dirty as his face. He clutched a brown paper bag.

"Well, shit," muttered Aiden.

The old man took a long look at the mess by our feet and

then looked up at us. A moment passed, and before either of us could use a compulsion to make the man forget what he'd seen, he shuffled around a knocked-over trashcan and then ambled off down the alley.

Aiden looked over at me.

Lips twitching, I shrugged. "I have a feeling he's seen stranger shit living along Skid Row."

"Guess so." Sighing, Aiden sheathed his daggers into their leg straps. "We need to get rid of this mess."

I looked down and then over. "I'm thinking we can just put it back where it came from."

"Sounds like a plan."

Picking up what I guessed was a front leg, I tossed it into the crevice while Aiden grabbed a head with both hands. Dragging and pushing the pieces of the hydra over to the crack, we quickly got rid of the evidence that a mythical creature had just been sliced and diced.

Aiden knocked a wave of dark hair out of his face as he turned back to me. "You know, when you killed Atlas, one of these things opened up, right where you killed him."

"The same happened where I put Hyperion down." I looked up as a police car raced past the mouth of the alley. "No hydra, though. Just daimons."

"But you didn't take a Titan out here or in Oklahoma, where another one of these damn craters opened up." Aiden folded his arms. "You're not at all concerned about that? The fact there's doorways to Tartarus popping up randomly and leaving some really bad damage behind?"

I stilled. "Why would you think I wasn't concerned?"

"You looked about as concerned as a sloth."

"Just because I know how to stay calm doesn't mean I'm not concerned."

"You don't even sound concerned, Seth." Impatience pinched Aiden's expression. "There are consequences for what you did."

"And like you and I discussed already, if Hyperion had done what he did to Josie to Alex, you would've done the same damn thing I did. So, you can drop the saintly bullshit and save the lecture." My notoriously short patience was reaching its end. "You're starting to sound like Apollo."

A muscle flexed along Aiden's jaw. "Just because I would've done the same thing doesn't mean it was the right thing to do. You took out Hyperion days ago. And we're still dealing with this?" He gestured at the torn ground. "Are we going to be doing this again in another couple of days?"

I sure hoped not, because I really didn't want to see what else was going to come through. Well, if it was a Pegasus, then I'd like to see that. As long as it didn't try to eat me.

Aiden was quiet for a moment and then sighed heavily. "Let's get out of here before Hades decides to make an appearance."

Now that made me laugh. "He wouldn't have the balls. Anyway, there's something I want to ask you—"

I felt the presence of another god a second before the runes sparked alive on my skin. I spun, stepping in front of Aiden as the air crackled with power—*absolute* power.

"But I *do* have the balls."

# 5

## Josie

Sitting with my legs curled under me, I hid my grin as Alexandria "Alex" Andros paced in front of me while I sat on a couch in a room I'd actually never been in before.

The University in South Dakota was on a huge, sprawling campus, so there were a ton of places I hadn't seen yet. Entire buildings I hadn't even stepped foot in.

But damn, I wished I'd seen this room before, because it was full of great ways to waste a day away with, everything from air hockey to Pac-Man. The arcade games behind me were quiet, as were the tables, but I figured even if they were turned on, Alex would've drowned out the beeps and thuds with her rant.

Saying Alex was annoyed would've been an understatement.

"I can't believe they left me here." Her pretty, heart-shaped face was flushed with irritation. "I could've helped them."

This was probably my fault.

If I hadn't started roaming around, looking to see if Seth had returned, I wouldn't have run into Alex, who was *also* roaming around, looking for Aiden. The moment I asked if she'd seen Seth, she'd put two and two together, and then her uncle Marcus, the dean at the University, had confirmed what she'd suspected.

Aiden and Seth had left to deal with an issue in Los Angeles.

"They're out there dealing with daimons on steroids and I'm here when I should be out there with them." She stormed past me again, stopping by the ping pong table. For a second, I thought she might actually flip it, but she pivoted around. "And they know that. Both of them."

Pressing my lips together, I resisted the urge to laugh as I folded my right arm over my lower stomach. Only Alex would be upset about being left out of hunting down and killing charred-up, gross daimons.

"Instead, I'm doing nothing but bitching and moaning. It's not like I can't fight. They don't have to worry about me getting hurt or something."

"Like they would with me?"

She stopped, her warm brown eyes widening. "No! I didn't mean that."

I lifted my brows. "It's okay. It's kind of true. That's probably why Seth didn't tell me where he was going."

"He probably knew you'd insist on going with him." Alex started pacing again. "You can fight, too. I've seen you." Letting her head fall back, she groaned. "Guys are such caveman douchebags."

I thought about the conversation I had with Seth last night. Would I have insisted *before*? Hell yeah. I'd want to be in the thick of it, even if it terrified me. I'd want to *prove* myself. Now? I would've wanted to help, but I wouldn't have insisted. Fighting a battle I wasn't even needed in didn't seem like a wise choice to make.

Wow.

I was more mature than I realized.

"Sorry, I didn't mean to insinuate anything. I'm just so freaking annoyed." Alex plopped down on the couch beside me. "I'm going to throat-punch Aiden."

I laughed then, unable to help myself.

She slid me a long look and then grinned. "I'm what most people would consider 'extra,' aren't I?"

"A little."

There'd been a time, not too long ago, when I was consumed with jealousy when I thought about Alex and her history with Seth. I mean, who'd blame me? Alex was gorgeous and a legit badass, a legend among half-bloods and pure-bloods.

And she'd been involved with Seth.

Like there'd definitely been some swapping of bodily fluid going on between them at one point, and it hadn't mattered that at the end of the day she'd always, irrevocably been in love with Aiden.

Alex was just, well, everything I wasn't.

Or at least that was how I used to see her, and see myself. Heck, at one point I thought Seth had been in love with her. I'd gotten over all of that, mainly because I stopped comparing myself to her. We may have been oddly related in a really weird and distant way and had some bizarre stuff in common, but we weren't the same. Alex and I were now friends, pretty close friends. She'd been with me when I found out I was pregnant.

And that had still been kind of awkward.

Alex leaned back into the couch, letting her head rest against the tall, thick cushions as her arms flopped limply at her sides. "I just hate sitting things out, you know?"

I didn't really know, not in the way she did, because all of this—the fighting, the killing, the *protecting*—was still new to me, but I nodded. Alex had grown up in this life. This was just an ordinary Tuesday for her.

Her sigh was impressive, sounding so much like her uncle when he was annoyed by one thing or another. That one thing usually being Seth. "I hope we figure out why these earthquakes are still…" She trailed off as her head swiveled to the door. "Well, this should be interesting."

I followed her gaze and saw a messy riot of curly blond hair. A grin raced across my face. "Deacon!"

Aiden's younger brother inched into the room, his silvery gaze the only thing that physically matched his darker-haired brother. "Are you guys busy? I have a surprise."

With Deacon, a surprise could be anything. Once he told me he had a surprise for me, and it was a painting he'd done of a Cabbage Patch Doll. It was strikingly realistic and a little unnerving.

"No. We're not busy," Alex answered, still sprawled beside me as if all the bones had been sucked out of her body. "We're *painfully* not busy."

Deacon eyed her and then shook his head. "I have a guest."

He stepped aside, extending a hand. I expected to see his super handsome and *always* calm boyfriend Luke, but that wasn't who crept tentatively into the room.

It was a girl about my height, with warm brown skin and raven-colored hair that fell past her shoulders in tight, springy curls.

"Cora!" Surprise rippled through me. The most recently acquired demigod—er, okay, she was kind of kidnapped—hadn't stepped foot out of her room since Deacon and Luke brought her here. The only people who she'd spent time with had been Gable, the son of Poseidon that we'd found in Malibu, and Colin, a half-blood who went to school here.

The girl, a daughter of Demeter, gave me an awkward one-armed wave. "Hey."

Luke was now in the doorway, beside the dark-haired and perpetually tan Gable. I imagined he got that skin tone from spending countless hours every day surfing. How incredibly cliché was that? Being the son of Poseidon *and* having a knack for water sports.

"Cora has decided to check out the campus." Deacon clasped his hands together. "Isn't that exciting?"

Alex glanced at me. "Yeah, that's really exciting."

I smiled at the quiet girl, who was obviously way out of her element. I couldn't blame her for holing herself up in the room and refusing to come out. It had been a shock when I found out the truth about this world of gods and halfs and pures coexisting among the mortal realm. I'd run from the truth. I just hadn't made it very far.

"I figured since a lot of the students are gone for summer break, it won't be as overwhelming. I'm her official tour guide," Deacon continued, draping his arm over the girl's shoulders. "Luke is my assistant."

Luke rolled his eyes.

"And Gable-boy is here for…why are you here?" Deacon raised a quizzical brow. "Moral support?"

Gable's bronzed cheeks pinked as he quickly found something about the brown carpet to be fascinating. "Yeah. Moral support."

Knocking a wayward curl out of his face, Deacon dropped his arm. "I thought we'd check out the chill rooms first, and low and behold, we find you guys."

"I don't think we've officially met." Alex rose from the couch and walked over to the girl, extending her hand. "I'm Alex."

Cora shook her hand. "I've heard about you."

"It was all me." Deacon winked. "I gave her the unofficial but true biography of Alex Andros."

"That worries me," Alex commented, stepping to the side. "A lot."

Luke snorted as he glanced around the room. "I feel like we're missing some people. Where's Aiden and Seth?"

Alex opened her mouth, but I jumped in. "I don't think you really want to go down that road."

"Uh-oh," Luke murmured, sitting on the arm of a nearby chair.

Alex lifted her chin as she popped her fists onto her hips. "They apparently left to go deal with some Tartarus daimons crawling out of a hole in L.A. or something." She paused. "Without me."

Cora's brows lifted. "Tartarus daimons?" She turned to Deacon. "You never told me about Tartarus daimons."

"Okay. Remember when I told you all about daimons? Well, these are the ones that were kind of dead, but they've escaped the Underworld," he spoke like he was talking about a new Xbox game or something. "They're like zombies, except when they touch you, it burns your flesh."

"Oh," she said, blinking once and then twice. "Alrighty then."

Concern flickered across Gable's face. "Like the ones I saw?"

"I'm guessing so," I answered, moving my arm as I scooted to the edge of the couch and unfolded my legs. "Seth woke me up briefly to say Marcus needed him. I fell back asleep and when I woke up, he was gone—"

"So was Aiden." Alex's jaw hardened. "Without me."

"Aw, poor little Alex was left out." Deacon grinned at her. "Do you need a hug? You need a hug so you feel loved and cared about and cherished?"

Holding her hands up, Alex quickly backed away. "I do not need one of your hugs. Nope. Not today, Satan."

Deacon started toward her, arms outstretched like a happy Frankenstein.

"Why?" I laughed. "I like his hugs. They're all warm and squishy."

"What? He must give you nicer hugs than me." Alex darted behind the couch, away from Deacon. "I'm pretty sure I end up bruised after his hugs."

Looking appropriately dejected, Deacon lowered his arms and pouted. "You gave me a sad."

Cora looked away from Alex to me, and her gaze dropped. Her eyes became the size of saucers, and at first I didn't get why she had that reaction or what she was saying, but then I realized she was staring at my stomach.

I stiffened. Oh crap! I'd forgotten about Cora's abilities. Besides the fact she could bring plants back to life, she was able to tell the health of a person, anything from them being sick to them being—

Her wide-eyed gaze swung to mine. "Are you…?"

My mouth opened, but words failed me. I didn't know what to say. Of course Alex knew, but the rest of them didn't, and this was not how I planned on telling them. Seth should be here for that.

"Are you what?" Luke frowned as he glanced between Cora and me. His eyes narrowed on me. "What is going on?"

Understanding flared across Cora's face. "God, I'm sorry. I really need to learn to keep my mouth shut. I just see things and blurt them out, and then *this* happens."

"Oh, boy." Alex hopped over the back of the couch, sitting so her butt was on the back and her feet were on the cushion.

I sat back, having no idea what to say. Seth and I had kept the pregnancy a secret, because we didn't want it to get out and somehow be used against us. Not that I thought Deacon or Luke would be careless with that information, but we just hadn't shared it with anyone other than Alex.

Who, of course, had told Aiden.

Besides, the pregnancy was still so early it seemed foolish to even be telling people. What if something happened?

Deacon's pout grew. "Okay. Now I'm feeling left out, and if you think Alex bitching about being left out is bad, you haven't seen anything yet."

"There has never been a truer thing spoken," Luke commented dryly.

"I feel left out too," Gable chimed in. "Then again, I feel like I never really know what is going on." He paused, his forehead creasing. "Probably because I don't."

"Um…" I glanced over at Alex, but she wasn't much help at all. If anything, I was thinking she now looked grateful that she'd been left behind to witness this.

Cora smacked her hands over her face, and when she spoke her voice was muffled. "I really am sorry, Josie."

"Wait a second…" Luke's brows lifted as the confusion faded from his expression. I saw the moment he figured it out. His lips parted on a sharp inhale. "Holy shit."

Deacon frowned. "What? Oh my gods, if someone doesn't tell me what is going on, I'm going to start a fire."

"Okay." I lifted my hands helplessly. There was no point for me to try to hide it. I wasn't that good of a liar. "I'm sort of pregnant."

Slowly, Deacon turned to me. His face was devoid of emotion.

"Sort of?" snorted Alex as she twisted toward me. "How are you sort of pregnant?"

I rolled my eyes. "Okay, I'm totally pregnant—"

"You're pregnant?" Deacon whispered.

"Yes."

"Like you're pregnant with an actual baby?"

I started to frown. "Versus being pregnant with what?"

"So, you're really pregnant? And you didn't tell me?" Deacon snapped out of whatever stupor he was in. "Oh my gods, how could you not tell me? And *Alex* knows?"

"Hey." The corners of her lips turned down. "What is that supposed to mean?"

Deacon stared at her. "Do I really need to explain that to you?"

I jumped in before that awkward explanation was given. "I

didn't mean not to tell you all." I glanced between both guys. "I just found out myself, and Alex happened to be with me. Seth and I haven't said anything because, well, there's been a lot of stuff going on."

A grin was creeping across Luke's handsome face.

"I bet Aiden knows, doesn't he?" He pinned a glare on Alex. "Because there's no way you would've kept any secret from Aiden."

"Well…" Alex trailed off, and I swallowed a snort.

Deacon shot her a dirty look before whipping around to me. "How did I not know?"

I winced. "Please don't be mad—"

"I'm not mad!" Deacon was kneeling in front of me in a blink of an eye, proving that he was, in fact, not a mortal. "Not at you. I'm just mad that I could've been obsessing over the baby shower, like, days ago."

A surprised laugh burst out of me. "Baby shower?"

"Of course! We're going to have a huge one." He clasped my hands and squeezed. "Like, the baby shower to end all baby showers. It'll be *Supernatural*-themed."

My brows flew up.

Luke's grin was now a full-fledged smile.

"How far along are you? Do you know if it's a boy or girl? When are you due?" Excitement filled Deacon's eyes. "Can I name it? If it's a boy, it has to be Sam or Dean. No other options."

"Geez," Alex laughed. "Come get your boy, Luke."

"I don't know how far along I am," I said, but that wasn't necessarily true. They didn't need to know that the exact moment of conception occurred right after Seth had knocked Luke and Gable out and while the rest of them were asleep, in the same house. "And I don't know when I'm due or if it's a boy or girl."

"Deacon." Luke dropped his hands on the slimmer boy's shoulders. "You need to calm yourself."

"But a *baby*." Deacon tipped his head back, grinning up at Luke. "They're going to have a baby." He paused, eyes widening as he locked gazes with me. "Seth is going to be a dad," he whispered.

"Yeah," I whispered back. "He is."

"Wow. And he knows?"

Alex toppled over onto the couch, landing on her side as she moaned, "Did you seriously ask that?"

"It's a valid question," Deacon shot back.

I nodded my head. "He knows."

Deacon smiled. "I bet he is so happy."

It was so obvious that was a genuine statement that I felt tears start to crowd the back of my eyes. "He is. I thought he was going to pass out at first, but he's happy."

"Good." Deacon lowered his voice as his gaze met mine. "You deserve it. He deserves it."

"Thank you," I said hoarsely, squeezing his hands.

"Okay. I have so many questions," Deacon said. "Like, are you having a pure-blood? A half? Wait. Will it be a demigod? Or a god? Are you going to birth a god?"

I opened my mouth, but I couldn't answer any of those questions, because I didn't know.

Neither did Seth.

There was just so much we didn't know about this child and pregnancy. Would it take nine months, or would it be longer or shorter? The nurse who administered the pregnancy test had seemed surprised that I'd begun experiencing symptoms so early on, but she had said that a demigod pregnancy could be different.

Which was why Seth and I were supposed to go to the infirmary today, and I guessed we would, if he ever got back here.

"I don't know," I said finally. "We haven't figured that out, and it's not like we can Google that."

"You know who'd probably know? Apollo." Alex's lips pursed as my chest squeezed. "But that would require him actually showing up for longer than five seconds, and then saying something useful."

"Yeah." I shook off the sting that always followed when I thought of my father's lack of involvement in my life. "It would be helpful, but it…it doesn't matter if the kid is a mortal or a god. We're going to love and cherish it no matter."

"Aww," Cora murmured. "That's sweet."

"It is." Deacon rose, stopping to hug me. And it was a good hug. One that was warm and squishy. When he pulled back, Luke took his place.

"Congrats. Seriously." He patted the top of my head like I was a puppy or something, and when he stepped back, he pulled Deacon along with him. "Happy for you guys."

Tears filled my eyes as Gable kept his distance as he offered his congratulations, as did Cora.

"Okay." I cleared my throat, really hoping I wasn't going to spend however long I was pregnant being overly emotional. "So, now that the cat is out of the bag on that—"

"Or the bun is out of the oven? Heh." Alex snorted. "That was clever of me."

We all stared at her.

"What?" She crossed her arms. "I thought it was hilarious."

"Aaaanyway," I drew the word out, changing the subject. "Any update on the demigod who's in Pluckley?"

Besides the fact that Pluckley was an interesting name for a village, it was supposedly one of the most haunted places in all of Britain.

Deacon was staring at me like he'd never seen a pregnant person before. "We were hoping to get an exact location of the dude before we head over there. Because you know how Aiden is," he said this to Alex. "So, we're trying to get as much information as possible."

"Has that happened?" Alex asked.

"Not exactly, since we don't have much to go on, but it turns out Gable is a computer genius." Luke turned to where the guy stood. "He's been running some searches."

Gable shoved his hands into the pockets of his jeans as Cora sat in one of those giant, "suck you in and never let you out" bean bag chairs. "Like Luke said, we don't have much to go on, which makes it hard to even search for something. We don't know what to look for, but I was able to hack into their local law enforcement computers."

Whoa.

That sounded serious.

Alex's brows knitted. "Did you find anything?"

"Yes and no." He glanced over at Cora. "There haven't been any missing person's reports filed in the last year, which has to be a good sign, right? That makes me think that the Titans haven't found him."

"Could be," I said, grabbing the end of my ponytail. "That would be good news if he has people who would've reported him missing."

"But he did find something interesting." Deacon looked over at Alex. "Wasn't planning to bring this up right now. Might as well, but I'm not quite sure I should even bring it up."

"What?" she asked. When no one responded, she rose to her feet. "Okay. You guys are starting to weird me out." She turned to Gable. "What did you find?"

"It could be nothing." Luke glanced at Gable, answering for him. "Just keep that in mind. It could mean nothing."

She tensed. "Okay."

"So, you know how Gable has an affinity with water, practically a dolphin or a merman?" Deacon said, and Gable's forehead creased at the description. "He's Poseidon's son, so duh. And

Cora-Bora over here is like a walking, talking Miracle-Gro. She's Demeter's daughter, so that also makes sense."

I started twisting my hair into a thick rope. "Yes, we know all of that."

"And you've just realized that some of your dreams are actually foretelling things that are going to happen," he continued.

A shiver curled its way down my spine.

It wasn't until their friend Caleb showed up from the Underworld with the means to remove the bands Hyperion had placed on me did I realize that my dreams were something more, because I had seen Caleb in a dream and I'd never met him before that moment he removed my bands. That wasn't the only dream to come true in some fashion.

But there was one that hadn't come true yet.

One where I was wearing a beautiful white gown, being held by Seth, and I...I was dying.

I shoved that thought aside. That wasn't something I needed to think about. At least not at this moment.

Deacon drew in a deep breath. "We know that Zeus and Hera's kids didn't make it, because those two gods put the cray in crazy. And that Ares took out four more during his I-Want-To-Take-Over-The-World phase. That's six down. We lost two more at the hands of the Titans. We know, according to what Apollo told Seth, that they were Hermes's and Athena's offspring. We have Poseidon's kid here. Demeter's kid, and of course, Apollo's kid. That doesn't leave very many gods left."

"It leaves a lot, actually," Alex said. "It could be Artemis or—"

"This is where the part about Gable discovering something else comes into play," Deacon interrupted.

I suddenly had a bad feeling about this. Call it instinct or maybe it was a weak premonition that my demigod abilities were capable of, but either way, I had a really bad feeling about what they were about to say.

"I didn't see any missing person's reports, but I did see a lot of police reports involving fighting and assaults, all within the last couple of months," Gable explained. "And I mean some serious fights. Like, entire bars throwing down. Street fights. People getting into arguments at intersections and it turning pretty violent. The police there are constantly responding to battery calls. It's a seriously, abnormally high amount. Like, you'd think the town was the most violent and not the most haunted."

The blood drained out of Alex's face so quickly I feared she might pass out. "No way," she whispered.

"Like I'm saying, it could mean nothing," Luke reiterated. "But for some reason, both Gable and Cora had begun to experience some of the abilities tied to their parent even though their powers hadn't been unlocked. It would be safe to assume that the same would happen to this demigod. And it made us think of…"

Alex drew in a sharp breath. "It made you think of Ares. That this demigod could be Ares's offspring?"

# 6

## Seth

Even if I hadn't seen him once before, I would've immediately recognized the god standing before us. He wasn't just a god.

He was the god of *gods*.

I was not expecting to see Zeus today.

The last time I'd seen him, he wore only white linen pants and appeared to be in his mid to late forties. The only thing different about him now was that his shockingly white hair was a little longer, brushing his shoulders.

The glyphs on my skin were going crazy in response, and instinct locked up every muscle in my body. There could only be one reason why Zeus was here.

He wanted to throw down.

The moment Aiden realized who was standing before him, he dropped to one knee and bowed his head.

I, however, did not move, because fuck that shit.

Zeus stared at me, waiting for the same treatment. I smirked. His all-white eyes snapped electricity as his nostrils flared. "Your ego will be your downfall."

"That's quite ironic coming from you," I retorted, folding my arms across my chest. "Then again, I guess it takes one to know one."

Aiden's audible inhale brought a smile to my lips.

The god's lip curled and then he looked at Aiden. His expression actually softened. "Rise, my child."

Rising to his full height, it didn't look like Aiden took a single breath as he stared at Zeus. He was awestruck, staring upon a being only a very few people ever would. Because of that, I didn't hold his reaction against him. As utterly useless as I thought Zeus was, he was an impressive sight to behold.

"You have done well today," Zeus spoke, his voice deep and commanding, as if he was the very thunder in the sky during a storm. "It's time for you to go home."

Zeus snapped his fingers, and Aiden was simply gone.

Poof.

There no more.

"I really hope you sent him back to the University," I drawled, not taking my eyes off the god. "Because if not, there's going to be a certain young lady you ordered *killed* that's going to be really pissed."

His lips thinned. "You speak of Alexandria, the true Apollyon? You think I enjoyed ending her mortal life? You would be wrong."

"I don't care if you liked it or not. You did it when you didn't have to do it. Not like that. Not after what she sacrificed—"

"You speak to me of sacrifice? What do you know of sacrifice? She did. She understood what sacrifice meant and what had to be done. So far, all you know is to run when you cannot control yourself."

Shit.

That little personal remark struck home. The truth in his words stung like a damn road rash.

"Have you had to kill someone you love for the better of the world? Have you had to answer for any of your mistakes? *Truly* answer for them? What have you given up, Seth, to lead? You know nothing of sacrifice."

Anger flowed through every pore, blanketing my skin, but I managed to keep my mouth shut. Because what could I say in response? Paying for my past sins had been temporary. In a way, it was almost like I'd been rewarded with my godhood. It was something that had worn on me every day since I became...this. Something I wasn't sure how to process myself.

Zeus's smile was faint, as if he knew the reason why I stayed quiet. And maybe he did. "We could not allow a God Killer to exist, but obviously, at the end of the day, her mortal death didn't stop anything." He stepped forward, and I unfolded my arms, tensing. "You still became the God Killer."

"That I did."

"Are you not afraid of me?" he asked after a moment. "You do know that I can kill you."

I held his gaze. Only absolute power could destroy absolute power. In the whole world, there were only three of us. Zeus. Cronus. Me. "And you know that I can kill you, so there has to be a damn good reason why you've decided to make an appearance after all this time."

Zeus sneered as lightning struck, heating the sky. "You would not win a fight against me, boy."

"Are you here to test that theory?"

For a moment, I thought Zeus just might do that. Fury poured into every line of his face. The air crackled with power and the threat of violence became a tangible being, but he seemed to suck it all back in.

A tense moment passed. "You only stand before me because

we need you to entomb the remaining Titans. That is why I allow you to live."

"Allow me to live? That's cute. You know what I don't understand? Why you don't entomb them yourselves—you and the remaining Olympians. You've done it once before."

"It took everything we had to entomb them, and that was with Ares's help," he answered. "It is too much of a risk now. If one of us were to fall, all would be lost."

"So, I guess the demigods are just disposable then?" My hands curled into fists as I thought of Josie. "They're cannon fodder. Who cares about them, right? As long as they get the job done. After all, that was what they were created for."

"They must do what is necessary as we must to ensure they do not fail."

I had no idea what that meant, and I had no clue where this damn conversation was going. "Why are you here? Is it because we just killed a hydra? That really wasn't our fault. Can't have that running around the mortal realm. If that's not why you're here, can you get to the point?" I smirked. "Because I am seriously trying to keep cool right now, but you're really pushing every one of my piss-me-off buttons."

"Of course I am," he retorted. "It would not be hard. You allow your emotions to rule every action. You always have, but that must be stopped."

Impatience sprung to life. What I wanted to do was get back to Josie. We had plans for today. Pretty fucking important plans. So, I didn't want to stand here and be lectured by a god who for the last how many thousand years stood on the sidelines and watched the world burn. "I feel like I've had this conversation before and—"

"This is your I-don't-give-a fuck face? Yes, you've had this conversation before, but it has not sunk through that thick skull of yours."

"Well, now that was just rude."

"You are a god now. You are capable of changing the course of this world and every life that exists with one simple act—an act you may not even think twice of. That kind of power comes with—"

"Great responsibility. Yeah, I know. I saw *Spiderman*."

His jaw throbbed with irritation. "That kind of power comes with great *consequence*. Something you need to see for yourself."

Zeus blinked out of existence and reappeared directly in front of me, clamping a hand on my shoulder. In a heartbeat, we were no longer standing in the alley near the Hotel Cecil.

The world came into focus as I shrugged off Zeus's grasp. I opened my mouth, about to demand to know where in the hell he'd taken me, but anything I was about to say died on the tip of my tongue as I looked around and saw...

*Destruction.*

All I saw was absolute, utter destruction.

Buildings crumbling and burning, sunken into the scorched ground. What must've been a beach at one time, and all the structures near it, had been razed, leaving nothing but splintered debris. The air smelled of burnt wire and sewage, and the echo of screams clawed their way into my brain, digging in deep.

Scattered among the rubble and burning piles were broken...bodies. Dozens of them. Maybe even hundreds. They were strewn across the ground, as if they'd been picked up and thrown. Arms and legs poked out from the ruins of houses and businesses. Bodies stuck in bent palm trees. Others floated in water that was in places it shouldn't be.

I stumbled back a step. "Gods."

Zeus said nothing as he stared out over the destruction.

Horror robbed the air from my lungs as I turned, seeing a city behind me. It was a fiery hellscape. "What is this?"

"This used to be Long Beach. It is no more."

I stepped forward, but found I couldn't move any further. I couldn't make sense of it, all the death and destruction. The air reeked with it. And I had seen some shit. I'd been responsible for some shit, but this…this was absolute, unbridled devastation.

I didn't want to ask the question crawling up my throat, but I had to. "Did I…did I do this? By killing Hyperion?"

Zeus was quiet for a moment and then he looked at me. "Would knowing that his death would trigger this change the course of your actions?"

Gods, I wanted to say yes—that if I'd known this would happen, I would've done something different, but I couldn't say that. Not honestly, because I didn't know. Because how could I regret killing the creature who'd tortured Josie, nearly killing her? How could I live with myself allowing him to breathe?

How could I live with myself after *this*?

"The ramifications of Hyperion's death are vast, and the mortal realm has yet to see all of them, but his death did not cause this. Not directly." A tinge of sorrow filled his tone, and I looked at him sharply. "This was Tethys. Her response to the death of her lover. Well, one of her lovers. I do believe she is still technically married to Oceanus."

My brows lifted.

"In a fit of anger, she caused a massive tsunami. The loss of life is…substantial." Zeus shuddered. "She would not have retaliated in such a manner if Hyperion had not been killed."

My throat thickened. "You really think she wouldn't have done this if he'd been entombed?"

"That I cannot answer. Perhaps she would've, but does the what-if matter in the end? You killed Hyperion, causing other damage and death, and she responded as such, destroying entire cities all up and down the coast."

Pressure clamped down on my chest. I didn't want to see this. I wanted to say something smartass. I wanted to show Zeus that I wasn't affected, but that would be a lie.

My insides were torn up, in shreds.

Because even if my actions hadn't directly led to this, they had indirectly caused this.

"We've all made mistakes—mistakes that have laid waste to entire civilizations. Mistakes that have destroyed countless lives. You are a new god, the start of a new *era*," he said, and I turned to him, almost against my will. "And you're already beginning to learn the hard way. You do not need to follow in our footsteps. I would think you of all people would want to avoid that." Zeus's voice was quiet. "You have a lot of reasons to be angry. I get it. Your mother was a cold, heartless woman. Your father a man you never got the chance to know. You were used as a tool in a war you did not know was brewing, and you struggle with countless decisions, but you cannot let your emotions rule you. Not anymore."

I was…I was utterly dumbfounded.

I knew that one day I would come face to face with Zeus again. Probably after we defeated the Titans. I'd figured he'd try to take me out because I was a threat to him and the rest of the Olympians, just like the Titans were.

I didn't ever expect him to be standing here, giving me…advice. This was perhaps stranger than seeing a hydra.

"Why?" I asked, genuinely curious. "Why are we having this conversation?"

"Instead of trying to fight you?" He finished my unspoken thought. "Because we need to work together. Neither of us needs to be looking over our shoulders when we should be focusing on the Titans. We cannot have anything like this happen again. But there should be a more personal reason for you to want to be better than me and my offspring."

Tension crept into my shoulders.

Zeus looked away, onto the devastation. "Is this the kind of world you want your child to be brought into?"

# Josie

Cora and Gable had disappeared with Deacon after he dropped the whole "the last demigod may be Ares's son" bomb. He'd left only after I promised to meet up with him later to discuss all baby-shower-related issues. I hadn't the heart to tell him it was way too soon to be discussing any of that. I guessed they were doing the tour of the campus.

Shortly after they left, Colin showed up, and he eventually perched himself on the arm of the chair across from the couch. The first time I met Colin, I hadn't actually spoken to him. He'd been there when that poor half-blood had been killed by a pure. Later, Colin had sought to protect me, before he knew I was a demigod, and he'd been there as a really good friend when Seth had broken things off with me. And he was still here even though he knew that Seth was not a fan of his.

Probably didn't help that Colin was nice to look at. His blue eyes were a striking contrast to his dark hair, and he had classic good looks. "So, you guys really think that demigod is Ares's son?" Colin asked as he slowly shook his head. He'd been filled in on everything. "Man, that's going to be rough."

As terrible as it sounded, I was glad that we all had something to talk about and focus on instead of my pregnancy. I just wished it wasn't something as messed up as this.

"Rough?" Alex laughed softly. Back to sitting on the couch, she rubbed the nape of her neck. "I know it shouldn't matter. This guy's not responsible for anything his father did. Hell, he doesn't even know he's a demigod or who his dad was, but…"

"I get it." I glanced over at Luke as he handed me a bottle of water. "It's not like you'd blame him for what Ares did, but it's still going to be hard. I mean, I think anyone can understand that."

Colin nodded in agreement.

"Yeah." Dropping her hands, she lifted her head. "I just wasn't expecting that. I don't know why. I just wasn't, because gods, that is messed up." She exhaled heavily. "I mean, really? Can we not catch a break here?"

"But you need to deal and I know you can," Luke said as I took a drink of my water. "You've dealt with crazier stuff, and if this guy is going to be anything like Cora, we don't need to freak him out."

"You mean, freak him out any more than you're going to by showing up and explaining that he's the demigod son of the worst god ever?" Colin asked.

I smiled at that. "Probably be best to leave out the whole 'your father was a psychotic god who nearly ended the whole world' part. Not sure if it's worth telling him what his father did, at least right off the bat."

"Agreed." Alex smacked her hands down on her knees. "Then again, maybe we'll get lucky and he's not Ares's son. The fighting could be co—"

The door to the room swung open, and a very tall pure-blood strolled in. Aiden. I shifted on the couch, expecting to see Seth behind him, but the door swung shut behind Aiden.

That was…weird.

No Seth.

Before I had a chance to question where Seth was, Alex shot to her feet. "You! Oh, you have a lot of explaining to do."

Aiden stood in the center of the room. "I just saw Zeus."

Boy, did that stop Alex right in her tracks, stopped all of us.

"What?" she asked.

Colin's brows knitted as he looked over at me. "Did he just say Zeus?"

"I did." Aiden blinked slowly, like he was coming out of a daze. "I saw Zeus, and I saw a hydra."

Now I was questioning my hearing. I had to have heard him wrong. Zeus? Like *the* Zeus? And a hydra? The several-headed snake thing?

Colin's mouth opened, but he didn't say anything.

"What?" Alex shrieked, snapping forward. She smacked Aiden's arm. Hard, too. The sound reverberated through the room, causing my eyes to widen. "You saw a hydra, and you left me here? I am so mad at you. So mad."

"Sorry," Aiden chuckled, catching Alex's hand and holding it to his chest. "Heading out to deal with the daimons in L.A. was a spur of the moment thing."

Alex tugged her hand, but Aiden didn't let go. "You had time to get me. So much time. I've never seen a hydra!"

"A hydra?" Luke was frozen on the edge of the couch, his eyes wide. "How in the world did you see a hydra?"

"It crawled right out of the ground, just like the daimons had, but it wasn't burnt up or anything like that, and it was definitely not a friendly hydra." Pulling Alex to his chest, he wrapped his arms around her. Probably to stop her from hitting him again. "We learned pretty quickly that not even Seth could kill it with a god bolt. We had to chop that sucker up."

My stomach dipped. What couldn't be killed with a god bolt? I guess a hydra couldn't.

"Well, that's kind of sad," Alex muttered, her arms still pinned to her sides.

"It was trying to eat us for dinner." Aiden grinned down at the top of her head. "So, don't be too sad."

"Hold on a second," I interrupted. "You said you saw Zeus?"

Aiden looked over Alex's head at me. "Yeah. He showed up afterwards. Was not expecting that. He...he looked younger than I thought he would."

"Were you expecting to see a hydra today?" Alex asked.

I rose. "Where is Seth?"

Aiden shook his head. "I'm guessing he's still with Zeus."

Unease exploded like buckshot in my gut, causing my breath to catch. "What do you mean?"

"Zeus showed up and pretty much sent me back here. I have no idea what he was doing there or what he wanted. Surprised the hell out of me."

My heart turned over heavily as the unease turned into full-fledged dread. Zeus and Seth? Alone? "That can't be good."

Wiggling free from Aiden, Alex turned to me. "I'm sure Seth is okay."

"Zeus can kill Seth." Setting the water aside, I started for the door, but stopped, realizing there was nowhere for me to go. I wasn't like Seth; I couldn't just pop myself to wherever I wanted to go. I stopped and turned back to them. "How long ago was this?"

"Five minutes? Maybe ten? When Zeus sent me back here, I ended up at the wall, just outside the Covenant."

A lot of things could happen in ten minutes. Like them having a major fight and destroying an entire city. Antsy energy buzzed through my veins. I had the sudden urge to turn on the TV to see if there were any more earthquakes or erupting volcanos.

Alex started toward me. "I'm sure Seth is fine. It would be so stupid of Zeus to try to kill him. The Olympians know they need the demigods, namely you, to entomb the Titans. Trying to kill your boyfriend would jeopardize that."

That made sense, but based on everything that I knew about Olympians, they didn't always make decisions that made sense. Like, they usually did the exact opposite. My heart sped up.

"Alex is most likely right," Luke said, and Colin nodded from where he sat. "It would be incredibly stupid for them to go after Seth."

Starting to pace just as Alex had been doing hours before, I nodded absently. "Why else would Zeus seek out Seth, though?"

Alex and Aiden exchanged looks. There was no missing that. I stopped in front of them. "What?"

"If I had to wager a guess to why Zeus would want to talk to Seth, it would have to do with the Titans," Aiden explained, folding his arms. "Namely what happened with Hyperion."

My spine stiffened. I knew that Seth shouldn't have killed Hyperion, and I knew that a part of him realized that too, but if Zeus showed up to lecture him, it would probably end badly for everyone involved.

Because while I knew that Hyperion had needed to be entombed, not for one second did I blame Seth for killing him.

In fact, I was *glad*.

Hyperion could've killed our child. He got what he deserved.

"Seth did what he had to do," I said, knocking my ponytail over my shoulder. "End of discussion."

Surprise widened Aiden's eyes, and he looked like he wanted to say something, but he wisely changed his mind.

Turning from him, I blew out an exaggerated breath as I started pacing once more. Frustration pulled at me. There was nothing I could do but sit around and wait while hoping something horrible hadn't happened to Seth.

Or hoping he hadn't started an all-out war with the Olympians.

"We-ell," Aiden drawled the word out. "Did I miss anything?"

"Kind of," Alex answered as I turned to them.

Luke sat on the edge of the couch. "We think we may know who the final demigod is. Or who his—"

A sudden scream from outside the room cut Luke off. My

heart launched into my throat as I turned, because that wasn't a playful scream. That was one of horror.

Aiden reached the door first and Alex was quickly behind him. Exchanging a look with Colin, we followed them out into the hall with Luke trailing behind us.

Since it was summer break, there were not a lot of students in the dorm. Probably half the normal amount. Only a few doors were open, with students sticking their heads out.

"What's going on?" Aiden demanded, slipping into the role of Sentinel like it was a second skin.

"I don't know." The girl clutched the door, eyeing us with wide eyes. Most of the students were getting used to having demigods and a god on campus, but you could still see their awed shock. "I think it came from the lobby."

We picked up our pace, and I was grateful that no one suggested I should stay back due to my *situation*. The lobby came into view and there was a small crowd. A guy was standing back, his arms folded and his jaw hard, next to a blonde with her hand over her mouth. My heart jumped when I realized they were standing in front of the entombed furies. The crowd parted as Aiden and Alex neared, stepping aside.

"No," whispered Alex, her hands balling into fists at her sides.

Colin stopped directly in front of me, his back stiffening. The lobby doors opened, and Guards came in as I stepped around Colin.

"Gods," I whispered.

Lying on the floor at the feet of the entombed furies was a girl. One who couldn't have been older than eighteen. Her reddish-brown hair was spread out across the white floor. Her skin was a ghastly shade of gray and it was clear that she was...she was dead.

And resting beside her was some kind of bronze mask. The

cheeks overly round, eyes just thin slits, and a closed, wide smile. There was a symbol in the middle of the mask's forehead, a circle with an off-center arrow striking through it.

Alex gasped, taking a step back.

"*Ares*," growled Aiden.

# 7

## Seth

The fact that Zeus knew about Josie being pregnant unsettled the hell out of me. No joke. He was one of the last beings on this earth, and in Olympus, that I would want to know, but...

Hell.

As shocking as this was to even admit, I didn't sense a threat to Josie or our child from him. I wasn't worried about Zeus when it came to my child.

That was something I never thought I'd believe. Then again, there was a whole lot of shit that had changed in a matter of minutes.

I stayed after Zeus left, helping where I could. It wasn't out of a sense of reluctant obligation. Not that I didn't feel responsible.

I did.

I stayed to help, because I *should*. Because I had caused this—this destruction and loss of life. I didn't hurt these people with my own hands or by my own will, but I had set the domino in motion.

Killing Hyperion had caused a ripple effect, one that had ended so many innocent lives. And damn, I'd been here…I'd been here before, with Ares. I thought I'd learned then that every choice I made triggered a chain reaction, good or bad.

Obviously, I hadn't learned.

I was faced with that reality.

And it burned through my skin, knocked my ass down a peg or two that it took Zeus of all damn people to drive that point home. *Fucking Zeus.* But what he'd said to me was true. All of it. Especially how I didn't want to follow in their footsteps. I didn't want to make the same mistakes they had.

I didn't want to become them, making decisions that ruthlessly slaughtered others.

And I was starting right then. I had no idea how many people I helped pull out of the rubble, but I knew exactly how many of them were beyond help.

Fifty-six.

Fifty-six of them were dead and four of them… Gods, four of them couldn't have been out of elementary school. Their faces were forever imprinted in my mind.

By the time I was done in what used to be Long Beach, I was covered in dirt, sand, and a healthy amount of dried blood. My skin and clothes were streaked with the mixture, and all I wanted to do was get back to Josie, to just…hold her and talk to her.

I should've popped my dirty ass right to the bathroom to shower first, but I closed my eyes and focused on Josie's face, letting myself slip into the void. I found her, and I felt the strange tingle of my cells scattering and fusing back together.

I heard her startled gasp before I saw her. "Seth."

Josie came into view a heartbeat before she threw herself on me. Folding my arms around her as I stumbled back a second, I buried my face in the crook of her neck and breathed deeply. Her smell. It was the lotion she used. Winterberries? Whatever it was, I loved it and right then I needed it to erase the scent of death. A shudder rolled through me.

"Hey," she whispered, curling her hands through my hair. "You okay?"

Tightening my hold on her, I cleared my throat. "Yeah. I'm perfect now."

She kissed the space just below my ear as she pulled back. Gently, she guided my head up. Then her eyes widened. "Why are you covered in dirt—wait, is that blood?" She leaned back. "Are you hurt?"

"No, babe. I'm not hurt. I'm—what the hell?" The rest of the room came into view. We weren't alone. "What in the hell are *you* doing here?"

Colin whatever the hell his last name was sat on the couch in *our* room. Had to give it to the guy. He didn't run out of the room in response. There was only a slight widening of his nostrils.

But man, I didn't like that guy.

"Something happened while you were gone," Josie answered, guiding my gaze back to hers. "A girl—a half—was killed. We were all together when she was found in the lobby."

"Her neck was broken," Colin added. "Alex and Aiden are with Marcus and some of the Guards. You just missed Luke."

"He left to go find Deacon." Josie stepped to the side, threading her arm around mine. "Deacon's giving Cora a tour."

"Cora came out of her room?"

Josie nodded.

Shit, what else happened while I was gone? "I'm guessing it was a pure who did it?"

Colin exhaled roughly. "Looks to be."

Shit. Shoving the hair that had escaped the leather tie back from my face, I shook my head. These fucking pure-bloods. "Did you know her?"

"No. She was a new student. Started summer classes," Colin answered, a muscle flexing along his jaw. "Completely screwed up. Gains her freedom. Comes here where she should be safe, and then she's fucking murdered because she has less aether in her blood? Gods."

There were a lot of things wrong in our world, but this was one of the worst. "No idea who did it?"

"I don't think so. Apparently the cameras in the lobby were destroyed and no one noticed it, so there's no video to check." Josie glanced at my torn shirt and pressed her lips together. "She was just...dumped there, right by the furies. At their feet, actually."

My brows lifted. That sounded almost like someone was taunting the gods.

"But there was something with her body," Colin spoke up. "There was a mask—a bronze one. Typical Greek mask, but there was a symbol carved into it."

Josie's arm tightened around mine, and I had a bad feeling about this. "What kind of symbol?"

Colin took a deep breath, and I prepared for whatever fuckery was about to come out of his mouth. "It was Ares's symbol."

Josie

I really had no idea how Seth would take the news of Ares's symbol being carved on a mask left with the body of a dead half-blood. And we hadn't even told him what Deacon and Luke suspected about the yet to be retrieved demigod.

And I still had no idea why he was covered in dirt...and blood, but I could only focus on one issue at a time.

Seth stared at Colin with such intensity that for a second I feared he might cause the poor guy to spontaneously combust.

"Are you sure?" Seth asked, finally speaking in a voice that was unnervingly flat.

Colin nodded. "I know what the symbols look like. That was

definitely Ares."

A muscle along Seth's jaw thrummed. "Ares is dead."

"I know—*we* know that." I squeezed his arm. "What we don't know is why his symbol would be on this mask."

Seth slipped free from my grasp. Walking to the small fridge in the dinette area, he grabbed a water. The back of him didn't look any cleaner than the front. "Do you know why Ares's symbol would be on that mask?" Colin asked, and I whipped toward him. "You spent time with him. I figure…"

Colin trailed off as I shot him a look of warning. He sat back, propping one ankle on his knee as he lifted his hands.

With his back to us, Seth took a long drink, finishing the bottle of water off in record time. "I did spend time with him. Not a lot, but enough."

I tensed. Part of me wanted to tell him he didn't have to go into this. His time spent with Ares was a dark shadow on Seth. It wasn't a place I wanted him to go to, but I stayed quiet, because if Seth possibly knew why Ares's symbol was on this creepy as hell mask, he needed to talk.

"Ares wanted…destruction. It wasn't something I realized at first. To be honest, back then, I'm not sure if I would've cared or not. He wanted to see the mortal world burn, thinking by causing men to kill one another, it would be easier for him to take over Olympus." Seth turned and leaned against the counter. "It was a shit plan, obviously, but we already know that."

My fingers found their way to the ends of my hair. I started twisting the strands.

Seth tipped his head back. "In the beginning, I fell for Ares's bullshit. That he wanted equality when it came to the halfs and pures. After all, that was how he got some of the halfs to side with him, but once he set things in motion, it became clear he viewed them the same way he did mortals. Less than. The pures who got close to him saw that. Many of the old-school leaders agreed. Council members. Some of them agreed so they wouldn't be killed and others, well, they agreed because of decades of their own prejudices."

He stretched his neck from left to right. "If Ares had won, he wouldn't have just stopped with the mortals. He would've slaughtered the halfs, even those who helped him achieve victory. Those deaths would've given him the greatest pleasure, to watch their faith and trust turn to fear and hopelessness."

Sickened, I sat on the couch. I had no idea what to say. Seth didn't talk a lot about Ares, and I knew this couldn't be easy. I wanted to go to him, but I sensed that right now he needed his space.

On the other hand, Colin knew what to say. "What a twisted fuck."

I thought that summed things up quite nicely.

A smirk twisted Seth's perfect lips as he met Colin's gaze. "You don't even know the half of it."

Colin swallowed. "So, you think that whoever left that mask supported Ares?"

"I took out a lot of people who sided with Ares," he replied dispassionately, and my heart squeezed. "Obviously, I wasn't able to get all of them. Some of them are still out there."

"So, it's possible? That whoever is doing this could've been a supporter of Ares?" I asked.

Seth folded his arms. "Could be."

"This isn't an isolated event," I pointed out, letting go of my hair as I twisted toward Colin. "Right? There have been multiple attacks."

"There have." Colin nodded. "A lot of them are resistant to change. Shit. Many of their families have lost all their servants and have to do their own shit now. No more free labor, so a lot of them are angry. But angry enough to kill? I don't know. There could be more behind this."

Seth was quiet for a moment, and then he said, "It's entirely possible that one of his supporters is somehow goading these younger pures into this, or that some pissed off pure-blood is cherry-picking Ares's beliefs to back what they're doing."

"Either way, we need to find out who is responsible here and stop them." I saw the girl's face in my head and I remembered everything else that had happened. "This has to stop. It's not okay. It's not something we can look away from and pretend it doesn't involve us."

Seth was still for a moment and then he nodded in agreement.

"Shit," Colin repeated, and then he stood. "I need to find Marcus and fill him in. I'll see you guys later." Colin nodded at me and then Seth, who had no response other than to open the door before Colin had reached it.

Colin halted for a minute, glancing over at Seth.

Seth winked.

"Thanks," Colin murmured, and then skedaddled out of the room.

I sighed. "You love messing with him, don't you?"

"Is answering that question honestly going to get me in trouble?"

I stared at him.

Seth grinned, but it quickly faded. "I'm sorry you had to see that girl."

"I'm sorry it happened to her. She was young, Seth. She just started going here and…this is how it ends for her. Why? Because she was a half-blood?" Disgust rolled through me. "It isn't right."

"No," he said quietly. "It's not."

And I still had to tell him about the demigod. "What happened to her isn't the only thing. Luke and Deacon think they've figured out who the last demigod is."

Tiredness settled into his features. "Am I going to want to hear this?"

"Probably not."

"Then pull it off like a Band-Aid."

I scooted to the edge of the couch. "They think it's Ares's son."

Seth's brows lifted. A moment passed. "You're shitting me?"

"No. I'm not."

"Why? Why do they think this?"

"There have been a lot of fights in the town he lives in. Like way too many, and they think it's his presence. Take Cora, for example. Even though her abilities haven't been unlocked, she was able to bring back dead plants." I paused, remembering what happened today. "Oh, and by the way, she can tell when someone is sick or pregnant. Luke and Deacon and Gable now know."

Seth stared at me.

"She didn't mean to do it. She looked at me and saw that I was pregnant, and kind of blurted it out." I shrugged. "Kind of freaky if you think about it."

He gave a little shake of his head. "All righty then. Hell, I don't know what to think." Pushing away from the counter, he walked over to the couch and sat next to me. "I don't care about them knowing. The other stuff? Strange how the dead still have a way of screwing things up." His head fell back and his gaze slid to me. "I'm guessing Alex heard about the demigod. How did she take it?"

"It freaked her out a little." Shifting toward him, I drew one leg up onto the couch. "I don't think she was expecting that."

Seth closed his eyes. At that moment, he looked so incredibly young. Dirty. But young. There was a vulnerability in the lines of his face that I knew he didn't let anyone else see.

"I can't say I'm surprised," he said after a moment. "I mean, it's like fate just keeps on screwing with everyone for shits and giggles."

My gaze dropped to his ruined shirt. "I'm sure Aiden or Marcus or someone is going to want to talk to you about Ares, but before then, what…what happened today? I know you saw Zeus. Aiden said so. Did you two…fight?"

Rolling his lower lip between his teeth, he turned his head away from me. "We didn't fight."

Shock rendered me speechless for several moments. "You didn't?"

"Sounds unbelievable, but it's true. Zeus didn't even attempt to go at me."

I leaned forward. "And you?"

"I didn't try anything. He wanted to talk."

My brows furrowed. "But then why do you look like you went toe to toe with a pile of dirt?"

The quick twist of his lips was good. "That came after Zeus left."

Reaching out, I poked his thigh. "You're going to have to give more detail."

His chest rose with a heavy breath. "Have you seen the news today?"

That wasn't a question I was expecting. "No, I haven't. Why?"

A second went by and Seth opened his eyes. "Zeus just wanted to talk. Well, it was more like he wanted to give advice, and I saw some things."

None of that was making sense. "What did you see?"

A muscle worked along his jaw, and I began to get really, really worried. "Death. A lot of unnecessary, preventable death."

I stilled. "What…do you mean?"

"Tethys caused a tsunami and destroyed Long Beach," he said, and my breath caught. "She was apparently angry over Hyperion getting killed, so she absolutely destroyed the area. Killed hundreds, if not more. That was what Zeus showed me."

I opened my mouth, but I was once again struck silent.

Seth lowered his head and looked over at me. "I know I didn't kill those people myself, but my actions caused their deaths. Some of them…they were kids, Josie. I pulled *children* out of broken and half-washed-away homes."

Sucking in a sharp breath, all I could do was stare.

"I know I didn't do that to them, but I caused that and I…" He exhaled roughly. "Zeus said something to me that was so damn right."

"What?" I whispered.

"He said I didn't want to follow in their footsteps, and I don't. They've spent thousands of years screwing things up by acting selfish or rash." His haunted gaze held mine. "And I did the same thing."

I stiffened. "Seth—"

"I did, Josie. We can all be honest here. With Atlas, I get a pass. I reacted right then and there, having no idea what I was at that time. I wasn't in the…right mind, but Hyperion? I knew what I was doing. I was getting revenge. I'm man enough to admit that. And the most messed up thing? I still don't regret killing him. I regret what my actions have caused, but I…" Leaning forward, he folded his hands under his chin and stared straight ahead. "Zeus knows you're pregnant."

I gasped. "Is that bad? That sounds bad."

"I don't think it is. I don't think he wants to cause either of us harm. At least not right now," he added, and I wasn't sure if I should feel relief or not. "And he asked me a question, Josie. He asked me if this was a world I wanted to bring a child into."

Closing my eyes, I sank into the couch. That was a horrible question to pose to Seth after showing him what Tethys had done because of Hyperion's death.

"And I don't want to bring our child into a world like that, but most importantly I don't want our child to grow up and have to learn what I've done. Who I am."

My eyes flew up. "You're an amazing—"

"I've done a lot of bad, Josie." He was still looking at me, his pupils slightly dilated. "A lot of bad shit, and I wanted to be better for you. Killing Hyperion may make you safer, but it didn't make me better."

"I know you have done bad stuff, but that isn't the sum of who you are." My heart was cracking for him. "You are making amends. You *have* made amends. You're not a bad person, and I know, without a doubt, that our child will never be ashamed of who his father is."

His throat worked on a visible swallow and when he spoke, his voice was hoarse. "I want that to be true. I need that to be true."

Tears scalded the back of my throat as I rose. Seth opened his arms, and I didn't care that he was dirty and covered with God knew what. I clambered into his lap, wriggling my arms behind him. He folded one hand behind my head, his fingers curling through my hair. He tugged me tight against his chest, so close I could feel his heart pounding. A deep shudder rolled through him, and my breath caught.

I wanted nothing more than to make him feel better, but how could I? What could I say? Any niceties would just be lies, and Seth would know that. No matter what, his actions had caused what happened in Long Beach and in L.A., and even if it was indirectly, it didn't matter.

Actions had reactions, and he knew this.

It was something he was going to have to live with. All I could do was lessen what I knew he was already doing to himself. All I could do was help him.

I kissed his dirty cheek and then his sweat-covered brow. Tears dampened my eyelashes as he tilted his head up and I brought my lips to his, kissing him deeply as I dragged my hands free from behind his back. I clasped his cheeks.

"There's only one option, then," I said, drawing back so we were eye to eye. "We'll make that true."

# 8

## Josie

Seth told me what he saw in Long Beach: the destruction and the death, the heartbreak he witnessed as people pulled their loved ones out of rubble. He knew the exact number of those he found who'd passed away.

Fifty-six.

Four of them were children.

My heart broke for them and it shattered for Seth, because this...this was a hard lesson to learn—a lesson that wouldn't be forgotten for a long time.

Comforting someone who was basically responsible for an unnatural disaster wasn't something I was particularly skilled at, but I quickly realized that all I needed to do was let him talk and just be there.

And I meant what I'd said to him earlier. I would do anything and everything to make sure that Seth saw that he was going to be the most wonderful father and that our child would never grow up to be ashamed of him or fear him.

When Seth finally fell asleep on the couch, I think it was

more a case of passing out from exhaustion than anything else. So I curled up against him, my hand on his chest. I feel asleep that way, feeling his deep and even breaths.

I wasn't sure how many hours had passed when I felt an arm snag me around the waist and tug me to the side. I ended up against a warm, hard chest, and I blinked my eyes open.

Thick, dusky lashes lifted and two amber-colored eyes met mine. "Hey," he murmured.

Sleep clung to my thoughts as I realized we were in bed, lying on our sides, facing one another, and Seth's hair was damp, his face free of dirt. "How did we get in bed?"

"I carried you in here a couple of hours ago. You've been dead asleep. Didn't even wake when I got your shoes and jeans off. Or when I took a shower." He tucked a strand of my hair back from my face. "Or when I got back in bed."

"Really?" I yawned. "What time is it?"

"Pretty early." His hand left my hair and he trailed the tips of his fingers over my brow. "Sorry to pass out on you on the couch."

"It's okay."

A different kind of smile played out on his lips. Not a bad one. More of a boyish one. "You're lying."

"Na-uh," I murmured.

"That couch is about as comfortable as a two by four." His finger skipped down the center of my nose. "Then again, I was there, so it was probably the best sleep you've ever had."

I let out a sleepy laugh. "Your ego never fails to amaze me."

His gaze searched mine as his finger found its way to my bottom lip. "You never fail to amaze me."

"Why? Was I snoring again?"

He chuckled. "No. But the fact something so beautiful can sound like Chewbacca getting run over by a van is pretty amazing."

"I do not sound like that." The sleep was finally clearing from my thoughts. "You're a liar-liar, pants on fire."

Seth winked, and I rolled my eyes. "But I wasn't talking about that. You just…you amaze me, Josie."

A goofy grin tugged at my lips. "I do?"

"Yeah." His finger dipped to my chin. "I just thought I'd let you know that."

"Thank you." Faint light tracked underneath the blinds, washing over the curve of Seth's cheek. "How are you feeling this morning?"

There was a time that Seth probably would've shut down and not answered the question. Made some joke and laughed it off. He didn't do that now.

"I'm okay," he said. His lashes lowered as he dragged his finger down the center of my throat. "Thinking about things, about what I saw, but I'm…okay. You?"

"The same." I placed my hand on his bare chest, and he jerked a little at my touch. I liked that, knowing that something as simple as me touching him had such an effect on him.

His gaze flickered over my face. "I owe you a thank you."

My brow puckered. "For what?"

"For last night. For just being there and listening to me." His finger skated around the edge of my collar. "You have no idea what that means to me."

I think I knew how important it was. "I'm always going to be there for you. No matter what. I love you, Seth"

Those three little words had been so hard to speak before. There'd been a time when I didn't have the courage to say them. Now I wanted to shout them from a rooftop like a goofball.

His eyes heated to a warm, tawny color. "Say it again," he whispered, pleaded really.

My gaze met his and I said it again and then again, and I kept saying it until his mouth silenced me. His lips were gentle on mine, a sweet sweep that was at such odds with his enormous strength and power, and even though it was such a gentle touch of his mouth to mine, I felt it in every part of me. Seth kissed me softly as he lifted up just enough so that I could see him. He leaned back. Guiding my hand off his chest, he clasped his fingers around mine and drew our joined hands to his mouth. He kissed the center of my palm.

"I will never get tired of hearing that." Lowering my hand back to his chest, to where his heart beat so strongly, he then folded his hand around the back of my neck. "And I'll never stop feeling it. What I feel for you increases every waking moment and sometimes that scares the hell out of me, but I love you. Yesterday. Today. A thousand tomorrows from now, I will be in love with you."

Warmth poured into me. Hearing those words was like basking in the sun, and Seth drove those words home with a kiss that went beyond the soft, gentle one we'd just shared. The way he kissed me was as if he was claiming me with the act, and I was claiming him in return.

What we felt for one another was said over and over again in every kiss and every touch. Somehow the blanket got pulled down and then Seth's hands gripped my hips. He pulled me to him, pressing his body to mine. The loose sweats he wore proved to be a thin barrier between our bodies, and the minty taste of his kisses and the way his hard body felt against mine made me greedy.

I wanted more—wanted him so badly that not only every part of me ached, but the wanting went beyond the physical, deeper, etching into my skin, seeping through my bones and settling in my muscles.

It was crazy how intense all of this could still feel—as if it were our first time kissing one another, touching one another. Maybe that was what being in love did. I had nothing to compare it to, but I like to think that was why. It had to be, because each time was like this, like it was our first and it would be our last.

"Beautiful," he said, voice thick as he trailed his fingers across the tip of one breast. I jerked as my heart jackhammered as his hand dipped, drifting over my stomach in a way that was reverent. His lashes lifted as his stare pierced me. "And I know in the upcoming months, you're going to become even more beautiful."

My heart swelled so fast and so big I thought I'd float right up to the ceiling. He meant that. There was no denying the truth in his words.

Then he was kissing me again, and these moments, those words he'd just spoken, were precious and powerful.

His lips skated over the curve of my jaw, toward my ear. A shiver danced over my skin as a heady flush followed, causing my muscles to tighten. "I know we have a busy day ahead of us."

"We do," I whispered back.

He kissed the corner of my lip as he drew back. "I know we need to get with the rest of them and talk about what happened here yesterday."

I cleared my throat as I let my eyes drift shut. "Yeah."

He started a line of tiny kisses that trailed from my chin down my throat and then further still. "And then we need to talk about this demigod."

My fingers dug into the comforter when his mouth found his way to one of my breasts, stopped and then lingered, drawing a shuddering gasp from me.

Then his lips skimmed over my ribs, hitting a ticklish spot. "We need to get that demigod before the Titans do. If he's anything like his father, we don't want the Titans deciding he's more valuable than being a battery pack for them."

That was true. Especially if he was able to influence others to become violent. That was a useful talent for those with nefarious goals.

He kissed just below my belly button. "But there's something we need to do first."

My thoughts were a bit scattered. "What is that?"

"You didn't go to the infirmary yesterday, right?"

"No." I opened my eyes and tilted my chin down so I could see him. "I wanted you to be there even if they just tell us we have to go somewhere else."

Seth looked up and grinned in a way that caused my heart to flop around. "Thank you."

"Of course."

His gaze coasted over me. "We need to do that first before the day gets crazy."

"Agreed." I caught his gaze and grinned. "We should get ready right now."

Chuckling, Seth rose once more, climbing over me. "Oh, we are not doing that right now."

"We're not?" I placed my hands on his warm shoulders.

His arms were huge and powerful as they came down on either side of my head, planting deep into the mattress. "I think I must've misspoken," he said, his lips brushing mine. "There is one other thing we are going to do first."

My stomach fluttered. "And what is that?"

"Well, it's something you're going to do first."

Air hitched in my throat as his mouth took control of mine. Folding my arms around him, I held him close. His tongue swept over mine. Then Seth was on the move again, sliding down and taking his sweet time doing so. Somehow my panties were gone. There was nothing between my skin and his hands and mouth. It had to be godly magic, because they seemed to disappear, and then I realized it *was* magic, because his tongue found the oddly sensitive crease between my thigh and hipbone. I lost my grip on his hair as he worked his way down my inner thigh, nipping at my skin and then soothing the illicit little sting with his tongue. Each sweep of his tongue was like touching a live wire.

I shuddered as his warm breath drifted over the most intimate part of me. "What…what am I going to do first?"

His lips tilted in a downright wicked, mischievous grin. "You're going to scream my fucking name."

## Seth

With Josie's hand firmly wrapped around mine, we followed the walkway to the two-story building adjacent to the training facilities.

It was still early and only a few students were out milling around, most of them heading to the cafeteria for breakfast.

The sun was bright, the air was warming up, and what I'd done to Josie in that bed still had my body thrumming. Yesterday was fucked up in a whole lot of ways, but today…today was already better.

"How many students do you think are registered here during the summer?" Josie asked.

I glanced over at her. She'd thrown her hair up in some kind of twist that looked like it was seconds from toppling off her head. Had to be some kind of girl magic that kept it up there. "Not sure," I answered. "If I had to guess, I would say probably a couple of hundred? Maybe a thousand or so."

"I don't know if that's a lot compared to a normal college." She glanced over at one of the statues of the muses. "But that seems like a lot."

"Some of the students probably don't have a home to return to." I pushed past the cold feeling that poured into my chest. "A lot of them were displaced during the war with Ares. I imagine they use summer courses as a way to have a place to stay."

She looked over at me. A moment passed, and she squeezed my hand.

"Why are you asking?"

One shoulder lifted. "The campus just seems empty. It's probably a good thing, with what happened yesterday."

I nodded. "True."

Stepping in front of her, I opened the door to the infirmary and led her down a wide hall, to another door that opened into a waiting room.

We walked up to the square window where an older half-blood sat. It was a little strange seeing a half in a position like this. Before the Breed Act, halfs were either Sentinels, Guards, or servants. They weren't in positions like this, and I doubted this was commonplace yet. The University would be one of the first places employing halfs. The rest of the communities would be slow to follow.

She looked up, and I immediately recognized that she must've been a Sentinel or Guard at one point. There was a daimon tag—a bite mark—on the woman's left cheek.

Fucking daimons.

They were assholes like that.

Her nervous gaze bounced between us. She sensed what we were. "How can I help you?"

"We'd like to talk with a doctor, if one is available," Josie said.

Still holding onto her hand, I placed one elbow on the ledge and leaned in. "In other words, a doctor needs to be available."

This time when Josie squeezed my hand, there was nothing reassuring about it. I sent her a wink.

She rolled her eyes.

The woman behind the window nodded. "I have a feeling we have one available. Take a seat."

Raising my brows at Josie, I backed away from the window, tugging her with me.

"Behave," she murmured as the secretary disappeared from view.

"Always."

She pinned me with a knowing look as she sat and reached toward her head, but stopped with a frown. I knew what she was doing. Whenever Josie was anxious, she messed with her hair, twisting the length. She must've forgotten she'd pulled her hair up.

Not wanting her to be anxious, I placed my hand on her back and rubbed. "Hey."

Josie looked over her shoulder at me. "What?"

"After this, we should make a pit stop and grab some bacon." Her eyes lit up. "Sold."

I chuckled as I continued rubbing her back. "Then we'll go find Alex and Aiden."

"Sounds like a plan." She bit down on her lip as she eyed the window. "Keep rubbing my back. I like it."

Smiling, I leaned forward and kissed her cheek. "Wasn't planning on stopping."

"Good."

Movement out of the corner of my eye caught my attention. It was the secretary. No sooner had the half reappeared behind the window when the door to our right opened and a female pure-blood appeared. She was wearing blue scrubs and a white lab coat. "You two need to see a doctor?" she asked.

I had a feeling that a doctor didn't normally come out and retrieve the patient, but then again, I doubted the infirmary was accustomed to a god and a demigod asking to see a doctor.

Josie slipped her hand free and stood. "Yes."

The doctor glanced at me and then nodded, holding the door open. "Together?"

"Of course." Josie motioned at me and then started forward. Rising from the not-so-comfortable chair, I followed behind her, making a promise that I'd keep my mouth shut and behave, because it was obvious that Josie was nervous.

The doctor waited for us in a narrow hall. If she was wigged out by being in our presence, she didn't show it. Her expression was one of professional interest and nothing more. "I'm Dr. Morales." She extended a hand.

"Josie." She shook the doctor's hand and then twisted to me. "This is Seth."

The doctor folded her cool hand around mine. "Nice to meet you both. Why don't you two step in here?"

Dr. Morales opened the door to a small room that looked like any other normal doctor's office. Josie hesitated for a moment and then walked over to the exam table and sat on the edge. I stayed close to her, keeping my hand on her back.

"So, what are you two here for?" Dr. Morales took a seat on one of those leather stools with wheels on the legs.

Josie glanced at me, and then drew in a deep breath. Her cheeks flushed a pretty pink. "I'm pregnant and he's…he's, um, the father."

I resisted a grin. Josie was just so damn adorable sometimes.

There was a flicker of surprise that rolled over the doctor's face. I was sure she didn't see a lot of people our age having children. Halfs had always been required to take birth control, and pures typically didn't have children until they were much, much older.

"I don't know if you know what we are," Josie added.

Dr. Morales crossed a leg over the other. "I know who you two are." A quick smile appeared. "I'm pretty sure everyone here knows who you two are."

"Okay." Josie looked relieved. "I don't think I'm very far along or anything, but we really don't know what we're supposed to do other than get an appointment with an OBGYN."

"There aren't any OBGYNs here," Dr. Morales said.

"We expected that," I intervened, still moving my hand along Josie's back. "Not like a lot of students here are having babies, but we figured it would be a good idea to get checked out and find out what our options are."

"Okay." Dr. Morales rose, reaching for the stethoscope around her neck. "What I can do is do a general exam and make sure that all the vitals for you are normal, and then we'll go from there, all right?"

Biting down on her lip, Josie nodded, and then it was time for me to step back and give them some space. Dr. Morales got down to work, listening to Josie's heart and then her lungs. Josie even got her ears checked, as well as about every orifice except for the interesting ones. Then Dr. Morales moved onto questions. Personal ones. Ones that made Josie flush even deeper.

Was this her first pregnancy?

Was she positive she was pregnant?

When did she think she got pregnant?

That was when I jumped in. "It's been about five to six weeks."

"You can sit up now," Dr. Morales said after palpating Josie's stomach. I had no idea what that did. "All of your vitals are perfect, and this is definitely an early pregnancy. Usually at this stage in a pregnancy, it's a wait and see period."

"What does that mean?" Josie straightened her shirt as I returned to her side and got back to the rub-down.

Dr. Morales sat back on the stool. "What do you two know about pregnancy among our...among our kind?"

I lifted my brows. "Well..."

Josie shrugged as she started gently swinging her feet. "Is it not like a...a mortal's pregnancy?"

The doctor smiled then. "In terms of pregnancy length? It's nine months. Some don't make it to full term, just like with mortals, and have the baby a little early. That does appear to be more common with our kind, especially the pure-bloods, and I imagine that will be the same for you two based on the amount of aether you both have."

"Wait." Concern rippled through me. I didn't know a lot about babies, but I knew delivering early could be bad, real bad. "How early?"

"Nothing too serious. Definitely in the third trimester, usually around eight months, but…" She exhaled hard. "Pregnancy between two pures is notoriously hard to carry out of the first trimester, and with half-bloods, it's even harder."

I stiffened, but I didn't let my hand still. "I didn't know that."

"I didn't think so. I know that pregnancy is not something that is often discussed among…" She trailed off, but I knew what she meant. Since I was a half-blood while I was Apollyon, pregnancy was forbidden. "No one really knows why. Some truly believe it's just Fate and nothing medical."

My upper lip curled. Fate. Gods.

"Is there something I can do to make sure I don't lose the pregnancy?" Josie asked.

"We've had women go on bed rest from the moment they found out they were pregnant and it hasn't made a difference. It's something that will either hold." Dr. Morales looked at me. "Or it won't."

That sounded like utter bullshit to me.

Josie glanced up at me, her eyes wide.

Dr. Morales focused on Josie. "Right now, you still have several weeks to go before you make it to the second trimester. I can tell you that typically women in their third trimester are more symptomatic."

"What does that mean?" I curled my hand around the nape of Josie's neck, smoothing my thumb along her pulse.

"More fatigued. Nausea and vomiting usually affect our mothers in the third trimester and not the first, like with mortal pregnancies. Backaches and other things like that, but you two…you two may be entirely different."

Josie inclined her head. "In what ways?"

"As far as I know, and granted, it's been a long time since I took Myths and Legends, but I do not recall there ever being a child of a demigod and a god."

Shit.

Both of us had been so sure that there had to be another case like ours. If there wasn't, that meant…

Josie's feet stopped swinging. "So, you're saying that we're the first?"

"First documented case that I know of." Curiosity filled Dr. Morales's gaze. "Anything is possible with the pregnancy."

# 9

## Josie

The best OBGYN.

That was what Seth had ordered when Dr. Morales said she was going to make some phones calls to find us an OBGYN. Dr. Morales assured us that would be the case, but at that point, I would have just been happy with any doctor who specialized in the whole birthing babies thing.

Seth and I were the first ever god and demigod to get together and have a child? That was... Wow, that seemed insane to me. Which meant that everything Dr. Morales said, about having difficulty carrying a baby to having more symptoms in the third trimester, could mean nothing.

Like the nurse before her, the one who administered the pregnancy test, Dr. Morales took a blood test just to confirm the necessary hormones were still present.

I didn't need the blood test to confirm what I already knew. I was still pregnant. Call it instinct or a soon to be mother's intuition, but I knew.

Seth and I didn't get the chance to really discuss anything the doctor had spoken to us about, since we went to the cafeteria to grab some bacon and ended up running into Alex and Aiden. They were on their way to see Marcus and that's where the four of us ended up, in Marcus's office.

Alexander, Alex's father, was there, a silent sentry who smiled in such a way that the moment he saw his daughter the skin around his eyes crinkled.

A pang lit up my chest as I watched Alex break away from Aiden, and go right up to her father and hug him. It wasn't the burning feel of jealousy or envy. But I did envy that, their relationship. I wanted that with my father. Heck, I would have liked to *see* my father. So, mostly, I just felt…sad.

I looked away as I walked to my chair, catching Seth's gaze. There was a soft look in his eyes, one that made me wonder if he knew what I was thinking.

His fingers brushed along my arm as I stepped around him. The touch was oddly soothing as I sat in one of the large, wingback chairs across from Marcus.

"Thank you," Marcus said, sitting down behind his huge, mahogany desk as he eyed Seth. "For not just appearing in my office, but instead walking through my door."

Aiden smirked from where he stood next to the other empty chair.

"I figured I need the exercise today." Seth folded his arms across his chest. "But I'll make sure to pop in when you least expect it later on."

Marcus shot him a droll look before looking over at Alex. She sat in the chair beside me. "I'm assuming you all are here to discuss what happened yesterday?"

So much had happened yesterday that I wasn't exactly sure which part they were starting with.

Alex spoke up, taking the lead as usual. "So, we think we have some information on the half-blood that was killed."

Sitting back, Marcus dropped one leg over the other. "Right now, I would love nothing more than to have the name of the perpetrator."

"That we don't have," Aiden chimed in.

"And what would you do if you had a name?" Seth asked.

Marcus's gaze slid to where Seth stood beside me. "What I would need to do is turn the person over to the authorities, but that is not what I would *want* to do."

Seth inclined his head. "Understood."

"Okay," I blew out a long breath. "Now that that's out of the way... The mask yesterday had Ares's symbol on it."

Marcus's jaw hardened. "It did."

"And after talking with Seth, we think that whoever this is, if it's a person or a group, they are following Ares," I continued. "Well, following some of his beliefs, that is."

"At the end of the day, Ares hated half-bloods. He viewed them the same way he did mortals. There were a lot of pure-bloods that agreed with him—with the idea that pure-bloods should be ruling the mortal realm and halfs and mortals should be subservient to them." As Seth spoke, his voice was flat and without emotion, but I knew talking about Ares was probably like stabbing yourself over and over with a hot poker.

Especially considering who was in the room.

"When I was doing *Remediations* for the gods, I took out a lot of his supporters, but not all of them," Seth finished.

"I wouldn't want to believe that was the case, that whoever has been responsible for what's been happening on campus here has anything to do with Ares," Aiden jumped in. "But we cannot underestimate what it means for Ares's symbol to be on that mask."

"And it makes sense." Alex leaned forward, her shoulders tense. "There have been a ton of problems here—"

"Not just here," Marcus cut in. "There's been similar issues and murders in some of the pure communities and at the Covenants."

"So, it would have to be somewhat organized," she went on. "Right?"

"Most hate groups are. Some are more organized than others, I imagine." Marcus rubbed two fingers along his temple like he was trying to scrub away a headache. A long moment passed and he dropped his hand to the arm of the chair. "One of the last things I ever wanted to hear was Ares's name."

"You and me both." Alex's voice was soft, and I knew Seth was thinking the same thing. "He may be dead, but I don't think we've heard the last of him."

# Seth

"What's the plan, then?" Marcus asked, getting down to business like he always did.

"Whether it's a group of pures who still follow Ares's beliefs or not, I think we need to start with the obvious. The pures that are here, on campus."

"Not just the students, but also the staff," Aiden agreed. We hadn't talked about this, but we were obviously on the same page. "So, we'll need a list of every single one."

Marcus raised a brow. "That is a lot of confidential information."

"I know it is." Aiden's smile was tight. "And I know sharing that info goes against a lot of rules, but we need to be able to check each of these people out."

"And look for what?"

Josie leaned forward. "It would depend on what you have on the students and staff here. Their backgrounds, where they came from, family information, and what not." Eagerness filled Josie's voice, drawing my gaze. "If you have that kind of information, we could build a profile."

Alexander's gaze sharpened.

"What do mean by a profile?" Alex twisted in her seat toward Josie.

"It's a tool the FBI and other law enforcement agencies use to help recognize people who are likely to commit crimes and to also recognize a pattern among crimes that happen," she explained. "It's basically built on psychological behaviors and what a profiler previously knows about others who have committed similar crimes."

Alex stared at her blankly, and my lips twitched.

"Okay. For example, there are already profiles out there for humans who commit hate crimes. You can take that profile and apply it to a pure-blood. I bet you'd find the same red flags—similar childhoods with earlier exposure to prejudice, they typically have no prior crimes, their bias usually isn't as overt as others, a situation where they felt wronged somehow. I could keep going." Her cheeks flushed pink. "But what I'm saying is we probably wouldn't have to talk to every single pure-blood here. With the necessary info, we could probably trim down the pool of possible suspects. I'm sure there are basic profiles out there out on the Internet, or if you had any connection with law enforcement."

Marcus inclined his head. "Actually, we do have some connections in law enforcement."

"Well…" Josie sat back. "I would reach out to them and see if they have a profile. Or better yet, if they're trained, they could possibly look over the info—"

"Wait. Josie, you studied psychology, right?" I spoke up, and Josie's wide gaze swung toward me. I nodded. "She can get a profile and figure out who we need to talk to."

Josie faced Marcus. A moment passed. "I studied psychology

and I did really well in my class."

Damn straight she did. My girl was smart.

"But I've never built a profile before, and even though I know the basics, with something like this you need someone trained. At the very least, to point you in the right direction."

I frowned at the back of her head.

Marcus appeared to consider that. "Handing over that kind of information is serious. To be honest, I'm more comfortable with you having access to these records than anyone else in this room."

Across from Josie, Alex's mouth dropped. "Well, I'm kind of offended."

I shrugged. "Meanwhile, I'm not at all surprised that you wouldn't be comfortable with me having that info."

"I'm actually surprised that you wouldn't trust me," Aiden said, and I rolled my eyes.

A faint smile appeared on Marcus's face. "Everyone except for Josie has a personal experience with Ares. I feel like this requires someone who wasn't a part of what he did, but I cannot hand over that kind of personal information."

Alex opened her mouth, but she was silenced when Marcus raised his hand. "What I can do is reach out to a few people I know who will be able to help us."

That was better than nothing.

"What are we going to do if we find out whoever is behind this?" Alex asked the moment Marcus lowered his hand. "Stopping it here may not stop it happening elsewhere."

"Well, if the profile works here and we can find the people responsible for the attacks, then why wouldn't it work elsewhere?" Aiden asked. "It could be implemented in any of the communities or schools that are facing these problems."

"But what will happen to them? As a mortal, I was as liberal as they come," Josie said, sitting back. "But if someone or a group of people is running around killing others because of how much aether is in their blood, then I feel like they've forfeited their right to live out their lives in a jail cell somewhere."

Everyone, including Alexander, turned and stared at Josie.

"What?" she said. "I'm not saying people aren't capable of changing, but once you murder someone? Yeah. No."

"That's bloodthirsty," I said to her. "And it really turns me on."

"Gods," Alex moaned. "We didn't need to know that, Seth."

I shrugged, and Josie flushed pink.

"We don't have the same procedures that the mortal court has," Marcus interjected. "We're a lot more…"

"Old school," Aiden said. "Hand for a hand type of stuff."

"Oh," Josie whispered. "Well then, that answers my question."

Marcus sighed. "As soon as you all get out of my office, I'll get to work on the personnel files."

At least that part was discussed and it felt like we were actually doing something about the damn pure-bloods here, but that wasn't the only thing on the table. "We need to talk about the remaining demigod."

Alex nodded. "We didn't get a chance to tell you yesterday, but there's a really good chance that the demigod is…Ares's son."

For a moment, I thought Marcus might actually curse. His mouth opened and then closed. Finally, he settled on, "*Gods.*"

"Exactly," Aiden muttered. "Ares is just raising his ugly, twisted head all over the place."

Marcus uncrossed his legs and leaned forward, resting his arms on the table. "So it appears." He let out a disgusted sigh. "Why do we think this?"

As Alex told her uncle, I could feel the mood in the room change. Without having to tell Marcus why it was so important we find that damn demigod yesterday, he got it.

"The Titans could use him in ways we haven't seen yet."

Marcus's lips pursed. "His abilities won't have the same impact on pures and halfs, but in the wrong hands he could create even more problems. The question remains—how will you find him?"

"Deacon is insistent on going over there." Aiden sighed as he leaned onto the back of Alex's chair. "I hate the idea, but he and Luke have a knack for finding the demigods. We need to get over there as soon as possible and find him."

"And I guess if he is Ares's son, I would recognize him." Alex started messing with her hair, the same way Josie did. "I know that sounds crazy, but I just…I'd recognize him."

Her father didn't look happy about any of that.

But I understood what Alex was saying. "I would recognize him, too." When she looked over at me, she nodded slightly. We both would know the second we saw the guy. "I can take them over. Save some time and money on a flight."

Marcus arched a brow. "Would it be wise for so many demigods and a god to be there? The Titans may not have found the location yet, but with so many of you there, it's bound to draw them."

"I'm going to hang back here," Josie spoke up then. "Not that I don't want to go to Pluckley and possibly see a ghost, but it's just not smart."

Aiden nodded. "Agreed."

"I think that is wise." Marcus nodded, but he didn't know the real reason why Josie wasn't going there.

I looked over at her, and she must've seen the question in my eyes, because there was the tiny lift at the corners of her lips and she nodded.

Shifting closer to her, I brought my gaze to Marcus. "You don't know this yet." I glanced at Alex's father. "Neither do you, but sooner or later, you'll find out."

Marcus lifted his brows while Alex folded her hand over her mouth, obviously hiding a smile.

Then I said the words I was quickly beginning to realize I really fucking enjoyed saying. Words I was oddly proud of. "Josie and I are expecting a child."

If I thought Marcus was caught off-guard by the whole Ares bullshit, I hadn't seen him truly shocked. Hell, I couldn't remember seeing him so thunderstruck before. Not even when I showed up with Josie the first time or when I popped into his office without warning when I'd been looking for her.

He stared at us like he didn't even understand how a baby was made.

Alex choked on a giggle.

"Is it that shocking?" I asked, one side of my lips kicking up.

"Yes? No." Marcus gave a little shake of his head, and I had no idea what that meant, but then he looked at Josie. "A child of a god and a demigod. That's—"

"Never happened." Josie grinned. "We know. We just learned that."

"And that...that will be something amazing." It was rare to see the Dean smile. It wasn't something he often did and usually it looked more like a grimace than it did a smile, but this was a real one, warming those usually chilled green eyes. "Now I see why you plan on staying back. I believe that is a mature and wise choice. How far along?"

"She's at about six weeks." Leaning over, I gently flicked her ear.

Josie shot me a look, but she was grinning. "I'm guessing I'm not due until around January, but I think we'll know more once we see a doctor who specializes in babies."

"Congratulations," Marcus said, rising from his chair. "I truly mean it."

Then he did probably the most shocking thing I'd ever seen the man do. He walked up to me and offered his hand.

What felt like an entire minute went by before I snapped

out of my stupor. In a daze, I shook his hand. Marcus had never shaken my hand. I was still standing there, staring at him like a dumbass when Marcus bent down, kissing Josie's cheek.

Aiden raised a brow as he looked over at me. When our gazes locked, he smiled and then looked away, placing a hand on the back of Alex's neck.

Drawing back, Marcus leaned against his desk. "Well, today has been full of unexpected revelations. A very good one." He met my gaze briefly, looking at me like he'd never seen me before, and then his gaze flickered over the room. "And some not so good ones."

"Starting to sound like an ordinary day," Alex commented. "Or, at least—"

A knock on the office door silenced Alex. I turned just as it opened. A Guard popped his head in. "I'm sorry to interrupt, but this could not wait."

"It's okay, Banks. What is going on?"

Banks stepped into the room, spine straight and shoulders stiff. I had a feeling the "not so good" part of the day was about to get worse. "We just received a call from one of our communities in Chicago. They said there's been an incident and they've lost contact with some of the people in different parts of the city."

I frowned as Alex twisted and looked at Aiden. Marcus became very still. "Do we have any more information?"

Banks nodded. "I think you need to see it. It's all over the news."

Marcus reached into a drawer and pulled out a slim remote. With one tap of a button, the upper doors on the mahogany cabinet to the left of the desk silently slid open, revealing a TV I'd never known was there. The TV turned on and a news channel appeared.

"Oh shit," Alex murmured under her breath the moment she saw the "Breaking News" banner along the bottom of the screen.

*Suspected terrorist attack near South Wacker Drive. Multiple injuries and casualties reported.*

No one needed to read the banner to see what was happening. The scene on the screen was one of chaos. People flooded the sidewalks, rushing out of the buildings and into the congested traffic that was at a complete standstill. There were glimpses of people covered in dust. As the camera whirled, there were brief glances of others just standing amongst those running, staring up, and then the camera went up.

Dark smoke poured out of several skyscrapers, darkening the sky and blotting out the sun.

Jaw clenching, I shook my head as I stared at the screen. The unseen reporter talked over the video. It was a suspected bomb— possible suicide bomber. Mortals. Sometimes I forgot just how violent they could be all on their own.

"This is terrible," Alex whispered. "There have to be so many people in those buildings."

The camera panned out over the crowd again, at the base of one of the burning buildings, lingering for a moment before zooming in on the smoke pouring out of the skyscrapers.

"Oh, my God." Josie shot from the chair so fast it could've toppled over. "Holy crap."

"What?" I turned to her.

"That man—that man in the crowd." She rushed toward the TV. "That was *Cronus.*"

# 10

## Josie

*M*y stomach felt like it was somewhere near my toes as I stood in front of the TV. I couldn't believe who I'd just seen.

"Are you sure?" Seth asked, suddenly at my side.

"Yes." I looked at him, eyes wide. "Never in a million years will I forget what he looks like."

His jaw tightened. "I believe you."

The camera was zoomed onto the building now. "Can you go back?"

"I believe so." Marcus was standing, staring at the remote with a slight frown on his face. "I think one of these buttons…"

"Geez." Alex rose from the chair. "Let me see the remote."

Marcus handed it over, and within a few seconds the images rewound.

"There," I said, my breath catching. "Stop."

Alex stopped and then paused it. Immediately I saw him in the crowd. An icy chill clung to my skin as I pointed at the man. "That's him. He didn't look like that when I saw him. He was frailer, but that is him."

Everyone crowded behind me, getting their first look at the man I knew as Cronus. "He was a lot slimmer when I saw him. He was frail, but that *is* him."

Cronus stood on a sidewalk, his shoulders broad now and muscles straining the pale blue shirt he wore, covering what had been a sunken chest. His skin had smoothed and filled out. That wizened beard was trimmed into a neat goatee and his white hair was cut shorter, slicked back from sharp cheekbones.

And the eeriest thing was how he was standing. "Is it just me, or is he staring directly out at the camera?"

"Hell." Aiden inched closer, his head tilting. "It does look like that."

"Hit play, Alex," Marcus commanded.

I missed it the first time, because it had been a shock when I saw him, and the camera had quickly moved away from him, but there was no missing it now once the image start playing again.

Cronus smiled.

"Gods," Marcus growled, stepping back. "They're responsible for this."

Alex hit rewind, stopping it back on the image of Cronus. His eyes were almost normal, but the irises were so black they were almost obsidian.

Seth turned to Banks. "What else was said to you by the community outside of Chicago?"

Banks swallowed hard. "Only what you see on the television and that they're unable to reach any of our kind within the city."

"If the Titans are in Chicago and the community can't get hold of the pures in the city, it's because the Titans already have them," I said, remembering the…the bodies of the pure-bloods scattered outside that house. "They'll feed off them. I've seen it." I spun toward Marcus. "You need to get those pures out of there. Now."

Seth cursed under his voice. "Where is this community?"

"It's near Lincoln Park, in a gated neighborhood," Banks answered. "It's pretty much a town within the city."

"So we could get them out without drawing too much attention?" Seth asked.

"I would think so." Banks looked to Marcus. "We could call ahead and let them know we're coming."

"We'd have to send in buses to get them out. With what is happening in the city, that's going to be a problem," Marcus said, his green eyes brilliant.

"They'll be expecting that," I spoke up, and Marcus focused on me. "I know I haven't been in this world long, but I've seen what they've done to pures. They could burn through them like they're nothing more than snacks. If the community can't get hold of the pures in the city, they're already lost. I'm sorry to say that, but they're already gone."

Banks blanched.

"Josie is right. We need to check it out first before we send more in. This could be a trap, and we'd basically be sending lambs to slaughter," Seth said. "I can go in and scope out the community. Make sure it's safe to bring in buses. You just need to figure out how to get the buses there."

My heart skipped a beat. Seth being in the same location as the Titans? I knew that what Zeus had showed him in Long Beach had shaken him up, but it was a risk.

A possible world-ending risk.

"It will be a strategic nightmare, but I can get it done," Marcus said.

"I want to go with you," Aiden announced.

Seth looked over his shoulder at him. "Are you trying to be my best friend?"

Aiden smirked. "I thought we already were best friends."

"I think that is a good idea," I suggested tentatively, earning a narrowed look from Seth. I squared my shoulders. "You have no idea what you could be going into, Seth. It could be nothing or it could be…" Pressing my lips together, I shook my head. "It could be horrific."

Seth didn't respond for a long moment and then he nodded. "For you," he said, his eyes holding mine. "Okay." He looked over his shoulder at Aiden. "You can come with me."

"If you take him, I should go." Alex squeezed past the chair and Aiden. "I am not—"

"I'm only taking Aiden." Seth's gaze hardened. "And before you even say it, it has nothing to do with you being a girl."

Her eyes flared to a burning whiskey. "I wasn't going to say that. I was going to say you're not taking me because you're being an ass."

My eyes widened.

Seth, on the other hand, showed little emotion. Apparently, he was used to Alex saying things like that. "It's too much of a risk."

"But going to Pluckley wouldn't be?" she shot back. "You had no problem with the idea of me or the guys going there."

Aiden turned to her. "Alex—"

"Don't Alex me," she snapped.

Keeping my mouth shut, I glanced over at Marcus, and we had a moment. Both of us were just going to stay quiet.

He tried again. "We have no reason to suspect that the Titans are anywhere near Pluckley yet. We know that Cronus is in Chicago."

"I can handle myself." Her cheeks flushed with anger.

"We know that." Aiden angled his body toward her. "No one would ever question that."

"And I'm not questioning your abilities. The Titans are going to sense me and they're going to sense Aiden. We don't need another demigod there," Seth explained. "It's going to be hard enough for two of us to stay under the radar there."

For a moment I thought Alex was still going to argue, but she finally relented. Not happily. When she and Aiden walked out of Marcus's office to retrieve Aiden's weapons, I was sure he was going to catch an earful.

Plans to leave for Pluckley were delayed until we knew what to do with Chicago, and I agreed to break the news to Luke and Deacon. Once we were back in our room, I scooted around Seth and stopped directly in front of him.

"I'm worried," I admitted.

"Babe." Reaching between us, he captured my hands. "You know I'll be fine."

That wasn't exactly true. "Cronus can kill you."

"He won't get near me." He dipped his chin so we were at eye level.

"You can kill Cronus," I reminded him.

Understanding flickered across his face. "I am not going to go after him. I know better. Now."

A huge part of me believed him, but Seth knew Cronus had fed off me and Seth was...well, Seth was *Seth*. "Promise me." I searched his gaze. "Promise me that you will get out of there before it comes down to a fight."

Seth rested his forehead against mine as he let go of my hands and cradled my cheeks. "I promise."

## Seth

Josie's fear ate away at me as I met back up with Aiden and then took both of us to Chicago. I didn't blame her for one second for worrying that I would lose my shit and kill Cronus.

Gods, to be completely honest, I wanted nothing more than to watch the fucking life seep out of his eyes. He'd fed on Josie, just like Hyperion had. So, yeah, I wanted to kill that bastard *slowly*.

But I wouldn't.

It would be like going against my nature, but I would keep my promise to Josie.

Aiden and I arrived just inside the gates of the community, and immediately, a cold chill powered down my spine that had nothing to do with the wind whipping the leaves on the tree-lined streets into a frenzy.

Something wasn't right.

Beyond the ten-foot stone fencing, I could hear blaring horns and the screech of sirens, along with the distant hum of conversation. But inside these walls?

"It's quiet," Aiden said, noting the same thing I did as he scanned the empty park we stood in front of. "It's way too quiet."

Not only that, but the wind carried the scent of burnt plastic and metal, and there was a faint smell of something else under it. A heavy metallic scent.

"Banks got the call from here," I said, walking toward the end of the park, past the empty playground. "Couldn't have been more than twenty, thirty minutes ago."

Aiden didn't respond as he kept a sharp eye out for any movement. We made our way to the Main Street.

"I have a bad feeling about this," Aiden murmured, eyes narrowing on a silent, dark-windowed coffee shop.

I stepped off the sidewalk and into the middle of the street. "Look at this."

Aiden followed. Down at the intersection, there were cars stopped. Doors opened. "What in the hell?"

I started forward, passing several brick row homes that appeared to be devoid of life. Reaching the driver's side of the last car, I walked around and peered inside. "It's empty."

"Like the damn Rapture took place." Aiden stalked up to the other side, one hand on the dagger at his thigh. He went to the next car and bent at the waist. He stumbled back. "Shit."

"What?" I looked up.

"Got a body."

Joining him, I looked inside and sucked in a sharp breath. There was a pure-blood male slumped over in the passenger seat, throat torn open, exposing tissue and congealed blood.

Part of me had already suspected what had happened here from the moment we arrived. There was no doubt now.

The Titans had been here.

I straightened, looking over my shoulder. Up ahead, at the next intersection, I saw a dark shape on the sidewalk, half-hidden by empty tables and chairs. "What about the other cars?"

Aiden moved ahead. "Nothing. The rest are empty."

Skirting around an abandoned SUV, I passed a toppled-over motorcycle. Unease formed in my gut as that heavy scent of blood increased.

The dark shape on the sidewalk was as I feared. A body. Another male, lying on his back, one arm outstretched like he was reaching for something or someone. This man's stomach was ripped apart, as if a wild animal had gotten hold of him.

Pale and jaw tight, Aiden continued forward, rounding the corner. Aiden came to a complete standstill, his hands falling to his sides, closing into fists. "Gods."

Instinct told me what I was going to see before I even laid eyes on the absolute destruction of life.

Aiden was struck silent as he stared at the bodies littering the street and sidewalks, his mouth moving as if he were trying to find the words.

I'd seen this before.

Bodies scattered and strewn about as if their lives had meant nothing and as if their bodies didn't deserve the most basic level of respect.

Except the last time I'd seen something like this, I had been responsible for it. While I'd been carrying out the *Remediations*, I'd left those who'd sided with Ares in such a state. And what had Apollo asked me that night he sent me to find Josie?

*Do you always have to be so messy?*

I didn't have to be. I shouldn't have been.

Muscle flexing along my jaw, I lifted my gaze to a body of a young woman. She hung from the side of a townhouse, her arms outstretched. Spikes were driven through her palms. The entire front of her body was covered in blood. Written under her body, scrawled in what I assumed was her blood, was a message in Greek.

Η μετακίνησή σας στη συνέχεια

Your move then.

I doubted it was a coincidence that the woman's long hair was blonde.

Red-hot rage burned through my veins as I dragged my eyes from the woman and turned back to the street. There was so much death.

The Titans hadn't just come here to feed.

"They came here to kill," I said. "That's what they did. They came here to kill and send us a message."

# 11

## Seth

Aiden stared up at the body of the woman. "How...how can they do this to someone?"

Sickened, I stepped forward and lifted my arm. I couldn't leave her up there like that. "We need to get her down."

"Agreed," he growled.

"I'll get the stakes out. She'll fall once it happens," I warned.

Shoulders tense, Aiden nodded. "Ready when you are."

I summoned the air element, pulling the stakes free. Her body immediately fell forward, but I slowed her descent. Aiden caught her limp body and then laid her carefully on the ground. I could see her face better.

Gods, she was young—younger than Josie.

Aiden folded her arms over her chest and then rose. "There's at least fifty bodies out here, and these communities have several hundred residents, if not more."

Scanning all the homes, I feared what lay beyond those closed doors was going to be just as bad as what is in the streets. "They probably took some when they—"

A musky, heavy, damp smell suddenly permeated the air. Aiden and I turned at the same time.

Two Sentinels stood in the center of the street, among the dead bodies.

Well, they *used* to be Sentinels.

Based on the inky blackness seeping into the whites of their eyes, whoever those Sentinels used to be, they were dead now.

"Shades," Aiden growled, unleashing the titanium daggers at his thighs.

"Why do they smell so badly?" I asked.

Aiden smirked. "That's a question I probably never want an answer to."

"True." A slow grin tugged at my lips.

One of the shades smiled. "Didn't like our handiwork? I don't think she liked it either."

I tilted my head to the side. "Oh, you're going to be a talkative one? Great."

Aiden shot forward, slamming into the shade. He shoved his blades deep into its midsection. The shade roared, knocking Aiden to the side. He hit the wall of a bookstore with a grunt. Chunks of cement gave way under his impact.

I arched a brow as he slowly picked himself up. "That didn't work out well, did it?"

Rising to his feet, Aiden flipped me off.

I grinned as I unhooked the daggers I hadn't forgotten to bring. Needing to work out the violent anger whirling inside me, I started toward the chatty shade. Adrenaline kicked my senses alive as it whirled on me. It cocked its head to the side, sniffing the air. I saw the moment the shade recognized who and what I was.

"You aren't going to throw me around, buddy," I said.

Charging the shade, I came up short with a curse when it simply vanished and then reappeared behind me. I spun around.

Blood bled through two puncture holes in the Sentinel's shirt.

"What the hell?" I'd never seen a shade do that before. Then again, I knew the older the shade, the more powerful they were when it came to manipulating the body it possessed and the environment around it.

I swung on the shade. It popped out of existence, reappearing a few steps to my left. Dropping down, I went for the legs of the creature, but before my kick could connect, the shade vanished.

The sound of its deep, throaty chuckle alerted me to where the shade now stood. Jumping to my feet, I aimed the blade for the midsection again. Over his shoulder, I saw Aiden rushing toward us.

Moving disturbingly fast, it spun and caught Aiden's blade, breaking it off. Then it had its hand around Aiden's throat, lifting him off the ground. Its body vibrated as it eyed Aiden. "Do you know what we'd do to boys like you in the pits? Spread those—"

Gripping the meaty wrists, Aiden pulled his legs up and used the shade's chest as a springboard. The action broke the creature's hold, and Aiden rolled into the fall, springing back to his feet.

I shot forward, jumping over a bike rack. I hit the stunned shade in the back, knocking it down. We both hit the hard cement sidewalk and rolled, coming close to the edge of a drop-off and the small creek below.

I could have easily tapped into akasha and ended this, but I wanted—no, I *needed* to feel the brutal savagery of a fight. I needed to get my hands dirty after seeing what they'd done to this place, to these people.

Flipping the shade onto its back, I slammed my fist into the shade's jaw, knocking its head to the side. I swung my other hand, the one holding the dagger, prepared to wedge the dagger deep in the fucker's skull.

The shade popped out, and I hit the ground, catching myself

at the last minute. "That is getting really annoying."

Reappearing above me, the shade grabbed me by the scruff of the neck, lifting my heavy ass clear off the ground in a surprising display of strength.

This shade thought it was a badass.

Arching my back, I swung my legs back, locking them around the shade's waist as I used both arms to break the shade's hold. I swung down, planting both hands on the dirtied floor. Using momentum and the shade's weight, I flipped the dumb son of a bitch head over heels.

Popping up, I saw Aiden engage the other shade that must've gotten tired of standing around.

I turned around, focusing on the hyped-up shade. "How about you stand still for about five seconds?"

"You're a *god*," it said, its voice deep and guttural. "Why don't you just take me out?"

"Good point." Snapping forward, I ducked under the shade's arm and wrapped my arm around its neck. "I guess I'm enjoying it." I squeezed as a horn blasted off in the distance.

The shade laughed. "You know what I enjoyed?"

"No," I grunted as it struggled in my hold. "And I don't really care."

"Oh, but I think you will." It laughed again. "I watched Hyperion drag your bitch across a field of bodies. How's that for enjoyment?"

What he said caught me off-guard.

The shade swooped down, tossing my ass right over his shoulder. "Dumbass," it hissed.

I hit the edge of a low brick wall hip first. Pain exploded through me, momentarily stunning me. In an instant, the shade was standing above me. Its hoofed foot landed a direct hit to my midsection, and before I could catch myself, I toppled over the edge.

The fall was only about four feet, but the landing still hurt like hell. For a moment I didn't move. Apparently I had been relying way too much on my godly abilities, because I was letting this shade get the upper hand.

Not anymore.

Springing to my feet, I ignored the pain and pushed up. Flying through the air, I landed on the retaining wall.

"Where do you think you're going?" The shade was heading for Aiden. "I thought we were going to play."

I briefly caught sight of Aiden moving behind the other shade, shoving his blade into its back. Dark, oily blood gushed from the shade's chest as a hole formed where the heart was.

The shade's roar of agony told me that blow had hurt.

Aiden yanked the dagger out and the Sentinel threw its head back. Its mouth dropped open as black smoke poured out of it. The Sentinel's body collapsed to the ground in a heap of useless muscles and bones, leaving only the scent of damp earth behind.

Where in the hell was a furie when you needed one? They liked to eat those things.

Aiden lifted his head, seeing me. "Are you still messing with that one?"

"Yeah." I shrugged, jumping off the brick wall. "We're working a few things out."

The shade looked between us. "I was just telling him how Hyperion used to beat the shit out of his bitch of a girlfriend."

Clutching the dagger, I stalked toward it. "You really do not know when to keep your mouth shut."

"You know what's going to happen?" The shade turned its back on Aiden. "You're going to lose this war and Cronus is going to make sure you're alive long enough to watch as he rips the intestines from her body."

The shade then disappeared.

"Behind you!" Aiden shouted as it reappeared.

I whirled around and swung, so damn done with this bastard and its taunts. Rage, potent and lethal, rolled through me in poisonous waves. "Fuck you."

I stopped thinking.

Launching forward, I gripped the shade's shoulder. I bent at the waist, pulling the shade close as I kicked out, my boot catching the creature just below the chin. Its neck snapped back with a sickening crunch. I spun around, feeling my face twist in a mask of rage as I slammed the blade through the neck first, just to hear its guttural scream, and then through the chest.

It, too, opened its mouth, but this one was not escaping to climb down the throat of some other innocent. Fuck no. Tapping into akasha, I hit the black cloud with the deadliest energy out there, utterly obliterating it.

"Fucker," I muttered, stepping back.

"Do you think there's—" Aiden's words were cut off by a grunt.

Spinning around, I caught sight of Aiden flying backward as if the Hulk had just punched him. He flew into the windshield of a SUV and then *through* it.

Shit.

I spun back, scanning the street. I didn't see anything and I didn't wait. Darting over to the SUV, I yanked the passenger door open, finding Aiden sprawled across the front seats.

He wasn't moving.

Double shit.

Grabbing Aiden under his arms, I hauled his heavy-ass body out of the SUV and into the street. I was about to get the hell out of there when a surge of power rippled along my skin. Glyphs appeared on my skin, and my head jerked around.

Air warped in front of me, and someone suddenly appeared

in a crackle of spitting energy. A tall, lean son of a bitch, rocking a blue Mohawk and leather pants. Nothing else.

I dropped Aiden.

He'd be okay.

Eventually.

The Titan stood staring at me, saying nothing as I straightened. Our gazes connected over the distance. I knew who this was based on the way he looked. Oceanus. He hadn't fed on Josie, but he'd done worse to the other demigod they had.

Much, much worse.

I tamped down my anger. "Nice hair."

Oceanus smirked. "I didn't think you'd come, but Cronus was right when he said you would."

"Now why would you think I wouldn't?"

The Titan's pitch-black eyes glimmered. "Do you know how long it took the Olympians to get the balls to face us?"

"Don't know. Don't care."

His head tilted to the side. "You're going to care."

"Is that so?"

He nodded. "You're not going to win this war."

"You sound confident in this," I said, catching movement out of the corner of my eye. A black mist crept between the buildings, coming from both sides of the street. It curled over the sidewalk, thin and wispy as tendrils flowed off the curb.

Shades.

Lots of shades.

"The Olympians are weakened," Oceanus said. "Without Ares, they have no hope."

"We don't need them."

Oceanus chuckled darkly. "The young demigods will stand no chance against us."

The shades were up to something.

They licked at the bodies, slipping over them. It was like a fog of shadows rolling over the still bodies, and that fog seeped into their bodies through the open mouths still frozen in horror.

"Like I said, you will not win this war. Not again."

"Are you trying to convince me or yourself of this?" I saw the finger on the nearest body twitch. A leg spasmed on another body.

"I'm not trying to convince you of anything." The freaky bastard didn't blink, not once. "I am here to make a deal."

# 12

## Seth

One by one, the fallen bodies of the pures rose, shuffling to their feet, a bloody and ghastly mess. They faced me in unison, an army of resurrected pures standing between the Titan and me.

I'd seen some shit in my day, but this—yeah, this was creepy as hell.

I went on high alert. "A deal?"

Oceanus dipped his chin in what I could only assume was a nod. "Bring us Zeus's head and you will have nothing to fear from us."

"You're serious?" A harsh laugh burst out of me.

Dark brows furrowed. "Do I sound like I'm joking? You bring us Zeus's head, and we will leave you in peace."

Behind me, I could hear Aiden waking up. My brain whirled to click everything he was saying into place. "And why would killing Zeus be enough?"

A smile crept across the Titan's face. "Do you know nothing?"

"Well, that was a rude statement."

"If Zeus dies, Cronus ascends to Olympus. We rule once more, as we should."

"And then you release the rest of the Titans and kill the rest of the gods?"

"We will give them a choice," he replied. "And they will choose their own fate."

"Why doesn't Cronus go after Zeus himself? Or is he scared?"

The ground trembled slightly under my feet, and I had a feeling Cronus was nearby. He'd heard that and hadn't liked it.

I smirked.

"Because we want you to choose your own fate, Seth. Side with us. You cannot defeat Cronus," Oceanus replied coolly.

Yeah, this wasn't adding up. "You know what I'm thinking? There's a reason why you want me to do this. Cronus doesn't want to face off with me. Is it because I killed Perses?"

His nostrils flared as the shades shifted restlessly.

"Or is it because of how easily I killed Hyperion?" I asked, letting some of my power slip through to the skin. My vision tinted white. "And he's afraid that I'll kill him?"

"You know what will happen if you kill Cronus."

I did, but he didn't know I cared. "Do I strike you as someone who worries about what would happen?"

"You should be." Oceanus lifted his chin. "We will usher in a new beginning, a *better* world."

A fine shiver danced across my shoulders as I thought of the prophecy Ewan the nymph had told me.

*The end of the old is here, and the beginning of the new has been ushered in.*

The prophecy was about me, wasn't it? Or was it about more than me?

"We will right all that the Olympians had done wrong," he continued.

"That's an extraordinarily long list," I replied dryly.

Oceanus inclined his chin. "Bring us his head or we will level this city, and from here we will destroy everything in our paths. You have until the *Kronia*. We'll be waiting."

\* \* \*

Oceanus disappeared after that, but I could tell he was still hanging around. I could feel him.

So, I made sure I took out all those damn shades, all fifty of them. Then I went to Aiden and we got the hell out of there. I focused on Alex and found her in her room.

She let out a little shriek when Aiden and I suddenly appeared in front of her. That scream turned into a gasp. "Aiden?" She rushed from the bedroom, hobbling along with one shoe on. "What happened?"

"I'm fine." He lifted his head. A purplish bruise shadowed his jaw. "I just need to sit down."

Alex's gaze met mine as she slipped an arm around Aiden's waist, taking some of his weight. "Titans?"

"And shades on steroids," I answered. "He'll fill you in, but I have to see Marcus."

"Okay." Concern pinched her expression as she led Aiden into the bedroom, stopping long enough to say over her shoulder, "Thank you, Seth."

I had no idea what she was thanking me for. Focusing on Marcus, I let myself slip into the void. A second later, I appeared in Marcus's office.

"Gods," he gasped, frozen mid-sitting down behind his desk.

"Sorry," I said. "No knocking this time."

Straightening his tie, he shook his head as he sat down. Marcus wasn't alone. Laadan and Alexander were in his office, and the television was still on. Scenes from Chicago played. "Should I be worried that you're back from Chicago so quickly?"

"Yeah, you should be worried." I came to stand between the chairs Laadan and Alexander were occupying. "There's no other way to say this, other than to just say it. The community in Chicago is lost."

"What?" Laadan's hand flew to her chest.

"I don't understand. Banks just spoke to them. No more than half an hour had passed between the time he got the call from them to when you and Aiden would've arrived." Marcus's brows furrowed together as he stared back at me. "What happened?"

"We found a community of…dead pures. The Titans didn't get in there to feed, Marcus. They slaughtered those pures."

Laadan paled as she lowered her chin. "Gods."

"There were shades there. Aiden and I fought them, and these weren't normal shades."

"Is it possible that there are some there still alive? The pures?" Laadan asked.

I nodded. "It's possible, but you send anyone in there to get them out, you're just sending more people to slaughter. I saw shades possess over fifty dead pures."

Alexander's eyes narrowed.

"Yeah, it was like something straight out of *Game of Thrones*," I said. "And again, these aren't normal shades. If there are pures still alive, there's a good chance they'll be dead by the time you wrangle up enough Sentinels and Guards to get there. Not to mention, if I were to bring them in, they'd feel my presence and know something's up."

"But we're going to leave them there? To be killed or fed off?" Laadan demanded of Marcus. "We cannot do that."

Marcus was quiet for a moment. "What do you believe will happen if we send reinforcements into Chicago?"

"My honest answer? They'd all die."

"Even if you go with them?" he persisted.

"If I went back there, the chances of killing another Titan increases. Trust me on that." I held his stare. "I know my limits and my patience. I also know that I…have a slight problem controlling myself when it comes to those bastards."

Surprise flickered over Marcus's face, and I figured it had to do with what I was admitting. "You think the Titans are in that community? Right now?"

"I know the Titans are holed up in that community. They're waiting."

"For what?" Laadan twisted back to me.

"Well, here comes the craziest thing that happened. Oceanus showed up and offered me a deal."

Marcus's hands flattened on his desk. "A deal?"

"They want me to bring them Zeus's head."

Laadan sucked in a shrill breath, and for a moment I thought the woman would faint. Marcus had a much more subdued response. "Is that so?"

"Yep. They said if I bring them Zeus's head, they'll leave us alone." I lifted my brows. "Of course, that means if I kill Zeus, Cronus will ascend the throne in Olympus. The Titans claim they'll give the rest of the gods a choice. Fall in line or die."

Marcus sat back. "If the Titans were to take control over Olympus, they would not remain hidden from the mortals. They'd throw the world back into the days of sacrifice and fear."

Which wasn't very different from when the Olympians interacted with mankind, but I figured Marcus knew that.

"What was your answer, Seth?" Marcus asked.

I arched a brow. "What do you think?"

He said nothing, and I could feel Alexander's stare drilling holes through me.

Crossing my arms, I had to remind myself that I didn't have

the greatest track record with them. "No, I did not agree to run off and kill Zeus."

"That's good to hear," Laadan murmured.

I smirked. "I'll be honest with you all. It has very little to do with Zeus, but mostly to do with the fact I'm not an idiot. Not for one second do I believe the Titans are a better choice. That any of us would be safe from them."

Marcus dragged his forefinger under his lip. "No, we would not be. This is an interesting development. What did he say would happen if you didn't do this?"

"Oceanus said they would destroy the city, and they wouldn't stop there."

Laadan closed her eyes, and I thought she might be praying.

"Did they give you a deadline?" Marcus asked.

"Yeah, they said I had until something called the *Kronia*. No clue what the hell that is."

Laadan lowered her hand to her lap. "The *Kronia* was, I believe, an old Athenian festival that celebrated Cronus. It was actually a lovely festival from what I've read. Everyone feasted and waited on their servants. Social restrictions were forgotten."

"Sounds like a fun time," I murmured. "Any idea of when this festival was held?"

Her nose pinched as she looked upward. "I do believe it was celebrated from the end of July through the beginning weeks of August."

"That's good news. We have time." More than a month, at least.

"We need to get the remaining demigod as soon as possible," Marcus insisted.

"We'll go in the morning." I started to leave, but I turned back to Marcus. "You're going to send Sentinels into that community, aren't you?"

Marcus's gaze lifted to mine. "I have to try."

"You'll be sending them to their deaths, Marcus."

He didn't look away. "If I gave them the choice, what do you think it would be?"

I already knew. "They'd go, even knowing the odds."

And that was the damn truth. Sentinels weren't suicidal. They were just dangerously brave. I had no doubt in my mind that, if Marcus presented them with the option, they would go and they would die trying to save others.

## Josie

I needed a shower.

Dust covered nearly every square of inch of my body, and it sucked, because I was going to have to wash my hair *again*.

That's what I got for practicing with the elements outside during a windy day. All the loose dirt had been stirred up by the wind, and it had coated my skin and hair.

And I hadn't even been outside for more than thirty minutes.

What I would've loved to do was take a bath. Of course, it would've been so gross, as dirty as I was, and this bathtub was so not for soaking, but the one at Seth's house in the islands?

I could marry that tub.

I turned on the faucet until steam filled the air, then stripped off my dirty clothes. As I snatched a towel and placed it on the sink for easy access, I couldn't stop the kernel of worry forming in my belly.

Seth hadn't returned yet.

There hadn't been any earthquakes, so I was taking that as a good sign. Not that I didn't believe he'd hold to his promise, but if a Titan showed up and went after him?

He'd do everything to keep his promise, but did Seth really know how powerful he was? Things could spin out of control before he even realized it.

Closing my eyes, I stood under the pelting spray of hot water and let all my worries wash away, right along with the dust and sweat. More than anything, I wanted to lose myself in Seth. I wanted him here, where I knew he was safe and I…

I sighed.

I was struck silly by the fact that I missed him even though he'd only been gone an hour or so, but I couldn't…well, I couldn't get enough of him. When we were apart, I did miss him desperately, and the longer we were separated, the more I hated it.

I guessed that was what being in love felt like.

A small smile tugged at my lips as I thought about him just holding me as we talked about the future, about our child. A strange thing always happened when he did that. I felt…normal.

Like we were normal and had a future.

Turning, I snatched up the body wash and soaped myself up. My skin was oddly sensitive, have been for, well, at least a couple of days. Probably had to do with pregnancy hormones. They were no joke, because right now, my body was aching for Seth in a way that was almost painful. As if he had branded me somehow and only he could ease the burn.

*Gods.*

That sounded ridiculous, and I was totally blaming hormones for that thought, but it felt true in that moment.

My head tipped back and I bit my lower lip as I placed the loofah on the little caddy. My hand slipped down my belly and then lower. My breath caught. The touch of my own fingers was nothing like what Seth could do, especially when he did that wicked thing with his thumb…

The mere thought of how he used his fingers made my head spin. Using my other hand, I ran it over my breast. Swallowing a moan, I rolled my hips. The tension coiled. I was so—

"You just can't stop thinking about me, can you?"

Shrieking, my eyes shot open and I pulled my hand away.

Seth stood just outside the shower stall; his golden hair fell around his chiseled cheeks, brushing the tops of his shoulders. There was a certain mischievous quirk to his full lips, but his gaze was like liquid fire, centered far below my eyes.

"You have got to stop doing that," I gasped, finding my voice. "Or I will put a bell on you."

"That was possibly the hottest thing I've seen in all my years." Seth pulled my hand away and climbed fully clothed into the shower. "You have no idea how badly I needed to see that."

I jolted at what he said and my heart dropped as my gaze coasted over his face. Was there blood along his temple? "Was it that bad?"

"Worse than that bad," he murmured.

My heart was racing, desire mixed with embarrassment and the returning concern, but then his gaze lifted to mine. I needed to know what had happened; however, instinct told me he needed something else entirely in that moment. I let the shame go and I pushed the concern to the back of my mind.

"Beautiful," he whispered. Water pelted him, but he didn't seem to notice. All of his attention was focused on me. "But this?" He brought my hand to his mouth, sucking a finger into his mouth.

"Oh, my…" My knees felt weak. Heat boiled my blood.

"I'm jealous." He dropped my hand and snaked an arm around my waist, lifting me off my feet. "Would've given just about anything to see how all of this started out."

I could barely breathe, let alone think. My senses were firing all at once and the feeling of being pressed against his soaked clothing set me on fire. "It really wasn't that exciting."

"Are you out of your mind? It was probably exciting on a heart-attack level." He dipped his head, brushing his lips over mine.

I opened my mouth, inviting him in as I slid my hands up his hard chest, clasping them loosely behind his neck. The taste of him was something I'd never grow tired of.

With that, his kiss turned urgent, deepening. Nothing could've prepared me for the raw intensity of his kiss, his embrace. And it scared me a little. Not of him or what I was feeling, but for what could've happened when he went to Chicago. He was kissing me like he'd been deprived of doing so, and that caused my senses to overload as his tongue slipped over mine. When he finally did lift his head, I felt dizzy.

Seth's smile was wolfish as his eyes connected with mine. Then, with one impressive surge, he had me backed against the shower stall. Using his knee, he pushed my thighs apart. The wet, smooth material of his pants made me groan.

"I missed you," I admitted, blushing as I threaded my fingers through the wet, silky strands of his hair.

He pressed a kiss under my chin. "I wasn't gone that long."

"I know."

His lips were against the hollow of my neck, hot and firm. "What did you do while I was gone?"

"I practiced with the elements." I tipped my head back and let my eyes drift shut. "I got covered in dirt."

He didn't move for a moment and then his lips were on mine, kissing me softly. Then he was back to trailing hot kisses down my neck, over my collarbone. His lips were so close to the tip of my breast, drifting over the swell. My breath became shallow and quicker as his tongue flicked over the beaded skin. My entire body shuddered.

"Were you thinking of me?" He teased. "Wait. Of course you were."

I was about to tell him that it was an incredibly dumb question, but then he drew my nipple into his hot mouth, and I didn't care. I gasped as pleasure rolled through me. His free hand slipped between my thighs, fingers brushing over damp skin. My gasp quickly turned to a moan.

He lifted his head, nuzzling my neck, under my ear. "You're so beautiful. Damn it, you're so fucking beautiful."

My entire body clenched. Hot, tight shudders racked my body. His fingers were barely touching me and I felt close to tipping over the edge. This wasn't *nice*—oh no, this was raw, full of painful need.

My hips surged forward, grinding against his thigh and his hand. Pleasure spiked, making me dizzy and breathless.

Seth growled low in his throat as he grabbed my hip, stilling my movements. His hand stopped moving. "Do you want more than this?"

Frustration caused my eyes to snap open. Was he being serious? Yes. He was. I pushed against his shoulders, but he stared down at me, the look on his face telling me without words what he wanted me to do. Part of me wanted to smack him. And the other…well, it wanted to drown in him.

He wore a wicked grin as his thumb smoothed over a very sensitive part, causing my body to jerk. "I'm waiting, babe."

"Yes," I whispered, glaring at him. "Okay. *Yes.*"

A satisfied smile split his lips. I expected his hand to return to what he had been doing, but his mouth started under my chin again, making a slow descent. He started all over. His hair brushed my chest as his lips drifted over my collarbone. A tiny feminine sound that sounded so foreign to my own ears caught in my throat.

Seth knelt before me, spreading my legs wide. Vulnerable—I was completely vulnerable to him. Lightning rushed through my veins as he spread my legs wider, grasped my hips. His tongue glided from my navel and then lower.

I remembered the first time he'd done this and he'd coaxed

me through it. Now, I didn't need any coaxing. I spread my legs further, giving him more access.

He kissed my inner thigh, nuzzling the slick skin. The air left my lungs as he moved just an inch. He captured my flesh with his mouth, and I cried out. Lost in the raw sensations, I grasped his hair and rocked my hips. He growled against me, and my back arched, heart pounded. Water beaded on my chest. The fierce heat was building and building until I feared it would consume me, and then my body felt like it liquefied. I couldn't breathe as every muscle locked up, ready for what was surely going to be a mind-blowing orgasm.

"Seth, oh yes…" I buckled and climaxed with such force I almost slid down the wall. He caught me, keeping his mouth on me while my body spasmed with sweet aftershocks.

Before the tremors even subsided, Seth stood fluidly and swept me into his arms. I wasn't sure how he managed to turn off the water. Had to be the fact he was a god. The next thing I knew, he was laying me on the bed. Dazed, I stared up at him. I was snared in his molten gaze.

He tore off the dark shirt he wore, letting it fall to the floor. My gaze followed the light dusting of blond hair that disappeared under the band of his pants.

I rose onto my elbow, grinning when he arched his brows at me. "You're sort of stunning," I said. "But I'm sure you already know that."

He stepped out of the wet pants and leaned over me, placing a hand on each side of me, caging me in. "You're one to talk."

I tipped my head back. "I love you, Seth."

He made a deep sound, brushing his cheek over mine. "I know."

I placed my hands on his chest, lowering them over each hard ripple. He pressed against my thigh, warm and hard. "You're supposed to respond with 'I love you, too.'"

Seth grasped my hips and rolled me on top of him. "I think I already did, in the shower."

I kissed the stubble along his jaw as I reached between us, palming him. His back reared off the bed. My heart was already racing again. "Not good enough."

He reached up, cupping the nape of my neck. His eyes were startling in the darkness of our room, consuming me. My heart tripped over itself. Lust hardened the edge of his voice. "I love you."

"That's better."

Sitting up in one fluid motion, he slipped deep inside me and captured my mouth, smothering my cry of surprise. He wrapped his arms around my waist, holding me tight against him as he flexed his hips upward while pulling me down. Toes curling, I gripped his shoulders as my surprise turned to pleasure.

"I love you now," he said, thrusting his hips. "I will love you always."

I pressed my forehead against his, my bottom twisting down. Both of our chests were rising raggedly. "Always? I-I love the sound of that."

He pulled back and our eyes locked.

Wordlessly, he cupped my rear, urging me to move faster. Unable to look away, I fell into those burning eyes. A sharp swirl of tingles rushed through my body. Under me, he moved his magnificent body at a furious rhythm. My release came fast and hard. My entire body stiffened.

Seth grasped my cheeks, bringing my face down to his, kissing me deeply. Lightning flew through my veins. My muscles clamped down on him as he found his own release. My cry mixed with his as he pumped his hips furiously, throwing me head first into another orgasm.

Sometime later, I stirred to lift my head from his chest, but his embrace tightened. I cleared my throat. "What happened in

Chicago?"

He didn't answer for a long moment, and when he did, part of me almost wished he hadn't. I almost couldn't process what he told me or the horror those poor people must've felt and seen. Worse yet, if Seth didn't do what they asked, more innocent people would die. Mortals. Pures. Halfs. Everyone.

"This is bad," I whispered.

And for the first time Seth didn't say it would be okay.

# 13

Josie

Standing among tall elm trees—trees so thick and full that only sporadic streams of light broke through their bushy limbs—I could feel the life slipping out of me. Everything had been so perfect, so beautiful, and now…

I was *dying*.

It happened so fast. I'd been standing in front of Seth, staring into those striking golden eyes, holding his hands, and then there was nothing but heart-stopping pain. Unexpected. Brutal.

Cool air raised tiny goosebumps along my bare arms. I tried to draw in a breath, but the air went nowhere as I looked down at the white gown that brushed the tops of my feet—the gown I'd been so excited to wear, so *ready* to wear.

Blood poured out of my chest, spilling down the front of the gown, ruining it.

Ruining everything.

There were shouts erupting all around us. Chaos as the very thick tree limbs seemed to rattle and shake. Seth was reaching for me, confusion fading from his face and giving way to a raw mixture of fear and anger.

Too late. Too late.

Pressing shaky hands against my chest, it did nothing to stanch the blood flowing from between my fingers.

Oh *gods*, I was going to die.

My knees gave out, but I didn't fall to the ground. Strong, warm arms folded around me, easing me down, holding me close. I blinked, trying to focus as I pressed against the warm, hard chest. Amber-colored eyes stared back into mine—eyes that had been filled with love and happiness moments before were now shining with terror.

With every stuttering breath I took, I knew I was coming to the end, that one of these breaths were going to be my last, and it was going to be all over.

"Seth," I whispered. "Don't let me go."

"No." His face contorted. Tears filled his eyes as he lifted my head, pressing his mouth to my forehead. "I'll never let you go, Josie. *Never.*"

My hands slipped away, falling to my sides. I tried to speak once more, to tell him that I loved him, that I'd always love him, but I couldn't force the words from my tongue.

"Josie." His voice cracked as he rocked us back and forth. "I love you. I love you and I won't let you go. I will never—"

Gasping for air, I came awake with a silent scream burning up my throat as I jerked upward. The sheet slipped to my waist as I planted a hand on my chest. My heart jackhammered.

Just a dream.

That's what I kept telling myself as I willed my heart to slow down and stared into the darkness in the bedroom. It was just a dream.

Shoving sweat-slicked hair out of my face, I twisted at the waist. As my vision adapted, I could make out Seth's profile. He was lying on his side, facing me. One heavy arm still lay over my hips and lap. He was sound asleep. A strand of blond hair fell over his cheek, touching the corner of his lip.

I wanted to wake him, so I could hear him say my name and to feel his touch. So I could erase the memory of the dream with all the wonderful things he made me feel.

But I didn't.

Easing down on my side so our faces were inches apart, I bit down on my lip. What if…

What if it wasn't a dream?

My breath caught as I closed my eyes. What if it was a prophecy, like the others? What if I wasn't dreaming, but seeing my own death?

\* \* \*

Sitting in the center of the bed, I tried to focus on braiding my hair, but it was hard.

Seth was virtually naked.

He'd just come out of the shower and all the man was wearing was a towel around his lean hips. A towel! It barely covered anything. And I had no idea how the towel was staying on as he prowled to the dresser. Those heavy biceps flexed as he lifted his hands, shoving hair that was darker-blond when wet, slicking the strands back. It was hanging so low, showing all those interesting dips and planes.

Staring at him made the dream feel like a lifetime ago.

My fingers stilled along my hair as I watched him pull out a black shirt. How in the world was I supposed to pay attention when I had that to drool all over?

Seth looked over his shoulder at me. "See something you like?"

"A lot," I told him, getting back to finishing my braid. "I see a lot that I love."

One side of his lips kicked up as he tossed the shirt on the bed. A pair of black boxer briefs landed next, followed by tactical pants.

A Sentinel uniform.

Yum.

I finished the braid with a hair band and then flipped it over my shoulder. "I wish I was going with you guys today."

He would've left for Pluckley immediately after the meeting with Marcus, but then everything had happened with Chicago. Late last night, Alex and Aiden had showed up to discuss going to Pluckley, the latter a little bruised but otherwise okay. I hadn't really paid attention to what they'd been talking about. What happened in Chicago was in the forefront of my thoughts.

What in the hell were we going to do? There was no way Cora or Gable would be remotely ready in a month's time to face the Titans, even if their abilities were unlocked. I'd been practicing with the elements since my abilities were unlocked and I still didn't have complete control over them.

And the Titans knew this.

Straightening, Seth turned to me. "That's the plan. Sort of shocked that Aiden relented on the whole allowing Deacon to go, but they're he's going with us."

"I'm surprised to." I dropped my hands to my lap. "I hope they're careful. I mean, I know Luke is badass and Deacon is in his own way, but he's…he's got a kind heart."

"You have a kind heart." Seth's fingers toyed with the towel at his hips.

"I do, but according to you, I'm also bloodthirsty." I gave him a cheeky grin.

"Yeah, that's right. You are. Huge turn-on."

"Only you would be turned on by something like that."

"Only I matter."

I rolled my eyes and my eyes almost kept rolling, because Seth dropped the towel, and *oh my*.

The tips of my ears burned as my gaze slipped over his chest and stomach and then further south. Wow. I bit down on my lip.

"I won't be gone all that long," he said, and hell, I had no idea what he was talking about. "I plan to take them over, scope out the town, and then Aiden's supposed to call me when they're ready. I don't plan on leaving you here alone."

Huh?

Seth chuckled. "You are not paying any attention to what I'm saying."

Blinking, I forced my gaze to his face. "Yeah, I am... Okay." I lifted my hands helplessly. "What do you expect? You're standing here naked and you're so nice to look at."

"*You're* nice to look at."

"But I'm fully clothed, so..."

"Shame." Planting his fists on the bed, he leaned in and kissed me. It was so soft and so sweet, it caused my stomach to dip. When he drew back, he repeated what he'd said. "I won't be gone long."

Letting my eyes drift closed, I rested my forehead against his. "You know I'm safe here, right?"

"Unless the walls are breached, and that has happened way too many times in the past for me to feel confident in their safety," he reminded me. "So I don't know if you'll be safe here."

A faint smile tugged at my lips. For some people, his over-protectiveness would chafe, but I found it sweet. "But *they* are more unprotected than me," I pointed out, opening my eyes. "If the Titans are close to finding this demigod, you guys could be in danger. As of right now, I'm not."

Seth didn't respond as his lashes lifted and his gaze met mine. A long moment passed. "I don't think the Titans will be straying too far from Chicago."

"We don't know that for sure. So I don't want you to worry

about me." I pressed my finger against the faint cleft in his chin. "But you also don't need to hurry back here because of me."

Dipping his chin, he nipped at my finger. "What are you going to do today?"

"I think I'm going to check out the library and see if I can find Medusa. If anyone knows how the demigods are starting to manifest abilities or how to unlock their abilities, she might." I pulled my finger free from his naughty little kisses. "And don't think I didn't notice you hadn't responded to what I said."

"Damn," he murmured, sitting down next to me as naked as the day he was born. "I was hoping you didn't catch that."

I lifted a brow.

His grin turn boyish. "All right. I won't rush back, but I'm not staying with them and it's not because I'm worried about you. But because I'll get bored and I'll miss you. And then I begin to wonder if you'll be taking a shower…touching yourself."

"Stop." Looking away, I grinned as I blushed. "How can you get bored in a town that's supposed to be one of the most haunted places in the world?"

"Probably because it's not haunted." Kissing my cheek, he pushed off the bed and finally started dressing.

I didn't know if I should be upset about that or not. "It better be haunted, or Deacon is going to be so disappointed."

Buttoning his pants, he shot a grin over his bare shoulder. "I'm willing to bet he's going to be disappointed." He reached for his shirt. "Do you think you can wait to find Medusa until I get back?"

"Seth." I pinned him with a dry look. "Last time I checked, Medusa hates dudes. Especially dudes like you."

He froze, arms shoved into his sleeves. "Like me?"

"Yes. Like you. She will never talk to me if you're around." I paused. "And honestly, I don't think she even likes you."

"She doesn't even know me." He pulled the shirt on over his

head. "How rude."

I laughed softly. "Is your ego bruised?"

He appeared to think about that. "Nah."

"Didn't think so."

His grin spread as he came forward again, placing his hands on either side of my legs. "Got a question for you."

"I might have an answer for you."

The damp strands of hair fell forward, slicing over his cheeks. "Did you wake up in the middle of the night?"

I was not expecting that question. "Did I wake you up?"

He tilted his head to the side. "A little. I was kind of half-asleep, but I had this distinct impression of you sitting up and then lying back down." He drew back, letting his hands slide off the tan comforter. "And I think you were staring at me."

"Oh, Lord," I muttered, feeling my cheeks heat. "Why didn't you say anything?"

"Why were you awake?"

Squirming, I lifted a shoulder. "I had a dream."

His gaze searched mine. "A nightmare? Like the ones before?"

After I'd been held captive by Hyperion, I had a lot of nightmares. I hadn't had any recently, but it didn't surprise me that Seth probably thought this dream was due to that.

In that moment, I knew I could tell him the truth about what I'd dreamt last night. I could get it off my chest, shaking off the fear that lingered like a cough that wouldn't go away, but that's not what I did.

"Yeah." I lowered my gaze. "It was just a nightmare."

Two fingers pressed under my chin, drawing my gaze back up. Seth's eyes were soft. "Next time, wake me up, babe. You don't have to deal with that alone. Okay?"

"Okay," I whispered.

I don't know why I had chosen not to. Maybe I knew because

if I did Seth would freak, and I didn't want that. Not when he was going out there, going to a place the Titans could be close to discovering. And maybe...maybe it was because I feared that, if I spoke it out loud, then it became more real.

Speaking it out loud made it something that could happen. That *would* happen.

## Seth

"I don't think I've ever been more excited about anything than I am right now." Deacon actually looked like he was about to pass out. "I am so ready for this."

I slid a look in Aiden's direction.

The bruise on his jaw from the day before was completely healed, and there was no mistaking the fondness in Aiden's expression as he shook his head. There was also no way you could miss the exasperation either. Aiden looked like he wanted to hug his brother and at the same time choke him.

"You're going to be so disappointed when you realize it's just a boring little village and nothing more," I said.

"Don't you dare say that," Deacon gasped, and beside him, Luke dipped his head. "You're going to jinx this."

Josie leaned into my side. "Don't jinx it, Seth."

Looking down at her, I raised my arm and draped it over her shoulders. She scrunched her nose at me. I sighed and then looked at Deacon. "You're going to see so many ghosts you're going to think you're in the Underworld."

"Damn straight." Deacon grinned as he nodded.

Alex rose from the couch. "All right, I think we're ready to get this show on the road."

Alex.

Forever impatient.

"Cora and Gable know where we're going." Luke turned to Josie. "And that we don't know exactly how long it's going to take, but they know you're still here."

"Cool. Colin's with them now, right?"

Colin? Hell. That guy.

Luke nodded. "Yeah, he's also going to keep them entertained."

"In other words, keep them out of trouble." Aiden sheathed a dagger in the holder strapped to his chest, fitted to be worn under his shirt and hidden. He reached for another dagger, and I smirked. This time I hadn't left mine behind. "I think it would be wise for them to stay in their dorms."

I opened my mouth to point out that I thought it would also be wise for Josie to do the same thing, but she must've read my mind, because her fingers dug into my skin. My gaze narrowed on her.

"I'll make sure they stay put and are safe." Josie completely ignored me. "Meanwhile, I'm going to see if I can locate Medusa and try to get some info out of her."

Deacon pouted. "Well hell, that might sway me to stay behind."

"Really?" Aiden jumped on that like a damn kangaroo. "I'm sure—"

"Pretty sure Medusa doesn't like guys," Alex cut in. "We're stuck with Deacon."

"Or I'm stuck with you two," Deacon corrected. "That sounds more like what is really happening."

"Okay." Luke stepped forward. "I think it's time for us to do this."

It was.

And I wasn't sure how I felt about that.

While Josie had been right and the gang heading to Pluckley was in more danger than her, I didn't like the idea of being over there. Hell, I hadn't even liked it when I went to the island to recharge.

Josie's hand slid along my back. When she spoke, her voice was low and only for me. "Remember what I said. Don't worry about me."

I turned to her. "You know that's never going to happen."

"You can try, though." She smiled as I picked up her braid. "Just like I'm going to."

I lowered my head, brushing my nose over hers as I said, "You do not need to worry about me, *psychi mou*. No matter what, I'm coming back to you. Always."

Her lips brushed mine as I found her hand. "I know."

"You guys need us to leave the room or something?" Aiden asked.

"Shut up," I replied and Deacon laughed as I cupped Josie's cheek. I wanted to tell her that I'd be back before she went to bed tonight, but truth was, we really had no idea what we were going to find when we got there. Could be a boring, quaint village, or worse yet, the Titans could be there.

Speaking so only she could hear, I said, "If there are Titans there, I won't kill them." I wanted to reassure her that I had...that I had learned something after what happened in Long Beach. "I'll put a hurting on them, but I won't kill them."

"I know," she repeated, squeezing my hand.

Damn.

She did *know*.

I loved this woman.

Stretching up on the tip of her toes, she placed her hand on my chest and kissed me. "Be careful."

"Always."

# 14

## Josie

*W*atching Seth and crew disappear before my eyes was more than just a little weird.

One second they were there, and Seth's intense gaze was focused on me, like he was making sure I was the last thing that he saw in the whole universe.

It kind of reminded me of watching a photograph fade before your eyes, and it only took seconds.

As I walked out of the dorm room, quietly closing the door behind me, I couldn't help but think about my life before I met Seth in the stairwell. If I'd seen someone fade away in front of me, I would've been convinced that I was experiencing the same symptoms as my mom.

My heart clenched, and I exhaled heavily. My poor mom. My mom had been sick. There was no doubt about that, but how much of her sickness was caused by the mental illness and how much was caused by what Apollo had done to her?

That was a question I'd never had an answer to, because I'd lost my mom before I even realized I had. Apollo had lied to me.

He'd told me that she was safe and…she hadn't been.

I didn't even really know how she died.

Maybe that was for the better. I didn't know.

The sadness that came with thinking about her lingered as I walked down to knock on Cora's door. A few seconds passed before the door cracked open. Only a sliver of Cora's face was visible. Smart girl.

"Hey," I said. "Can I come in for a few minutes?"

The door opened as she stepped aside. "Sure."

As expected, Cora wasn't alone. Colin sat in the chair closest to the door, and Gable was on the couch. The television in the room was on, turned to a news station that was covering the attack in Chicago. Mortals had no idea it was the Titans, and I had no idea if that was a good or bad thing at this point.

I glanced at the coffee table, spying a huge book. "*Myths and Legends?*"

"Figured they could use some light reading." Colin smiled. "They've been reading through it, and I've been answering what questions I can."

"Light reading?" Cora snorted as she squeezed past me and plopped down on the couch. "That book weighs as much as a newborn."

"I know. It could be a deadly weapon if used right," I said.

Gable nodded. "We've been reading it. Learning a lot of stuff—insane stuff we never would've believed true for one second before, well, before everything."

"Tell me about it." I leaned against the wall. "Up until I met Seth and ended up here, I thought all this stuff was just old, crazy legends."

"And you guys didn't even know that people like me existed." Colin kicked a booted foot up on the coffee table.

"I still don't know how all of this was kept secret." Cora shook her head as she stared at the book. "It just seems so impossible."

It *was* unbelievable when you thought about it.

"Did everyone leave?" Colin asked.

I nodded. "Yep. Just a few minutes ago. I was just stopping by to see how things were going."

"Good," Gable answered, and then paused. "I guess."

Cora glanced over at him and then refocused on me. "Have you guys heard anything more about what happened to that girl?"

"Did you fill them in on the whole symbol thing?" I asked Colin.

"I did. I figured it was best they knew everything."

I did, too. Knowledge truly was power. I caught them up on what we'd discussed with Marcus. "Hopefully that will help us figure out who is behind it, so we can stop them."

"That's pretty smart." Cora's dark eyes were alight with interest. "Has to be a hell of a lot easier than interviewing half the campus."

"Right?" I smiled, sort of proud of myself.

I stayed for a little bit, talking about my plans to see if I could ferret out some information on how to unbind their abilities fully. Neither Gable nor Cora knew mine had been unlocked when Apollo had thrown a dagger straight at my heart, effectively ending my mortal life. I figured we'd cross that bridge with them if it came to it, because while knowledge was power, that kind of knowledge just wasn't necessary at the moment.

After promising to come back later, I asked to talk to Colin out in the hall. He rose, following me outside. "What's up?" he asked.

"Have you heard about what happened in Chicago?"

Scratching fingers through his hair, he frowned. "The terrorist attack?"

He didn't know. I glanced down the hall, making sure it was still empty, but I kept my voice low anyway. "It was the Titans."

"What?" His eyes widened. "Are you serious?"

I nodded. "They also took over a pure community. I don't think it's something Marcus wants everyone to know, and I…" I drew in a deep breath. "I feel terrible for even suggesting this, but I don't think we should let Cora and Gable know it's the Titans."

He tilted his head. "I don't know, Josie. They need to know what they're going to face."

"I agree, but they don't need to be terrified," I reasoned. "They're basically mortal—they spent their whole lives being mortal and we're throwing so much at them. Trust me, them knowing the Titans are responsible for what happened in Chicago could be too much for them."

Colin was quiet and then he nodded. "You have a point. We don't want them to shut down, or to run."

"Exactly."

"Thanks for letting me know, but damn." He tipped his head back against the wall. "These Titans are no joke."

"No, they're not."

He sighed. "I was thinking about working with Cora and Gable later, some basic fighting moves. What do you think?"

"I think it's a good idea."

"Cool." He pushed off the wall. "See you in a bit?"

"Yep." I left him to get back to doing the Q&A thing.

I had a game plan for today.

The hallway outside our rooms was empty, but the lobby was always packed, even during the summer. I skirted around the entombed furies. To me, they looked like beautiful angels praying with their hands folded under their delicately curved chins, wings tucked back and stone expressions serene. However, from what I had been told, their presence served as a warning. The gods were upset about something, and everyone had told me I didn't want to see them unleashed.

Seth figured their presence had something to do with the

animosity between the pures and the halfs, but the gods had never seemed to care about that before. So who knew? But considering the whole Ares's symbol thing on the mask, he could be right.

Seth had also insisted that these furies would be nothing like my friend Erin. That, once unleashed, they would come after anything in their way, including me. I couldn't suppress my shudder as I walked past them, heading for the glass doors.

No one said anything to me; they never did. Heck, the whole time I'd been here, Colin was the only one who had spoken to me, but I could feel their gazes on me.

It was kind of funny in the way only irony could be.

When I'd first arrived at the University, the students here pretty much ignored me. I was invisible to them. A ghost. Before, all they'd cared about was Seth, and that used to tick me off to no end. But now? They knew I was a demigod and Apollo's daughter, so I got the same wide-eyed stares Seth received.

Honestly, I kind of wished they'd go back to ignoring me, because it was more than a little unnerving. Stepping outside, I squinted and immediately wished I had grabbed sunglasses. I bet if Seth was with me, he could just will them out of thin air.

Because he was so special like that.

Welcoming the pleasant, warm air, I took my time as I followed the pathway to the library. It was…goodness, it was lovely to have warmth without stifling humidity.

It made me long for lazy days, lying out in the sun. Lazy days that involved Seth and…and our child. The three of us on a blanket, dozing the day away. The moment that image filled my mind, a burst of sweet yearning nearly swept my legs out from underneath me.

How could something so simple as spending a day doing nothing have such an impact on me? But it did. It really did, and I wanted it so badly I could taste it.

*One day*, I promised myself. One day I would have that, and to get that, I needed to figure out how in the hell we were going to entomb these Titans.

The only person that I knew besides my absentee father who might have some clue on how to do this, or if there was another way, was Medusa.

There was a wicked sense of *deja vu* as I hoofed it up the massive steps and entered the library. I remembered doing just that when I was looking for her the first time.

All I was missing was Deacon.

Chilly, musty-scented air greeted me as I stepped just inside the huge library. Everything on this campus was crazy big.

Seeing the massive, stacked shelves that stretched all the way to the ceiling made me think of Radford University and the many, many evenings spent inside its library, cramming for exams. A small smile pulled at my lips and a feeling of nostalgia rose.

Strange thing was, I…I didn't miss Radford.

The realization stopped me dead in my tracks. I missed Erin and the few close friends I'd made, but I wouldn't go back if I had the choice. My life was so different now and it could be insanely dangerous, but it was *better*. Maybe one day I'd go back to college. It wasn't like demigods couldn't get degrees, and I already knew some people in this community who'd totally benefit from some counseling sessions, but my life wasn't lacking or incomplete because I wasn't in college. Realizing that was… It was a wow moment for me.

Truth was, I'd been feeling that way for a while now, but it was almost, like, *wrong* to admit. Screw that. I wasn't going to spend time forcing myself into some kind of shell I no longer fit in.

My steps were a little lighter as I started walking.

The last time I'd gone looking for Medusa, she'd found me roaming aimlessly through the stacks, but this time I knew where to go.

Passing the empty tables, I glanced around and noted that there were hardly any students in here. Granted, enrollment was low in the summer, but I thought it might be more than that. What had Deacon said about the libraries? The halfs were weirded out by them, but the pures were never bothered? Something like that.

So strange.

I headed down one of the aisles and did what I always do whenever I am around so many books.

Grinning like an idiot, I ran my fingertips over the spines of the books, all way to the very end of a row. I hung a right, heading for the space under the wide, ornate staircase. My steps slowed and then I stopped. I blinked once and then twice, because I knew I couldn't be seeing what I was.

"What the hell?" I gasped.

"Shush," someone, somewhere, reprimanded me.

I scanned the shadowy space. This didn't make any sense. The doors...they were *gone*. How was that possible? I hurried forward, scanning the bare, seamless wall. There'd been three of them before. Three. This was insane.

Spinning around, I stalked down the narrow space between the shelves and back wall, peering around the rows as I looked for the person who had shushed me. I found her using the air element to put books away on the top shelf.

"Excuse me," I said, gaining her attention. "What happened to the doors that were underneath the stairwell?"

"Doors under the stairs?" She picked up a book that looked like it weighed about twenty pounds. It lifted like a feather, floating to the top shelf.

"Yes." I turned, gesturing back toward the wall. "There were three doors there. They're gone."

The older lady frowned as she picked up another book. "I

don't know what you're talking about. There have never been any doors there."

# 15

Seth

The stone parish church the five us of appeared behind had to be hundreds of years old. The thing was obviously still in use and in great shape, but damn, it was old.

"You just had to bring us here?" Alex's wide gaze was trained on the ancient gravestones scattered around the church, rising up out of the thick grass like misshapen teeth. Most of the tombstones were unreadable, the words and dates lost to time.

"I figured this was the safest location to appear in," I explained. "The village isn't big. Once we leave the church grounds, we're pretty much in the town, and the last thing we need is to appear out of thin air in front of mortals"

"It's so strange how you're actually thinking about these things." Aiden tilted his head. "I'm used to you not—"

"Giving a fuck?" I supplied for him.

"Yeah. Basically."

I lifted a shoulder. Truth was, in the past I probably would've enjoyed scaring the shit out of some mortal, but now? The possible fallout of scaring the shit out of a mortal wasn't worth the momentary amusement.

"But this is the creepiest thing I've ever seen," she said, seemingly aware of Aiden and me.

"Really?" Aiden's brows lifted as he twisted toward her. "Pretty sure the giant spiders in the Underworld were the creepiest thing we've ever seen."

"Oh. Yeah." Her brow pinched. "Forgot about those."

Aiden stared at her.

"How in the world did you forget about that?" Luke asked, and then he turned. "Dammit. Where is he going?"

Deacon was already halfway through the uneven rows. He looked over his shoulder when Luke shouted. "This is the most amazing thing I've ever seen," he yelled back, and I frowned. "You guys have to see some of these tombstones."

Luke sighed heavily as he glanced at Aiden. "That's your brother."

"That's your boyfriend," Aiden shot back.

"True." He let out another sigh. "I better go get him."

It took a few minutes to round up Deacon and get going. "Lead the way," I said to Luke, who I knew had done a lot of research on the village. *Valuable* research. Unlike Deacon.

Who could list the ghosts that supposedly haunted Pluckley.

The screaming man.

Shadow people.

The schoolmaster who hung himself.

The Red Lady.

The White Lady.

Meanwhile, Luke knew where to go. "I figure the best place for us to scope out is this pub I saw. Seemed like a smart place to go. It's kind of in the middle of everything."

So that's where we headed while Deacon beguiled the group

with different ghost stories he'd heard.

My first impression of Pluckley was exactly how I'd imagined it. Rolling green pastures. Homes that are nearly as old as some of the trees, and narrow roads. The place was quaint, and I think Josie would've liked seeing it.

She probably would've liked to hear Deacon tell his stories, too.

I hung back as we walked along the road, keeping an eye on everything. There were no weird feelings or surges of energy, but I was staying alert.

"The houses look like something out of *The Hobbit*," Deacon was saying, and I grinned. They sort of did. "And I thought it was rainy and overcast in Britain?"

Luke patted Deacon's shoulder. "The sun does come out here."

Alex responded to something Deacon muttered under his breath, and I was at once grateful to see that there appeared to be a lot of tourists snapping pictures, because if not, we would stick out like sore thumbs. I'd be worried about all the attention Deacon was drawing.

Gods.

My lip curled.

This "being responsible" thing was fucking exhausting.

Aiden slowed down, falling in step beside me. "Feel anything?" he asked. "Like yesterday?"

"Nothing so far." We hooked a right, and the brick buildings crowded the road. I glanced over at Aiden, and saw he too was eyeing everything closely. "That could change."

"True." He kept his hands loose at his sides. "I wanted to say something to you."

Gods only knew what this was going to be. "Do I even want to know?"

A faint grin appeared. "I'm proud of you."

I almost stopped walking when I looked over at him. I had

no words. None.

He let out a low chuckle. "Shocked you into silence? I'm going to take advantage of that before you tell me to shut up. You didn't go after Oceanus yesterday. The old Seth would've. And the old Seth would've thrown down with Zeus, no matter the consequence. You may have even killed him. At least, you would've put a hurting on him. The fact it appears you just *talked* with him shows how much you've changed, and I was wrong."

Aiden wrong?

Tartarus just froze the fuck over.

"I was wrong when I said it appeared you weren't concerned and didn't care," he continued. "So, I wanted to say that I'm proud of you."

I let his words sink in and then I said, "Shut up."

Aiden smiled as he looked away.

## Josie

There had never been doors here?

No.

No way.

My mouth dropped open. I hadn't been the only one to see them. Deacon had been with me the first time, and both of us had seen those doors. And besides, I'd walked through them with Medusa.

I snapped out my stupor. "There's another librarian that works here. She's this tall." I lifted my hand as far as I could get it over my head. "And has really...curly hair. She wears sunglasses. Is she working?"

The librarian's dark brows rose. "There's another full-time librarian, but that doesn't sound like Lilly. There's Janice, and she's here on the weekends and on Tuesday and Thursdays, but she has pin-straight hair and she's shorter than me."

Whoever she described was not who I was looking for, unless Medusa could shapeshift. And what did I know? Maybe Medusa could.

Another book flew up to the shelf, this one ending up on the shelf second from the top. "Are you sure whoever you're looking for works here?"

Well, I had no idea if Medusa actually worked here or not. "Maybe not," I said, backing up. "Thanks for your help."

Turning around, I cut over to the left and then headed past the empty tables once more. What in the hell was going on? Had Medusa left the library, therefore taking the doors with her?

If so, that sucked.

Because what did that leave me with? A big fat nothing, because with Medusa gone, that left it up to my father to randomly appear and impart some useful information. Which was as likely as me deciding to never eat bacon again.

This was big. Huge.

The demigods' icons, what they needed when their powers were unbound, were in that place Medusa had taken me to.

And that place had been under the library…and yet somehow outside it.

It had been one of the gateways to Olympus.

Full of frustration, I all but stomped my way back to the dorm. Once inside, I walked to the center of the sitting room and then I looked to the ceiling.

"Apollo?" I called out, wincing because I felt kind of foolish. My gaze flickered over the ceiling and I waited. Nothing. "Dad?"

Reaching for my braid, I ran my fingers over it as I tried again. "Apollo? If you can hear me, I could really, seriously use to talk to you right now."

Silence.

I moved closer to the doorway to the bedroom like I could, I don't know, get better reception to Olympus or something. "I really need to talk to you about the demigods and the Titans. We have no idea how to entomb them or how to unlock their powers."

Still nothing.

The frustration began to give way to anger. "And the doors in the library are gone. How can the demigods get access to their icons if Medusa isn't here? How in the hell can we fight the Titans? What are we supposed to do? It's not like we can train them to fight. It would take months, if not years, to get them to the point where they can go toe to toe with a Titan. And not to mention, they're basically human. They can't be expected to be able to fight like we'd need them to."

And still, there was no response.

I dropped my braid and my hands curled into fists as I stared up until the stupid—so stupid—burn behind my lids forced me to close my eyes. "Do you know? I'm pregnant. I'm going to be a mother and Seth is going to be a father and you..." My voice cracked as a knot formed in my throat. "You're going to be a *grandfather*. Do you not even care?"

Opening my eyes, I stood there in silence as I lowered my chin. Hot tears crawled their way up my throat—stupid tears. So stupid, because I wasn't even sure why I was so bothered by the lack of response. Yes, he was my father, but he hadn't raised me, and he hadn't given me any real indication that he was remotely interested in forging any type of father/daughter relationship.

But damn, it still hurt.

Letting out a ragged breath, I wiped at my damp cheeks. "Pull it together," I ordered myself. "No time for tears."

After taking yet another deep, cleansing breath, I flipped my braid over my shoulder and then left my room. Knowing that Cora and Gable were good to go with Colin, I was going to do the next best thing I could do since Medusa was currently a bust and my father was off doing who knew what.

I was going to practice with the elements.

Clouds were beginning to fill the sky when I walked outside again, blocking out the sun and dropping the temperature. Since I was going out to the field that tended to get windy on a calm day, I wished I'd grabbed a hoodie or something, but I kept walking. Maybe the clouds would clear.

Nearing the infirmary and cafeteria buildings, I rounded the corner of the building, passing a group of students who were clustered together, off to the side on the lawn. I reached the edge of the sprawling portico that surrounded the entrance to the cafeteria. I stepped out—

From between the thick marble columns, a heavy, metal outdoor chair flew across the walkway, smacking into a nearby tree.

"Holy crap!"

Something big barreled right at me. I jumped to the side, planting myself against the building as I narrowly missed being taken down by a...by a *person*. Pushing off the wall, I spun just as the person slammed into the walkway with a sickening *crack*. Marble underneath him splintered.

Whirling around, my lips parted on a sharp inhale as I stared out over the courtyard in front of the cafeteria. People were everywhere. Halfs. Pures. Sentinels and Guards in the middle of them, shouting orders. It was absolute chaos.

And I'd walked right into the middle of it.

# Seth

The sun had gone down, and flames were flickering from the brick fireplace despite the fact that it was summer, and if I saw another basket of fish and chips come out of the kitchen, I might actually burn the building down.

So far, the trip to Pluckley had turned up...nothing. The patrons of the pub were, frankly, so mortal I was bored to tears. No fighting or even shouting. Well, there was a game on the TV, and that had caused some yelling, but nothing to raise an eyebrow. Not even a ghost, much to Deacon's disappointment.

And Alex and Aiden had left for a little while and did some scouting around the few local businesses. Nothing suspicious there.

I was more than ready to get out of there and get back to Josie, but...

There was a weird feeling building between my shoulder blades. Had been for the last two hours. As I sat in the wooden chair, drinking bitter ale, this sharp tingle began and hadn't gone away. It reminded me of the feeling you get when someone is eyeballing the fuck out of you.

Except for curious glances from the townsfolk, no one was paying a damn bit of attention to us. I kept looking over my shoulder and seeing nothing. The only thing I managed to do was commit the faces of the patrons to memory.

If the demigod was here, he was nicely hidden, and short of going door to door, we needed a better plan.

"What's the game plan?" I asked once Alex had returned from the restroom.

Aiden leaned back, draping his arm along the back of Alex's chair. "I think we can give it a couple of more hours, but I don't see the point of staying the night."

Deacon looked up from the menu of desserts. "I am *so* staying the night."

"Deacon—"

"You'll have to pull my cold, dead body out of here if you think I'm going to miss the chance to stay at the B&B down the road. Do you know—?"

"I really do not think they want to hear about whatever ghost may be haunting that place," Luke cut in as the tingle between my shoulder blades intensified. He ignored Deacon's narrowed gaze. "We can head out. Check out the town again. Maybe—"

A sudden heavy *thud* drew our attention. I looked over my shoulder just as a bar stool rolled across the uneven floorboards. My gaze flew to the bar. Several men stood there, their backs to us.

Aiden pulled his arm off Alex's chair as she twisted in her seat. "Could just be someone drunk."

"Could be," Alex murmured.

A man in a dark shirt stumbled back a step just as a shorter, older fellow with gray hair picked up his tall mug of frothy, amber liquid.

"What is your problem, Kent?" the younger man demanded. "You're acting like an utter twat."

"Whoa." Deacon's eyes widened. "That's hardcore."

Said twat turned, gripping his mug. "You're taking a piss at me."

"What?" whispered Alex. "Did he just get peed on?"

I snickered. "That's not what it means."

Aiden shot her a quick grin before refocusing on the bar.

Whatever the younger guy said in return was lost in laughter and jeers coming from the peanut gallery at the bar. Nothing was too out of the ordinary about this. Seemed like just a drunken argument.

"Bloody arseholes." The younger man shoved his fist out, making the universe sign for jerking off before he turned from the bar.

Without saying a word, the old man—the man old enough to fucking know better—tossed the drink *and* the glass straight at the back of the younger man's head.

The man jerked forward, his knees smacking off the floorboards as he gripped the back of his head.

"Holy crap on a cracker," gasped Alex, shooting out of her chair.

"Why you go an' do that?" someone at the bar demanded, stepping back with a scowl. His blond hair was a mess, like he'd been out in a wind tunnel.

The old man, who was starting to remind me of Santa Claus, waved the man off. "Stop sticking your beak in, you massive bellend."

Blondie shot forward, slamming his fist right in Santa's face. The old man pinwheeled backward. He was going down. Probably going to break a hip.

I kicked my feet up on Alex's empty chair and crossed my arms.

Aiden was fast, though, flying out of his seat and catching Santa by the shoulders before he fell and hurt himself.

"Careful there." Aiden straightened him, letting go when he appeared sure the man wasn't going down.

Santa spun, his red face blotchy. "Who are you?" He looked Aiden up and down with an impressive level of distaste only a British person could muster. "Nothing but a silly cu—"

"Don't finish that sentence," Aiden advised. "Seriously."

"Yeah?" Santa shot back, as belligerent as ever.

Aiden stared down at the portly man, his voice flat. "Yeah."

Someone let out a shout that would've made a banshee proud. Luke rose just as the man who'd taken a glass to the back of the head charged the bar with a stool high over his head.

Alex shot forward, snatching the barstool out of the man's hands as blood trickled down his neck. She put the stool down. "Now, that's not nice. You could really hurt someone."

The man turned on Alex and then he looked at her, really looked at her. "Well, you ain't no minger."

I had no idea what "minger" meant, but Aiden didn't like the sound of that. He was next to Alex in a nanosecond. Wrong move, because Santa was still on the move. He picked up the barstool.

"Oh, shit." Luke's eyes widened as Deacon reached over,

picking a cold fry off my plate and popping it in his mouth.

Santa winged the barstool at the bar. That thing flew through the air like a damn Frisbee. The bartender ducked at the last second, and the stool crashed into the shelf lined with liquor. Glass shattered and liquor spewed into the air.

Well, that had escalated quickly.

The bartender popped up and vaulted over the bar. *Vaulted*. He tackled Santa, crashing into the table next to where we sat. Plates broke as a burly, redhead snatched his beer off the table before it was lost.

Luke ducked as a bottle flew over his head. He turned to me. "You going to get up and help anytime soon?"

"Not yet." My gaze trekked over the bar, searching out any new faces. I was sure I'd seen everyone come in, but obviously I had missed someone.

Because if they'd been right about who this demigod was, he was in here.

Deacon reached over our table and picked up my barely-touched plate of food. "Keeping it safe for you."

"Sure," I murmured, scanning the bar.

He backed away, cuddling the plate close to his chest.

"Gods." Alex swung, catching a tall, scrawny guy who was making a beeline for Deacon by the scruff of the neck. She tossed the guy back, and he slid along the now-slippery floor. "Seth, are you enjoying yourself?"

"Immensely," I murmured.

Then I saw him.

Well, saw the *back* of him.

He was tall and his dark hair brushed the collar of the back of his white shirt. He'd easily dipped under a thrown punch that connected with some poor guy's face. He was carrying a mug of what appeared to be beer.

Every godly instinct in me told me that was who we were looking for.

A slow smile spread over my face as I finally got my ass out of the chair. "Guys, I think we got a winner."

# 16

Josie

watched in stunned silence as a half-blood jumped off the portico and power-bombed a pure into the marble walkway, cracking the stone. Like, legit picked the pure up over his shoulders and then slammed him down like he was in some pro-wrestling match.

"Holy crap," I whispered. I started to look away, but something odd caught my attention. The pure on the ground was wearing a mask.

The same mask I'd seen by the body of the half-blood girl. Before I could even process that, everything around me changed.

Intense heat blasted the air. Out of the corner of my eye, I saw a damn fireball heading straight for the half's back. I reacted without thought.

Raising my hand, I summoned the water element. Power rushed through me as the air around me dampened and constricted. It was like a tiny rainstorm erupted out of thin air, dousing the fireball before it hit the half.

Water.

Holy crap.

I'd finally used the element of water correctly.

I wanted to throw myself a little party, but there was no time to be proud of myself.

The fire-happy pure turned to me as the half spun around. Lifting his hand, the pure halted the moment he got a really good look at *who* I was, and he froze right there. He too was wearing *that* mask.

It was the same bronze mask, covering the entire face with just thin slits for eyes. The cheeks were overly round and the closed mouth formed a grotesque smile. Etched into the center of the mask's forehead was that damn circle with an off-center arrow striking through it.

Seeing it by itself was one thing, but seeing it on someone was a whole different experience.

"Well, that's a mask of nightmares," I said.

The masked man shuffled back a step, and then tucked tail and ran, dodging between sprawling halfs and pures.

Starting forward, I scanned the open campus grounds and realized that several of the people fighting were masked. Dozens of them.

"Thank you," the half said, wiping a hand over his forehead as he stared at the wet spot on the walkway. "Shit. That would've killed me."

I started to ask him what had happened, but I saw a different half fly past us, her midsection pressed to the top of her thighs. It was like there was an invisible string attached to her waist, yanking her back toward the entrance of the cafeteria. She was a Guard dressed all in white, and the woman was going so fast through the air that I knew if she hit the building, it would break every bone in her body.

I had to do something.

Spinning, I tapped into the air element, but it was too late. The female Guard hit the wall. Blood splattered where the back of her head connected with the brickwork.

I jolted as I sucked in a sharp breath.

Someone screamed, but the words were lost as horror filled me. The Guard fell, crumpled in a bloody, messy heap.

"Gods." Anger pumped through my veins as I pivoted.

Some part of me clicked off as I stalked past the half. There was fury just burning through my skin as I neared a fighting half and a masked pure. The pure was on top of the half. The clouds above parted. Sunlight glinted off a blade—*an actual knife*—as the pure swung his arm.

This wasn't fighting.

They were trying to kill the halfs—they were killing them, just like they'd killed that girl and caused the death of the other half-blood when I first arrived here.

And Seth had been right yesterday in Marcus's office. I was *bloodthirsty*.

I wasn't thinking about what I was doing as I gripped the shoulder of the masked pure. I was just so *pissed*. There were Titans out there, hell-bent on taking over Olympus and the world, and they were fighting? Over what? Because one group had more aether in their blood?

This was so damn stupid it went beyond tragic.

My touch startled him. His downward swipe halted as his head swung in my direction, and I found myself staring down into those weird slits.

"Asshole," I said, and then I tapped into the air element.

The masked pure flew backward, hitting the ground and then rolling several more feet. The knife was lost in the grass.

I continued walking, catching another masked pure off-guard. I threw him backward, into the center of the walkway. The man was stunned as I crouched over and gripped the edges of the mask. The pure grunted as it ripped off his face.

I stared into the emerald-green eyes of a pure-blood that couldn't have been much older than me. That got to me, cutting so deep. This guy was so young. "What is wrong with you?"

The pure blanched to a pale, sickly white.

Metal heated under the unnatural fire I summoned. Flames rippled over the mask, and within seconds ashes slipped from my fingers.

"Holy shit." The pure scrambled backwards, on his hands like a crab, and then he rolled. Pushing to his feet, he took off running.

I smiled as I wiped my hands off on my jeans.

I felt like a badass—like Maggie from *The Walking Dead*. I was leading the—

Hands landed onto my shoulders, pulling me backward. I lost my balance and went down hard, landing on my butt with jarring force. The sunlight was blocked by a shadowy form, and the next thing I saw was a large boot coming down, aiming straight for my stomach. A burst of panic lit up. Not for me, but for my child.

Rolling to the side, I grunted as the boot caught my hip. The spike of dull pain was nothing compared to how bad it could've been. I rose onto my hands and knees and then pushed up, springing to my feet. An odd feeling shot across my stomach. Not a pain, exactly, but more like a pulling sensation. There was no time to dwell on it. I darted to the side. Knowing I needed to avoid hand to hand combat, I summoned the air element.

The masked pure jerked and then folded as if his legs had been cut out from underneath him. He hit the ground where I'd just been. Lifting my gaze, I saw Colin.

"Hey," I said, placing my hand over my stomach. "Thanks for that."

Concern pulled at his face. "Are you okay?"

"Yeah." Breathing heavy as I lowered my hand from my stomach. Unless Alex or Deacon had told him, he didn't know I was pregnant. Taking another look at him, I saw that his shirt had dark splotches all over. Blood. My stomach dipped. "Where are Cora and Gable?"

"They're in Cora's room. Or they better be. I was trying to grab them something to eat." Shaking his head, he thrust his hand through his black hair. "It's crazy. They attacked in the cafeteria. About fifty of them, all wearing those damn masks. Just started stabbing halfs and Guards."

Another wave of horror rose. "Fifty?"

"Where are Seth and the crew?" Colin asked as he whipped around. A Sentinel had caught one of the masked pures, bringing the bastard to the ground.

It took me a moment to recognize the Sentinel, but it was Alex's father. Alexander.

"They aren't back yet." If Seth was, he would've already lost his patience and laid waste to the pures. "We can take care of this. We have to."

Colin turned back to me. "We can. We—"

"Everyone, get inside! Get inside!"

Twisting at the waist, I saw a Sentinel racing across the grounds. Whatever relief I felt at seeing him was short-lived. "They're coming!" he shouted, panic pouring into his voice. "They're coming!"

My heart lurched at the terror in his voice. I took off, running toward him. Colin was right behind me. "Who's coming?"

Fear filled the Sentinel's eyes as he reached my side, grabbing my hand. The kind of fear that shot a cold shiver down my spine. "Not that way. You do not want to go that way!"

"What are you—?"

The sound of what reminded me of a wounded animal tore

through the air. Several wounded animals. High-pitched and shrill. *Screams*.

Terrified screams mingled with something darker, something inhuman. A screech echoed through the air, drowning out the screams.

Masked pures began dropping to their knees, clutching at their heads as they tried to cover their ears.

Off in the distance, I thought I saw something dark against the gray skies. Large...birds? There were three of them, their wings gliding—

"Holy shit," I stumbled back a step. "Those aren't birds, are they?"

"No." The Sentinel tugged on my hand. "The furies have been unleashed, and they are pissed!"

Colin's mouth dropped open. "The furies?"

"They'll take out everything in their paths. We need to get inside." The Sentinel was moving, pulling me behind him. "The Library."

I got my feet working again, but I had to look over my shoulder, because I just had to. Their wings moved silently as they drew closer and closer. One broke off, zooming to the ground like a torpedo.

Screams intensified.

We reached the steps as Alexander joined us. Tiny hairs on my arm rose as a sharp tingle erupted along the back of my neck. Instinct guided me as my grip tightened on the Sentinel's hand.

"Stop!" I shouted.

A dark shadow fell over us. Colin was at the top of the steps when he froze. A stuttering heartbeat passed. A furie landed in front of the closed library doors, and she was not as I expected. Not at all.

This furie was beautiful, all golden hair and peachy skin.

Absolutely stunningly beautiful in her white, diaphanous gown. She had the lithe grace that always seemed inherent to Erin. The furie's wings were frail-looking and transparent, her expression serene.

She zeroed in on Colin, tilting her head as she seemed to size him up. She…she sniffed the air. Long blonde hair toppled over her shoulder.

"Tricky. Tricky. Tricky." She laughed and it sounded like wind chimes.

"Back up," the Sentinel said, voice low. "Colin, back *up*."

I had to agree with the Sentinel. I'd seen how badass Erin was, and she was a friend. These furies? I had no idea what they were capable of, but they had just been just freed from their tombs, so I imagined they'd be a bit…aggressive.

Colin took a measured step back, and behind me, I could feel Alexander crouching. We weren't the only one on the steps or on the porch who had the same idea. We were just the ones who were holding still.

"Don't move," the Sentinel said, his gaze trained on the furie, and I was beginning to think he had experience in dealing with them. "Everyone just stand very still—"

A half darted away from the wall of the library, rushing toward the steps.

Thick blonde curls lifted from the furie's shoulders and then she shot forward, moving as fast as I'd seen Seth do many times over. Her bare feet left the stone porch as she flew up and forward, those massive wings spreading out on either side of her.

She changed in an instant.

Peachy skin shifted gray and wings thickened, also turning gray. Slender fingers formed razor-sharp claws. Blonde hair darkened and curls—holy crap, the curls were like Medusa's. They were snakes.

The furie grabbed the half by the head. Sharp claws dug into the girl's scalp. Bright red blood trickled down the sides of her face. The girl's scream was cut off as the furie's wrists twisted.

With the slightest pressure, the furie had snapped the girl's neck.

"Oh my God," I whispered, stomach churning.

Everyone moved at once, but the furie was simply faster. She snatched up another—this time a masked pure-blood. She took him into the air, ripping him in two.

The furie was on a mission, heading straight for Colin.

Hands tugged on my shoulders, and my gaze met Alexander's. The man couldn't speak, but I got his message. *Run*. The four of us turned, and I had no idea where we were running to, but I was down with this plan.

What I had just seen...

We made it halfway down the steps when I heard a strange, rough sound turn into a scream. I looked behind me, and my freaking heart stopped. The furie had Colin.

"No!" I screamed, whipping around.

The Sentinel grabbed for me, but I was fast when I wanted to be. I darted around him as the furie lifted Colin into the air by the chest. Colin struggled, grasping at the furie's bony hands, but it was no use. Red ran down his arms, dripping to the stone porch.

No. No. No.

Colin was good. He wasn't out here, harming anyone. He was a *protector*. Kind. And he'd been nice to me from day one even though Seth had made it extremely hard on him.

"Josie! No!" The Sentinel yelled, but I raced back up the steps.

The furie lifted her head as I tapped into the deadliest element inside me. Akasha. The ripple of power expanded inside me, building until it erupted. I screamed as I threw my hand out. White light poured from my palm, and it struck true, arcing over the distance and slamming into the furie's shoulder.

Screeching in pain, she dropped Colin, but I didn't let up as rage and fear mingled with the powerful energy. I was vaguely aware of Alexander and the Sentinel rushing forward and grabbing Colin, but he...he wasn't moving.

The furie came at me howling, but the white energy poured over it, stopping her in her tracks. The power recoiled, snapping back at me. I teetered back a step as the furie crashed to the stone, falling into a pile of slender arms and broken wings. It didn't move.

I'd killed it.

I'd killed a furie.

Oh crap, was that bad?

The answering screeches from the other two furies sent chills down my spine. One was down, but there were still two. I figured they were going to be pissed.

Heart pounding, I turned just as the two furies stopped in mid-flight. They were a couple of yards away, and I tensed, having no idea if I could take two of them at once.

But they weren't gunning for me.

Wings cutting silently through the air, their heads tilted up as if they were hearing something. Mouth dry, I waited for them to attack.

There were two flashes of blinding, bright light and then...

Then they were gone.

Having no idea what had just happened, I decided not to look a gift horse in the mouth. I hurried down the steps, to where the Sentinel and Alexander had Colin laid out. Both were kneeling, so all I could see was Colin's legs. Obviously he wasn't as hurt as I'd feared, because they weren't taking him to the infirmary. They were just kneeling there.

"How is he?" I asked, running my damp palms over my hips. I felt weird. Shaky. "Is he...?"

The Sentinel looked over his shoulder at me, his face pale as he shook his head. My steps faltered. I saw all the red first. It was too much. Covering his chest and stomach and down the front of his pants. So much blood, it pooled under him, and Alexander was kneeling in it, and his hands—his hands were still on Colin's chest. He was pushing down, as if he could stop the river of blood, but there was no stopping it.

My hands floated to my mouth, but they froze halfway, because I saw Colin's face. I saw his eyes. They were wide and fixed on the sky, and I knew in my heart of hearts that it was too late.

I had been too late.

# 17

## Seth

"Get these people under control," I ordered, stepping over the sprawled form of some guy who'd just gotten knocked out.

Alex whipped around. "What?"

I kept walking, slipping out the door and into the night. A handful of seconds had passed between when I'd seen the guy leave and when I stepped out, but the road in front of the bar was empty.

Frowning, I looked down the old cobblestone sidewalk. Left and right were vacant and... "Shit."

Wispy mist slowly crept across the road, and tendrils licked up the curb and coiled around my ankles. There was nothing supernatural about the fog, but it sure as hell was creepy.

The door opened behind me and Deacon spilled out, plate of food still clutched to his chest. "I was sent to check on you—whoa, look at this fog."

"It's just fog, Deacon." Frustrated, I tried to see through the damn mist, but apparently X-ray vision wasn't a godly ability.

Where in the hell had the guy gone?

"I don't know." Deacon wandered to the left as he picked up one of his fried fish filets. "This is spooky. Like, this is the kind of atmosphere perfect for a ghostly sighting if I've ever seen one. I bet the *walker* is around…"

Shaking my head, I let instinct guide me as I stepped off the curb while Deacon prattled on about some ghost that walked around and, I don't know, screamed in people's faces?

I crossed further into the mist, reaching a market of sorts that had been open when we entered the pub, but the large, square windows were now dark. I passed a bench and stopped at the corner of the alley. The weird-ass tingle was still dancing between my shoulder blades, but I still didn't see shit as I crossed the alley. It was so damn quiet out here I was beginning to wonder if I'd hallucinated seeing the guy in the bar.

Shit. Maybe it *was* a ghost.

A ghost who walked into bars and stole drinks.

Sounded like a cooler ghost than the one who ran around screaming in people's faces. I turned back to the pub. Maybe he went in the—

"Looking for me, mate?"

My back stiffened. Son of a bitch was right behind me, and I didn't even hear him. I pivoted around, and there he was, standing near the bench I'd just passed.

The moment I saw him, I knew.

Fuck.

Even in the faint light, I knew he was Ares's son. Even if what had happened in the pub hadn't happened, I would've known the moment I saw him.

The guy looked like a younger version of Ares. Dark hair. Dark eyes. Cold face.

Shit.

The damn Fates had their messed-up hands in this. I knew it. Only they would ensure that, out of all the demigods, it would be Ares's son who survived.

He must've walked down the alley and waited, and he still had the mug of beer in his hand.

"Maybe," I said, keeping my hands at my sides.

The guy took a drink of his beer. "Who are you?"

I said nothing. Staring at him and realizing who the hell his father was caused bitterness to mix with anger, but at the same time, I felt…nothing beyond that. Fucking nothing.

He sat the empty mug on the bench, but he didn't take his eyes off me. "Or should I ask, *what* are you?"

Interesting. "That's a strange question to ask."

"Is it?" The guy stepped around the bench, but he didn't come any further. "I don't think so."

So, we were going to play the evasive game? "What makes you think that?"

The guy tipped his chin up. "Well, ever since about March, any time I get around people, they end up trying to kill one another, but you and the group you were with? Didn't seem to affect any of you."

Ever since March? Something clicked into place then. Josie's abilities had been unlocked about that time. Had her becoming a demigod triggered the abilities of the rest? That would make sense.

I was done with beating around the bush. "You didn't affect us because we're not mortal."

If those words came at any surprise to the guy, he didn't show it. Which could only mean…

"What is your name?" I demanded.

One side of his lips kicked up in a smirk that was so damn familiar I almost snapped forward and punched it off his face. "My name is Erik."

"Where are your parents?"

"Dead."

"Do you know who your father is?" I demanded.

Erik didn't answer.

"*I* know who your father is."

Only then did I see a reaction from the guy. His nostrils flared. "What is your name?"

"Seth."

Recognition flickered across his face and then he exhaled heavily. "Bloody hell."

# Josie

I walked numbly behind Marcus, not feeling a single step. Not really feeling anything.

We were in the main building, inside the closed lobby, and every single pure-blood who'd taken part in the attack and was still alive was unmasked and on their knees, their hands secured behind their backs.

Colin had said there'd been around fifty of them that had attacked, and there were forty-two apprehended. Those forty-two had managed to kill nine half-bloods and two pure-blooded Guards. And the furies had killed...

I swallowed hard.

They had killed many.

"I want every single one of them questioned and then locked up," Marcus ordered, his voice terse with barely restrained fury. "I will be contacting the families of every single one of you. Personally."

One of the pures, a young man with dark hair, smirked, and Marcus's response was immediate. He snapped forward, slamming his knee into the pure's chin, knocking his head back.

The old Josie would've gasped and been surprised by Marcus's reaction. Now? I wanted to do the same.

I wanted to kill all of them.

Marcus's fist balled in the pure's hair as he yanked his head back again. The smirk was gone from his now-bloody face. "Did that amuse you? Because you're going to be far from amused by the end of this day, when we make use of the cells that are right underneath you."

A girl at the end trembled as tears spilled down her cheeks. "I'm sorry. Please. I'm sorry—"

"Stop." Marcus let go of the pure, and he slumped back, blood dripping onto the floor. Marcus straightened. "While I appreciate your outburst of remorse, I don't care at the moment."

Marcus pivoted, his movements stiff as he motioned to me to follow. Taking one last look at the pures, I followed Marcus over to where Alexander waited.

I couldn't look at him.

Because when I did, I saw the dried blood on his hands and forearms. I stared at the floor.

"Make sure they go hard on the girl who was crying. She'll be the first to break," Marcus told Alexander. "None of them gets a pass. Do you understand?"

Glancing up, I saw Alexander nod. The man's gaze met mine, and a thousand words were spoken in those eyes. Each one pierced my chest, proving that I was still feeling. I wasn't numb at all. Pressing my lips together, I struggled to hold it together.

Marcus bowed his head as Alexander stalked off. "I have never hit a student before."

I blinked. "He deserved it."

"That is true," he replied. "But I shouldn't have done that."

Surprised that he'd mention that to me, I glanced over at the pures. They were being made to stand. "I want to kill them all. I know I shouldn't, but that's not what I want."

Marcus was quiet for a long moment. "And I do not think I'd stop you if you did."

Neither of us spoke for a long moment.

"Have you heard from Seth or any one of them?" he asked.

I shook my head. They couldn't take a cellphone with them. Whatever it was that Seth did when he traveled that way messed with cells, apparently making them unusable afterward.

"And our demigods? They're safe?"

"Yes." I'd gone to check on them after the attack. They were okay, but I...I'd had to tell them what happened.

Colin was...

Colin was gone.

That had to be one of the hardest things I'd ever done.

His body was in the...cold room in the infirmary, and his life was over. "He didn't deserve that," I said, my voice hoarse. "None of them deserved what happened to them, but those furies..."

"They don't see good and bad. They are perfect killing machines. Blind justice."

Shivering, I folded my arms across my chest. There was a coldness in my chest that couldn't be warmed. "Erin wasn't like that."

"She was your roommate at college?"

"Yeah. She was like...she was like me, just like anyone else." A weird sensation rippled across my stomach. It wasn't painful. More of a...discomfort. I shifted my weight from one foot to the next. "She didn't run around, killing everyone in sight."

Marcus turned to the locked lobby doors. I followed his gaze. All I could see was a sea of white-garbed Guards and Sentinels dressed in black. "Your friend had been around mortals. She'd learned empathy. She adapted. These furies are the furthest thing from human, Josie."

I'd seen that with my own two eyes.

"Colin was an amazing student here," Marcus said after a moment, and my breath caught. "But more importantly, he was a good person who knew what loss was and still pushed through it."

My lower lip trembled. Colin's family was killed in the war with Ares, and now he was gone, killed not in a war but by a furie who had been unleashed because of hatred and bigotry.

"He was someone who had an extraordinarily bright future ahead of him." Marcus's voice thickened, and I had to think he'd seen too much of this already. How many students during the war with Ares had ended up the same way? Too many, I was sure. "He will be rewarded greatly. I know death is different in the mortal world, but I assure you that he will be reunited with his family and he will be given—"

A sudden, sharp pain lanced across my lower stomach, startling me. Gasping, I doubled over, clutching my belly. What in the world? I waited, eyes peeled wide as I thought someone called out my name. The pain was gone as quickly as—I cried out as another burning stab traveled along my pelvis.

"Josie!" Marcus was suddenly right by my side, touching my shoulders. "What's wrong?"

I forced a breath out as fear pinged around inside me. That pain—oh, *gods*—that pain was not normal. "I don't know. I think…I think it's the baby."

# 18

## Seth

Alex stared at Erik, her expression one of reluctant curiosity, and she looked more than just a little disturbed.

Erik had taken us back to the flat he rented in one of the stone homes a few blocks from the pub. Alex lingered in the back of the room, near a blown-up black and white poster of David Bowie, while Aiden and the guys sat down with Erik.

"He looks like him," Alex whispered. "It's crazy, but he looks like Ares."

Folding my arms, I leaned against the wall. "I know, and I have more crazy for you." I looked over at her, keeping my voice low. "He says his presence started affecting people around the same time Josie's abilities were unlocked. Doubt that was a coincidence."

Her gaze met mine. "Doubtful."

"And more crazy?" I looked over to where Erik sat, his eyes as dark as the damn sky outside. "Erik, tell them about Ares."

Aiden twisted at the waist, his brows raised as he looked over in my direction. I nodded.

"I knew my father." Erik leaned back, resting an ankle on his knee. "Met him more times than I could count. He told me what I am and who he was. My father was a god."

Tension rolled off Alex as she stepped away from the wall. "Your father was a psychotic mass murderer who was hell-bent on committing genocide."

Erik glanced over Aiden's shoulder, at Alex. "I'll have to take your word for it."

Deacon raised his brows from where he sat. "You have to take more than her word for it. He was everything Alex said."

A muscle flickered along Erik's jaw. "He told me about some of you." He looked over to where Alex and I stood. "He told me about you two. Apollyon?"

"Apollyon." I chuckled, and then I blinked out of existence, reappearing directly in front of Erik.

"Bloody fuck." Erik jerked back.

"I'm not the Apollyon anymore." Reaching down, I picked up his foot and dropped it on the floor. "I'm a god. Just like your father. Except he's dead, and that girl back there, who is now a demigod, killed him. So, you're going to do more than take our word for it."

"Seth," Aiden warned, and Luke cursed under his breath.

"Do you understand me, *mate*?" I asked again, letting just a little bit of my godhood slip in. I knew what Eric saw. Eyes that were now all white.

Eric inhaled sharply, but he didn't look away as he looked up at me. "I understand."

"Good." I smiled then, and by the time I turned around, my eyes had returned to normal. "There's a lot we need to discuss, but that's not going to happen here."

Erik looked around the room as a little bit of unease seeped into his features. "What do you mean?"

"Maybe we should hold off on that," Aiden suggested, slapping his hands on his knees.

"You want to hold off? Fine," I replied. "But I've already been gone too long, and I need to get back. You want to stay? Up to you."

Alex came forward. "We can't stay here too long. Not all of us. It's too much of a risk."

"Why? Why is it a risk? You said my father is dead—"

"It has nothing to do with your father." Luke rested his hands on the back of Deacon's chair. "It has to do with the Titans. Did your father tell you about them?"

"Yeah. He told me who they *were*." Erik frowned as he rubbed a hand over his chest.

"Well, they're free and they're hunting down demigods like you to use as portable battery packs," I explained, grinning while Deacon grimaced. "We have no idea if they've figured out where you are, but they have this nifty ability to track demigods, and besides you? They are two more. They're going to find you, and since I'm not allowed to kill any more of them, they're probably going to take you. So, you're either coming with us or not. Either way, I'm leaving, with or without you."

"What Seth is trying to say," Aiden began, "is that—"

Without warning, a fissure of energy flowed through the room. Glyphs erupted all over my skin, spinning and gliding in a dizzying rush. A god was coming.

No more than a second later, a column of shimmery light appeared in front of the closed, curtained doors, and then it faded to reveal Apollo in his full god glory—a massively tall man with hair the color of the sun and white eyes spitting static into the air.

Poor Erik about came out of his skin, lurching to his feet, face pale and obsidian-colored eyes wide. He may have seen his father several times throughout his life, but he wasn't used to gods randomly appearing in front of him.

I didn't get a chance to say a word to Apollo.

He turned to where I stood and said, "Josie needs you now. Go."

At those words, my fucking heart stopped in my chest. I didn't question his command. Didn't take a moment to even respond. I focused on Josie, and let myself slip into the void.

The immediate startled gasp I heard didn't belong to Josie.

Opening my eyes, I saw an unknown male first, He was a pure dressed in pale blue scrubs—nursing scrubs. The rest of the room came into view. It was small and white, with only a cabinet and a sink along one wall.

"Gods." The pure-blood stumbled back, crumpling what appeared to be a plastic cup.

The room suddenly made sense. It was the infirmary.

"Josie!" I shot around the pure and saw her. My stomach dropped in one of the worse ways I'd ever experienced in my entire life. "What happened?"

She was propped halfway up on the narrow bed, a thin blanket tucked in around her waist. I scanned her. Cheeks were flushed with color. No visible signs of trauma. I didn't know if that was good or bad news.

I picked up her hand. "What's wrong, Josie? Why are you at the infirmary?"

She glanced at the pure before drawing in a deep breath. The entire damn world stopped at that moment, because the question formed even though I couldn't speak it out loud.

*Did something happen to the baby?*

The pure cleared his throat. "I'll give you two some time. Dr. Morales will be back as soon as she can."

"Thank you," Josie replied.

The pure nodded in my direction as he slipped past the bed and out the door, closing it quietly behind him.

"Babe." My damn hand trembled as it coasted over her cheek, my heart pounding in my chest. "Tell me what's going on, because my head is going in so many directions right now, and none of them are good."

"Seth." She curled her hand around my forearm, her fingers cool. Her shoulders tensed. "Did you guys get back from finding the demigod? Bring him back?"

"We found him. He's not here yet. We'll talk about that later, but that's not what I care about right now."

Josie's brows knitted. "If you weren't done, why are you here?"

"Your father told me to come here."

Her eyes grew wide with surprise as her hand slipped off my forearm.

I dragged my thumb along her jaw as my heart still raced in my chest. "Tell me what happened."

Those bright blue eyes met mine. "You don't know what happened here while you were gone?"

I coughed out a short laugh. "I don't know anything."

She looked away then. "There was an attack—the pure-bloods. They apparently caught a bunch of half-bloods off guard in the cafeteria. They killed...they killed nine half-bloods and two pure Guards, Seth. They stabbed them to death or used the elements. I managed to stop some of them."

"You were fighting?" I felt sick. Was she hurt? Was our child hurt? "*Psychi mou...*"

"I had to do something, Seth. I walked right into the middle of it. I wasn't going to run away and hide."

Of course she wasn't.

Josie was brave, and that was dangerous, because she didn't even realize it.

She swallowed as she pressed her lips together, and my feeling of unease tripled, burning through my veins like acid. Sitting down on the edge of the bed, by her hip, I picked up her hand again. "There's more?" I asked, sensing that there was.

Josie nodded as she squeezed her eyes shut. "The furies were unleashed."

Every part of me froze.

That was the last thing I'd suspected her to say. I'd seen first-hand what the furies were capable of when they were unleashed from their tombs.

Devastation.

"They came out of nowhere, and they were brutal." She tipped her head back against the extremely flat pillow. "It didn't matter. They were just ripping through people. We got caught outside with them."

I brought her hand to my chest. "Who were you with?"

Those beautiful eyes opened and slid to meet mine. "There was a Sentinel." She frowned. "I don't even know his name. He knew me, but I…" Josie sighed. "There was him, Alexander, and—" Her voice cracked. "And Colin."

Immediately I knew.

I knew without her having to explain anything that something really bad had happened. I closed my eyes as I brought her hand to my mouth, pressing a kiss to her knuckles.

"The furie went right at Colin, and I tried to stop it," she whispered, voice thick. "I killed it, Seth. I killed it. I killed a furie."

My eyes opened. "Oh, Josie, babe, you did what you had to do."

"I know." Tears filled her eyes, thickened her voice. "But I was too late. The furie had a hold on Colin, and it killed him."

Heart sinking, I leaned over as I let go of her hand. Cupping her cheek, I pressed my forehead to hers. I'd never liked the guy. Wasn't exactly based on something he'd ever done. My dislike was on my end, but he'd been a good friend to Josie, and I didn't want her to lose anyone else, because she'd already lost so much.

"I'm so sorry." Tilting my head, I kissed away the tear that tracked down her cheek. "I'm so sorry."

"He didn't deserve that, Seth. The pain he must've felt—the fear? He didn't deserve that." Her breath caught as she gripped the front of my shirt. "None of them deserved that."

"I know." I smoothed my hand along her jaw as I kissed her other cheek. "It shouldn't have happened."

And I couldn't help but feel like I should've been here. I didn't say it, because she didn't need to hear that right now, but damn it, whenever Josie needed me the most, I was gone. She didn't need me to always be there to protect her, but I wanted to be. I wanted to be there to protect her from seeing this harshness, from being in danger.

Worse yet, none of this explained why she was lying in this bed.

Part of me didn't even want to ask, because I wasn't sure what I'd do. Yeah, after seeing what I had seen in Long Beach, I knew to control my temper, to not just react out of emotion.

But if something happened to our child, I couldn't say what I would do. Every action had a reaction, and I knew my reaction would rock the whole damn world. The fear that was building inside me was something I'd never experienced before. It was raw and consuming as I drew back just enough that I could see her face. I tried to prepare myself for what I was terrified to hear. I took a shallow breath as more tears formed on her thick lashes.

No matter what, I would hold it together. I would be here for her if the news was bad. I wasn't going to fly off the handle and abandon her. I wasn't that person anymore.

"Talk to me." I guided her gaze to mine. "Are you okay? Is our child okay?"

# 19

## Seth

Josie's hand spasmed around my shirt. "I'm okay," she whispered, tugging at me. "The baby is okay."

I didn't hear her right.

There was no way I did.

A shudder rocked me. "Josie…"

"I got knocked down by a pure-blood," Josie continued, watching me. "I wasn't hurt, but I felt weird. There wasn't time to really think about what happened, because then the furies came."

I tensed all over again. "Is that pure still alive?"

"I don't know."

I would find out. "And what happened?"

"Everything with the furies happened, and then I was with Marcus. He'd rounded up all the pure-bloods who were a part of the attack and they were being led off to be questioned when I felt this sharp pain in my stomach."

Holding onto her hand, I breathed in the minty scent of the infirmary. Shit.

"At first, it went away, and then I felt it again," she explained.

"Along with this weird pulling sensation. It scared me, and Marcus—he was really good. He got me right here and had the doctor see me even though they are crazy busy with all the injuries."

It might make me an ass, but I really didn't care about any of the other injuries right now. My stomach pitched once more. "And it's not the baby?"

A tentative smile pulled at her lips. "The doctor doesn't think so. She thinks I actually pulled a muscle." Her laugh was hoarse. "Didn't know a demigod could pull a muscle, but apparently we can. I guess I overreacted."

"You didn't overreact." I squeezed her hand as cautious relief seeped into me. "You feel like something's wrong, you get to the doctor. I'm thinking you did the right thing." Wishing the doctor was in here, I smoothed my thumb along her palm. "Are you sure everything is fine with the baby?"

"She and the nurse did an exam, a blood test, and gave me another pregnancy test. There was nothing in the exam that she found concerning and both the blood and pregnancy showed positive." She shifted on the bed, still holding onto my shirt. "You can't see the baby's aether any longer, can you?"

"I only saw it when your powers were unlocked. Both your aether and the baby's faded after a few moments." I drew in a shallow breath. "What about that scan thing they do for women when they're pregnant? I think it's called an ultrasound?"

"Actually, the doctor is coming back with that, I think a pelvic one, just to confirm that there's…a heartbeat." She bit down on her lower lip. "You know she's not an OBGYN, so she only can do the basics, but she's been really busy with everything."

Wait. What did she say?

"A heartbeat?" When she nodded, I was glad I was sitting, because my damn knees were feeling weird again. I brought her hand to my mouth again and kissed each of her knuckles. "Okay."

She was watching me closely. "But it may be too soon, she told me, to see the heartbeat. I'm barely at six weeks. From what she was telling me, the ultrasound can sometimes detect a heartbeat at six to seven weeks."

I nodded.

There was a knock on the door, and a moment later it opened to reveal the middle-aged pure-blood rolling in a cart. Dr. Morales drew up short when she spotted me sitting on the bed, her eyes widening. She stopped, her hands tightening on the sides of the cart, and she didn't look like she was moving any farther into the room.

"Hi." Josie let go of my shirt and sat up, leaning around me. "Seth just got here."

"I see that." The doctor let go of the cart. "I'm sorry. When I see you, I don't know if I should shake your hand or bow."

My grin spread. "I do like when people bow—"

Josie smacked my back, and I thought for a moment Dr. Morales would pass out. "You don't need to do any of those things."

"Well, that's no fun." I grinned at Josie, extending my hand. "Anyway, you're here to tell me that my child is okay, aren't you? And if we're lucky, we'll hear its heartbeat today?"

Taking my hand, Dr. Morales cleared her throat and then got down to business. "Yes. Like I told Josie, everything about the pregnancy seems fine, but we're going to see if we can hear a heartbeat today."

"Good," I murmured. "That's real good."

"Seth," Josie sighed. "Let go of her hand so she can do her job."

"Sure thing." I let go with a wink.

The doctor looked like she might faint.

Josie elbowed me in the side and whispered, "Behave." Then she said, louder, "How is everyone else doing?"

"We haven't lost anyone who has been brought in, so that's

good news."

"Yeah, it is." Some of the tension seeped out of Josie, but I saw the sadness lingering in her, a sadness I would do anything to take away.

Dr. Morales wheeled the cart to the other side of the bed. "You still feeling better?" she asked as she began to fiddle with the machine on top.

"Yes. I feel completely fine."

"That's good." She clicked a couple of buttons and then turned, looking at the stool waiting in the corner. I rolled it over and her wide gaze shot to me. "Um, thank you."

"No problem." I stood, figuring the doctor needed the space, but I didn't go far. I moved to the head of the bed. "So, what will this entail?"

"It's completely noninvasive. I use this wand here," she explained, gesturing at the piece of equipment. "And roll it over Josie's stomach. It will transmit the image to this screen here."

"Cool."

Josie glanced at me.

I grinned down at her.

She shook her head. "But it might not show a heartbeat, right?"

"Depends at this stage. This test should give us a clear understanding of when you conceived, unlike our last time, even if it's too soon for a heartbeat." Dr. Morales looked over at me. "Either way, like we discussed earlier in the week, she really should be seen by an OBGYN soon. This early on in a pregnancy, it's not a big deal, but the sooner the better. I've made some calls like I promised, and I expect to hear back from them very soon."

"Hoping that call comes soon." I crossed my arms. "Real soon."

"Me too." Smiling at Josie, she reached for the blanket. "May I?"

Josie nodded. "Yep."

The doctor pulled it down and then rolled Josie's shirt up,

exposing her lower stomach. "This is going to be a little cold. Just a heads-up."

Must've been a lot cold, because Josie jumped when the gooey liquid hit her skin. Picking up the wand, Dr. Morales moved it in circles along Josie's stomach.

Josie glanced up, giving me a quick grin. "I'm glad you made it back for this."

"Yeah, I am too, babe." My emotions and head were all over the place. Total rollercoaster from start to finish. Had the fright of my life when I saw Josie in this bed, and now…maybe I'll get to see my child's heart beating.

Today was a strange day.

"I should be able to see a gestational sac no matter what," the doctor was saying as a grainy image began to appear on the screen of the ultrasound. "Good news, guys. I can say without a doubt that the pregnancy is viable."

Josie exhaled roughly. "You can?"

Dr. Morales nodded. "Yes—and there." She smiled as she twisted at her waist, pointing at the gray and black blobs. "This here is the sac, and see that little blinking right there?"

I squinted. There was something there. No idea what, though. "Yeah, I see it."

"I do, too," Josie said.

"That is the baby's heartbeat."

*The baby's heartbeat.*

The floor had to have moved under my feet. The whole room moved, but good gods, there it was. Our…our child's heartbeat. I honestly had no idea what was what on that screen except for the part that flickered, and the image of that blinking splotch was firmly implanted in my brain.

"Really?" Josie whispered, finding my hand without taking her eyes off that screen. She gripped tight.

"Yes." Dr. Morales moved the cursor. "Let me see if I can measure this. It's been a long time since I've done this, but...I think you're about six weeks, give or take five days."

Josie bit down on her lip as she stared at the screen. "That's what we thought."

"You thought right." Dr. Morales moved the wand along Josie's stomach and the picture on the screen flipped. Green lettering appeared on the screen. "The heart rate is one hundred and twenty-one beats per minute. That's a really good, strong heartbeat."

Josie's chest rose with a heavy breath as her gaze moved to mine. "That's our baby."

"Yeah." My voice sounded thick. "Yeah, it is." I blinked, because my vision had gotten a little wonky there for a moment.

Josie folded her other hand around mine as she squeezed her eyes closed. I bent down, brushing the hair off her cheek with my other hand. I kissed her cheek and then rested my forehead against hers. Dr. Morales was saying something about printing off the picture, and she reiterated how she expected to hear from the doctors soon, but my gaze was locked with Josie's. In that moment, no one else was in the room and everything that had happened outside of it didn't matter.

Emotion swelled in my chest to the point it was almost painful as I whispered against her lips, "Boy or girl?"

Josie let out a laugh that danced across my lips. She threw an arm around my neck, burying her face in my shoulder. I sat on the edge of the bed, folding my arm around her shoulders.

I didn't let go of her hand.

She didn't let go of mine.

# 20

## Josie

It was unbelievable how in one day I could go from experiencing fear and hatred and heartbreaking loss, to witnessing something so breathtakingly beautiful as my baby's heartbeat, I almost couldn't believe it.

Seeing my baby's heartbeat didn't take away the hurting Colin's death had left behind, but it was a much needed reminder that there were still miracles out there.

There was still life in all of this.

And sitting on my bed, freshly showered and wrapped in a fluffy soft robe while Seth checked on Cora and Gable, I clung to that piece of knowledge. There was still the beauty of life.

My child was still okay. More than okay, according to Dr. Morales. His or her little heart was beating strong.

Pushing my wet hair back from my face, I lifted my gaze to the ceiling. I didn't want to close my eyes for any real amount of time, because even though I was clutching at that good feeling, the image of that furie sinking its claws deep into Colin's chest waited for me. I knew if I let my thoughts wander I would hear the sound of the half-blood's bones shattering as she slammed into the wall.

And I knew if I wasn't careful, I would think of my father.

Of how I'd called out to him this afternoon and he hadn't responded. Of how he didn't come to my aid when the furies were unleashed. I would think of how he had to have been watching, because he'd gotten Seth.

But he hadn't appeared to me.

The door opened before I allowed that train wreck of a thought process to take hold, and within a heartbeat Seth was strolling into the bedroom. His gaze immediately found me in the softly lit room.

"How are they?" I asked.

"Good." Walking around to where I sat, he bent down and kissed me on the temple. He straightened. "They know to stay in their rooms for the rest of the evening."

That was good to hear. "Do they have food, though? Should we—"

"They have food, babe." Turning, he began to unhook the daggers around his waist, the ones hidden under his shirt. "They have everything they could need right now."

Except for Colin. He'd been so good with them.

I fiddled with the sash on the robe. "I think I need to be there with them." I started to scoot off the bed, but Seth turned and the look in his eyes stopped me.

"You need to be right where you are."

"I'm fine, Seth. There's nothing wrong with me except for a sore muscle."

"I know you're okay, but today has been shit for you." Seth twisted, placing the two titanium daggers on the dresser. He reached around to his back. "There's no harm in taking it easy for a few minutes."

I guessed he was right, but I felt like I'd been taking it easy half the time already. Shoulders slumping, I sighed. "Tell me about this other demigod."

Seth placed a gun on the dresser, next to the daggers. "It was who we expected. Ares's son."

"I expected as much, but I was really hoping that wasn't the case." I watched Seth lean against the dresser as he toed off his boots. "How was he?"

"Other than causing an entire bar full of old men to throw down like they were in a wrestling match, and then being a smartass?" Bending down, he tugged off his socks. "He's seems all right."

"I feel like there's a 'but' coming."

One side of his lips kicked up. "He knows who his father was. Actually met Ares a few times."

"Whoa." My eyes widened as I pulled my legs up onto the bed. I tugged the edges of the robe over my knees. "That's probably bad, isn't it?"

"I really don't know." He pulled the leather band from his hair. Gold strands glided forward, resting against his cheeks as he dipped his chin. "He knew of me—of who Alex and I used to be. The amount of stuff Ares could've told him is insane. At the end of the day, he's going to be a wild card. Either way? We can't let the Titans get their hands on him. Not with his abilities."

Biting down on my lip, I nodded. "You said...you said Apollo showed up?"

Seth looked up as he tugged off his belt. "Yeah. Came out of nowhere. Told me to get to you and I did."

I opened my mouth, closed it, and then tried again. "Do you think he's still with them?"

"I damn sure hope so, because I'm not going back there anytime soon to get their asses." He dropped the belt on the dresser. "I figure Apollo can bring them back."

"But what if he doesn't?"

"That's their problem."

"Seth."

He flashed me a quick grin that I lost sight of as he reached behind his head, gripping the collar of his shirt. He pulled it off over his head. "If I don't hear from them in a couple of hours, I'll go back and check on them, but I seriously doubt Apollo is just going to leave them there."

My gaze flickered over all the glorious bare skin on display as Seth tossed his shirt aside. It landed somewhere on the floor, in front of the bed. Dragging my gaze away from Seth, I stared at the space the shirt had disappeared to. "I went to the library this morning, after you guys left. Not only did I not find Medusa, the doors she'd taken me through were gone."

"Gone?"

"Yep. Completely gone. Like they'd never been there, and when I asked the librarian about Medusa, there was no one who works there that looks anything like her." I wrapped my arms around my knees. "And when I got back here, I...man, I feel so stupid, but I called out to Apollo. You know? Like, I asked for his help. I mean, how can we entomb the Titans when there aren't even six demigods left to naturally unlock their abilities? What are we supposed to do? So, I called out to him, and he...he didn't answer."

I didn't hear Seth move, but he was suddenly there, sitting on the bed beside me. His fingers curled around my chin, guiding my gaze to his. "Babe..."

"I didn't really expect him to. I figured he doesn't even pay attention." I lifted a shoulder. "But he is paying attention. He knew something had happened to me. Instead of coming to me, he went to you. Why?"

Pain flickered across Seth's face. "I don't know why. I wish I did. Damn, do I ever."

Closing my eyes, I leaned forward, all but face-planting his shoulder. Harsh words festered in my chest, and I didn't want to give a voice to them, but they slithered up my throat. "I hate him."

"*Psychi mou.*"

"I know I shouldn't. I know that makes me a bad person, but I hate him."

"It doesn't make you a bad person." He folded his arms around me, pulled me to him and lifted me up at the same time. I ended up in his lap, my face still fused to his shoulder and my robe slipping down one arm. "It just makes you mortal."

"But I'm not mortal."

His lips coasted over the inch of bare skin at my shoulder. "You know what I mean."

"I do." I turned my head so my cheek rested on his shoulder. "He didn't save my grandparents. They died. He lied to me about my mother. She died. I really don't even know if Erin is okay or not. He could be lying about that too." I drew in a shaky breath. "And you said Zeus knew I was pregnant. That means Apollo *has* to know. Does he not even care?"

Seth's hand tangled in my wet hair. "He cares. I'm not saying that because I'm trying to make you feel better, babe. But I think he cares. He just has a shit way of showing it."

Tears burned the back of my eyes as more words bubbled up. I whispered, "I don't hate him."

His arm tightened around my waist. "I know."

I swallowed hard.

"Hug me back," Seth said, voice soft in my ear.

I gave a half-hearted attempt at pressing against him.

Seth chuckled. "Hug me back, Josie."

Letting out an absurdly loud sigh, I let go of my robe and wiggled my arms free. I threw them around Seth.

"That's my girl."

I hugged him tight as I shifted around so my knees slid along either side of his hips. "What are we going to do, Seth?"

"That's a loaded question," he said as he scooped the strands of hair out from under the robe.

It really was, but I figured I'd start with the obvious. "What are we going to do with the Titans? Great. We have Ares's son. Awesome. But we don't have enough to unlock their abilities. The whole plan is bad."

Seth slightly pulled back so he could kiss my cheek. "The plan has been shit from the beginning, really."

I couldn't help it. That made me laugh. "It has."

"We'll figure something out."

Leaning back, I slid my hands off his shoulders, to his chest. His skin was warm under my palms. "We keep saying that, but we aren't figuring anything out."

"Kind of hard to argue with that statement."

I smirked, but it quickly faded. Lifting my hand, I traced the line of his jaw with my finger. His eyes drifted shut and thick lashes fanned the smooth skin under his eyes.

"I keep saying it, because we have to," he said, "We don't have a choice."

Seth was right.

We had to figure out so much that it left little room to focus on the pain and fear or anything else, but what had Seth said when he walked in?

I had time to take it easy?

In all honesty, we really didn't have the time. Every waking second needed to be focused on finding a way to entomb the Titans and stop the pure-bloods who were attacking the half-bloods.

A sharp pain pierced my chest, and it felt so real that I sucked in air. The image of Colin started to form, his face waxy and eyes unfocused—

I cut off that train of thought, refocusing on Seth. He was staring at me in that intense way of his, the way that made me feel like he could see inside my very head.

I didn't want to think or feel any of the heartache waiting for me or the fear of the vast unknown waiting for both of us.

Not right now.

My gaze traveled across his face, committing the angles and planes to memory with more than just my eyes. I traced the curve of his cheek with the tips of my fingers and then mapped the bridge of his brow with my thumbs. From there, I trailed my finger along his upper lip and the fuller bottom one.

"I like that," he said, his voice rough as he tilted his head back, eyes closed as he exposed his throat to me. "It feels good."

I could tell that he did thoroughly enjoy this, because he was hard against the curve of my ass.

Then again, I had a feeling that if I looked at him a certain way, he *enjoyed* it, and I loved that. I may have been an awkward, uncomfortable mess ninety percent of the time, but Seth always, *always* made me feel beautiful and wanted, desired and cherished.

Dragging my fingers down the center of his throat, I lowered my mouth to his, kissing him softly. Seth made this pleasant little humming sound against my mouth. I kept lowering my fingers, marveling at the way his stomach muscles clenched in response. My palms pressed back against the loose sash on my robe. Seth's lips parted on a soft inhale, and I took advantage of it, dipping my tongue in as I wrapped my fingers around the sash, pulling it free. The robe parted and, with a wiggle of my shoulders, it slipped down my arms, stopping at my elbows. I reached between us, my fingers going for the button on his pants.

Seth groaned into the kiss as he gripped my arms, pulling my hands away and holding me back. Breaking the kiss, he opened his eyes. They were pools of liquid amber.

"Babe," he murmured, his gaze dropped and drifting over my bare chest. "What are you doing?"

"What does it look like?"

His chest rose sharply. "I think I have a good idea, but we really shouldn't be doing that right now."

"Why not?" I pressed my mouth to his, and Seth's opened, welcoming the kiss.

He was breathing heavier. "Do I need to remind you that you were just hurt? And Dr. Morales said—"

"I have a pulled muscle, Seth." Smiling, I rocked against him, rewarded by another deep rumble coming from within him. "And we can take this easy."

"Josie," he all but groaned. "You know I want you. Always. But when Apollo came for me tonight, I thought...I feared the worst."

I squeezed my eyes shut.

"Those seconds that it took for me to get back here, I feared the worst. That there'd be no more moments like this," he continued, stopping to groan as I moved. "They were only seconds, Josie, but they felt like an eternity."

"Seth," I whispered against the knot in my throat. "Then let's take back those seconds and make them ours."

He started to respond, but I brought our mouths together, silencing his fears, and we kissed...we kissed like we'd never have the luxury of doing so again.

"I don't want to think about anything right now," I told him, moving away from his mouth to nip at the delicate skin of his throat. "I just want to feel the good that we have. I just want you, Seth. I just want these moments."

Seth shuddered as he let go of my arms. "How can I say no to you?"

"You can't." I reached for the button on his pants again. "Because you love me."

"I do." One hand curled around the back of my head as the other slipped inside the robe, settling on my waist. "I love you so fucking much I think it's killing me sometimes."

I shuddered and almost lost sight of what I was doing, but I got his pants unbuttoned and the zipper tugged down. Seth's arm tightened around me as he lifted up just enough for me to get his pants down to his thighs. His entire body jerked when I reached between us, wrapping my hand around him.

"Josie," he growled my name.

I rose up. His breath fanned my throat as I positioned him where I wanted him. Seth's other hand found its way between the halves of the robe and tightened on my hip as I slowly worked my way down his length, inch by inch. I got halfway down and started over. I had to.

Seth groaned. "Gods, you really are killing me."

My gaze flew to his. "Am I...am I doing this right?"

"There is literally nothing about this you could do wrong."

I stopped moving. "Really?"

His head tilted and his lips brushed across mine. "Well, if you bit me, and not in the fun way—"

"Seth," I laughed.

"No, babe. There is nothing you could do wrong."

I grinned then, but the grin slipped from my face as I gasped at the pressure, the fullness, and I let go, sinking down the rest of the way.

Seth shuddered all around me as his hands opened and closed on my hips. For a moment, I couldn't move as liquid heat poured through my veins.

Then I had to move.

I wasn't exactly all that skilled and I really wasn't the one to take charge like this, but I pushed past the uncertainty and just relied on instinct and what my body wanted to do.

And it knew exactly what it wanted.

Him.

Always him.

Shifting forward, I lifted up and then pushed back down, gasping at the delicious tug and pull as my chest flattened against his. My fingers sifted through his hair as our foreheads pressed together.

"You feel so damn good," he whispered in the space between our mouths. "Every single time, Josie."

We took our time.

We did take it easy.

And Seth…*gods*, Seth just held me as I moved on top of him, lifting and rolling my hips, taking it slow and taking him deep. Somehow it made everything all the more intense, more consuming, and the sweetest fire burned its way through me. When I finally broke apart, I shattered into a million little pieces. It was like every part of my body experienced release. Maybe even a part of my soul found some semblance of peace.

Sometime later, Seth was on his back and I don't remember exactly how he got his pants off, but they were balled up at the foot of the bed. My robe was still caught around my elbows, but I was too lazy to shrug it off.

As I lay there, still sprawled on top of Seth, tracing tiny circles on his upper arm, my thoughts began to wander. I didn't even try to stop them, not even when I started thinking about the Titans.

The only good thing we had going was that not all the Titans had been unleashed. We had Tethys and Oceanus and Cronus left to deal with. Three. We also had a buttload of shades, but when the Olympians fought the Titans before, the Olympians went up against all of them.

How did the Olympians defeat the Titans?

I knew what I had read in the *Myths and Legends* book and

what I'd been told. That it took all of them to take them down, but...

I tried to remember the legends I'd read ages ago, before I realized that gods were real. I couldn't remember the details, but something wasn't adding up. It was like a word lingering on the tip of my tongue. "Seth?"

"Hmm?"

"How did the Olympians defeat the Titans?"

He didn't answer for a moment. "That's a random question."

"It is."

"All of them fought the Titans and were able to entomb them," Seth said, his fingers flexing along my thigh.

I considered that. "I feel like I heard or read something else. Like, something way before...all of this began."

"You probably did. A lot of the legends mortals know are based in some truth, but got exaggerated over the years." He let out a yawn. A moment passed. "I forgot to tell you this, but Ares's son? Erik? He started experiencing his abilities around the time yours were unlocked."

"Really? That's strange." It really was since that's not something Apollo had ever mentioned. He'd said it would take six demigods and they'd all have to be together, so how did my abilities affect the other demigods?

But Erik was really just getting the shitty end of the deal. His presence caused violence, but—

Something occurred to me.

"I just thought of something."

Seth's hand stilled on my thigh. "Does it involve doing what you just did? Because I'm going to need a few more moments to recover."

"No." Pushing against his chest, I ignored his groan as I sat up. Excitement thrummed through me as the idea took hold and spread. "It has nothing to do with the demigod. Not really, but more of what is happening here."

He gave me a lazy look from under his lashes. "Okay."

I took a deep breath. "If Ares's son affects people and makes them violent, what if that's what is happening here? At the Covenant? What if something like that is influencing the pures here and making them act this way?"

# 21

## Seth

Josie dragged the huge-ass *Myths and Legends* textbook out from under the bed and plopped it down next to me.

"How did that book end up under the bed?" I asked, looking up at Josie. She'd fixed her robe, but she'd barely tied the sash at her waist, so the halves of the robe were gaping in very interesting, very distracting ways.

"I don't know." She crawled across the bed, sitting cross-legged beside me. "It fell off the bed one day and I was too lazy to pick it up."

I grinned at her.

"What?" She ducked her chin as she started opening the book, flipping through the pages. "This book is heavy."

I could've pointed out that she had the air element at her disposal, but I figured she'd be likely to knock me upside the head if I did.

I leaned back against the headboard. "What are you looking for?"

"I'm looking for…this!" Picking up the sides of the book, she dropped it on my stomach.

Grunting, I grabbed it before it slid back onto a very sensitive part of me. I looked down, scowling when I saw that it was open to several paragraphs about Ares. "Josie." I looked over at her. "Ares's son hasn't been to the campus."

"I know, but he's not Ares's only son. Okay. So, when Deacon was telling me about Alex and Aiden and, well, you, he told me what happened to Alex after she fought Ares the first time. That she'd been, I guess you could say, infected by two of his sons." Leaning over, she scanned the page and then pointed at the section about Ares's children. "Phobos and Deimos, right?"

Tension crept into my shoulders as I stared at their names. "A thousand years could pass, and I won't forget those bastards."

They'd done a number on Alex, preying on her fears and amplifying them. Worse yet, they'd made her think she was pregnant. It had been…fuck, it had been horrible. The fallout for both Alex and Aiden…

Josie pulled her hand back. "Apollo had summoned them out of her, right? He looked at Alex and knew she'd been infected."

I nodded. "Artemis had seen something in Alex, but it was Apollo who saw them."

"Do you think it's possible that they are here, infecting someone and influencing others?"

Shaking my head, I looked back at the page. Ares had quite a few children, as did most of the gods. Being alive that long, you could accumulate quite a brood. "Anything is possible, but they only infected Alex. Not saying they couldn't have a larger impact if they wanted to."

"But it's not impossible, right?" Josie's eyes glimmered with excitement. "It could be any number of his kids. Phobos instills fear. Deimos can cause terror, which by the way seems like the same thing to me, but whatever. And then there's Enyo, or however you pronounce her name. She was his sister and lover, and *ew*, but she can cause discord. Discord, Seth."

I wanted to believe that Josie was on to something. That all we had to do was find this one person or entity and everything would magically be resolved.

But it rarely worked out that way.

She pulled the heavy book off my stomach and held it in her lap, curling her fingers around the edges. "And if we could get one of the gods to come here and do whatever summoning mumbo-jumbo they need to do, we could stop what's been happening here and all these deaths. And Colin's death wouldn't be for nothing."

Damn.

I saw it then, what was shining in her eyes and why she was so desperate to believe that she had the answer to fix this. She wanted revenge for Colin's death. She wanted his death to mean something in the end.

And she wanted to be the one to bring him justice.

I got that.

I really did.

Tugging the book from her grasp, I closed it and placed it aside. I shifted closer to her, leaning over and planting my weight on one arm.

"Why'd you do that?" she demanded.

My eyes met hers. "I know you want to find the people or person or god responsible for Colin's death. I completely understand that." Cupping her cheek, I then slid my hand to the back of her head, tangling my fingers in her hair. "I want to find those people too."

She stiffened. "You didn't even like Colin."

That was true. "I still want to find the person responsible. I just don't think you're going to find the answer in that book, babe."

Her shoulders slumped as she looked away, and I hated seeing the sadness creeping into her expression. "Why can't it be one of them?" she asked after a moment.

"It could be, but…Josie, there has been a long history of violence and hatred toward the halfs. Centuries worth of bigotry and discrimination. Some of that was fueled by the gods. And some of it is because there are a lot of pures that are just fucking disgusting assholes. There's no one causing them to be this way. They chose to be this way."

Josie gave a little shake of her head. "How can anyone choose to be so full of hatred that they murder people?"

"I don't know." I kissed her cheek. "I mean, I guess I kind of do know."

"What?" Josie pulled back, her eyes searching mine. "What do you mean by that?"

I lifted a shoulder. "I did terrible shit when I was with Ares. I killed people, Josie. I can blame Ares, but it wasn't like I wasn't in control of myself. I'd been swayed to believe certain things and I acted on them. Some of these pures have been swayed to believe in certain things. They can be taught differently. I was, but does learning and changing wash away my crimes?"

Josie opened her mouth, but I already knew what she was going to say.

"I know you believe that it does for me," I said. "But I know I still have an extraordinarily long road ahead of me when it comes to making up for everything I've done."

She didn't say anything as she scooted her way toward me. Quietly, she clasped my cheeks and kissed me. And that soft sweep of her lips led to a much deeper one that also led to a hell of a lot more than a kiss.

Hours later, I ended up lying beside her while she slept. My mind was too all over the damn place to get any shut-eye, so I was awake when someone knocked on the door.

Easing my arm out from underneath her, I wasn't all that surprised that all she did was snuggle down in the bed, wiggling those damn hips of hers in a way that made it so fucking hard to get out of the bed.

But I did.

Because I was mature like that.

Finding my pants on the floor, I pulled them on and then made my way out to the sitting area. I opened the door and found Aiden standing there.

"Well, apparently you guys made it back here."

"Yeah, obviously," he said as I stepped out into the hall, closing the door behind me. "Is everything okay with Josie?"

"She's okay." I dragged a hand through my hair, shoving it out of my face. "There was an incident here." I told Aiden about what had happened with the pures and with Colin. "Josie is fine, though. Turned out to be a pulled muscle."

"Damn." Aiden bowed his head as he placed his hands on his hips. "Colin seemed like a good guy."

I made some sort of noise of agreement.

"This crap with the pures is the last thing we need."

"No doubt. So, did Apollo bring you guys back?"

Aiden nodded. "Yeah, he managed to, uh, *convince* Erik that it would be a very wise choice for him to come with us."

Leaning against the wall, I crossed my arms. "I don't know how I feel about him being here. I know he can't be out there, not where the Titans can find him, but I also don't like the idea of him roaming around. We have enough problems without an untapped demigod who might be pissed off about being here."

"Agreed. He's currently on the second floor, under Luke's watchful eye. We put Erik near Deacon and Luke." Aiden glanced down the hall. "Alex went to see if Marcus was still up, but I guess, considering everything that just went down, she's going to be gone a while."

"Probably."

Aiden focused on me. "That's not the only reason why I'm here."

I was still leaning against the wall, but every muscle tensed.

"Apollo wants to see you."

My jaw clenched, and a moment passed before I could trust myself to even respond. "Does he now?"

"Yeah," Aiden gruffed.

"He's obviously not here. I don't feel him."

"Well, I'm guessing he's coming back. Said to have you meet him in my room."

My molars were starting to ache. "Now, I find this strange. He's never had any problem just popping into my rooms, no matter what I'm doing. Hell, he usually takes great pleasure in that."

"Yeah, I find that strange too."

Looking away, I shook my head. The fucker was avoiding Josie. I pushed off the wall. "Let's go."

Aiden sighed. "This should be fun."

Damn straight it was going to be just fucking dandy. I prowled down the hall, and the moment Aiden opened the door and I stepped in, a fissure of energy rolled down my spine. The glyphs bled through, swirling over my skin.

Apollo appeared in front of me, in the center of shimmering lights, in all his golden glory. The moment he became visible, I slammed my fist into the fucker's jaw.

"Gods," Aiden stepped back and to the side as Apollo's head snapped back.

Apollo turned his head back to me, his all-white eyes narrowed as he rubbed his jaw. "Was that necessary?"

"Not really, but it made me feel so fucking good."

Apollo dropped his hand. "I see some things never change."

"Yeah, ditto, fucker." I stepped up, going toe to toe with him. "Because I see you're still doing the 'played-out absentee father' thing."

The sun god's nostrils flared. "You should go do something, Aiden."

"Sounds like a plan." Aiden backed up to the door. "I think I'll go see if Alex is with Marcus."

I didn't acknowledge any of that. All I heard was the door close behind Aiden. "You don't want Aiden to be here when we talk about how your *daughter* calls out to you, time and fucking time again, and you never answer?"

"I'm here *because* of my daughter," Apollo growled, and he took a visible step back from me. "I told you once before, boy. Don't even begin to think you know what I would do for her or have done—"

"I don't give a flying fuck what you think you've done or are doing for her." Anger flowed through me like lava. "You obviously know she's pregnant. You obviously know that she needs you in her life." The last part nearly killed me to admit, but it had to be said. "And you're not there."

Apollo turned from me, and without saying a word he walked to the couch and sat. Several moments passed as he stared straight ahead, as if he were focusing on something only he could see. "Is the baby okay?"

I curled my hands into fists and strived for patience I didn't have. "The baby is okay."

He closed his eyes. "I could…feel her panic earlier. I knew it had to do with the baby. That was why I came for you."

"Great. Glad you did that so I could be there for her, but that doesn't answer why you didn't go to her yourself."

Opening his eyes, he looked at me. They were somewhat normal. The same vibrant shade of blue as Josie's. "You don't understand."

"No shit. I don't understand. The furies were unleashed, Apollo. You do know they could've seriously injured her. Possibly killed her." I stepped toward him. "She watched one of her friends die. So, yeah, I don't understand why you didn't step in."

"It's not as easy as you think it is." He turned his head. "I know she was calling for me this morning. She wanted to know how the demigods' abilities can now be unlocked."

"You have the answer to this?" I demanded. "One that you couldn't tell her yourself?"

"I'm telling you." Apollo's glacial gaze met mine. "The demigods' abilities cannot be unlocked now. They cannot fight the Titans."

# 22

## Seth

There was a good part of me that was sure I had not heard Apollo correctly. I needed him to repeat himself.

"Come again?"

"The demigods' abilities cannot be unlocked. There needed to be six of them for that to happen naturally. Now, as you've probably guessed, some of their abilities began to take shape when Josie became a demigod, but as far as them being able to control the elements or harness akasha, they would need to be fully unbound and that will not happen."

I stared at him for a good minute before I could find the words. "Why not? There has to be… Wait." I barked out a harsh laugh. "Fuck me with a rusted fork, I get it."

Apollo's brows lifted. "The image you just provided me was something I could've lived without ever experiencing."

I ignored that comment. "What you're saying is that, for the demigods to have their abilities unlocked, it would require the gods who donated their sperm or their egg to unbind them.

That would mean the god would be weakened." I smirked. "Can't imagine Poseidon signing up for that."

The god's eyes narrowed. "It's more than just that, Seth. Or have you forgotten that Ares is dead, and therefore cannot unlock his son's abilities?"

"I haven't forgotten, but three fully charged demigods is better than one, right?"

"Right," he agreed coolly. "Do you think I haven't wished they'd follow my lead? Or that I haven't asked?"

"I've given up on guessing what you may or may not do."

"I have spoken to them," Apollo responded.

And I knew without asking what their answers had been. "Then what do we do? Because what other options do we have? Or are you saying that entombing the Titans is hopeless? You do realize they just took over the community in Chicago? You guys do realize they are responsible for what happened there."

"Yes. We are aware of it."

"And that's not enough for them to unlock the demigods? Do you know what they offered me?" Apollo's jaw locked down, and I had no idea if he knew the deal I'd been offered. "Oceanus wants me to bring them Zeus's head. I have until some festival at the end of July. If I don't do it, they will destroy Chicago, and they won't stop there."

Shockingly, he didn't ask if I was going to take the deal.

"And now you're telling me there's no chance of the demigods getting their abilities? Then what is the point? If that's the case, then give me a heads-up and I'll take Josie and go someplace that it'll take decades for the Titans to find us."

"You'd do that, wouldn't you?"

I met his gaze and then I really thought about what I'd said and what I'd do. And then, damn if I didn't think about what Zeus had said to me. "That's what I would want to do. That's what instinct tells me, but I don't...I don't want my child to grow up in a world that could end at any given minute. I don't want a world where Josie has to look over her shoulder every second of the day. So, I guess my answer is no. I wouldn't do that. I would want to, but I couldn't. I'd figure out a way to entomb the Titans."

Apollo held my stare for a moment and then looked away. "What you would do for love and for your child is...admirable, Seth. That I can say."

I stared at him.

"Love usually doesn't make people better. People want to believe that it does, but in the end, love usually makes people selfish. And for us? Gods? Love is more of a poison than a gift," he said, and I had no idea how to respond to any of that. "What would you do to ensure that your child is birthed into a better world?"

I didn't hesitate. Not for one second. "I would do *anything*."

# Josie

My chest sort of hollowed out as I stared at Seth. We were supposed to hook up with Alex and Aiden so I could finally meet Ares's son when Seth dropped the bomb that Apollo had been here, at the Covenant, and that there was no other way of unlocking the remaining demigods' abilities.

We stood in the hallway, just by the stairs leading to the second floor. It was early in the morning, so the hall was quiet while we waited for Aiden and Alex.

"He was here, at the University?" I felt like I needed to clarify that. Maybe he meant that he'd talked to Apollo in an alternate dimension or something. "Like, right here, in the same building as me?"

Seth nodded.

I opened my mouth, but closed it. A moment passed. "And

you didn't come get me?"

"You were sleeping."

Mouth gaping, I blinked slowly and then I shot forward, smacking his arm. "And you didn't think to wake me up?"

Seth caught my hand as his eyes met mine. "I'm sorry."

"You're sorry?" Irritated, I tried to pull my hand free, but Seth held on. "I can't believe you didn't wake me."

"I know." Seth pulled me to his chest, clamping one arm around my waist, trapping my arms so I didn't hit him again. He still held onto my hand as he dropped his chin to the top of my head. "And I *am* sorry, Josie. I really am."

I didn't get it. Why would Seth not wake me up? He knew how badly I wanted to see my father, to talk to him—to force him to talk to me. Seth more than anyone knew.

Then it hit me.

Sucking in a sharp breath, I pulled back, and I did so with enough force to break Seth's hold. Understanding dawned, and damn, it hurt. "He didn't want to see me."

Pain flickered across Seth's face, and I knew I was right. "Josie—"

"I'm right, aren't it?" My entire chest burned.

Jaw grinding, he looked away and didn't answer, and that wasn't good enough. I wanted to hear him say it. I didn't know why, but I needed to hear him say it.

"He only wanted to talk to you, but didn't want to see me. That is why you didn't wake me up."

"Josie, babe, I…" He trailed off, finally looking at me again. "Don't make me say it."

"Why?" My heart pounded in my chest and the burn had crawled into my stomach. "It's the truth, right? What's so wrong with saying it?"

Seth stepped toward me, and I knew he was going to pull me

back into his arms, and if he did that, I was going to cry. Because I was a mess and I wanted my dad to be a dad, but Alex and Aiden's door finally opened and they stepped outside.

Relieved by the interruption, I spun toward them. "Hi!"

Both drew up short and looked between Seth and me. Probably had to do with my overly bright greeting.

"Hey." Alex smiled faintly. "I hope you guys weren't waiting long."

"Not at all," I chirped, ignoring the frustration that rolled off Seth.

Aiden looked from Seth to me. "We are so sorry to hear about Colin," he said, his voice heavy with compassion. "We didn't know him well, but he seemed like a really great guy."

"He was." I pressed my lips together, not wanting to think about Colin. I knew that was wrong, but it hurt too much to do it. I drew in a shallow breath. "So, you guys ready to head up?"

"Yep." Alex stopped beside me, her heart-shaped face tilted up as she placed her hand on my arm. "Everything okay with you?"

Swallowing the knot in my throat, I nodded. "Yeah. I'm okay; the baby is okay."

Alex squeezed my arm. "I'm happy to hear that."

And I knew she meant that, which made me want to cry again.

Good Lord, was this pregnancy hormones? Or was it everything to do with Colin and my father? Probably a mixture of all of those things, but thankfully, we got to walking up the stairs.

Unfortunately, Seth lingered back and said, "We need to talk," his voice low as Alex and Aiden rounded the first flight of stairs.

"I don't think we do." I didn't look at him as I gripped the railing. "I know the answer. It is what it is."

"Josie…" He moved so fast, he was beside me and then he was right in front of me. "I don't like seeing you this way."

"I don't like feeling this way. I just…" Casting my gaze to the window on the landing, I shook out my shoulders. "I'll be okay."

Seth lightly touched my cheek. "Tell me how I can make you feel better about this. Tell me, and I'll do it. Anything."

My heart squeezed in response to his words. If I told him jumping on one foot would make me happier, I really think he would've done it. "I'm not mad at you."

"I know that." The door above us creaked open. "This isn't about me."

It was all about Apollo. Closing my eyes, I shivered when he brushed his nose along the side of my cheek and then kissed the corner of my lips.

"Let's go," I said. "They're waiting on us."

Seth didn't move for a long moment, his warm breath dancing over my lips, and then he pulled away. Taking my hand, we walked up the steps. Alex and Aiden hadn't stayed in the stairwell, but they waited out in the hall. Obviously they knew something was up and were giving us space.

Feeling my checks heat, I cleared my throat. "Do you think he's awake?"

"Yeah." Aiden walked ahead, to the third door on the left. "Time difference. It's actually in the afternoon for him."

"Oh. Good point."

I had no idea what to expect when Aiden knocked on the door; a few moments later, it opened, but I had not expected to get an eyeful of male nipple and a whole lot more.

"What the hell?" Seth cocked his head to the side.

Ares's son stood in the doorway wearing nothing but a towel folded around his hips. The guy was lean and tall. He was also fairly good-looking, with high, cut cheekbones and a wide mouth.

And apparently he didn't realize he was about five seconds away from death, courtesy of either Seth or Aiden.

"Did you forget to put clothes on?" Aiden clipped out.

Erik arched a dark brow in Aiden's direction. "I just got out of the shower," he said, and oh my, he had an accent. *Nice.* "Do you have a problem with that, mate?"

"I do." Seth stepped in front of me, blocking my view, and I rolled my eyes.

"All righty," Alex murmured under her breath as she turned slowly and raised her brows at me.

I grinned.

Sighing, Aiden pushed open the door, edging Erik out of the way. "Go put some clothes on. *Gods.*"

Erik smirked, but he disappeared back into the bathroom. I looked around the room, seeing a small piece of black luggage. Was that all he brought? I guessed he wasn't planning to be here long.

Erik wasn't gone long. He walked back into the sitting area, wearing a pair of jeans. And that was all.

"Really?" Seth murmured, his lips thinning.

I wanted to point out just how often Seth failed to wear a shirt, but decided against that. I stepped forward, offering my hand. "I'm Josie."

The newly acquired demigod took my hand as he checked me out. "Quite nice to meet you, love."

"It's not going to be nice if you keep holding her hand," Seth said from behind me.

I turned, pinning him with a look. Seth raised his brows in return. I shook my head as I looked back at Erik. "Please ignore him. He's crabby in the morning."

"I'm sure that's what it is." A half-grin appeared on Erik's lips as he glanced over at where Aiden stood next to Alex. "I was hoping someone would bring me breakfast."

Seth snorted. "You better do more than hope."

"So I'm allowed to leave this room then?"

Aiden answered before Seth could. "Not yet. As we told you,

there is some stuff going on here. It wouldn't be wise for you be out there by yourself."

Sitting down on the couch, Erik stared up at us and there wasn't an ounce of concern on his face. He glanced at me. "So who's your father?"

They hadn't told him? Surprised, I glanced at Seth, but he was eye-balling Erik like he was a single-celled organism he hadn't decided if he should squash or not.

"My father is Apollo," I answered.

"Really?" Erik chuckled as he leaned back. "My father was not a fan of yours."

I blinked. When Seth had told me that Erik had met Ares, I'd been somewhat surprised, but I figured it may have been a one-off thing. I mean, Ares sounded legit psychotic, so I couldn't imagine he'd been spending much time with his son.

"Did you see your father a lot?" I asked.

Erik lifted a shoulder as he rubbed a finger along his brow. "I guess so. Wasn't like every day or every week, but he was around. Anyway, what's the plan?" he asked. "I'm assuming no one brought me here just to keep me stashed away in a room."

"Well, we're thinking we'll start training you, along with the other two you'll be meeting today," Aiden said, sitting on the arm of the chair. "At least in the basics when it comes to hand-to-hand combat."

"Your full demigod abilities are still bound, but you don't need them to defend yourself," Alex chimed in. "We can teach you."

As they talked, a hot, ugly feeling unfurled in the pit of my stomach. I knew I should be paying attention, because I felt responsible for these demigods, even this one who was looking back at Aiden like he hadn't signed up for any of this, but my brain was tripping over what Erik had said about his father.

Ares had formed a relationship ,Erik.

*With.*

Crazy, murderous Ares.

Meanwhile, my father did everything under the sun to avoid being in the same room with me.

I shifted my weight from one side to the next, trying to pay attention to what they were saying, because I was pretty sure they were starting to argue, but my head…it just wasn't in this right now. My skin felt stretched too tight, brittle and about to break.

In that moment I realized I was going to lose it, right there, in the middle of the room with a stranger who had a better relationship with his murderous, psycho dad who was *dead* than I did with mine, who was very much alive and mostly not a psycho.

I had to get out of that room.

"Excuse me," I murmured, and then I left the room. I didn't wait for a response from anyone, but I knew Seth followed.

He caught up to me a few steps away from Erik's door. "Josie, are you sick?"

For a moment, I had no idea why he thought that, but then I realized my face felt flushed and he probably thought I was about to vomit. Morning sickness. Duh. "No," I said quickly. "I'm not sick."

There wasn't any relief in his striking features as he walked to where I stood. His hair loosely brushed the curve of his jaw. The moment those churning amber eyes met mine, I felt my self-control begin to crack a little. "Don't compare what is going on with Apollo to what Ares and Erik had. That's not a road you want to go down."

Was I that transparent?

Yeah, like a window.

I sighed. "My head is just not where it needs to be right now. I'm okay, Seth. I just…I just need a few minutes. Please?"

One look at his face told me that he didn't want to leave me alone, and I could appreciate that. I really could, but I just needed space to get my head back where it needed to be. "I didn't get the chance to tell you this earlier, but he did ask about you, Josie. He asked about you and the baby. He is thinking of you and he is concerned, he is just shit at showing it."

I drew in a stuttering breath. Somehow him asking Seth about me made it all the worse, because he was thinking about me. "I just need to walk." My vision blurred. "You said you'd do anything, and that is what I need."

Seth's shoulders tensed and it was obvious he didn't like it, but then he nodded.

I mouthed "thank you" and started to back up, but Seth caught me around the waist and tugged me to his chest. He lifted me clear off the floor, to the point my feet dangled. His mouth was on mine, hot and firm, and making my head spin. Electricity thrummed between us. I opened, and his tongue spread over mine. Despite the sorrow infecting my chest like a poison, molten lava moved through my veins. His kiss was demanding, possessive—devouring.

When he put me back down, I was surprised my legs were still working. All I could do was stare up at him, flushed for a whole different reason.

"I love you," he said. "Just want you to remember that."

"Always," I whispered.

"Find me when you're ready."

More than a little shaken, I nodded as I backed away and then hurried off, my lips feeling swollen and my pulse pounding.

I really had no idea where I was going, but I eventually found myself in the gated courtyard, the one that bloomed beautiful flowers all year round and smelled like the best parts of a florist shop.

Walking past the bench, I stopped and stared at it. This was where Colin and I would sit and talk during the time Seth had pushed me away.

Colin was…he had been a good friend.

Blinking back tears, I sat down on the bench and shoved the hair back from my face, clasping the strands to my neck. I closed my eyes as I breathed in the warm air. Maybe I was being overly emotional. Or maybe I would be handling this latest development with Apollo better if Colin hadn't just been murdered.

I squeezed my eyes shut, but tears snuck through. I wondered, if I just let myself cry, I'd move on and clear my head. Then I could focus on what was important, like the fact that the demigods had no way of their powers being unbound.

But I felt like…I felt like that little girl again, the one who didn't understand why her father wasn't a part of her life and who her mother wished she hadn't had.

It was like being right back there, unwanted.

Letting go of my hair, I wiped at my cheeks and sat up straight. I looked down at my stomach and placed my hands there, just below my belly.

My child wasn't even born yet and I couldn't imagine not wanting to see him or her, to not be a part of their life. I just didn't—

"Josie?"

I looked up at the sound of my name, seeing Laadan rounding the corner. I expected to see Alexander behind her. Whenever I saw her, he wasn't far behind the raven-haired woman.

They had a…thing.

Wiping at my face, I plastered on a smile. "Hey," I croaked out, and then cringed. "What's up?"

Sympathy creased her face as she approached me. Her long hair was pulled back in a smooth ponytail I could never master. Even in jeans and a blouse, there was an innate elegance to Laadan that made me feel like I had the grace of a baby donkey.

"I'm sorry to intrude," she said softly, "but Marcus and Alexander are looking for you and Seth."

Figuring it had to do with what had happened yesterday, I

pushed my daddy issues aside. "Seth is with Alex and Aiden and, um, Erik." I didn't know if she knew who Erik was. "What's going on?"

"I don't know how to tell you this, but Marcus thought it was best for you to hear this before it gets out like almost everything inevitably does."

I started to frown. I had no idea where she was going with this.

Laadan clasped her hands together. "Colin…Colin's body is missing."

# 23

Seth

$\mathcal{I}$ don't remember the walk back to the main Covenant building, but I knew the minute Alexander had found Seth, because he suddenly appeared beside me in the stairwell, frightening Laadan so badly she would've fallen down the stairs if Seth hadn't caught her arm.

"Sorry," he said, steadying her before turning to me. "I just heard."

All I could do was shake my head. I had no idea what to say. How in the world did Colin's body disappear? We were heading to Marcus's office and I was hoping he could shine some light on what happened.

"Do you think someone took it?" I winced as Laadan walked ahead. "I mean, took his body?"

"Someone had to." He placed his hand on my lower back. His features were drawn. "Why, I have no idea."

We were silent as we walked the rest of the way. Marcus was on the phone when we entered his office, his head bowed and his fingers pinching at the skin between his brows. Shortly after we arrived, Alex and Aiden joined us while Laadan lingered near Marcus's desk, her expression tight with concern.

"Where's Erik?" Seth asked as I stood next to him.

"Luke is with him," Alex answered, sitting in one of the chairs. "And Deacon is with Cora and Gable, getting them breakfast and sorted for the day." She paused, glancing at Marcus and then me. "We need to talk about Erik after this."

"Understatement of the year," Seth muttered, and I turned to him, wondering what the hell I had missed after I left the room to have my mini-breakdown.

Marcus hung up on the phone. He looked at Laadan. "Thank you." Sitting down, he drew in a deep breath. "That was our campus security. They're revealing the tapes for us to see who had access to the morgue area."

I shivered. Morgue. Ugh. "Why would someone do this?" I asked, not expecting an answer. "I mean, God. Why would anyone take a body?"

Aiden shifted his weight as he eyed Marcus. "I hate to even think this, but based on what's been happening here, I can't imagine this is going to end remotely well."

Understanding flickered through me as I stared at him. He meant that one of the pures who were against the halfs might've taken Colin's body? Horror and anger beat at me as I turned to Marcus. What could those pures possibly want with Colin's body? A hundred gruesome ideas sprung to life.

"If they do something to his body," I started, my voice barely recognizable to my own ears. "I swear to the *gods*, I will lose it."

"We don't know anything yet for sure," he reasoned, his tone calming. "Right now, we have all the pures who were involved in the attack yesterday in custody. I know that doesn't mean we have all of them who have been taking part."

"Are you sure he was dead?" Alex asked suddenly.

I wasn't the only one to turn and look at her.

"What?" She threw up her hands. "Bodies just don't get up and walk away! And, you know, stealing a body is pretty extreme."

"Thank you for clarifying that for us," Marcus said dryly.

"Yes," I said, folding my arms across my stomach. "He was dead. Your father saw him. There was no way…" I gave a shake of my head as Seth dropped his arm around my shoulders. "He was dead."

Seth pulled me in to his side, and I felt his lips brush my temple.

"Then we need his body," Alex stated. "And I'm not trying to be Captain Obvious, here. If we don't…"

"We will find his body," Laadan assured us. "We have to."

"Wait." I turned to where Alex sat. "Besides the obvious of not being able to bury him, what will happen if we don't find his body?"

She stared at me a moment. "You don't know?"

"I'm guessing not."

It was Seth who answered. "Remember when we buried Solos?" When I nodded, his gaze then searched mine. "We have traditions that must be followed for our fallen to pass over."

My heart lurched into my throat as I remembered them placing coins over Solos's eyes to ensure he'd have a warrior's welcome. "What will happen to him if we don't do that?"

Aiden turned away.

Seth's shoulders tensed. "He will be stuck at the River Styx, unable to cross. He will be in a form of purgatory for eternity."

# Seth

Marcus assured us that he'd let us know as soon as he heard back from security, once they finished reviewing the tapes. I didn't think we needed to wait to know what happened.

One of those fucking pures had taken his body to do gods knew what with it. After everything that Josie had been through, this was the last thing that needed to prey on her mind.

I wanted to pull Josie aside and get her to talk to me, to open up about how she was feeling, but we had another issue to deal with now.

The four of us sat in one of the smaller common rooms in the dorm. Josie sat on one side of the couch, her legs pulled up to her chest.

"What's going on with Erik?" she asked, and I could tell that her mind was still back in Marcus's office.

I stood across from her. "Besides the fact he's arrogant, unpredictable, really doesn't want to be here, and has the ability to piss off everyone…" I trailed off, realizing everyone, including Josie, was staring at me expectantly. "What?"

Josie grinned a little as she clasped her hands together in front of her knees. "You're pretty much describing yourself."

"Am not."

Alex snorted from where she had plopped down next to Josie. "Yeah, you are."

I opened my mouth and then rolled my eyes. "Whatever. My point is he's really a wild card right now and there's something about him I don't trust."

"And that has nothing to do with him answering the door almost naked?" Alex piped up, grinning.

I tilted my head as I stared back at her.

"Look, it's a rare day when I agree with anything Seth has to say, but I do," Aiden chimed in. "There *is* something off about him."

"And that also has nothing to do with him answering the door in a towel?" That was Josie who nearly parroted Alex's statement.

Aiden shot her a deadpan look.

"We're confident in our sexiness. Thanks," I shot back, smiling tightly. "Anyway, as I was saying before I was unnecessarily interrupted, I don't trust this guy."

"He relented way too quickly once Apollo showed," Aiden added. "And I don't think it has anything to do with the fact that Apollo is a god. He agreed, packed up his stuff, and then came here. But he has no interest in learning anything."

"Well, maybe he's just overwhelmed," Josie suggested, lifting a shoulder. "It's a lot to handle, even if you know you're a demigod."

"To be honest, it almost like he already knows about the Titans and what's expected from him," I said, and when I glanced at Aiden, he nodded. "Hardly anything seems like a surprise to him."

Josie frowned as she let go of her knees, letting her legs cross. "What do you mean, he already knows?"

"It's just a feeling. Like nothing we say to him comes as any real surprise." He gestured at Alex. "You've had to be thinking the same."

Alex reached for her hair. "Yeah, I hate to be a part of the paranoia crew, but I've got that feeling too."

"Really?" Josie asked, twisting toward her. "What could that mean, though? Ares died before all this stuff happened with the Titans."

"Shit, the options are endless," I said, brows knitting together as I stared at Alex and Josie. Both of them were messing with their hair. "But Ares knew that Perses had been released. He could've foreseen something like this happening—Perses going back to free the others." As much as I hated saying the next part, I had to. "We know Ares had a relationship with Erik. What we don't know is all that Ares had told him."

"That's a good point." Alex rocked slightly, from left to right. "But even if Ares filled his head with a ton of nonsense, he has to understand this isn't going to end well."

"You'd be surprised by how effective nonsense can be…" Brows lifting, I watched Alex and Josie twist their hair. I couldn't get over the fact that both of them were literally doing the same thing. "Okay. You guys are freaking me out."

They stopped and looked at one another, not mirror images, but way too damn similar. It was unsettling as fuck.

Aiden must've seen it too, because he blinked as he shook his head.

"What?" Alex demanded, dropping her hands to her lap. "What are we doing? We're just sitting here, waiting for you two to get to the damn point."

Josie's grin spread.

"You guys have very similar mannerisms," I pointed out. "I don't know how you two haven't noticed it."

Josie lowered her hands as her lips pursed. "Well, now we will."

Tipping her head to the side, Alex stared at Josie. "It's because we're awesome."

"Okay," I sighed, moving on. "I think we just need to keep an eye on Erik. As Aiden said, there's something off about him, and it has nothing to do with his burgeoning abilities."

"He doesn't have an effect on any of us, right?" Josie asked. "I wasn't around him long enough to figure that out."

I nodded. "It seems to only affect mortals, but then again, he hasn't been around a lot of us. We really don't know."

"That's why we should limit his contact."

Alex nodded. "I think that's a smart idea, but we can't hold him captive in that room."

"Well, Alex and I are only here for a couple more months," Aiden said, bringing up the fact their time up here was limited. "Alex and I can keep an eye on him until then."

Alex murmured an agreement, and while that was all good, I was still very uneasy about Erik being here. Could just have been the fact I thought the guy was an asshole.

Or something simple—the fact that he was Ares's son.

Or it could have been more.

Either way, I did not trust the guy as far as I could punt kick him.

"Well, while we're all here, you might as well tell them what Apollo said earlier." Josie rested her cheek on her elbow. She wasn't looking at me as she spoke. Her gaze was focused on a painting of one of the Muses behind me. "They need to know exactly what we're dealing with."

"What?" Alex asked, sitting up like steel had just been dropped down her spine.

Aiden's gaze sharpened. "Why do I have a feeling whatever you're about to tell me is just going to irritate me?"

"Because this is the world we live in," I replied, smirking. "Apollo confirmed some pretty bad news. The demigods' abilities cannot be unlocked…organically, at least, since there's not six of them. Demeter and Poseidon would have to do what Apollo did, which would weaken them. Apollo doesn't think that will happen."

Josie's nose wrinkled, but she didn't say anything.

Alex was quiet for a moment, and then she all but exploded, shooting to her feet. "Then what in the hell are we supposed to do about the Titans? Josie is the only fully charged demigod—"

"Actually, that's not true. There's us," Aiden pointed out.

"But we don't have icons or whatever the hell the others are supposed to find once their abilities are unlocked." Alex started pacing. "And Erik's abilities obviously can't be unlocked because Ares is dead. What in the hell are we supposed to do?"

Aiden cursed under his breath as he dragged a hand over his head. "It was a long shot in the first place, having only four demigods to face off with the Titans, but now?"

"It's not that we don't think you aren't badass all on your own," Alex was quick to say to Josie, who was still focused on the painting. "But this just went from a chance in hell to a snowball's chance in hell."

Josie tilted her head and then she looked at me. "Wait. I have an idea. It's kind of crazy." She glanced at Alex and Aiden. "And it's kind of right in front of our faces. Apollo didn't say he *asked* Demeter and Poseidon, right?"

I thought back to our conversation. "No. He said he spoke to them, but he didn't say he asked them."

"Then I know what we need to do," she said, meeting my gaze. "We need to ask them ourselves."

# 24

## Seth

"Ask the gods?" I repeated.

Josie nodded. "I know it sounds crazy, but what if we're able to convince them?"

I opened my mouth, but I really had no idea what to say in response to that. Josie sounded like she was suggesting we ask Marcus if it was okay if we redecorated our rooms here. As if it was no big deal.

"What other option do we have? Look, I would love to find a way to entomb these Titans without fighting them, but so far we're coming up with nothing." Josie rose to her feet. "And we have to do something. I know that having three of us fully unlocked is not what we need, but it's better than nothing and there's only three Titans left."

"And one of them is Cronus," I reminded her. "You know, *the* Cronus."

"I know," she said, her gaze meeting mine as she popped her hands on her hips. "But what other choices do we have?"

"She might be onto something. Maybe you two can convince

the gods to unlock their abilities," Aiden said.

Alex had stopped pacing. She too stood with her hands on her waist. "The gods have never been all that helpful in the past. You really think we're going to get two of them to agree to weaken themselves?"

"But things are different now," Josie said.

Things *were* different now. Hell. Everything was, but would the gods really listen to us? When they never had before? But what had Apollo asked me? What would I do to make sure the world was a better place for my child?

I said *anything*.

Turning, I rubbed the heel of my palm over my chest. The thing was, I didn't want Josie facing the Titans at all. We'd talked about this.

"Like I said, facing them is the last thing I want to do," Josie repeated. "And I also know that only having the three of us is really not looking good, but we wouldn't be alone. We have you, Seth. We have Alex and Aiden. And we have Luke." She paused. "We even have Deacon."

Aiden sighed. "As much as I hate having Deacon involved in something like that, he has gotten really good with the fire element. If anything, he'd definitely distract the hell out of the Titans."

"True," Alex laughed, but she quickly sobered. "But Cora and Gable are nowhere near ready. Not even remotely."

"But do they have to fight the Titans? It's something I've been thinking about. They have to get their icons, and maybe that's the key." Excitement thrummed through Josie's tone, and I knew, once she felt like she was onto something, there was no stopping her. "We don't know. Apollo sure as hell hasn't told me or anyone else how exactly we entomb the Titans."

"Even if the icons magically send the Titans to their tombs, they're not going to stand there and let it happen," I pointed out, my voice harsher than I intended.

"Gee, really? I thought they would get down on their knees and beg us to send them back." Josie's lips thinned. "But if Cora and Gable's abilities are unlocked, then the only thing we really need to focus on is their ability to use akasha. Hand to hand combat needs to be taught, but it should be the last thing we expect them to use when fighting the Titans."

"I hate to be Realistic Rachel, but even if you guys agree to go ask the gods, there's one problem with that." Alex lifted her brows as I faced her. "How are you going to get to Olympus?"

"That *is* an issue," Aiden agreed. "I seriously doubt that Apollo will answer our summons and bop us over there."

Slowly, I looked over at Aiden. "Did you just say *bop*?"

"Shut up," he replied.

"I thought it was kind of cute." Alex made her way over to Aiden's side. "I like the word." She threw her arms around Aiden's waist. "Bop. Bop. Bop."

Staring at her, my brows lowered. Sometimes I wondered if Alex was dropped on her head a lot as a small child. I knew she was as a teen. I'd seen it happen. Often. And it probably explained a lot.

"Guys." Josie waited until all our attention was on her. "I know where there's a gateway."

## Josie

"The library?" Alex pulled her arms free from Aiden and visibly shuddered. "I hate libraries."

Aiden looked down at her fondly. "Not always."

Her cheeks flushed a pretty pink, and I had a pretty good idea that something must've gone down between them in a library.

"The library? The one here?" Seth asked.

I nodded as I crossed one arm over my waist. I knew he wasn't happy with me revisiting the path that led to a face-off with the Titans, but unless we figured out another way, this was the only path before us.

"When I met Medusa, she took me to this place that was underneath the library, but it was actually outside. Super weird, but that's where I saw the Pegasus," I said, and a faint smile curved Seth's lips when I brought up the Pegasus. I'd been so excited to see one, I had talked about it for hours. "Medusa told me where we were. She said it was a gateway to Olympus."

"Whoa," Alex murmured.

"Wait." Seth brushed a strand of his hair back from his face. "I thought the doorways leading to this place Medusa took you were gone?"

"They were." That was the only wrinkle in my plan. "I didn't see the doors and the librarian I saw acted like they'd never been there, but they have to be there."

"We could always knock down the walls," Aiden suggested.

Alex looked up at him. "I can totally see Marcus's face when you ask him for permission to knock down walls in the library."

Seth was quiet for a moment and then he said, "You know, I'm always of the mindset it's better to ask for forgiveness than permission."

\* \* \*

Once Seth and I were alone in our room, I turned to him and immediately asked, "Are you really okay with this plan? Knocking down a wall? Going to Olympus?"

Seth walked into the small kitchen area. "I am always down for blowing stuff up and pissing people off in the process."

I arched a brow. No big surprise there. "Besides that part, what are you thinking?"

"Honest?"

I nodded. "Yes. Honest."

"You and I talked about facing the Titans. Both of us want that to be the last damn option." Opening the fridge door, he grabbed a water. "But right now, it is the *only* option. Thirsty?"

"No."

He paused, fridge door open as he looked over at me.

I rolled my eyes. "Okay. Yes. I'm thirsty."

Seth winked as he grabbed another bottle. "I hate the idea of you having to do anything that puts you in danger." Walking over to me, he handed me the bottle. "To be honest, it terrifies me, but if I would do anything to make sure our child grows up in a world not terrorized by Titans, I know you would do the same."

The plastic bottle crinkled under my grip. "You know I don't want to do anything to jeopardize the baby."

"I know." Taking a drink, he then placed the bottle on the small, brown end table. "But that doesn't mean at some point you're not going to be in a situation where it's dangerous. You stayed here and it wasn't exactly safe."

It hadn't been. Not when you had jerk-face pures running around and Furies being unleashed. Unscrewing the cap, I then took a drink. "So, we should go ahead and do this. Alex and Aiden said they'd keep an eye on Erik, and we have Deacon and Luke with Cora and Gable. There's no point in delaying this."

"We should probably wait until the library closes before we head in there and try to blow up walls."

"Good point." I grinned, but it quickly faded. "And if there isn't anything behind those walls? I honestly don't know what to do at that point."

Seth took my hand and led me over to the couch. "Then we come up with something else." Sitting down, he pulled me into his lap. I held onto the water as I slid against his stomach. "That's what we do."

Sometimes Seth made things sound so simple. I took a drink of the water as I leaned against him, letting my head rest against his shoulder. "You know what I've been wondering?"

"How I'm so awesome?"

I laughed softly. "No. I already know why." I ran my fingers along the label on the bottle. "Do you wonder why the Titans have been so quiet after taking control of Chicago? We haven't heard a single thing. And when you guys went to get Erik, they didn't show up."

"I do wonder." He looped an arm around my waist. "I think they're scared after what happened to Hyperion." His thick lashes shielded his eyes. "I'm not saying that to be cocky. I don't think they expected me to be able to do what I can. Killing Hyperion caught them off-guard. They've entrenched themselves and are lying low."

"Or they're planning something other than laying waste to the city." A shiver curled its way down my spine as I turned to put the water on the end table next to the couch and saw a red light blinking on the phone. "Hey, we have a message."

Stretching over, I hit the play button and a female voice filled the room. "Good morning, this is Dr. Morales and this message is for Seth and Josie. I have good news for you. I've found an OBGYN who is ready to see you two as soon as you like. Give us a call back and we'll give you the contact information."

The message ended, and my gaze found Seth's. Those lashes had lifted, and the amber eyes churned with emotion. A slow grin tugged at my lips. "Our life is so...it's so weird."

# 25

## Seth

The morning started off more than just weird.

Luke and Deacon stood shoulder to shoulder before Josie and me, and I knew before they even opened their mouths, this wasn't going to be good.

Probably because both of them were up this early.

"We just ran into Laadan and Marcus, and we just learned the most messed-up thing ever," Luke started.

"Really? The most messed-up thing?" Josie was finishing her braid, wrapping a band at the end, securing the strands. "There's been a lot of messed-up things lately."

"Yeah, but this takes the cake." Deacon leaned into Luke. "Marcus heard back from campus security. They reviewed the tapes."

"And they found what?" Impatience crowded my tone. Josie and I had plans today and a lot to get done.

"They found nothing," Luke answered.

"Nothing?" Josie frowned as she rested her hands on her hips. "What does that mean?"

"It means no one entered the morgue other than one of the

doctors, and they left about ten minutes later. Not carrying a body out." Deacon glanced at me. "They checked the film to see if anyone messed with it, and there were no cuts or anything like that. His body just…it disappeared."

My mouth opened, but I had no idea how the hell to respond to that. At all. Bodies didn't just up and disappear.

"Is that possible?" Josie exclaimed.

Deacon's eyes widened. "Not as far as I know."

"But…how?" Josie twisted toward me. "How could his body just disappear inside the morgue?"

"I don't know." I dragged a hand over my head, clasping the back of my neck. "I mean, we all have seen some strange shit, but this…" I was actually kind of speechless.

"Yeah." Luke shook his head. "We told Marcus we'd let you guys know. He's going to have the doctor who was in the morgue interviewed to see if he possibly had something to with it."

But…

There was an unspoken "but" there, because the film would've captured Colin's body being removed.

Luke and Deacon parted ways with us at that point, and we headed outside. Josie was quiet as we walked to the infirmary. I knew she was thinking about Colin—about him and her father, about the demigods and the Titans. Her head had to be in a million places.

"We'll figure out what happened to Colin's body," I told her. "It couldn't have just disappeared."

"I know," she whispered, and I knew she wasn't entirely confident in that belief.

Neither was I.

Worst part was we had so much going on, it was something neither of us could focus on at the moment, which also had to cause a hefty amount of guilt for Josie.

Dr. Morales was busy with a patient, but the receptionist handed over a slip of paper with the doctor's information on it. As we walked out, I asked, "Where's the doctor?"

Josie studied the little card. "Looks like the doctor's office is in Manhattan." She peeked up at me. "I've never been to New York."

"First time for everything." I nudged her with my hip as we made our way down the path. There was no one out but Guards and Sentinels. Marcus had put a curfew in place due to the violence, but it was early in the day and there was not a student to be seen. "Manhattan is pretty cool. You'll like it."

"Dr. Morales wrote a note on the back of the card." She flipped it over. "She says we can call their office at any time, and they're expecting to hear from me."

I nodded at a Guard we passed. "Want to call them now?"

"I…I think we should do what we're planning to do first." Reaching behind her, she slipped the little card into the pocket of the loose dress she wore. "We'll call the doctor's office afterward."

"You want to wait?"

Nodding, she smiled, but it didn't quite reach her eyes. "Yeah. It's something to look forward to. You know, just in case we get nowhere with the gods, we'll end the day on a high note."

That brought a smile to my lips as I reached over, tugging her braid. "I like the way you think."

Her smile warmed then. "It's because I'm brilliant."

"Now, don't get too ahead of yourself."

Gasping, she smacked my arm as we rounded the courtyard and the library came into view. "Ass."

I laughed.

Josie shook her head, but with each step we took, the lightness faded from her. "This was…this is where Colin died."

Gods. Clasping her hand, I didn't know what to say as we walked down the wide path. There were cracks in the marble I didn't remember seeing before.

"There was so much…blood and gore, but they've cleaned everything up. It almost looks like nothing happened." She pressed her lips together as we reached the steps. "But I can…I can still see it." Staring at the wall of the library, she let out a shaky breath. "And we don't even know where Colin's body is or how it just vanished."

Stopping at the top, I turned to her and pulled her forward. Folding my hand around the back of her neck, I pulled her head down and kissed the top.

She lingered, our chests close but not quite touching. A moment passed and then she stepped back. "I'm okay." Her gaze lifted to mine. "I mean, I'm okay to do this."

"I didn't think that you weren't."

"Really?" Josie's laugh was hoarse. "I've been a hot mess since yesterday—well, probably before then."

"You haven't been a hot mess," I corrected, flashing a quick grin. "No one, especially me, would hold it against you. You've been through a lot. If someone thought you weren't dealing, they either aren't paying attention or they've lived a sweet life and never had to deal with shit."

"Thank you." She stretched up and kissed my cheek. "I just want you to know that my head is screwed on right for this. I'm ready."

"Damn straight you are. Let's do this."

We made it about five feet and discovered our first obstacle. "The door is locked." Josie stepped back with a frown, scanning the sign that read CLOSED. "Must be because of what happened yesterday."

"Locks really aren't an issue for me." Taking her hand, I winked. "Hold on."

Josie's soft gasp was lost in my laugh as I used the godly way of entering the building. She squeezed my hand so hard I thought she might actually break a bone when we reappeared just inside the doors.

"That is still so weird," she said, swallowing. "Okay. Wow. The closed library is actually going to work in our benefit."

"Yeah, it is. I really didn't want a librarian screaming while I blew a hole in a wall."

Josie chuckled as she pulled her hand free and started to walk between the empty tables. "Would've been entertaining, though."

I snickered as I followed her. "Marcus is going to be so mad."

"Maybe not." She looked over her shoulder. "If we come back with good news, I think he'll get over the damage we're about to cause."

I didn't know about that. Marcus was not a fan of destruction of property, but oh well.

"This is where the doors were," Josie said as she walked under the staircase and pointed at the wall. "Three of them. Right here."

I eyed the area. "And it was the center door?"

Josie nodded. "Yes."

"All right. Stand back." Lifting my arm, I waited until Josie was behind me and then I let a bolt of akasha smack into the wall. It was like a crack of thunder, and dust plumed into the air. Bricks evaporated under the energy. Pulling the energy back, I found I hadn't created the biggest gap in the wall. Just big enough for both of us to slip through.

As the dust settled, Josie stepped out from behind me. "Hot damn. It's still here."

A brightly lit hallway appeared beyond the dust. "Finally," I said. "Something is going right."

"I know." Josie stepped around me. "From what I remembered, there is really nothing in this hall until you reach the end." She walked ahead, her pace brisk. "Crap. I forgot."

"Forgot what?" I stopped behind her.

"Dammit." She turned to me. "See that marble wall? Medusa touched it or waved her hand and a door appeared. Maybe..." She sprang forward, smacking the wall.

I arched a brow. "That didn't work."

She scowled. "Then why don't you try it? Maybe it will work for you, because you're so damn special."

Smirking, I sauntered past her and placed my hand on the wall. "Open sesame."

"Really?" She slowly looked at me.

"You have a better—whoa." I jerked my hand back. The atmosphere appeared to ripple, warping the marble. Electricity charged the air, and the glyphs sparked alive, racing across my skin.

"It's doing it!" Josie whirled, her eyes bright.

The wall was definitely doing something. The marble expanded and then shrunk back. A tear appeared at the top and then split down the center, peeling back to reveal a wooden door with vertical slats held together by a dark metal. Hinges creaked as it opened.

"Holy shit," I murmured, glancing down at my hand. "Maybe the world needs to stop making fun of 'open sesame?'"

Josie looked at me weirdly as she started forward. A flame, unsettled by the burst of air, flickered from a large torch jutting out from a wall. There were more torches, placed every so many feet. Their soft glow bathed statues of—"Dear gods, these are the men Medusa turned to stone."

"Yeah, I think we should definitely pick up our pace," Josie quipped.

My eyes widened on the back of her head. I was pretty confident that Medusa could even turn gods to stone.

The further we went down the hall, I realized the same glyphs that currently had my skin buzzing were etched into the walls. An odd shiver tiptoed down my spine.

"I really hope they don't take my presence as an all-out declaration of war."

Josie stopped as her mouth dropped open. "I didn't even think about that."

I grinned. "Well, it's a little late for that."

She stared at me and then sighed as she started walking again. "You know, I think if they had a problem with us being here, they would've already intervened."

Hopefully that was the case.

We reached another door and Josie pushed on it before I had a chance to tell her to slow down. The door swung open, and...and glittering sunlight poured in from a grassy meadow of blue and purple wildflowers.

At first I couldn't move. It was like every muscle locked up, and then I was moving without realizing it, as if I were somehow compelled to enter.

The moment the sunlight touched my skin, I inhaled deeply, and it was like taking the first hit of the purest drug. Energy rushed through me, drenching my skin and seeping through my muscles before settling into my bones.

I came to a complete standstill again.

My skin hummed with energy as I stared at the trees crowding the edge of the meadow. I felt...I felt like I did after I fed.

Josie turned to me. "You okay?"

"Yeah." My voice was hoarse as my gaze shifted to her. "It's the...it's the aether. I can feel it."

"I felt it too, even the first time here. The air is heavy with it." She bit down on her lip. "This is where I saw the Pegasus and the twelve icons. Medusa said that whenever there was activity near the gateways—"

Wind picked up, stirring the thin wisps of hair around Josie's temples and shaking the heavy tree limbs. Instinct propelled me forward, to stand in front of Josie.

Something was coming—something very powerful.

And it wasn't a Pegasus.

A column of shimmering light appeared in front of us, and in the center stood a god.

"Hermes," I said as the shimmering light faded into nothingness. "Long time no see."

# 26

## Josie

My eyes widened as I stared at the *messenger*. I remembered reading about him in the Myths textbook. He was the second-youngest of all the Olympian gods and was also known as the "divine trickster."

To me, he resembled what I imagined angels looked like.

He was tall and had a head full of curly blond hair, reminding me of Deacon. Those all-white eyes creeped me out.

One side of his lips curled up. "Has it really been that long, Seth?"

"Not long enough," Seth muttered, and I shifted my gaze to him. "What do we owe the honor of your presence?"

The god laughed. "I am here to escort you."

"To where?" Seth demanded.

"To commune with the gods, where else?" That half-grin spread. "Is that not why you two have come here? They're waiting."

"That is why we came," I answered before Seth said something ridiculously antagonistic. "I think we're just surprised that they would be, uh, accommodating of our unexpected visit."

"Unexpected?" Hermes laughed and the sound carried. "Your visit is not unexpected."

"Well, that's not creepy or anything," Seth replied dryly.

Hermes winked. "Come."

He didn't give us much of an option. Turning, he walked toward the tree line, and I had no idea if we should follow him or not. My heart felt like it was going to claw its way out of my chest. Were we just going to blindly follow this god? I exchanged a long look with Seth. He nodded as he took my hand and squeezed.

I guess it really was too late to change our minds.

Following Hermes, I wondered how far we had to walk or where we were being led, but as soon as we stepped under the first tree, the air started to ripple around us. I sucked in a startled breath as the trees above us fragmented.

"Seth," I gasped, eyes going wide.

His hand tightened as he tugged me to his side while the limbs and leaves faded. Deep blue skies appeared. The grass under our feet hardened and turned to marble. Tree trunks thinned out, replaced by thin olive trees and columns covered in grapevines. Statues appeared out of thin air, six on each side of the pathway, each one as tall as a giant.

"What the hell?" Seth demanded.

"It's an illusion, the forest," Hermes explained, sounding bored. "If you were to get this far without a guide like me, you'd walk an eternity trapped in the illusion."

"That…that wouldn't be good." I eyed the statues, quickly realizing that each one held something in their hand. A helmet. A bow. A harp. A trident. A spear. "These statues…"

Hermes looked over his shoulder. "This is the Isle of the Gods and *that* is the Great Pantheon."

"The Great…" Seth trailed off as a massive structure came into view.

It was a massive dome-shaped building supported by thick columns. The structure was a pristine white, as if dust or rain had never touched it. The dome appeared to be made of some sort of glass as it seemed to reflect the clouds…except there were no clouds.

Off in the distance there were soft trills from birds, but I didn't see a single one as we neared the Pantheon. There was a rustle, though, coming from behind the trees. My head swung to the right, and I stopped short, catching a glimpse of something white and winged.

"Seth," I whispered, pulling on his hand as I pointed. He followed my gaze. "I think it's a Pegasus."

"Really?" He strained his neck, his eyes flaring wide. A white wing lifted high, and I turned to Seth. Awe settled into his expression, and I couldn't look away from the boyish excitement filling his golden eyes. "I…" He gave a little shake of his head. "It's beautiful."

I grinned at him, thinking that it was him that was truly beautiful.

"Children," called Hermes from the top of the wide, long steps. "There is very little time to linger."

Seth blinked and his gaze found mine. There was something soft in his stare, a quality that was rare to Seth, and then he bent his head, kissing the corner of my lips. "We better get going. They can be impatient."

Nodding, I started walking again and took the time to prepare myself to come face to face with the Olympians…and my father. That was, if he was here. My pulse was racing as we joined Hermes. He stopped in front of titanium doors. They glided open, and a rush of cool, sweet-smelling air washed over us.

I thought I might have a heart attack.

Seth stepped forward, and he had to tug on my hand to get

me to move. It was like being in a dream. I was walking, but really didn't feel any step I took.

None of this felt real.

The inside of the dome was brightly lit, and my eyes went to the ceiling first. Fluffy white clouds drifted across the glass. I got a little hung up on that, because there were no clouds in the sky outside.

Then I lowered my gaze.

And I was no longer thinking about the weird ceiling and the questionable clouds. Eleven gods sat before me on marble thrones. Without having to ask, I knew who the two were in the middle.

Zeus and Hera.

Regal. That was all I could think as I stared at the two. Both were inhumanly stunning, tall and elegant.

I was so glad I decided to wear a dress, but I really wished I'd done something more with my hair.

Flanking either side of them were the remaining gods and…and my *father*. He sat to the right of Zeus, at the end, and the moment I saw him, I didn't see any of the other gods.

Apollo did not look at me. He did not look at Seth. He seemed to stare above us. I opened my mouth to say something, but caught myself before I did.

I wanted to scream at him. I wanted to run up there and shake him. I wanted to hug him and then slap him, but I had enough common sense to realize this wasn't the time or the place.

Seth let go of my hand and moved in a way that he was standing more in front of me than beside me. It was a protective move, and based on the way his shoulders tensed, it was also one of challenge.

"Seth. Josie." Zeus's voice carried like thunder. "I assume the reason you two are here must be of extreme importance."

"Or extremely reckless," Hades answered with an accent that

reminded me of Erik's. "Considering who is standing before us, I'd go with reckless."

"If I didn't know better, I'd think you're still upset over losing Aiden and me as your servants," Seth replied, and I could hear the smirk in his voice. "I bet that ticks you off daily."

Hades, who I'd seen briefly before, leaned forward in his throne. His smile upped the whole creep factor. "You have no idea, but be careful, *Seth*. It's funny how fate can change so quickly."

I stiffened, not liking the way that sounded.

A beautiful blonde with waves of hair sighed heavily. "You sound like a child who didn't get their prized toy, Hades."

Oh wow.

Hades looked over at her, his handsome face slipping into an impressive frown. "Do you want to talk about prized toys, Aphrodite?"

That was...

My head whipped back to the goddess in the gauzy white dress. Oh, my word, that was *the* Aphrodite?

She giggled, lifting a shoulder. "I haven't lost any of mine."

Hera arched a brow.

Crossing his arms over his chest, Seth cocked a head to the side as a male god I'd never seen before chuckled. He was dressed like he'd just gotten back from a Jimmy Buffett concert, complete with cargo shorts, sandals, and an ultra-bright orange and red Hawaiian-style shirt.

"Do you actually have something of value to add to the conversation, Dionysus?" Hades demanded.

The god of partying snorted. "No. I'm not going to even pretend that I do."

My brows lifted.

"That's not even remotely surprising," another goddess chimed in as she pinched the bridge of her nose. She was dressed like a mortal in a high-powered business position.

Dionysus looked over at her. "You know what I think, Athena? You have a massive stick shoved—"

"Don't finish that sentence," a goddess who I was pretty damn sure was wearing overalls cut in. Like, legitimate overalls. "Use your words better."

"Use your words better?" Dionysus let out a high-pitched laugh. "You're as corny as a cornfield."

Another god snapped something in return, and suddenly it was like Seth and I weren't even standing there. They were too involved in bitching at each other, determined to have the last snarky remark.

Seth sighed as he glanced over his shoulder at me.

All the while, Apollo sat there silent and staring above us like he wasn't even there. I couldn't really believe it—that the gods really were this petty. I'd heard Alex and Deacon's stories—even Luke and Seth had talked about how they behaved, but I'd always figured it was some sort of exaggeration. I mean, they were gods—ancient beings who could either destroy the entire world or rebuild it.

And they were sitting up there arguing like a bunch of spoiled brats.

I couldn't take it a second longer. My patience stretched and then snapped. Stepping forward, I went shoulder to shoulder with Seth. "Are you guys done yet?"

Seth jolted beside me, but I got their attention. Their incessant bitching stopped. All eleven stared at me.

A trickle of unease curled down my spine. "While you guys are bickering over toys and cornfields, Cronus has taken over an entire pure community and is threatening one of the largest cities in America. I'm sure you guys are aware of this."

"Josie," Seth warned under his breath.

I ignored him. "We came to you for help. Not to get front-row tickets to family fight night."

Out of the corner of my eye, I thought I saw a faint smile ghost across Apollo's face, but that could've been wishful thinking.

"You are…" Hera placed slender arms on her chair as she inclined her head. "You are very much like your father."

I stiffened at that.

"And you?" She looked at Seth. "I never thought there'd come a time when you stood in front of us, quiet and not threatening us."

"The day is still young," Seth replied.

Hera laughed softly. "We are aware of what Cronus has done."

"Then you have to be aware of why we're here," Seth interjected. "We need you to unbind the remaining demigods."

"That's not going to happen," a god who'd been silent spoke up, drawing my attention. I could see the resemblance to Gable.

Seth dipped his chin. "That's it, Poseidon?" he asked, confirming my suspicion. "It's not even up for discussion? What about you, Demeter?"

The goddess in the overalls smiled sadly. "You do not understand why we refuse to do this."

"You keep saying that. All of you. That we don't understand," Seth snapped. "How about you explain it in a way that we can?"

It was Apollo who answered. "Because it would not make a difference."

Hearing his voice was like a punch to the chest. It had been so long since I'd heard him speak.

"The demigods would not last in a fight with the Titans. Not when there are so few of them. I told you," Apollo said. "The demigods cannot abide."

"You didn't tell *me* that," I said, sucking in a sharp breath as he finally looked at me. I held his eerie white gaze for a moment and then focused on Demeter. "We need their abilities unbound to stand a chance. If not, the Titans will destroy Chicago and they won't stop there."

"Or Seth could always bring them my head," Zeus offered.

"That's starting to sound more and more like the better option," Seth returned.

The clouds in the glass ceiling thickened and the light dimmed as I fought the urge to elbow Seth. "So both of you are going to refuse to unbind your demigods?"

"Our refusal is not something we do lightly, child. We know our children will fail now that we have lost so many of them." The sadness in Demeter's smile crept along her face, and I honestly believed that she was saddened by all of this. "Poseidon and I would be severely weakened, as was your father. We would be among the first to fall if it came to a battle with the Titans. We have to prepare for that moment and be at our best."

Swallowing the sudden knot in my throat, I dared a quick glance at Apollo. He was watching us, his expression intent. "Then if you think it would be pointless to unbind the demigods, and that you're preparing to go to war with the Titans, then why don't you do something now? You defeated them before."

"Now that's a good question." Seth smiled the kind of smile I knew ticked off most people.

"We had Ares then," answered Athena, and then she glanced down to where Zeus sat. "And we did not defeat the Titans alone."

Seth started to frown. "What is that supposed to mean?"

"It means the fables mortals teach are partly correct." Athena lifted a bare shoulder. "And the teachings that are taught in our schools are not a hundred percent accurate. More like seventy percent or so."

I opened my mouth and sort of stared at them while I tried to figure out what to say. Hadn't I felt like something had been missing in the whole Titans versus the Gods mythology I'd read in the Myths textbook?

"What part of what we were taught was not true?" Seth demanded. "The one where you used the helmet of darkness to steal Cronus's weapons?" he asked of Hades, causing the god of the Underworld's lips to thin. "Or is you striking him down with lightning the false part?"

Zeus's jaw hardened.

"We fought the Titans for a decade, neither side making ground. It was a bloody, destructive war." Hera grasped the arms of her chair. "That is true, and eventually, we did entomb the Titans. There is a mixture of the real and the unreal in both legends."

"We had help," added Apollo, and I felt his stare shift to me. "There are legends among mortals that involve the Hekatoncheires and the Cyclopes."

I blinked slowly. "Hekatach-what?"

A slight smile curved his lips. "Hekatoncheires were basically giants."

Now that he said it, I sort of remembered reading that somewhere when I was younger.

"The Hekatoncheires wanted revenge on Cronus as he had kept them imprisoned. They were eager to help. The Cyclopes built weapons for us," Apollo explained. "Once the giants were involved, the war was quickly ended."

Seth unfolded his arm. "Wait a minute. This entire time, all we needed were some giants and a Cyclops or two? That's it?" Seth sounded like he was seconds away from exploding.

The goddess beside Apollo tilted her head. "Seth, it's not that simple. The Cyclopes fashioned the weapons we used and the giants were more fierce and more powerful than the Titans, but we cannot simply call upon them to fight again."

"And why not, Artemis?"

That was, I guessed, my aunt? Then again, they all were related and having sex, and I really didn't need to think about that at the moment.

"While the Hekatoncheires were eager to help, they still needed to be swayed," Zeus said, and I swore he might've paled a little. "They required a sacrifice."

"Of course they did," muttered Seth. "What? A few virgin priests and priestesses?"

Zeus stiffened. "Foolish young god."

If that insulted Seth, he didn't show it. "Where are these giants now?"

"They are in the Underworld," Hades answered. "And before you make some inane comment about us unleashing them, you must learn what it took for us to sway them in the first place."

Hades then smiled at Seth, and a chill rippled down my spine. It was like a sudden burst of cold air hit me, and all I could think of was that old saying. The one where people say it felt like someone had walked over their grave.

That was how I felt.

And I knew beyond a doubt that whatever they were about to tell us was going to change everything.

# Seth

As usual, I didn't like what the gods were saying or where any of this was heading.

"How did you sway them?" I demanded, wanting to find out what the hell I was going to have to do so I could just get it done. Then I could start spending the rest of forever with Josie, starting with preparing for our child.

Zeus studied me. "They requested a sacrifice from a being of absolute power. They gave me a choice. It is the same choice they will give now, and it is a sacrifice I cannot make again."

"What?" Josie asked, nervous energy rolling off her in waves. "What did you have to do?"

Zeus didn't take his gaze off me. "I had to kill the only thing I ever loved."

My skin turned to ice as I stared up at him. What had he said to me the day Aiden and I had faced the hydra?

Josie frowned as she glanced at Hera. "I don't understand."

"I am not his true love," Hera replied with a laugh. "Never was."

I wasn't entirely surprised to hear that Hera wasn't Zeus's true love, but I'd never heard this before.

"You wouldn't have," Zeus said, as if my thoughts were on my face, his voice low. "She was erased from all history, her name never spoken. If you want the Hekatoncheires, you will need to make that sacrifice."

My skin turned to ice as what he'd said began to sink in. I looked at Josie, and she was staring up at the gods, her beautiful face pale. I saw the exact moment she understood what they were saying. Her entire body jolted, and I remembered what Zeus had asked me before.

*What do you know of sacrifice?*

My eyes widened as I looked up at him. No. No fucking way. He could not mean what I thought he did. He could not be suggesting that I sacrifice Josie and our unborn child. Raw energy coursed through me.

"The sacrifice would fall on you," Zeus said, "as you are the other absolute being in the position to make the choice."

I latched on to the last part of what he said. "You said a choice. What choice is there? Because what you're suggesting is not going to happen."

"You must sacrifice what you cherish most." It was Apollo who answered. "Or you must sacrifice yourself."

The damn floor shifted under my feet. What kind of fucking

choice was that?

"No." Josie whipped toward me and grasped my arm. "Let's go, Seth. We'll find another way."

"There is no other way," Hera spoke up. "Not to defeat the Titans, and he knows that. Once the shock fades, you will know that too."

"Yes." Josie whirled on Hera. "Last I checked, the Titans gave us a hell of a better option."

Zeus raised a brow, but I spoke before he could. "Josie, babe—"

"No!" she repeated, her blue eyes glimmering. "This is stupid! We can find another way. We have to. Come on." She pulled on my arm. "Let's go."

Go where? Back to the Covenant where we would wait until the deadline came to pass?

The demigods couldn't face the Titans. Even with their abilities unlocked, it was a long shot. The Titans would destroy Chicago and they'd keep going. It would get to the point where I would have to kill Cronus, and his death would bring catastrophes we'd never seen before.

There was another option.

Yeah, I could kill Zeus. Take his head to Cronus, but I... Fuck, that wasn't me anymore. I didn't want to be that man. Not for Josie. Not for our child.

I wanted to be a better man.

I wanted to be better than *them*.

My gaze lifted to Zeus. "You were given the same choice?"

"I was," he answered after a moment. "And it was a choice I regret to this day."

"Like I said, be careful of how quickly fate turns on you." Hades smirked as he crossed one leg over the other. "But you've found yourself in this position before, have you not? It was either you or Alex, and you did not have the fortitude to make the sacrifice that she had to."

I flinched.

Those words were so damn true.

Alex had gone to fight Ares knowing she would die, and she'd done it. She hadn't known that Apollo had given her ambrosia. She had made that choice.

One I couldn't make back then.

Josie was talking again, and I looked at her, really looked at her. Gods, she was beautiful and kind, and so damn loyal. So much so that I'd never realized how lucky I was to have her.

Suddenly there wasn't enough air in the Pantheon, or in my lungs. I couldn't breathe as Zeus watched me intently. Out of all the possible scenarios, I'd never dreamed of this.

Everything had been leading up to this.

I knew in my bones that was the case. From the moment Ares made sure I was born, to this very second, it was leading to this moment. Maybe this was why it had been Alex before. What if this was why I became a god? And maybe…just maybe this was how I would truly redeem myself.

Sacrifice the one I loved to save the world, or sacrifice myself to save her so that she could raise our child in a better world.

There wasn't even a choice.

Apollo had asked me what I would do to protect Josie and our child, and I had said I would do anything.

And I meant that.

"Why this?" I asked, voice hoarse.

"Because love is selfless, and an act of love is the ultimate sacrifice," answered Zeus.

"Then what happens?" I asked, dragging my gaze from Josie's wide eyes. "What happens if I sacrifice myself?"

"You make that choice, and you will bear the same fate as her," Zeus said, referencing the woman he had once loved. "You will be erased from history and your name will not be spoken among the gods, but if you choose this, then the Hekatoncheires will rise and we will fight beside them once more, entombing the Titans."

"Okay," I said, lifting my chin. "I will do it."

# 27

## Seth

"What?" Josie cried out. "What did you just say?"

I couldn't look at Josie. Not right now. Apollo closed his eyes while Hera tipped forward once more.

"Are you sure?" Hera demanded. "If you speak the words once more, it will set in motion a chain of events you cannot stop. Your death is the end. Gods do not go to Tartarus. Our end is the final end. When we die, we cease to exist."

"Seth! Please, stop." Josie pulled on my arm, her voice cracking with anguish.

I grasped her hand, holding on. "If I do this, you will make damn sure that Josie wants for nothing. That she will be safe and our child will be safe."

"I will ensure it myself," Zeus spoke.

"Seth!" Josie darted in front of me, clasping my cheeks. She forced my gaze to hers. "You do not need to do this. Don't you understand me? This is not how this—"

"This is what I have to do, *psuchí mou*." I lightly gripped her wrists, pulling her hands from my face. "It's the only way to end this."

Tears glimmered in her eyes. "It cannot be the only way."

"Josie," Apollo called out.

She stiffened and then slowly turned to face her father. She didn't speak as her chest rose and fell sharply.

"If he does not do this, there will be nothing but destruction and death. Millions will die, and that is before Cronus forces Seth's hand. The Titans will come for you, and Seth will kill Cronus." Apollo rose from his throne. "Tens of millions will then die as his death rocks the earth from its very core. I have foreseen it."

A long, tense moment passed, and then Josie said, "Now? Now you dare to speak to me?"

Energy crackled dangerously, and the rush of power wasn't coming from me. It was all Josie.

Artemis shifted in her throne as a look of unease settled into her expression.

"I am sorry," Apollo said.

Josie sucked in air as she tried to step forward, but I held her wrist. "You knew?" she demanded. "Did you know this all along? From the very beginning? You knew how this would end?"

Apollo looked away.

I thought for a moment Josie might explode, but she seemed to rein it all in. "I hate you."

I pulled Josie back against my chest as Apollo sat down. I turned her to me, but she yanked herself free. Stepping back, she wrapped her arms around her chest. She stared at the floor of the temple, breathing raggedly.

Drawing in a ragged breath, I dragged my gaze to Zeus. "I will make the sacrifice."

"Then so be it."

Josie's muffled cry faded as a male appeared before the gods.

I'd never seen him before. He was young. Possibly a teenager. His eyes were…well, he didn't have eyes. Where they should've been, there was nothing but sunken-in skin. He held an open case, and resting inside was an icicle-shaped dagger. The wickedly sharp point was a different color, as if it had been dipped in something.

"The dagger is an ancient one," Athena said, her voice cautious. "Fashioned from Thanatos's sword, it is deadly."

"You will have until sundown to complete the sacrifice." Zeus rose from his throne and stepped off the dais. "We will know when it is done."

My eyes burned, but it wasn't because of what I was going to do to myself, but what I knew it was going to do to Josie.

Zeus picked up the dagger and offered it to me, handle first. As I took it, he leaned in and whispered for only me to hear, "Your son will think of you with great pride."

## Josie

It was like being stuck in a waking nightmare. Everything was a blur and at the same time startlingly sharp and clear. I was vaguely aware of Seth coming toward me and wrapping his arm around my shoulders and pulling me against him. I didn't fight him this time, and when I took my next breath we were no longer in the Pantheon, but we were back in the dorm room we shared.

Seth let go and stepped back from me. I watched him place the dagger on the bed.

He didn't take his eyes off me. "Josie—"

"Why?" I whispered, his face blurring as a rush of raw tears blinded me. I was so pissed off at him, so furious, and at the same time I was horrified. I was shocked, and none of this—none of this seemed real.

"This is not what I want," he said. "Gods, Josie, this is not how

I thought today was going to go."

"You didn't?" I laughed, and it sounded broken. Wiping at my cheeks, I walked to the bed and sat down. "This isn't right."

Seth came to me and knelt on the floor. He looked up at me, but I could barely look at him, because if I did, I would completely break down. "You can't do this."

"I have to," he said, holding my hands. "It's the only way."

I lowered my head. "How can you be sure of that?"

A long moment passed before he answered. "It's crazy, but I know this…this is right. This is what my entire life has been leading to—"

"You honestly believe your entire life has been leading up to the moment where you can sacrifice yourself?"

"Yes and no." He placed his hand on my cheek, guiding my head up. "My life really didn't have much meaning until I met you. I always hated the idea of fate, but it feels like this is fate. It makes sense."

Hands shaking, I clutched my knees. "It doesn't make any sense, Seth."

His sharp intake of breath cut through me. "Babe…"

"No. It doesn't make sense. At all," I said, gripping my knees until my nails bit into my skin. It took several tries for me to say it, and when I did it was barely a whisper. "We were supposed to have forever."

Seth closed his eyes.

"We were going to defeat the Titans and then we were going to come back here. We were going to pick a room for our child and we were going to do normal things, like shop for baby stuff, and let Deacon throw us a baby shower. We were going to be together." My voice cracked. "And you were going to be there when I had our child. You'd be there. You wouldn't be dead."

Seth's fingers slipped from my cheeks as he rose. Turning, he dragged his hand through his hair.

"There...there has to be another way," I insisted. "This has to be some kind of twisted test that we have to figure out." I stood, my knees shaking. "Maybe that's all this is. Some kind of sick test and we can figure this out, right? We—"

"It *is* a test, Josie." He faced me, his sculptured face painfully open. My breath caught at the finality in his expression, and I shook my head, already knowing what he was going to say. "There is no other way. Apollo was right. If I don't stop this now, it will end with me killing Cronus."

"So, what?" I demanded. "Then we kill him—"

"I know you do not want that, not when millions will die."

"Then kill Zeus! That's still on the table. We kill Zeus and then we take his head to Cronus."

"No." He caught my shoulders, holding me still. "That is not who I am anymore."

Panic clawed through me. "If I had to kill—"

"I want my child to grow up knowing I made the right choice. I want my child to think of me and be filled with pride," he said, drawing me to him. "I want our child to look up to me. Killing Zeus isn't going to do that. Neither is killing Cronus."

"I won't let you do this, Seth. I can't."

"You have to. I know you don't want me to. And that you don't want to hear this." He grasped my face, tilting my head back. "But there is no other way."

I couldn't stop the tears as I grasped the collar of Seth's shirt and pressed against him. His arms circled me, holding on to me just as fiercely as I gripped him. "Do you want to die?" I whispered. "Is that it?"

"Gods, no. All I've ever wanted to do is be good enough for you—for our child." Seth smoothed his hand down my hair, cupping the back of my neck. He pressed his lips against my damp cheek. "And if I have to give up my life to make sure you and our child have a long one in a better world, then I will gladly do it."

"You *are* good enough, Seth. You *already* are."

"I will be," he said quietly.

Crying out, I pushed him away. "That's not right! You can't be okay with this." I backed away from him, keeping my hands up as if I could ward off what he was saying. "You're just going to give up?"

"I'm not giving up, *psychí mou.*" Pain shone in his eyes, pain for me and not him. "I'm telling you that I know this must be done."

"No!" I screamed it even as it slowly started to sink it. There was no way out of this, not when he saw this as a way to ensure the future for me and our child. "Seth, *please.* Don't you want to see your child?"

He grabbed me, pulling me into his arms. "I saw...I saw our child's heartbeat." His voice thickened. "That's going to be... It has to be enough and it is. It's more than I ever could've hoped for."

The finality of this slammed into me. This was happening. There was no way out of this. He was going to do it, and I broke. Deep, soul-crushing sobs racked my body as Seth held me. I buried my face into his chest, gripping his shirt once again.

"Shh, *psychí mou,* it's okay. It's going to be okay." He rocked me gently soothing me as each sob tore me apart from the inside out. "I'm here. It's okay."

But it wasn't okay. It would never be okay. Never again.

He placed his lips against my temple. "We still have right now, *psychí mou.* And we'll have forever in our memories."

I pulled back, unable to catch my breath against the pressure clamping down on my chest. "Right now," I whispered.

He smiled, running his fingers along my bottom lip. "We have right now. By the time the sun sets, it...it needs to be done."

I started to protest, because I needed more time, but I *listened* to him. I *heard* him even though it felt like I was dying.

Right now—the beginning of what would be the end.

I captured his hand and closed my eyes, placing a kiss against his fingertip. Right now was all we had. Grief exploded, tearing me apart again. I had never known such pain that wasn't psychical, not even after I learned that my grandparents or my mom had died. No. This was so much more. Like dying inside, piece by piece until there was nothing left of me.

I drew in a shuddering breath and released his hand. Reaching down, I grabbed the bottom of his shirt. Quickly, I pulled the material up over his shoulders, letting it slip to the floor. Then without words, I moved to the button on his pants. They too fell to the floor.

Starting with his chin, I kissed every square inch of his flesh until I was on my knees before him. If all we had was right now, then I would give him everything I had in me. *Everything.*

"Josie," Seth breathed unsteadily, threading his fingers through my hair as I took him in my hands first, holding him tight as I moved my hand wickedly slow.

When his breath sucked in sharply, I took him into my mouth as I drew my hand back. His hips thrust up, but I didn't hurry and I didn't worry for one second about how inexperienced I was at this. That didn't matter. Between warm breaths, I teased him with my tongue before taking him in once more, as far as I could. I flattened my tongue to draw him out, working him slowly until the sounds of his rough groans overshadowed my pounding heart.

With a near-feral sound, he gripped my shoulders and pulled me away, lifting me up to claim my mouth. He walked me back, removing my dress and bra with amazing quickness. Guiding me onto my back, I lifted my hips as he tugged my panties off with one sweep.

Molten lava shot through my veins as his heated gaze met

mine. Need pulsed through me, dizzying as heat pooled between my thighs. There was a roaring in my ears as he knelt on the bed, his large hands on either side of my thighs. He lowered his head, his mouth blazing a path from my thigh to the most intimate part of me, and my back arched clear off the bed.

Seth captured my hands, holding them down as his tongue delved deep, teasing me until I moved unashamedly against his mouth, tipping my hips up and spreading my thighs. His name leaked out from my lips, over and over again like a whispered prayer.

Finally, after what felt like forever, he let go of my wrists, and I took control. Rolling him onto his back, I climbed up his hard body, kissing him with everything I had. Then, only after I had tasted every crevice of his mouth did I move down his body, slowly inching down on his thick length.

I placed my hands on his chest, grinding down. I gave him everything I was feeling, every part of my being. Words, for me, were not enough to describe how much I loved him. Not enough to tell him how much losing him was going to kill me. I used my body to show him how deep my love ran, and I prayed that it was enough. That he could feel it. That he knew it.

Seth sat up in one fluid motion, cupped the back of my head as he thrusted. "You've always been the best of me, Josie. I love you."

The tears fell again. There was no stopping them as I wrapped my arms around him. Our bodies moved as one, hearts pounded in sync. He kissed me, devoured me as if he hoped to take my taste with him.

He quickened his strokes. Our breathing turned ragged as we clutched at one another desperately. In a searing burst of pleasure, we came together. Minutes passed as he held me tenderly, our bodies still joined together, and then I felt him hardening. I lifted my head from his chest and looked at him questioningly.

Without saying a word, he rolled me onto my back. He smoothed his thumb over my parted lips as he started to move with slow, unhurried strokes that burned my body. Lifting my hips, I crossed my legs over his hips and took him in deeper.

His pace picked up, surging over and over, going deeper and deeper until I didn't know where he ended and I began. This seemed so right. So perfect. And it wasn't fair what had to be done. It wasn't right.

The release shattered through my body and heart. I cried out as his body jerked against mine. And when we both came back down to earth, we started all over again. I was desperate to remember the feel of his skin against mine, the way it tasted and felt and smelled. Using my hands, my tongue, I worshipped every inch of him, and still it wasn't enough.

It would never be enough.

He pulled me into his lap, sliding in with one stroke. I moaned. "You're so beautiful and you're so strong. Don't ever forget that. No matter what. Never forget that."

Tears pricked my eyes until they blinded me. "Seth…"

"Promise me." He cupped the back of my head, exposing my throat so that he could rain kisses down the length of my neck. Again and again, we made love to each other until the first shadows started to bleed through the windows.

And then it was time.

Wrapping myself around Seth, I sobbed against his skin. My insides were twisted, cold. "I can't. I can't do this."

He cradled me to his chest. "You don't have to. I'm not going to do it here. I'll leave. It'll be easier that way."

I leaned back, placing my hands on his shoulders. "How can you be okay with this?"

"Easy." He kissed the tip of my nose and brushed my tears away with the back of his hand. "I love you. And love is selfless."

That only made me cry all the harder, because I had never been selfless in my love. Never. "You don't deserve this."

A faint smile curved his lips. "Some would say this was a long time coming." Seth gently placed me on the bed and sat up. He gazed at the dagger for several seconds. "I'm going to leave. You don't have to—"

Panic erupted as I scrambled onto my knees. "No—no! Don't leave. Please. I can be here." I pulled it together, brushing the tears off my cheek. "I can be here."

He looked at me. "I don't want you to see this."

"And I don't want you to be alone." Sliding off the bed, I picked up my dress and tugged it on, my heart pounding and my stomach churning. I faced him. "Please. Please don't leave. I need to be here. I need—" I drew in a slow breath. "I need to be here for you. I need to be a part of this."

"Josie…"

"I'll never forgive myself if I don't." And that was the truth. I squared my shoulders. "I will help you."

Seth closed his eyes briefly, and for a moment I thought he was going to tell me no, but then he nodded. He stood and picked the dagger up. "Then it's time."

Slowly, numbly, I stood as he knelt on the floor beside the bed. I followed him down, pressing my body against his. "I don't want you to… I don't want you to…go," I said, because I couldn't force myself to say the correct word.

"I know." Seth kissed my tear-soaked lips and pulled back far enough that his breath warmed the space between them. "Close your eyes."

I squeezed my eyes shut, but the tears still leaked through. My heart completely ripped open, beyond repair. Out of everything that I'd experienced, this was the one thing that would kill me. We would defeat the Titans and save millions of lives, but I'd never be the same. A huge part of me would die a slow death, because I no longer knew what life was without Seth.

But I wrapped my hands around his.

And his hands were wrapped around the dagger

"I love you," he whispered hoarsely, pressing the sharp edge against his chest, above his heart. "I will always love you."

A ragged sound escaped me, more animal than human as I opened my eyes. "I love you. Oh God, I love you so much."

"I know. I know, Josie."

"And I will tell our child all about you. Every day. Every second, I will tell our child how great you were and how much you loved them," I said, taking short, broken breaths. "Our child will know you. I promise."

"Thank you." Seth shuddered. "I love you."

Hands trembling around his, I felt him pull back, and at the last minute instinct took over. I tried to stop him, but it was…it was too late.

I screamed as he impaled the dagger deep into his chest, and the last thing I saw was his eyes, those beautiful amber-colored eyes. I thought I saw a flicker of surprise.

Then there was a flash of bright light that momentarily blinded me, followed by an intense blast of heat. I pitched forward as the dagger slipped from my lifeless fingers.

I was alone.

I curled into myself, a scream of vast agony and despair still pouring from me, tearing from my very soul.

Seth hadn't even made a sound, ensuring that the last words I'd ever remember him saying were him saying that he loved me, and now…he was gone.

Seth was gone.

# 28

## Josie

"**J**osie." The soft voice came again, this time closer. "Josie, let me help you."

Squeezing my hands into fists, I didn't respond to Alex's quiet pleading. She'd been checking in on me for several hours now, throughout the entire night. Each time she got a little bolder, going from knocking on the door to eventually getting a key and opening it and coming into the room. This time she'd bent down and touched my shoulders.

And I still didn't respond.

I couldn't.

Alex left the room, and I stayed where I had been since Seth had…since he *left*. I stayed curled on the spot he'd knelt on.

I guess Alex knew what had happened.

Or they'd heard me screaming earlier.

More likely that Apollo had gotten in contact with them. I didn't know.

None of this felt real. None of it except the pain. That was too raw and too consuming for it not to be real. And there was no escaping it.

I couldn't move. I couldn't sleep. I couldn't think about anything other than Seth—other than the first time I'd seen him and the first time I'd heard him speak and then the first time he'd kissed me.

Those moments played over and over, chronicling every minute I'd spent with him and how every second we'd been apart now seemed like such wasted time.

And I cried.

I cried so much I didn't think it was possible for a person to produce that many tears, and just when I thought I'd cried myself out, I would think of his last words, how he thanked me and said he loved me, and then I'd start crying all over again. My eyes were swollen. My throat burned and my head felt like it was thick, but the tears were endless.

The pain was endless.

As I lay there, staring at the dagger, I thought about the dream I kept having. The one where I wore a white dress and I'd been…I'd been dying.

The dream hadn't been about me.

It had gotten some things right. The white dress. I was wearing that. The tears. They would not stop falling. The numbness. Beyond the pain and grief, there was just a vast nothingness. But in my dream, it had been me dying, covered with blood. In reality, it had been Seth and there had been no blood.

My prophetic abilities sucked.

Uncurling one arm, I slid my hand down the front of my dress, to my stomach. I closed my eyes again. I don't know how much time went by, but there was another knock on the door and then I heard a different voice call out this time.

"Josie?" Deacon was in the room, inching closer.

A few moments passed and then I felt his light touch on my

shoulder, and I opened my eyes. I stared at the dagger.

Deacon sat behind me. He reached down, brushing aside the stands of hair that had come free from my braid.

I took a breath and it scorched my throat. "Seth's…he's gone."

"I know." Deacon's voice was hoarse. He continued to smooth his hand over my hair.

"It wasn't supposed to be this way." The dagger began to blur. "None of this. It was supposed to be the demigods and me who defeated the Titans. That was the whole point of *everything*." Anger burned low in my chest. "That was why…Seth was sent to get me. That was why we found Gable and Cora and Erik, but none of that matters."

"It still matters," he replied. "We may not be using them to entomb the Titans, but we saved them *from* the Titans. You saved them." He paused. "Seth saved them."

My heart squeezed. Deacon was right. Retrieving the demigods hadn't been pointless. We'd made sure they didn't face the same fate that the other demigods had faced.

Knowing that didn't lessen any of the pain, though. A shudder rolled through me. "I can't believe he's gone."

Deacon bent down, resting his forehead on the side of my head.

"This can't be happening," I said, shaking. "I keep thinking this is a nightmare. That I'm going to wake up and all of this will just be a nightmare."

"I know," he murmured, throwing an arm around my waist. "It doesn't seem real. Seth was…" His voice cracked a little. "He deserved so much more than this."

Another tremor rocked me. "He did—oh, God, he did, but I…" I hated saying the next words. "I don't think he knew that. I don't think he ever did."

"He didn't."

I squeezed my eyes shut against the rising tears. "I don't know what to do. I don't know how to get over this."

"You don't." Deacon lifted his head. "I never got over the death of my parents or Solos or Caleb, but it's gotten easier. It's gotten better."

My chest ached like it had been ripped open. I couldn't think of a day when this was going to feel better. When this wouldn't hurt like a raw wound.

"I'm not going to ask if you're okay," Deacon said after a moment. "I know you're not, but I'm here for you. We all are here for you, Josie."

"I know," I whispered.

Deacon folded his hand over mine. "You haven't lost him. Not really. You're always, always going to have your memories, and most importantly, you're going to have this." He gently pressed on my hand, flattening my palm against my stomach. "You're going to have his child, Josie. You're always going to have a part of him. Don't lose sight of that."

God.

Deacon was right again, and in a way, that hurt more than anything, because I would have my memories of Seth. I would have a piece of him, but all our child would have would be what I had to share about Seth, and while that had to be enough, it wasn't going to be.

Seth had deserved to know his child.

And our child deserved to know him.

\* \* \*

The gods responded fifteen hours, forty-three minutes, and fifteen seconds from the exact moment I said goodbye to the only man I loved. It was only then that I rose from the floor and showered, taking my time to change into pants and a shirt—Seth's shirt. It had been the one he'd worn the day before, and it still smelled like him. I pulled my hair into a ponytail.

Upon returning to the bedroom, I couldn't look at the bed that was still disheveled from our lovemaking. The dagger was where it had fallen. I took a breath and then walked over to it. I picked it up as my gaze fell to the spot where Seth had knelt. Part of me kept expecting him to reappear, run to me and pull me into his arms.

It didn't happen.

A knock on the door drew my attention. Placing the dagger on the dresser, I went to the door. It was Alex. There were shadows under her puffy eyes.

"Hey," she said, and then she sprung forward, throwing her arms around me. She hugged me tight. "I'm so sorry, Josie. Gods, I'm so sorry."

I think I murmured something, but I have no idea what I said. When Alex pulled back, I had to look away from the fresh tears in her eyes. I wasn't the only person experiencing the grief tearing me apart inside. Alex had known Seth longer than me. The two of them had a weird history, but they were like two sides of the same coin.

"I don't know what to say." She stepped back.

Pressing my lips together, I shook my head. A moment passed before I could trust myself to speak. "I don't think there's anything anyone can say." My voice sounded hoarse and unused. "There's a god here."

Alex wiped at her cheek as she nodded and cleared her throat. "Yes. He's waiting in our room."

Tension crept into my muscles as I faced her. "It's my father?"
"Yes."

Drawing in a shuddering breath, I turned away. "I guess we shouldn't keep him waiting."

"Josie…"

"It's okay." I started walking toward their room.

She caught up to me easily. "But it's not okay."

I closed my eyes, stopping. It took a second to respond. "I know. It's not. It's far from okay, but I have to be right now."

When I opened my eyes, she was staring at the floor. "All right," she said finally. "Let's go."

I wasn't ready to see anyone, especially my father. I was furious just thinking about him, but I was mostly just hurt. So damn hurt. Some of it was irrational. He hadn't been able to stop this? To suggest something better? Then there was the fact I suspected that he'd known how this would end with Seth. He'd known all along.

Alex opened the door and the first person I saw was Aiden. His silvery gaze was somber as it landed on me. He didn't say anything as he came forward. His hug was nearly as tight as Alex's, and when he let go, he cupped the sides of my face, holding my gaze to his.

"He loved you and this child in the purest and most powerful way." He caught a tear that had snuck free, wiping it away with his thumb. "And you made him into a person capable of that kind of love. Don't forget that."

My lip trembled as I swallowed down the knot in my throat. "I won't."

Aiden bent his head and kissed my forehead. Luke was there the moment he stepped back, folding his arms around me. He said something to me, but I couldn't hear it over my pounding heart. I scanned the room as he stepped back, my gaze connecting with eyes identical to mine.

Apollo stood in the corner.

I slipped free from Luke, unable to look away from my father.

He didn't move as he met my gaze. "I know I am the last person you want to see and what I'm about to say doesn't change what you've gone through, but I am truly sorry for the pain you're feeling."

I opened my mouth, but I didn't have the words. Actually, I did, but if I spoke them, I would scream them—I would scream until my lungs caved in. I couldn't afford that right now.

Not when I knew why Apollo was here.

Dragging my gaze from his, I watched Luke sit next to a quiet Deacon. "Have you got the—whatever they're called? The giants?"

"Not yet," Apollo answered. "But that's why I'm here. I want to let you know that we *will* defeat the Titans. By the time the sun sets tonight, they will be entombed."

All that was good to know… Wait. "I'm going with you guys."

Apollo opened his mouth. "I don't think—"

"What you think really doesn't matter," I said, my tone harsh—harsher than I even wanted it, but I wasn't in the mood to be told what to do by anyone. "I am going."

Deacon shifted forward. "Are you sure you are ready for something like this?"

Valid question, since he'd spent the better part of the day lying on the floor with me. "I have to see this through."

Alex and Aiden exchanged a look and I knew they were gearing up for a discussion listing all the logical reasons why I should stay behind.

"You don't understand. I need to see this through." I curled my hands into fists as I looked around the room. "I need to see what Seth gave his life for."

"Okay," Alex said not even a second after I finished speaking. "You're going."

Apollo's gaze shot to her.

"Don't even argue with me," Alex snapped. "Josie needs to go, and she's going to go."

He looked away, jaw hard.

"We can hold off, though. This can wait until you're ready,"

Aiden offered. "We don't have to do this right now."

"But there are probably still pures alive in that community. The longer we wait, the more likely it is they won't survive this. The Titans probably aren't expecting us to return so quickly. If anything, they'd been expecting...Seth, and not us." I forced myself to breathe through the pain centering in my chest. "The longer we wait, there's a chance they could find out what Seth has done and prepare."

"Is that a possibility?" Aiden asked of Apollo.

His bright blue eyes fixed on mine. "Anything is possible."

That wasn't true.

If *anything* was possible, Seth would be standing here with me. He wouldn't be—

I cut those thoughts off with a shake of my head and squared my shoulders. "Let's get this done."

Apollo lowered his chin. "Do you have the dagger?"

"It's in my room."

His gaze lifted to mine. "We're going to need it."

* * *

If I was being honest with myself, I needed this distraction. Not that it wasn't about the pures who could still be alive in the community. I wanted to get this over with because of them, but I also...I needed this.

I needed to see this through.

We arrived just inside the gates, the five of us. Deacon stayed behind to keep an eye on the other demigods.

The first thing I noticed was how eerily quiet the community was. Looking behind me, I saw the tall stone gate and I could hear the distant sounds of traffic and life, but in here?

It was like a grave.

"Was it like this before?" I asked.

Aiden nodded and started walking. "Yes. But there were shades here before. We need to be careful."

Luke and Alex flanked both of my sides as we walked past the empty playground and turned onto what I was guessing was the main street. It wasn't like Seth had told me.

The streets had been cleared. No abandoned cars or bodies.

And there were definitely people here.

They sat on the outdoor patios and at the dining tables, and lounged on the corners of the streets. Dozens of people.

And I used the term "people" loosely.

I breathed in deeply, stomach churning at the distinctive musky scent that saturated the air.

They all turned at the same exact moment, their eyes like pools of oil.

Alex unsheathed her daggers. "I'm guessing it wasn't quite like this last time."

"No." Aiden did the same.

I clutched the dagger Zeus had given Seth while Luke palmed a Glock.

"So, when are we going to summon these giant people?" Luke asked under his breath as the shades stood and faced us.

"Soon," Apollo murmured.

I was hoping soon was really soon, because these shades were giving me the creeps. They were all just standing there, staring, and the silence became deafening.

One of the shades, who must've been a middle-aged pure-blood, moved. He stepped off the sidewalk. Luke's thumb glided over the handgrip of the Glock.

The man cocked his head to the side and then he took off, running straight at us at an inhuman speed. I started to lift my free hand, prepared to tap into akasha, but Apollo snapped his fingers.

The man imploded.

Like sucked right into himself and *crumpled*.

Alex lowered her dagger as both of us looked at him. "Really?" she said, mouth dropping open. "That's how you get rid of shades?"

He arched a brow. "How else would I?"

Now my mouth was hanging open. "Seriously? This entire time and all you had to do was snap your fingers?"

"Why, yes. All gods can."

I frowned. "Seth can't—" I sucked in a sharp breath as I realized I'd said that in the present tense. "Seth couldn't do that."

An emotion flickered across Apollo's face, but it was gone before I could figure out what it was. "He would've been able to. If he had had more time to learn."

If he had had more time…

My hand tightened around the dagger. It felt like I'd just stabbed myself in the chest.

Apollo's head suddenly swung back around as the ground trembled under our feet. Energy poured into the street. Goosebumps erupted all over my arms. The air began to warp, and I saw the blue Mohawk first.

Fury exploded inside me. That Titan had done terrible, horrific things, and he wasn't alone. The female Titan appeared behind Oceanus, and my lip curled back with a snarl.

She had destroyed Long Beach.

She had made Seth feel like shit.

I wanted to kill them both.

Oceanus smirked as he eyed my father. "This is an interesting development."

"He came here to die." Tethys laughed. "In front of his daughter. Cute."

Oceanus looked the rest of us over. "But where is—"

"Now, Josie," Apollo commanded.

Sending him a brief glance, I did what he'd instructed me

to do earlier. I stalked forward, and then I let all that anger and hurt and *fucking* despair empower me. Meeting Oceanus's stare, I swung the dagger high and then brought it down, letting out a scream as I slammed the dagger into the asphalt with everything I had in me.

The dagger cut through the cement and stone, sinking deep. I saw Oceanus's eyes widen in surprise. I saw him mouth one word.

*No.*

I smiled.

The force of what I'd done came back up, thrusting through the asphalt and up the length of the blade. It slammed into me, knocking me backward and flat on my ass.

The blade shot into the air, where it vibrated and then stilled. It hovered as if an invisible hand held it. Then it exploded into a million fine pieces, nothing more than dust.

"Was that supposed to happen?" Luke asked.

Apollo widened his stance. "Just wait."

Eyes wide, I shoved myself up onto my feet. Behind Tethys, the air warped once more and my breath got lodged in my throat as Cronus appeared.

"What have you done?" he asked, that pitch-black gaze burning mine. "What has he done?"

The shades threw their heads back and *howled.* Their screams sent chills down my spine.

"That's not creepy or anything." Alex shuddered. "When are those—?"

The shades charged.

Alex and Aiden shot forward, catching the first wave of shades. Alex slammed the hilt of a Covenant dagger deep into the chest of the first shade. Aiden spun like a graceful dancer, releasing his sickle blade. It caught the shade under the chin. With one clean strike, the head went in one direction and the body went in another. Luke started unloading, striking one shade after another, in the centers of their foreheads.

One blew past Alex, gunning straight for me. Newly honed instinct took over. I lifted my hand and tapped into akasha. Every cell in my body sparked alive as power flowed from my core. A bolt of charged energy arced from my palm, smacking into the center of the shade's chest. It flew backward, past Oceanus.

It started as a tremor, like a train was running nearby, but the tremor grew until it became hard to stand. The shades stopped attacking, their screams fading as they stared at the ground. Unbalanced, I threw my arms out as I looked at Apollo.

"Please tell me *this* is supposed to happen."

Apollo nodded.

The street swelled as if some great pressure was pushing it up. We stumbled back as the street collapsed, settling. The road was cracked, and all I could hear was Luke's ragged breathing.

Chunks of asphalt spewed into the air, mowing down the shades who hadn't been wise enough to back away. Dust blanketed the sky, and out of the floating dirt came a hand.

A hand that was about the size of my torso.

Aiden threw an arm out, shielding Alex. "Holy…"

"Daimon balls," Alex whispered.

Another hand smacked down on the ground, rattling the buildings. A large, soot-covered head appeared. It came out of the torn street, a massive creature that had to be more than twenty feet tall.

I really hoped there weren't any helicopters flying nearby because there'd be no hiding this guy.

My eyes nearly popped out of my head as my gaze drifted down, and I immediately wished I hadn't.

"Whoa," Alex murmured.

The giant was buck-ass naked.

Another set of hands came out of the torn ground. A second

giant joined the first and then a third appeared.

Aaand all of them were naked.

"I guess they don't make clothing big enough for them?" she asked, and a small, hysterical-sounding giggle escaped me.

Oceanus shouted something and then turned. The shades rushed forward, toward the giants. Some fell into the hole in the street. Others were smarter, going around the rift. They swarmed the giants, attacking their legs and climbing up.

Apollo cocked his head to the side and then sighed. "*He* always has to make a fashionable late entrance."

A fissure of pure energy shot down the road. Static crackled, and my heart nearly stopped in my chest. Behind Cronus, a column of shimmering blue light appeared. When it faded, Zeus stood there.

"Where do you think you're going?" He smiled as lightning crackled from his palms and wind blew the strands of his hair.

Cronus drew up short. "Not again."

"History does have a habit of repeating itself." Zeus smiled.

"Look!" Aiden shouted.

Black dots appeared in the sky above us, circling and swirling, coming closer and closer to the ground with each cycle. They weren't dots. They were large winged creatures.

"Furies." Luke cursed.

Before we had a chance to run for cover, they carpet-bombed the shades trying to slow down the giants, snatching them up with their clawed feet and throwing them into the air. Oily blood arced out, dotting the broken ground. A shadow passed over me and the ground shook as a furie landed directly in front of me.

I gasped. "*Erin?*"

The furie winked. I barely recognized her features, but it was her in her true form. "Be right back."

Using powerful legs, she launched into the sky. Within seconds, she had a shade in her grip. I stared at her, shocked that she was, in fact, very much alive.

My father hadn't lied about that, at least.

The first giant broke free from the shades and rushed forward, each step jarring the earth. It was heading straight for Tethys.

A burst of white light shot from Apollo, striking Tethys in the back. She stumbled. She didn't fall, but Apollo had cornered her. Zeus was doing the same, hitting Cronus over and over with lightning.

Apollo and Zeus weren't killing the Titans. They were trapping them, not allowing them to escape.

Alex walked past me and picked up an overturned bench. She sat down, plopping her cheek on her fist.

"Getting comfortable?" Aiden asked.

She lifted a shoulder. "Not like they need our help."

"For once." A rare grin appeared on Luke's face as he watched one of the giants snatch up Tethys in a meaty hand. The female Titan shrieked and flailed, but she was not getting free. "It's about time."

The four of us were actually on the sidelines as Apollo and Zeus, along with the furies, took over. I couldn't help but think if Seth were here, he would've passed out from seeing this.

A sad smile tugged at my lips. He wouldn't even believe what he was seeing. That finally, after all this time, after all the deaths and the sacrifices, Zeus was down here, *fighting*.

And all it took was Seth…sacrificing himself.

The knot of raw emotion expanded in my chest as I lowered my hand to my stomach.

The final battle lasted maybe minutes. Corralled into one area, it took nothing for the giants to capture each of the Titans. They held them in their hands, and from where I stood, the Titans looked like screaming children as they were taken back into the tear in the road. Cronus was the last to go, his screams of rage overshadowed by the screams of the shades as the furies took them out, sucking them down their throats as they tried to escape the bodies they'd possessed.

"Do you think they get indigestion from that?" Alex asked.

I thought that was a valid question.

The ground trembled once more as Zeus walked forward. As he neared the rift, he waved his hand over it. Shimmery blue light settled over the tear like a million fireflies. The road…repaired itself. Stone and cement churned, spreading over the tear, and within seconds it was like giants had not just crawled out from there. Even the yellow paint marking the lanes was flawless.

"That could come in handy," Luke murmured under this breath, and then he quieted as Zeus approached us. Even Alex sat up straight and then rose to her feet.

"They will take the Titans back to their tombs, where Hades is awaiting their return," Zeus explained, and then looked over his shoulder. "The furies will hunt down the rest of the shades. A few have escaped, but they have no place to run."

Alex opened her mouth, but for once, nothing came out of it.

Zeus looked at me. "It is over, Josie."

It was.

I don't know what I was expecting to feel. A sense of completion? Relief? Righteousness? As if knowing Seth's sacrifice wasn't for nothing was suddenly going to lessen the burden of facing a…a possible eternity without him?

But I felt…I felt *nothing*.

I looked over Zeus's shoulder, and I didn't see any of the furies. I saw my father. He was staring back at me.

"This was because of him," Zeus said quietly, drawing my attention. "He made this possible, and you will understand one day why this had to be this way."

"I will never understand." Tearing my gaze away from Zeus, I shuddered as I faced my father. "I want to go…home."

# 29

## Josie
### *Two months later*

"Kyría, is there anything I can do for you?"

Sitting in the sand, I lifted my gaze from the frothy waves and squinted. Basil stood beside me. "What did I tell you, Basil?"

His brows pinched. "To stop…waiting on you?"

"Yes." I nodded for extra emphasis. "You're not my servant. None of you here are my servants."

Since Apollo brought me here after the showdown with the Titans, Basil and every person—er, priest and priestess—who lived here treated me like a queen who had finally come home.

Which was a good thing in the beginning, especially when I first walked into the bedroom that I'd shared with Seth and had an utter breakdown. If it hadn't been for Basil and the priestess named Karina, I don't think I would've made it to the bed. And as much as it shamed me to admit it, if it hadn't been for them making sure I ate during those first dark days here, I would've just stayed in that bed, wasting away.

And if it weren't for the child I carried inside me that was what I would've done. Withered up and died when the pain of losing Seth was fresh, like it happened yesterday.

Except, with the help of those who lived here and my friends, I did get out of that bed, and even though there were days when I wanted nothing more than to give up, I didn't.

I was still here.

I was going to be here.

"But we wish to serve you," Basil said, and he'd only said that about a million times.

"I know, but it's...weird."

Basil stared at me like he couldn't process how that was weird. He then changed the subject. Like he always did when we had this conversation. "We stocked the pantry and fridge this morning. We did not forget those cheese snacks this time."

A grin pulled at my lips. He was talking about Cheetos. "Erin is sure to appreciate that."

He smiled brightly. "I am pleased to hear that. Does Erin plan to stay long this time?"

"I'm not sure. I guess it depends on her being...summoned."

Basil nodded with understanding. Erin had been here since the moment Apollo had brought me here. Besides the happiness of being able to reconnect with her, her presence came in handy. She also had the nifty ability of easy transportation, able to take me wherever I needed to go.

That was how I got to my first appointment with the OBGYN in New York. The appointment had been equally amazing and depressing, and Erin had been there through it all.

Just like Basil and Karina.

Sometimes I wondered why they were still here.

I bit down on my lip as I looked out at the ocean. "Can I ask you something?"

"Anything, *Kyría.*"

"Why are you all still here?" I asked, wincing at how bad the question sounded. "I mean, I'm happy that everyone is here. I don't know what I would've done without you all, but Seth is... He's gone, and you all were here because of him."

Basil knelt beside me, and when I looked at him, his gaze held mine. "Just because he is not here with us does not mean he is gone. He is the God of Life and he is the God of Death. This is just a moment in that cycle."

What he said was confusing as hell, but none of the staff here, or the priests and priestesses behaved as if Seth was...dead. They acted as if he was just on vacation or something. Like he was coming back.

But Seth wasn't coming back.

I knew this, because if Seth was coming back, he would've done it by now. He wouldn't be out there and not be with me. He wouldn't have missed the first real doctor's visit. He wouldn't have left me like *this*.

Knowing all of that, there was a still a part of me that was just like everyone here.

Waiting for Seth to return. Like he was simply *gone* and not dead.

Basil lightly touched my arm, and I blinked, refocusing on him. I realized that he'd been talking. "I'm sorry. I kind of zoned out there."

"It's okay, *Kyría.*" The man was the definition of patience. "We're also here because of you. We want you to know that. We are your family, not by blood but what exists in here." He thumped his fist off his chest. "And family of the heart and soul does not leave. No matter what."

\* \* \*

"Tacos or wings? This is an important decision, so don't say I don't care." Erin stood in the massive kitchen, holding a package of soft taco shells in one hand and uncooked chicken wings in the other. "Wait. Can pregnant ladies eat chicken wings and tacos?"

I laughed as I poured myself a glass of freshly squeezed orange juice. "As long as it's cooked properly, yes, I can eat it."

She lowered the taco shells as she eyed the bag of chicken. "I think chicken is probably a healthier choice."

Closing the door, I walked over to the island and hopped on the bar stool. "Not sure chicken wings ever constitute a healthy choice."

"If it's baked, it's healthy."

"I don't think that's how that works."

She frowned as she put the chicken into the fridge. "Why not?"

"Because there's a lot of stuff that's baked that is terrible for you."

"Name one."

"Cookies. Pies. Cake. Lasagna—"

"You're a life-ruiner," she interrupted, grinning. "We'll do chicken wings and a salad."

I took a sip of my juice as she came over to the island and sat beside me. "How was everything at the University?"

Erin had popped over there earlier to scope things out. "Still no fighting, even with all the students back in class."

"No incidents?"

"None." She crossed one leg over the other. "Maybe Deacon and Luke are onto something. They think it has to do with my sisters making an appearance. Many of the pures have never seen a furie before. Could've been a wake-up call to get their life right."

It was hard to think of those entombed furies as Erin's sisters, because of what they had done to Colin. Erin was nothing like them.

The last time Erin had swung by the campus, Marcus had let her know that he'd heard back from one of his contacts and had gotten the profile of the pures who'd be likely involved in the crimes against the halfs. Several interviews had gone down, but there hadn't been any breakthroughs.

"This is good news, though." I ran my finger along the rim of the glass. "At least it seems safe for the students there."

"It does, but..." Erin sighed when I glanced over at her. "I don't know. I feel like we're missing something, and I'm not taking about your friend's body, either."

I shifted my gaze from her. Every square inch of that campus had been searched for Colin's body and nothing had been found. I feared what happened to him was going to be one of those mysteries that were never solved.

"Anyway," Erin said, nudging me with her arm. "Cora and Gable are a thing now."

"Really? That's good."

"Yep."

Come to think of it, I wasn't entirely surprised. Gable was always staring at her when they were around each other. "How's Erik doing?"

Erin rolled her eyes. "Good, I guess? I can't stand his arrogant ass longer than five minutes at a time to really know how he's doing, but the three of them seem to be fitting in at the University."

I arched my brow at her, thinking her reaction to Erik was a little strong. I was happy to hear that they were doing well there. Even though there was no threat to them, they needed to learn about their heritage and what abilities they did have.

"Alex and Aiden's time is almost up," she continued. "They're having a going-away party and they really, really want to see you before they go."

I nodded, unsure of how to answer. Talking about visiting

everyone was about as fun as talking about my father, who I hadn't seen since he brought me here.

Erin was quiet for a long moment. "Everyone misses you."

Uncomfortable with where this conversation was going, I looked away. "I miss them too."

"Do you?"

"Yes." And I did miss everyone.

"Then why haven't you've gone to see them? Or had me bring them over here again?"

I opened my mouth, but anything I was about to say died on the tip of my tongue. Erin knew why. The last time I'd seen Alex and Aiden, they'd been here, along with Luke and Deacon, and they wanted to talk about a funeral for Seth.

We'd had one for Colin even though there'd been no body, about two weeks after the Titans were entombed. Then about a week later, Alex had broached the topic of doing one for Seth.

"I know it's not something any of us wants to think about," Aiden had said. "But it will help give closure. Not just to you, but to everyone else."

I'd shut down.

"They're not going to push the whole funeral thing." The fact she knew what I was thinking about was evidence of how well she knew me. "You know that, right?"

"I know." Picking up my juice, I took a long drink. It was time to be honest. "I just feel bad."

Her dark brows knitted together. "For what?"

"Being selfish, for starters." I dropped my elbow onto the island and planted my forehead into my palm. "I know they need to say goodbye to him, and a funeral is closure. They need it, and I'm holding them back."

Which was proof that I hadn't entirely accepted that Seth was gone.

"You're not holding anyone back. Having a funeral isn't necessary," Erin argued.

"I know that, but doesn't Seth deserve that? The remembrance? The recognition?"

"What do you think Seth would've wanted?"

"Not a funeral." I shoved my fingers through my hair as I squeezed my eyes shut and coughed out a harsh laugh. "He'd rather have people have a massive fight in his honor."

Erin snorted. "Sounds like him."

"I just don't know." I dragged my hand down my face. Guilt and unease churned inside me. Thank God I still hadn't gotten any of the typical pregnancy symptoms other than feeling tired. I was already causing my stomach to be upset enough without hurling every morning. "I just...I miss him."

Erin leaned into me, resting her chin on my shoulder. "It's okay to miss him. You're going to for a long time."

The backs of my eyes burned. "I don't want to feel like this forever."

"You won't." Throwing an arm around my shoulders, she squeezed me. "I promise."

I smiled at her, but I wasn't sure it would ever change. Maybe I really need to let go. To move on. And maybe...just maybe doing something like the funeral was the right thing to do.

At this point, I was willing to try anything, because I needed to get better before this child made its entrance. I had to. Because I didn't want to repeat history. I didn't want to become my mom, emotionally and mentally absent.

I had to get it together.

* * *

Later that night, after a rather ridiculously long bath where I might've dozed off, I checked myself out in the standing mirror tucked into the corner of the massive bathroom.

I was starting to show.

The corners of my lips tipped up as I twisted to the side. My stomach had never been flat and it sure as hell wasn't now. There was a slight bump, like a food baby, but that wasn't what it was even though I ate more wings than any one person should ever consume.

Splaying my hands across my belly, I exhaled roughly as the image of Seth formed in my head before I could stop it. I could almost see him in the mirror, standing behind me, his hands where mine were. He'd kiss my cheek, tell me I was beautiful, and then kiss my stomach before showing me just how beautiful he thought I was.

I turned from the mirror and grabbed the shirt off the sink. It was one of Seth's. Just a plain white shirt. When I slipped it on, it reached my thighs and wasn't the most attractive sleepwear, but it was Seth's.

It wasn't that late, but I climbed into bed anyway. Throwing the covers over my legs, I rolled onto my side and watched the ocean breeze lift the curtains. My mind wandered, and when it started to linger on the conversations with Erin and Basil, I switched gears.

Baby room.

I knew exactly which room I wanted to decorate. Seth's childhood room. Right now, it was dark and rarely visited, but I thought using that room would breathe new life into it. Erase the years of loneliness that clung to the walls. I thought Seth would approve of the choice.

When I had my next appointment with the OBGYN, I hoped I might be able to learn if I was having a boy or girl. My lower lip trembled as I thought about the game Seth and I used to play. I closed my eyes. I still played it. Every night since the last time.

My voice was thick as I said, "Boy or girl?"

"Boy."

A jolt ran through my entire body in response to the deep voice, and my heart cracked wide open because it was a voice I'd never hear again—a voice I'd give almost anything to hear again.

Which meant I was now hearing things. Great. That was all I needed.

The bed suddenly shifted. My eyes flew open…and the world stopped moving.

Time stopped.

Even my heart seemed to have ceased beating for a full ten seconds. Then it picked back up in rapid succession. I couldn't catch my breath, couldn't believe what I was seeing.

He sat beside me, head lowered but the features painfully unmistakable. Perfect. Beautiful. Loved. Golden-colored hair brushed his shoulders. The curve of his jaw was hard and firm. Cheekbones I'd touched and kissed in what seemed like a different life were the same.

Light exploded inside me. A rush of emotions pulsed through me, stunning me into silence and immobility. Happiness, disbelief, love, fear, and confusion all warred to take center stage.

It was him.

Or I was also having visual hallucinations now.

That was possible.

But he *looked* real.

I inhaled sharply, rising up on my elbow as I caught the scent of lush spice and the crisp smell of fall.

He *smelled* real.

"Seth?" I whispered.

Those well-formed lips curved into a smile. "*Psychí mou.*"

He sounded real.

I was moving before I even realized it, before I let the impossibility of the situation take hold. I threw myself at him, and dear Lord, if he wasn't really there, I was going to end up on the floor, but there was no stopping me.

Warm, strong arms swept around my waist, stopping me from toppling off the bed. My legs were tangled in the blanket, but I was flat against his chest, my hands on his shoulders.

He *felt* real.

My vision blurred as I stared at his face. "Is it really you? Are you really here?"

"It's really me," he said, those amber eyes luminous. "And I'm really here."

# 30

## Josie

My heart was racing so fast, I was getting dizzy, and I thought there was a good chance that I might hurl all over the bed.

Seth was sitting on our bed and he was holding me, his hands splayed across my lower back.

This just didn't make sense.

I didn't understand.

Lifting my arms, my hands shook as I touched his cheeks. The skin was warm and smooth as I dragged my fingertips over the curve of his jaw. His brows lifted as I touched his lips, all the while telling myself that this was a dream, because this was impossible.

And if it was a dream, I didn't want to wake up.

My gaze roamed down his throat, over his bare shoulders. I vaguely recognized the white linen pants he wore. I'd seen my father in them before. I dragged my gaze back to his, and those eyes were like pools of warm honey.

He kissed a fingertip. "Josie, babe…"

I jerked as tears blurred the features of his striking face. "I don't understand."

His head tilted to the side, and I heard his sharp inhale. "Don't cry." His hands left my back and went to my cheeks. He chased the tears with his thumbs. "Babe, don't cry. Please. You know how I hate it when you cry."

And that made it me cry all the harder, because this...this couldn't be real. Seth was gone. He was dead. I'd seen it with my own eyes, and weeks had passed. *Months*. Whatever this was, it couldn't be real.

"Is this some kind of cruel trick?" I whispered, shuddering. "Are you going to disappear? Are you going to fade away—?"

"This isn't a trick. I swear." He caught another tear, smoothing it away. "I'm not going anywhere. I'm not disappearing on you. I'm not leaving you. Never again, Josie."

Hope dared spark alive deep in my chest, but so did a terror I'd never tasted before, because hope—it could kill me. I jerked back, slipping out of his grasp as I put some space between us.

I stared at him with wide eyes. "I can't do this again,"Tremors rocked my entire body. "I can't lose you again. I won't survive it. I'm barely surviving it now. I can't—"

Seth moved fast.

One moment he was sitting on the edge of the bed, and then the next he was caging me in, one hand planted on the headboard behind me, the other curled around the nape of my neck.

He brought his mouth to mine, and there was nothing slow or soft about the way he kissed me. It was raw and brutal. Our teeth knocked together, and there was a good chance my lips would be bruised in the morning, but he kissed me without an ounce of restraint or reservation. My already-turbulent senses spun out of control. I was immediately overwhelmed.

He *tasted* like Seth.

He pulled back just enough that, when he spoke, his lips

brushed mine. "It's *me*. You used to call me Sethie and I called you Joe." His voice was full of gravel. "You used to tell me all the time you didn't like me, but you did, you *always* did."

Another shudder rolled through me as I opened my eyes.

His stare was fierce. "You were tagged by a daimon, at the motel with condoms in the reception area. When you first learned how to use the elements, you always tapped into fire when you were trying to summon air. Luke never wanted to be around you when you were practicing."

A choked-sounding laugh escaped me.

"It's *me*," he repeated, his grip on my neck tightening. "You wanted me even when I wasn't worthy of you. When you told me that we were going to have a child, I fell flat on my ass. And because of you, and only you, I became a better man. It's me, *psychí mou*. I am here, and I am never leaving you again."

My eyes widened as the truth of everything he said broke through the panic and fear. The hope didn't just spark now. It flamed gloriously, and when I broke this time, I split wide open in an outpouring of raw emotions.

And it *was* Seth who pulled me into his arms. It *was* Seth who held me so tight there was no space between us. It *was* Seth who was there, alive and breathing.

# Seth

Burying my head in the mass of hair, I breathed in Josie's scent, letting it wash over me. Damn. I'd never thought I'd hold her again. I'd never thought I'd hear her voice or feel her soft curves.

When I pushed that dagger into my chest, I thought that was it. And it was. For a while.

I held her until the tremors subsided and the tears slowed. Then and only then did I pull her away so I could see her face.

Gods, she was beautiful.

I wiped away the lingering tears and then tucked her hair back from her face. "Babe, you're breaking my heart right now."

"I'm sorry." Her voice was hoarse. "I thought... I mean, you were gone, Seth. You died."

"I did." I dragged my thumb over her cheek. I couldn't stop touching her. "Kind of."

Her hands opened and closed against my chest. "I don't understand. If you weren't dead, then where were you? Where have you been?"

"Gods, Josie, it's going to sound crazy." I looked down at her, and I grinned. "Are you wearing one of my shirts?"

Her brows knitted together. "Yeah, but that's not really important right now."

I wasn't sure I could agree with that. Touching her after being separated from her for so long already had my engine revving, but seeing her in my clothes? So turned on it was almost fucking painful.

"Seth," she said, and when I lifted my gaze to hers, those stunning blue eyes were warm. "If there was any thought in my mind you weren't Seth, it is now gone."

I grinned as I drew my thumb under her lip. "I thought I died. That was how it felt at first. There was you, your voice, and then there was nothing. Just fucking nothing, and then it was like I woke up."

She slid her hand over my arms as she sat back. "Woke up? Where?"

"I was nowhere. I mean, I was awake on a conscious level, but I had no... Gods, this is insane, but I wasn't corporeal."

Josie blinked slowly. "Meaning you didn't have a body?"

"Yeah, meaning that." I shook my head. "At first there was just nothing but whiteness. I was surrounded by it, and I woke up, but I had no idea who or what or where I was. I guess it was kind of like being born, but slowly I started to remember things. Pieces of my childhood and my...my mother. Then things started to click into place. I remembered me. I remembered you, but I was just trapped in this nothingness."

"Seth," she whispered. "That sounds terrible."

"It was." For the next million years, I wouldn't forget how it felt. "I was so damn pissed and frustrated and I...I felt helpless. A part of me was obviously alive and all I wanted was to get back to you, to our child, but I couldn't get out of the nothingness."

Her eyes glimmered, and I drew in a ragged breath. "Gods, I have no idea how long I was there. Felt like years, but then something hit me. I am absolute."

Josie stared at me. "Um, okay?"

I laughed, and gods, the sound even startled my ass. I hadn't laughed since before we went to the Olympians. Almost didn't recognize the sound. "I am absolute, and only another absolute being can kill me. Thanatos's sword is the sword of death, but he is not absolute. Once I realized that, I sort of...pieced back together. There was a flash of bright light, and then my naked ass was lying in Zeus's temple."

She jolted, her eyes widening. "Holy crap. You're right! Only Cronus or Zeus could kill you... Wait. You sort of killed yourself, and *you're* absolute. Wouldn't that count?"

I picked up her hands. "Apparently not. At least, according to Zeus."

Josie was still for a moment and then she squeezed my hands. "Did Zeus know this from the beginning? Know that you weren't going to die, but you'd get...stuck?"

"Yeah," I growled. "Yeah, he did."

"What?" she shrieked. "Are you *fucking* kidding me?"

"I wouldn't kid about something like this." I brought her hands to my mouth and kissed the tops of her fingers. "You were right, Josie. It had been a test—a test to see if a self*less* or self*ish* act would be committed. It was a test that Zeus himself had failed."

Never in my life did I ever think I'd say I saw genuine remorse in Zeus, but when he came to me in his temple and told me that he'd chosen wrongly all those thousands of years ago, I heard the raw pain in his voice. If he'd done what I had done, only the gods knew who he'd be today.

And who'd be sitting on the throne beside him.

"I came back as soon as I could." I brought her hands to my chest. "I'm sorry it took me so long to find myself and to figure it out. I'm so damn—"

"Don't." She rose up to her knees. "You do not apologize. You gave your life, thinking that was it, to put an end to the Titans and to give me and our child a safe future. You do not ever apologize. You came back to me. You made it back. What I don't understand is why no one told me. Zeus could've. And if Zeus knew, then my father had to." Her cheeks flushed with anger. "Of course. He's the God of prophecy. He knew. Oh my God, I am going to kill him."

My lips twitched. "Bloodthirsty. Gods, I missed you."

"He could've told me. He could've hinted at it. He could've given me hope!" Her gaze searched mine. "I was… It felt like I *died* right there with you, Seth. It felt like—"

"Stop." Dropping her hands, I grasped her shoulders, I leaned in, resting my forehead against hers. "Don't go back to that place. I'm here. You're here, and nothing in this world or beyond was going to stop me from coming back to you."

She trembled. "I love you. I love you so much, Seth. I love—"

I kissed her and I didn't stop there. It had been far too long since I'd felt her skin against mine, and dammit, I wasn't wasting another second.

Josie must've been feeling the same thing, because she reached for my pants at the same time I went for her shirt. We froze for half a second, and then Josie tipped back her head and laughed.

My damn breath caught in my throat at the sound. "You first."

She bit down on her plump lower lip as she lifted her arms. I got a hold of the hem of her shirt and lifted it off. Then I looked my fill, quickly realizing my memories didn't do her any justice. Those smooth shoulders. Those breasts and her—

Wait.

Her body...her body had changed.

Now my damn heart stuttered in my chest. Her breasts were fuller, and there was this little bump below her navel.

"Gods..." I stared at her, at the first real signs of our child growing inside her. My vision blurred as I placed my hands on her slightly swollen stomach. "Look at you?" My voice thickened. "I missed this—when it happened. When did it happen?"

She placed her hands on mine and a slight tremor radiated from them. "Kind of feels like I woke up one day with the stomach, but it was slow. I had my first appointment with the OBGYN in New York."

"And?"

"Everything is perfect so far."

Blinking back tears, I bent and kissed her stomach. I hated that I had missed that appointment. I wasn't going to miss another one.

Her fingers threaded through my hair. She guided my mouth back to hers, and as she kissed me she went for my pants, tugging them down my hips. When they got hung up on my knees, I willed them off.

Josie's laugh was like basking in the sun.

A heartbeat later, I was thrusting inside her. There'd be time to take it slow, to get reacquainted with every inch of her body, but not now. Neither of us could wait. Urging me on, she wrapped her legs around my hips.

We met each other, thrust for thrust. The rhythm increased until we were slick with sweat. Her hands were everywhere—in my hair, trailing down my back, and gripping my ass. And my mouth was everywhere—trailing kisses down her throat, capturing her taut nipple as my hands cradled her hips, and holding her still as I ground against her.

Lost in the blinding pleasure, I looked down when I lifted up far enough that I could see where we were joined together. The sight of my dick moving in and out of her was erotic and intimate. Higher and higher I went until she threw her head back. Spasms blew through her, rocking through me. Her gasping moans quickly escalated, and I quickly followed, my hips pumping furiously. It was like the never-ending orgasm. Quite some time passed before my movements ceased and I was motionless above her, my heart pounding.

She dragged her palms across my cheeks, catching my hair and tugging it back. "I *really* missed this."

Easing out of her, I laughed as I shifted my weight onto my arms. "Not as much as me."

Josie smiled up at me as she played with the edges of my hair. "I don't want to close my eyes."

"Me neither." I shifted onto my side and brought her with me, lining up our faces. I touched her cheek. "There's something I need to do. Something I've wanted to do for a while now and then. For a while, when I was stuck in that nothingness, I thought I missed my chance. That I wasted so much time. I'm not wasting another second."

"What?" she asked, placing her finger on my lower lip.

My chest expanded. "I want to get married. Not six months from now. Not a week from now. I want to get married as soon as we can," I told her, and I thought she might've stopped breathing. "I know this isn't the most romantic of proposals, but will you marry—"

"Yes." Josie shot forward, knocking me flat on my back as she scrambled on top of me. "Yes!"

# 31

## Josie

"It's beautiful," I whispered, awed by my reflection. My gaze found Erin's in the mirror.

She looked like she was about to cry. "It really is."

Alex stood beside Erin, her grin impish. "There are so many buttons. How much do you want to bet Seth just gets impatient and rips that dress off?"

Heat blossomed in my cheeks and I ducked my chin, laughing. Seth wouldn't rip this dress off if he got impatient. He'd will it off with his mind, because he was special like that.

"I just hope I don't see his bare ass again," Erin quipped. "Not that I'm complaining about his ass. It *is* a nice ass, but that was awkward."

Alex turned to Erin, expression expectant. "Now how did you see his ass?"

My gaze centered in on my reflection as Erin explained how she'd learned Seth had returned from, well, being sort of dead. It had been the following morning, and since Seth and I had stayed up late that night just talking, we'd slept in. Concerned that I hadn't gotten up yet, Erin had burst into the bedroom and got an eyeful of Seth's bare behind.

That was an awkward welcome back.

Especially since Erin had been so shocked by Seth being there, she sort of just stood there gaping while Seth got up to find the shirt I'd been wearing.

Other than that, the last couple of days had felt like the best kind of dream. I got to hear Seth's voice again, feel his touch and drown in his kisses. We got to play our name game, boy or girl, each night, before we fell asleep. Seth had been there when we opened his childhood bedroom door and had the room cleaned and aired out.

Seth was beside me, once more.

Basil and Karina hadn't seemed all that surprised by Seth's return. It made me think of how they'd given off the impression of waiting for him.

Maybe they knew.

Or maybe they hadn't given up hope. There was a part of me that felt a little guilty about the fact that I *had* given up. Not a hundred percent, but I had been beginning to accept that Seth was gone.

It took a few days for me to fully accept that Seth wasn't going to disappear on me. That this wasn't some kind of cruel cosmic joke. I still woke up in the middle of the night, clamoring to touch him just to make sure he was still there. I still got nervous when he wasn't within eyesight, and Seth seemed to realize that, because he rarely strayed too far for too long. That was incredibly needy of me, but I don't think anyone would blame me since I'd just spent two months believing Seth was dead.

Probably would be a long time before I stopped waking up in the middle of the night to reach for him.

But I wasn't going to focus on any of that today. My stomach fluttered with a mixture of anticipation and nerves. The dress I was wearing was gorgeous, simple yet elegant. I'd never worn anything remotely like it before. A strapless white gown gathered under the delicately beaded bodice, it whispered along the floor as I turned slightly.

A *wedding* dress.

I couldn't believe that Seth had proposed only three days ago, and I already had a tailored wedding dress, thanks to Laadan.

And I was about to get married. Today. In under an hour.

"Are you nervous?" Alex touched my arm, drawing my attention.

I nodded. "I am. A little. I don't know why, but I am."

"I think all brides are nervous," Alex said as she reached up, straightening the pale white rose crown th Laadan had picked out and now rested on top of my head.

I'd left my hair down, knowing that Seth liked it that way, and I was going to be married barefoot, in one of my favorite places.

On the beach, with Seth's home, soon to be *our* home, overlooking us as we actually got married.

What had started off as a proposal had become a full-fledged wedding—a mortal wedding.

Even though Seth and I had wanted to spend the next month locked up in our bedroom, we wanted to let everyone know that Seth was, in fact, not dead. So we'd headed to the Covenant, and after giving everyone the shock of their life, Seth had given them the second shock of their lives.

He'd proposed.

Aiden had looked like he'd choked a little. Alex had broken into a fit of giggles, and Deacon immediately rushed off to find Laadan, shouting something about planning a wedding.

From that moment on, things had sort of spiraled out of our control—the whole wedding business. Seth and I hadn't exactly planned on doing the actual wedding thing. We'd figured we'd exchange vows and rings, and that would be all.

Deacon was not having that.

And he had not been pleased to learn that we weren't going to wait months for a massive wedding to be planned. Seth had given him two and a half days.

But he'd risen to the challenge. With Laadan's help, a wedding was planned.

I turned to Alex and Erin. Both were wearing pretty dresses the color of the pale white roses in my hair. They weren't bridesmaids. Seth and I had pulled the brakes on doing the whole bridal-party thing, but Laadan had snuck in those super cute headpieces, so the girls were wearing them too.

The woman was a miracle worker. Right now, she was down on the beach with Deacon, making sure everything was perfect.

"This is…this is crazy, isn't it?" I asked the girls.

"The best kind of crazy." Alex sat on the bench in front of the bed. Her eyes glimmered with emotion. "When you showed up with Seth, I…" She trailed off, shaking her head. "I'm just glad he's alive and back to his arrogant self."

"Me too," Erin chimed in.

I arched a brow at her.

She giggled as she picked up their smaller hair garlands. "Look, I still think he's an arrogant asshole, but he's *your* arrogant asshole."

Alex snorted as she took her garland. "I hope you do the toast."

I eyed Erin, shaking my head when I saw the eagerness in her eyes. "No." I turned to Alex. "Thank you again. Tonight was supposed to be your and Aiden's party."

Rolling her eyes, she waved her hand dismissively. "We don't need a going-away party every single time we head back. That's all Deacon, and besides, you made Deacon's year. You know how he is with parties and stuff."

I grinned at her. "I'm kind of afraid to see the wedding cake."

"You and me both," Alex snickered.

There was a knock on the door and we heard Luke call out, "You guys good in there?"

"Yeah." Alex turned to the door.

Luke stepped in. Dressed in a pair of dark slacks and a loose white button-down, I almost didn't recognize him. His gaze found me and his features softened. "You look beautiful, Josie."

"Thank you." I clasped my hands together to stop them from trembling.

"You about ready?"

I glanced at the girls. "I think so?"

"Yes—wait." Erin popped forward, straightening the crown yet again. Apparently I had an oddly shaped head or something. "Okay." Erin's smile was bright. "You look perfect. Everything is perfect."

"Yeah, it is…" I trailed off as my smile faded a little. Turning back to the mirror, I swallowed the lump forming in my throat. Everything was perfect except…

My father.

My father should have been here.

Because he seemed to know everything that was happening, it wasn't like he didn't know *this* was happening.

Then again, we hadn't parted on good terms. We hadn't even really spoken to one another when he brought me here, but I thought…I thought maybe he'd show.

Maybe he would. There was still time. Either way, I wasn't going to let anything ruin today.

Taking a deep breath, I turned away from the mirror. "I'm ready."

\* \* \*

Priestesses and priests stood along the cliffs, their golden robes billowing softly in the warm, salty breeze.

They bowed as we passed them, one by one, and my stomach was twisted up in so many knots as we walked down the steps. The fact I didn't trip over the hem of my beautiful dress and roll down said steps was a freaking miracle.

Erin and Alex walked ahead with Luke, out of sight around the bluff so they could take their seats. There was no music, just the sound of waves and the low hum of conversation, but I knew as soon as I rounded the jagged outcropping of rocks, I would see them—I would see Seth waiting for me.

Oh, my gods, I was legit getting married in every sense of the word. There wouldn't be documents filed in the mortal world, like a marriage license, since Seth didn't, well, exist to them. Or something like that. Who knew? But paperwork would be filed with the Council. It would be legal, but I didn't need a piece of paper. I didn't even need a ring or this wedding. I just needed Seth.

This was all just a bonus.

A great bonus.

Grinning, I looked down at my stomach. The way the dress fell, it completely hid the small baby bump. I touched my stomach and whispered, "You ready?"

The wind picked up, stirring the strands of my hair and I lifted my gaze. The sand sparkled under the bright sun and felt warm under my feet.

This was *real*.

My chest swelled to the point it felt like I would float straight up into the endless blue skies. I started walking, rounding the bluff. A white runner was laid down the middle of two sets of white chairs.

Looking back, I'd remember seeing Deacon sitting beside Luke, holding his hand. I'd remember seeing Alex and Aiden

looking over their shoulders at me, both of them smiling as they
started to rise, as did Alexander. The always-radiant Laadan beam-
ing as she held onto Alexander's arm. I'd recall seeing Erin beside
Erik, who was sitting with Cora and Gable. I'd remember seeing
Basil and Karina standing off to the right of Marcus, who stood
in front of a vine-covered trellis. He was the officiant.

But right now? Seeing them didn't register. There was only
one person I saw.

The air in my throat hitched as Seth turned to face where I
was, and nothing, absolutely nothing mattered other than him.

He was dressed in a tux, and I'd never seen him like that. I
hadn't even expected him to be wearing that, figuring he'd set-
tle for something looser, but he looked like he stepped off the
cover of *GQ*. The cut of the suit fit his broad shoulders down to
his tapered waist. His golden hair was pulled back into a short
ponytail, and even from where I stood, I could see the heat and
love in his amber eyes.

I don't remember walking down the white runner. I was just
suddenly standing in front of him, looking up into his eyes, my
hands trembling as he took them in his, and I swore his eyes were
brighter than ever.

"*Psychí mou,*" he murmured. "You steal my breath."

A shiver danced over my shoulders. "The suit. I like it. A lot."

One side of his lips kicked up. "How much?"

"A lot," I stressed.

"Show me later."

I flushed.

Marcus cleared his throat, and I jerked, having completely
forgotten about him. "You two have an audience, in case you've
forgotten."

My eyes widened while Seth chuckled. Laughter from our
friends reached me, and I felt the blush deepen.

"You two ready?" Marcus asked.

"I've been ready," Seth answered, squeezing my hands.

"For forever," I whispered back.

Marcus started the ceremony, speaking in ancient Greek. The words fell between Seth and me, and not once did we take our eyes off one another. There was that feeling again, of it just being him and me in this entire world. Just the two of us, and when Seth leaned in toward the end, kissing me like there wasn't a single person watching us and cheering us on, I realized with startling clarity that we'd made it. We'd made it to the *end*, against all odds, and we were man and wife, and we had an eternity of this—of the deep, soul-scorching kisses that twisted my stomach up in the most wickedly delicious ways.

Someone shouted, and it poked through the pleasant haze. Something about it sounded off. Wrong.

Seth lifted his mouth from mine and turned his head. The hand at the nape of my neck tightened. I saw the surprise shoot across his face. I followed his gaze—everyone's gaze.

I jerked back, breaking Seth's hold as I saw who stood at the end of the runner. It didn't make sense, but it was *him*. "Colin?"

Dressed like he was the last time I'd seen him. The only things different were that his shirt wasn't ripped and he wasn't covered in blood.

Colin smiled as he tipped his head to the side. "I didn't want to miss the wedding of the century."

"What in the hell?" Seth demanded.

I stepped forward, still holding onto one of Seth's hands. "Is that really you?"

"Yes."

Deacon's brows raised. "I guess everyone is returning from the dead now."

Colin chuckled. "I wouldn't say I've risen from the dead. You can't even say Seth has, since he didn't die and I didn't die either. Not really."

"What?" I asked. "You were so dead, and I'm so confused—"

"Wait," Erin was saying as she stood, her head moving to the side. "You're not right." She edged around a confused-looking Erik. "There's something very wrong about you."

"Furies," Colin said with a sigh. "Such pains in the ass, with their nifty ability to see through falsehoods."

Unease exploded in my chest. "What are you talking about?"

Seth stepped forward, his eyes narrowing as he let go of my hand. "You better answer that question really quickly."

"That's not Colin," Erin said. "That's not a half-blood."

"Funny," the thing who looked like Colin said. "If the furies had been unleashed earlier, you guys would've figured it out."

Suddenly, I remembered how the furies had appeared to gun for Colin. One of them spoke—the one I killed. What had it said? *Tricky.* The furie had said the word "tricky."

"What are you?" I demanded. "And where is Colin?"

"Colin died a while ago. Before you even met him." The thing smiled and then his features seemed to warp and distort. "You see, I needed a body. I needed a body no one would suspect." It lengthened, becoming taller and leaner. "I needed to blend in."

Someone cursed. Sounded like Alex.

Dark hair grew, falling down noticeably slimmer shoulders. "All of you may have killed Ares, but you did not end his legacy." The voice softened, becoming more feminine. "You did not kill all of us."

A woman stood in front of us, a tall gorgeous woman, and she found Alex in the audience. "You got to know his sons well, but you never got to meet me."

"Is that so?" Alex reached for her daggers, then realized she was wearing a dress and had no daggers. Her hands closed into fists. "And who the hell are you?"

"I'm Enyo, the goddess of war and destruction, the harbinger of discord." She tipped her head back. "I'm Ares's sister."

"And his lover," Deacon muttered not too quietly. "Y'all are freaks…"

"I was right!" I turned to Seth. "Didn't I suggest it was something related to Ares causing all the problems between the halfs and pures?"

"And so was I," Seth growled. "I knew there was a reason I didn't like you."

"Oh, you're about to have a bigger reason," she said, laughing. "Ares had so much hope for you. So many plans, and you betrayed him. You might not have been the one to kill him, but you set into motion what led to his demise. And you?" Enyo said to Alex. "I would love nothing more than to take you out."

"I'd like to see you try," Aiden snarled.

Enyo smirked. "But I'm smarter than that."

The goddess spun toward Seth and me, throwing out her arm. An arc of energy pulsed and crackled in the air. A god bolt. Deadly to everyone here except Seth. I didn't see it when it left Enyo's hand.

With a roar of rage, Seth let go of a god bolt of his own. It slammed into Enyo, encasing her in light, and I knew she was a goner. Seth had killed her before she had a chance to tuck tail and run, but it…

But it was too late.

I felt it.

It happened so fast. I'd been standing in front of Seth, staring into those striking golden eyes, holding his hands, and then there was nothing but heart-stopping pain. Unexpected. Brutal.

Cool air raised tiny goosebumps along my bare arms. I tried to draw in a breath, but the air went nowhere as I looked down at the white gown that brushed the tops of my feet—the gown I'd been so excited to wear, so *ready* to wear. I stumbled back.

Blood poured down the front of my chest, ruining the gown—ruining everything. My wide gaze swung to Seth's. His eyes were filled with dawning horror.

The dream. *The dream*. I'd seen this. With the exception of the elm trees, this was the dream. I opened my mouth, but everything felt wet.

I'd seen *this*.

And I knew what was happening.

How this would end.

There were shouts erupting all around us. Chaos as the very world seemed to rattle and shake. Seth was reaching for me, confusion fading from his face and giving way to a raw mixture of fear and anger.

Too late. Too late.

Pressing shaky hands against my chest, it did nothing to stanch the blood flowing from between my fingers.

Oh *gods*, I was going to die.

My knees gave out, but I didn't fall to the ground. I knew I wouldn't. The part of my brain that was detached from all of this expected to be caught, and I was. Strong, warm arms folded around me, easing me down, holding me close. I blinked, trying to focus as I pressed against the warm, hard chest. Amber-colored eyes stared back into mine—eyes that had been filled with love and happiness moments before were now shining with terror.

"Seth," I whispered. "Don't let me go."

"No." His face contorted. Tears filled his eyes as he lifted my head, pressing his mouth to my forehead. "I'll never let you go, Josie. *Never*."

# 32

## Seth

Those stunning blue eyes were wide as they fixed on mine, fear and panic crowding them.

"Hold on, baby." I placed my hand over her sternum. Blood immediately seeped between my fingers. I looked up, panicked. "We need a doctor!" I shouted.

Basil was already running back toward the house. Several people were frozen, their expressions mirroring the horror pinging around in me.

This couldn't be happening.

Not after everything, this wasn't happening.

Alex and Aiden were beside us. They were shouting, but their words weren't making sense to me. Erin was there, as frozen as one of the entombed furies.

Josie shuddered, her entire body rocking mine. My gaze flew to hers. Her eyes were closed. "Josie! Open your eyes. Babe, come on. Open your eyes for me. Please."

Her eyes didn't open.

Terror turned my skin to ice. "*Psychí mou*, please open your eyes. Please, baby. Open your damn eyes."

She didn't move.

Her chest didn't rise.

"Oh my gods," Alex whispered, dropping down to her knees.

Hands slick with blood, I checked for a pulse, sliding my thumb along the side of her neck. I felt… Oh gods, I felt nothing. No pulse.

Nothing.

"No. No. No." I fell back on my ass, pulling Josie into my lap. She was so limp. Her arms hanging loose at her sides. I looked up at Alex and then Aiden. His silver eyes were shadowed. "I don't know what to do." My voice cracked. "Tell me what to do."

He shook his head wordlessly.

"She can't go without oxygen for long. Her… The baby…" I turned back to her, dragging her hair out of her face. "I've got to get her breathing again."

"Mouth to mouth," Alex suggested, her voice thick. "You can try—"

A fissure of energy rippled across the beach. The glyphs appeared on my skin. There was a flash of light and then a shadow fell over us, blocking out the sun.

Apollo knelt between Alex and Aiden, his gaze focused on Josie.

"Help her," I begged him. I didn't care that I had never begged a day in my life before. "Please, Apollo. Help her."

He touched her forehead. "Her soul is leaving, Seth. The wound is deadly. Your child is already—"

"No!" I shouted, my grip tightening on her. "She is not dead. Our child is *not* dead."

He smoothed the blood from her forehead, blood I had tracked there. "I've seen this," he said, trailing his fingers down the side of her face. "I've known this was going to happen. You do not

understand how hard it is to know how your daughter and grand-
son will die."

I stared at him. "No."

His gaze shifted to mine. "It is Fate, Seth. It is the prophecy
written eons ago."

"No." Rage filled me as I rocked back. My cheeks were damp
as my vision blurred. "*Fuck* Fate! *Fuck* prophecies! I will not lose
her or my child. *This* will not be taken from us. I swear to gods,
I will—"

"You will do nothing," he said calmly, his eyes turning all-
white. "For it is not your prophecy. It is mine. And it is your son's.
For love is the root of all that is good, and the root of all things
that are evil. Love is the root of the Apollyon. Fate is afoot," he
continued, moving his hand to Josie's sternum, over his icon that
was engraved in her skin. "Things cannot be undone. Fate has
looked into the past and into the future. History is on repeat."

"What the hell?" snapped Alex, recognizing the prophecy that
she'd heard years ago at the Covenant in North Carolina.

Fine hairs rose all over my body as Apollo's voice carried
through the salty air.

"Know the difference between need and love." Apollo began
to glow. From the top of his golden head, down through his
entire body, he became as bright as the sun. "For what the gods
have feared has come to pass. The end of the old is here, and the
beginning of the new has been ushered in." His voice rose, carrying
out to sea and over the cliffs, just as Ewan the nymph's voice had.
"For the sun child and the new god will give birth to a new era
and the great creators will fall one by one, reshaping our homes
and hearths, reaping man and mortal alike."

I shuddered as the glow radiated from his hand and enveloped
Josie in warm golden light, blurring out her features as I held her
in my arms.

"A bloody path was chosen," Apollo said, and lightning ripped across the rapidly darkening sky. Night fell, pitching the world into darkness. "The Great War fought by the few *has* come to pass, and in the end, the sun has fallen, and the moon will reign until the new sun rises."

My skin burned from holding onto Josie, but I didn't let her go. I would not let her go. I'd promised her I wouldn't let go, and I would never do it. Never.

Apollo's voice had weakened as the light pulled back from Josie and traveled up his arm. I could see Apollo's features again. He stared down at Josie. "She carries the god of music, truth, and prophecy, the god of sun and light, plague and poetry, and when he comes of age, he will take his rightful place among the Olympians. He will rule until end times."

The bright glow receded from his eyes. The whites were milky and flat. "Tell her that I have always been proud of her. That I have always loved her. Tell her that I give this to her not out of obligation, but out of love for my child. Tell her that, Seth."

I opened my mouth, but fuck, I was out of words. All words. Across from me, Alex fell to her butt, a broken sound coming from her, because Apollo... He was...

Coming apart.

Flaking piece by piece, drifting into the air around him. The night cleared as rays of sunlight streamed down, reflecting off the glittering sand. Apollo was slowly, right before our eyes, becoming nothing as he returned to the light all around us.

"The new sun..." Apollo said, his voice faint as he simply disappeared. "...has risen."

Josie jerked in my arms, and my gaze shot back to her face. Color returned to her skin, spreading across her face and down her throat, a pink flush that brought life back to her body. I trembled. Her eyes flew open as she dragged in a huge gulp of air. Her chest rose and fell heavily.

"Seth?" she whispered, voice hoarse.

*Fuck.*

Lifting her against my chest, I buried my face in her neck as I lost all control. Didn't even care. I fucking *sobbed* as I held her.

"Seth." Her voice was muffled. She managed to pull back and lift her arms. She clasped my cheeks and tilted my head up. Seth? Why are you crying?"

A hoarse laugh escaped me as I pressed my forehead against hers. "I love you, Josie. I love you."

# 33

## Seth

The rising sun crested along the horizon, turning the sky a burnt orange and deep violet as a warm breeze washed over my skin, stirring the gauzy curtains of the open doorway behind me. Having woken an hour or so ago and unable to lie still, I found myself out on the balcony, listening to nothing but the rolling waves and distant call of waking birds.

I wanted to be in there, asleep beside Josie, but my damn brain just would not shut down, damn near replaying every moment of my life the last couple of years. From the moment I found out I was the Apollyon, to when I first stepped foot on Deity Island and beyond, it was "Seth's Greatest Hits," and then not so much, on repeat.

It was like I was trying to figure out how, after everything that had happened and everything I'd done and after every good and bad moment, I had still gotten here.

Closing my eyes, I tilted my head back, letting the warmth of the sun bake my skin. The future was…it was *here*.

Sounded corny as hell to think that, but it was true.

How did I get so lucky? It was a question I'd asked myself a hundred times since I met Josie, but after I'd almost lost myself only to almost lose her and our child, it was a question I couldn't shake. There were so many people who were better than me who had lost so much.

But here I was still tasting the bitter fear and rancid hopelessness as I'd watched the life start to seep out of Josie's beautiful eyes. Probably be a hundred years, maybe even a thousand before I forgot that feeling. Hell, there was a chance I never would, but Josie was safe. Our child was safe.

And I wasn't living with that fear and hopelessness. I wasn't living that life of loss that Josie had experienced while I'd been trapped in that nothingness. Instead, we were...

We were home.

This island, this house, had never felt like home to me. Hell, no place had felt like a home, but this house? It had been a cold and barren place, no matter how bright the sun shone on it or how many people filled the rooms. This house was just the bones of a home, nothing of substance inside, tainted by memories of a cold mother and a fate I'd never asked for.

Until now.

Never before would I've thought of the house where I'd spent many lonely years as something I want to come back to, start a family in. I used to think of this place as a ghost, one that always haunted the fringes of my thoughts.

Not anymore.

Now it felt like a home, because my entire world was curled up a few feet away, sleeping peacefully. It even looked differently when we arrived yesterday. Brighter. Warmer.

*Home.*

This was going to be the place we would always come back to when we left. This was going to where we would raise our child, and I knew in my bones that every nook and cranny of this house that was once cold and empty would be filled with life and love. But home wasn't really a place.

It was really a person.

Opening my eyes, I found myself back in the bedroom, standing at the foot of the bed. Josie was lying on her side, the sheet twisted around her hips. One of her lovely legs peeked through the sheets. Tempting. So damn tempting. Everything about her. Even the way her arms were crossed in front of her bare chest, her hands balled loosely. That amazing hair of hers, a wild array of blondes and browns streamed across the pillow.

Gods.

Unable to help myself, I moved closer to her.

A raw knot of emotion crawled up the back of my throat. Damn tears stung the back of my eyes as I brought one knee onto the bed and then sat beside her.

She was *psychi mou*.

She was my everything.

Reaching over, I curled a finger around a strand of hair lying across her cheek and tucked it back behind her ear. Her hips wiggled, and her fingers curled on reflex. The corners of my lips tipped up as the sunlight creeping across the bed reflected off the diamond on her ring finger.

She was my wife.

A hoarse laugh parted my lips. *My wife.* Gods, I never thought I'd be married. Pretty sure the vast amount of people who'd met me would've never thought that, but here I was.

Lucky.

My hand drifted down her arm, over the curve of her waist to the flare of her hip.

Josie let out this soft little sound as she eased onto her back. Thick lashes fluttered and then lifted. Bright, beautiful blue eyes

focused, and I was blessed with a sleepy smile. "Hey," she murmured.

"Hi there." I swallowed, but the damn knot of emotion was
still there, choking me.

She turned her head to the open doorway. A frown pinched
her face. "What time is it?"

"It's early. The sun just rose." I placed my hand on the other
side of her hip.

"Mmm."

"I didn't mean to wake you." That was the truth. "You should
still be sleeping."

Lifting her arms above her, she stretched that beautiful body
of hers, arching her back and giving me one hell of a show. Her
breasts jutted up, all rosy and perfect as she bit down on her plump
lower lip. The sheet slipped, revealing her lower stomach. There
was a larger…bump there, a roundness that stole my breath in
the best possible ways. There wasn't a scar left from Enyo's attack.
Not a single blemish save for Apollo's mark.

"You're staring at me," she said.

I was always staring at her.

Especially when she was naked and pregnant with our child.
Kind of couldn't help myself.

When I didn't answer, she lowered her arms. The lingering
sleepiness vanished. Her brows knitted and then she rose onto
her elbow as she cupped my cheek. "Are you okay?"

"Yeah," I said thickly.

Her gaze searched mine. "You sure?"

"I am." I folded my hand over hers. "I'm just…thinking about
everything."

One eyebrow rose as she sat up. Hair fell over her shoulders.
"That's a lot to be thinking about."

Lowering our joined hands, I kissed the center of her palm

and then pressed her hand against my chest, above my heart.

"Why are you awake?" Her gaze searched mine. "Talk to me, Seth."

"It's nothing. Everything is okay."

"Really?"

"Yeah. It's just that…" I caught a strand of her hair and gently tugged on it. "I'm so damn lucky. I can't stop thinking about that."

She was quiet for a moment. "You think it was all luck?"

"I don't know," I answered truthfully.

"We're both lucky." She scooted closer. "But it's not all luck that got us here. I think we worked damn hard to be here. We both *fought* hard to be here."

That we did.

We had the scars that didn't show on the skin to prove it.

"And we had help. Loads of it," she continued, placing her other hand on my thigh. "And my father…"

It was hard to think of Apollo. There was a part of me that still got irrationally irritated just hearing his name, and the other half missed the annoying son of a bitch, popping in and out without any warning, but what he did for Josie and our son could never be forgotten. "Yeah, he really came through for us, didn't he?"

She nodded, and I hated seeing the sadness creeping into her expression. I'd given her Apollo's message once she remembered what had happened. It had been hard, watching as she fully understood the sacrifice Apollo had made. He'd given his godhood to save her and our child, and from what we could tell, his life as well.

And it hadn't just been hard for Josie.

Alex and Aiden couldn't process it even though they saw it with their own eyes. The god had been a part of their lives longer than Josie's, and for Alex, it was also like losing a father.

It was hard for everyone.

Even me.

"I wish I had…time with him." Her gaze dropped. "To actually get to know him. You know? Because I really didn't know him at all."

"I'm sorry." It seemed inadequate to say, but I was. "He loved you. At the end of the day, he proved that and then some."

"I know."

"I just wish he'd showed it in a different way." And that was the damn truth. "Like, I don't know, taking you out for ice cream or some shit."

Josie coughed out a hoarse laugh. "That would've been nice. Spending any real time with him would've been… Well, I really wanted that." She cleared her throat as she lifted her gaze to mine. "So, it wasn't just luck. We fought to be here. People sacrificed everything for us to get here, and not just my father."

No, it hadn't just been Apollo who had given his life. Solos. Colin had, before we even met him. Countless others. Some were nameless, but their sacrifices were just as important.

But Josie was…she was right.

I wasn't saying some of it wasn't luck. I used to think there was no such thing, but I knew better. And maybe some of it was even fate. I knew enough to know fate was a real thing. Fate could be reshaped, but it was a damn freight train at times, running right over you.

But we did fight to get here. I fought to get here. It wasn't just luck or fate. "It was us."

She nodded. "And it's over. It's really over, Seth."

Words I'd never thought I'd have the luxury of hearing.

"No more creepy shades. No more Titans," she continued, sliding her hand along my inner thigh. "The Olympians know their place and we know ours."

"Yeah, we do." My cock thickened as her hand came precariously close. "Our place is here."

"It is." She leaned in, kissing the corner of my mouth. "And whatever crazy things may come our way, we're going to face them. Together."

If the remaining Olympians were smart and played their cards right, they'd make it their top priority not to piss either of us off.

Alas, the Olympians were not known for being smart or playing their cards well, even though the last time we'd seen them, things had been cool. One never knew what they were going to get from the Olympians, but I'd be ready for them if they ever tried to step out against us.

Or if they tried to stop our son from taking his rightful place among them when he was of age.

I caught the fierce glint in Josie's eyes and corrected myself. *We* would be ready for them.

"Together," I agreed.

Her head tilted back as her gaze roamed over my face. She cupped my cheek again and then traced the curve of my jaw with the pad of her thumb.

Turning my head, I caught the tip of her finger between my teeth. Passion clouded her eyes as I nipped down.

"You need to stop doing that," she said, pulling her hand away and sliding it down to my chest.

I raised my brows. "Why would I do that?"

"Because for some reason, these pregnancy hormones have me wanting sex for, like, nearly twenty-four hours a day," she said, and hell if that didn't go straight to my dick. "You do something like that, and I just want to climb on you like a sex-deprived manic."

"Okay. I don't care what you say." Wrapping my hand around the nape of her neck, I kissed her. "I am so fucking lucky."

Josie laughed against my mouth. "Because I'm horny all the time now?"

"Yeah." I pressed my forehead against hers and drew in a long, slow breath. "And for the fact that, after all of this, you've never given up on me."

"I could never give up on you." She kissed me again, nibbling at my bottom lip. "Not just because I love you, but because you're worth fighting for, Seth. You're worth loving, and if takes a hundred years to prove that to you, I will."

Her words were a lightning bolt to my chest.

"Hell," I growled. Snatching the sheet that had pooled at her waist, I tossed it aside. The silk sheet floated in the air beside the bed and then fell quietly to the floor.

Needing to be inside her more badly than I needed my next breath, I willed my pants off.

Josie laughed as she fell back onto the bed. "That is a nifty talent, Seth."

"That it is." I climbed over her, stopping to kiss her lower stomach. "You're jealous of it, aren't you?"

"Well, yeah." Her fingers threaded through my hair. "Who wouldn't be?"

Moving up, I placed a kiss on the raised mark between her breasts. "But I like to think I have far better talents then undressing myself with a thought."

"You do." She tugged on my head, guiding my mouth to hers as I settled between her thighs. "But that would make getting ready so much easier."

My laugh was lost in her kiss, and then I got lost in her. Everything started off slow. I took my time, because hell if we didn't have all the time in the world to slow everything down, to enjoy one another without a threat hanging over our heads, and to simply live.

So, that's what we did.

I sipped from her lips, drank from her breathy sighs, and fed from her cries as I worked my way down her, exploring every dip and curve like it was my first time. And in a way, it sort of felt like that.

It always felt like that.

I'd never grow tired of those soft sounds she made, or the way her skin tasted. I'd never grow tired of her. Never.

By the time I slid inside her, we both were grasping at one another, hands greedy on slick skin, our breaths short and urgent.

Josie cried out my name as I thrust into her, and the sound was like touching a live wire. Those long, beautiful legs wrapped around my hips. I moved over her, arms shaking, hips pumping slow and deep.

She was having none of that.

Rolling me onto my back, I laughed and grasped her hips as she took control. She planted her hands on my chest. Head thrown back and back arched as she rode me, I'd never seen anything more beautiful. And when she came, clenching and throbbing all around me, my release powered down my spine.

I sat up, wrapping my arms around her as tight as I could. Her head dropped to my shoulder as her body trembled all around me. I pulled her down, grinding up and sealing our bodies together. There was not an inch of space between us when I came, shouting her name.

I fell back, bringing her with me as the aftershocks shook me to my very core. Good gods, I was rattled in the best possible way.

Clearing my throat, I glanced over at Josie. Breathing just as heavily and fast as me, half her body was strewn across me and her legs were tangled with mine. That was something about her I loved. Somehow she always managed to get her legs all wrapped up in mine. A lazy grin tugged up the corners of my lips. She was the best kind of octopus.

"Gods." I dragged my hand up her spine as I turned my chin, pressing a kiss to the top of her head. "I could do that again and again and again."

"Same." She snuggled down. "That was…"

"Extraordinary? Heart-stopping? The best sex of your life?" I suggested helpfully.

She giggled. "All of those."

"That's what I thought."

"Your ego never fails to amaze me."

Dragging my fingers along the center of her back, I chuckled as I let my eyes drift shut. There was a good chance that I might've dozed off, because when I opened my eyes again, the sunlight had shifted from the bed to the floor and Josie was smiling at me, her chin propped against her fist, resting on my chest.

"Have you been watching me sleep?" I asked, retuning my hand to her back, because I knew she liked that.

"Maybe just a little."

Lifting my other hand, I dragged it down my face. "How long was I sleeping?"

"A couple of hours. Not too long."

"Shit. Really?"

She nodded. "I wasn't staring at you the *whole* time."

"Well, that's a relief." I paused. "Sorry about that."

"It's okay, Seth." Josie smiled as she pulled back. "You can take naps. We have forever to be awake and annoying each other. Like literally. Forever. And soon, we'll have a little version of ourselves to also annoy and take naps with."

I don't know why, but it struck me right then that we really did have forever—fuck, we really did. Not the blink and you missed it life. Not a future that ended hopefully when we were both old and gray, our muscles weak and our bones frail. We really did have forever.

"Yeah." My voice thickened as I tugged her back down, right where I wanted her. Flesh against flesh. Heart to heart. "Yeah, we do."

Josie kissed my chest, and another thing struck me as I lay there. Something fucking wondrous in a way.

I...I had gotten everything I could ever want in the end.

Me. The one some called the villain for a long time.

But it was true. I had the love of my life in my arms. My wife. I would have a child soon. I had a real future, one that I would look forward to every day.

I laughed before I could stop myself.

Josie lifted her chin. "What?"

"I was just thinking." Smiling, I curved my hand around her arm, holding her tight to me. "I got *everything*. Every damn thing I never even allowed myself to dream. Crazy."

Josie wrinkled her nose in that cute way of hers, and my smile grew. She let out a happy little shriek as I rolled her onto her back. Staring into the eyes of the woman who was truly a gift, I made a promise I'd never break. "I'm going to spend the rest of eternity proving to you just how much I deserve all of this."

Tears filled her eyes. "You already do, Seth."

# EPILOGUE

## Seth

"**D**o you think you'd ever want one of these?" Deacon asked Luke, never taking his eyes off the little, wrapped bundle in his arms.

Luke looked over to where I stood. His brows lifted in surprise. "I think so, but not for a fairly long time from now. Like a real long time from now."

I grinned.

"I don't know." Deacon lowered his face to the bundle resting in the crook of his arm. "I would like to get me one of these."

"You make it sound so simple," Luke replied. "Like you can go to the local grocery store and pick one up."

"Nowadays, that could happen," I commented dryly.

"Don't antagonize him."

Deacon went back to making those ridiculous cooing noises— noises I'd found myself making more than a time or five hundred. Sometimes I'd do it without even realizing it.

"I can't wait for Alex and Aiden to see him," Luke said, crossing his arms. Deacon hadn't been able to keep his hands off the newest addition to the Army of Awesome, but Luke was a bit standoffish, staring down at the wrapped bundle like it was some kind of unknown weapon of mass destruction. I couldn't blame him for that. "This kid is going to be spoiled considering he has, like, four or five godparents."

The corners of my lips tipped up. "Yeah."

Deacon lifted his gaze as the swaddled bundle started to wiggle around. "I think he wants his daddy."

Smiling, I walked over to Deacon and bent, picking up my son. *My son.* Those two words never failed to rock me to my very core. I cradled his wiggling body to my chest, and he immediately settled. "I think he wants his mommy."

"Can't blame him for that," Deacon teased as he leaned back against the couch. "How is Josie doing?"

"She's doing perfect."

And that was true. They'd only gotten to visit with her a little last night. When the whole labor thing started, I had to keep telling myself that Josie was going to be okay. That she had survived so many crazy things that labor was going to be breeze for her. The first real contraction, though? I about passed the fuck out seeing how pale she got. Watching her go through the labor and not being able to do anything other than hold her hand hadn't been easy. It actually scared the shit out of me.

And I wasn't the one delivering a baby.

Josie was my hero.

Brushing my lips over the dusty blonde head of my son, I closed my eyes and mentally thanked every freaking deity there ever was for bestowing this gift upon me. When I opened my eyes, both men were watching me, their stares soft.

"I better get him up there to her," I said, clearing my throat. "Help yourselves to whatever you want."

"We plan to," Deacon replied, and I rolled my eyes.

I started to turn.

"Seth?" Luke called out, and I faced him as I gently shifted my son in my arms. "I don't think I've said this yet, but I just want to tell you that we love the name you picked. Apollo... he would approve."

In that moment, my son opened his eyes. They weren't the brilliant shade of blue like his mother's and grandfather's. They were the same color as mine. A tawny, amber color.

My son had my eyes.

"Yeah," I said. "It is the perfect name. See you guys in a little bit."

Leaving the room, I passed Basil in the hall as I made my way to the stairs. He bowed even though I shot him a look of warning against doing just that.

At this point I thought he was just doing that shit to get on my nerves.

"Let's go see your mom, little man," I said, climbing the steps. "She's probably missing you."

I got an incoherent baby gurgle in response, which made me grin. The little man was a happy baby so far. Well, until he was hungry. That was a different story.

As I entered the hallway, I saw Erin coming my way. Things were... better between us, as in she wasn't trying to kill me, but we weren't going to be best friends anytime soon.

"I was just about to start looking for you," she said, stopping to curl her finger around a baby fist. "I think it's almost feeding time."

"Sounds about right."

And that was about the extent of that conversation.

Like I said, things were getting better between Erin and I, but we were by no means friendly with one another.

Nodding at Erin, I made my way to the bedroom, opening the door without touching it. I immediately saw Josie.

She was sitting up, her fingers making quick work on the thick braid. Gods, she was beautiful. Just sitting there, her chin tipped down and her face marked with concentration, she was the most stunning person I'd ever seen.

Josie looked up and a smile raced across her face as she secured the braid. "Hey you."

"Brought you something."

"Is it my child?" she asked, wiggling her fingers at me.

"Maybe." I sat beside her and carefully handed over our son to her. There was a pressure in my chest as I watched her entire face light up as she smoothed a hand over our son's head.

"Is it just me or does he seem to already have more hair?" she asked, glancing over at me.

Planting my hand in the bed near her hip, I leaned in. "He does have a lot of hair. Seems to be growing faster than him."

She laughed. "He's going to have a little man bun before long."

I shook my head, grinning as our son curled his hand around Josie's finger. "How are you feeling?"

"Good." She lifted his hand to her mouth, kissing those tiny fingers. There was a happy, little giggle that came from the crook of her arm. "Perfect, really. You know? I just… everything just feels perfect right now."

It really did.

Leaning over, I kissed her cheek and then stayed there. "Deacon and Luke approve of his name."

"I figured they would." She turned her head toward mine, and kissed me. "I think Alex and Aiden will like it too."

"They will." I kissed her back and then pulled away just enough to see our son staring up at us, his gaze steady and sharp. The kid seemed to know exactly what we were talking about. "I want you to do me a favor, little man," I said to him. "The first time Aiden holds you, I want you to take the biggest crap—"

"Seth," Josie laughed. "Don't you dare finish that sentence."

I chuckled. "Your mom is a life-ruiner."

"And your dad is going to be in a lot of trouble if he keeps it up," she said, widening her eyes when our son let out another gurgle, as if he were responding. "Oh, yes he is."

I kissed her cheek again and then I moved my hand close. Our son immediately reached for my fingers. He gripped both of our hands. "Leon," I said, lifting my gaze to Josie's. "Leon is the perfect name."

# *About*
# JENNIFER L. ARMENTROUT

# 1 New York Times and # 1 International Bestselling author Jennifer lives in Martinsburg, West Virginia. All the rumors you've heard about her state aren't true. When she's not hard at work writing she spends her time reading, watching really bad zombie movies, pretending to write, hanging out with her husband, her Jack Russell Loki and their retired police dog, Diesel. In early 2015, Jennifer was diagnosed with retinitis pigmentosa, a group of rare genetic disorders that involve a breakdown and death of cells in the retina, eventually resulting in loss of vision, among other complications. Due to this diagnosis, educating people on the varying degrees of blindness has become of passion of hers, right alongside writing, which she plans to do as long as she can.

Her dreams of becoming an author started in algebra class, where she spent most of her time writing short stories....which explains her dismal grades in math. Jennifer writes young adult paranormal, science fiction, fantasy, and contemporary romance. She is published with Tor Teen, Entangled Teen, Disney/Hyperion and Harlequin Teen. Her Wicked Series has been optioned by PassionFlix. Jennifer has won numerous awards, including the 2013 Reviewers Choice Award for Wait for You, the 2015 Editor's Pick for Fall With Me, and the 2014/2015 Moerser-Jugendbuch-Jury award for Obsidian. Her young adult romantic suspense novel DON'T LOOK BACK was a 2014 nominated Best in Young Adult Fiction by YALSA. Her adult romantic suspense novel TILL DEATH was an Amazon Editor's Pick and iBook Book of the Month. Her young adult contemporary THE PROBLEM WITH FOREVER is a 2017 RITA Award Winner in Young Adult Fiction. She also writes Adult and New Adult contemporary and paranormal romance under the name J. Lynn. She is published by Entangled Brazen and HarperCollins.

# Acknowledgements

I need to thank the readers who started with the Covenant Series all the way back in 2011, who followed Alex and Aiden's story as it turned into Seth and Josie's journey. The Titan Series never would've happened without you guys. Especially those who used to celebrate Aiden's birthday with cake, defended Aiden and Seth in book boyfriend battles over the years, and those JLAnders who like to always argue who is better, Seth or Aiden. I hope, by the end of this, we can say they're equally awesome, and Alex and Josie are two very lucky ladies. This is the end, for now.

A big thank you my editor and said editor's editing prowess. Ha! A thank you to my agents, Kevan Lyon and Taryn Fagerness. Thank you to Christine Borgford for her amazing formatting skills, Sara Eirew for her design, and Franggy Yanez for his photography awesomeness. Thank you to Stephanie Brown, even though I think she wanted to hurt me a little by the end of this book. Thank you to Kate Kaynak, Hannah McBride, Jen Fisher, Valerie and Vi and Jessica, Laura Kaye, Sarah J. Maas, KA Tucker, Vilma Gonzalez, Lesa Rodrigues, Stacey Morgan, Jillian Stein and Liz Berry, Andrea Joan, Jay Crownover, Cora Carmack, and many, many more who help me stay sane while writing, and thank you to Drew Leighty, who embodies Seth in a freakishly accurate manner.

The Titan Series was more than just a book series. It was what kicked off the ApollyCon event, and even though the Titan Series has come to an end, ApollyCon will carry on.